COLIN THUBRON

Colin Thubron is an acknowledged master of travel writing, and the author of eight celebrated novels. He has been numbered among 'the current masters of the short novel' (*TLS*), and called 'one of our most compelling contemporary novelists' (*Independent*), as well as writing the classic travel books, *Behind the Wall* (winner of the Hawthornden Prize and the Thomas Cook Travel Award), *The Lost Heart of Asia*, *In Siberia* (Prix Bouvier) and *Shadow of the Silk Road*. Colin Thubron was President of the Royal Society of Literature from 2010 to 2017.

COLIN THUBRON

Night of Fire

VINTAGE

1 3 5 7 9 10 8 6 4 2

Vintage
20 Vauxhall Bridge Road,
London SW1V 2SA

Vintage is part of the Penguin Random House group of companies
whose addresses can be found at global.penguinrandomhouse.com.

Penguin
Random House
UK

First published in Vintage in 2017
First published in hardback by Chatto & Windus in 2016

penguin.co.uk/vintage

A CIP catalogue record for this book is
available from the British Library

ISBN 9780099532651

Printed and bound by Clays Ltd, St Ives plc

Penguin Random House is committed to a sustainable future
for our business, our readers and our planet. This book is made
from Forest Stewardship Council® certified paper.

MIX
Paper from
responsible sources
FSC® C018179

For Margreta

'Just as there are phantom limbs there are phantom histories, histories that are severed and discarded, but linger on as thwarted possibilities and compelling nostalgias.'

Adam Phillips, *On Balance*

Contents

Landlord

*It began with a spark, an electrical break like the first mur-
mur of a weakening heart that would soon unhinge the body,
until its conflagration at last consumed the whole building.
Years ago, at the end of the Victorian century, the house had
been built in dignified isolation, but later developers split its
storeys into separate flats, and the once-grand staircases now
ascended past empty landings and closed doors. It was slipping into stately old age. Its balconies sagged behind their
wrought-iron balustrades, and chunks of stucco pediment
were dropping off on to the dustbins fifty feet below. The
garden behind, which had once been the landlord's pride,
lay half forgotten, and its shrubs – photinia, daphne, rose-
mary – burgeoned unclipped over the lawn.*

*Somewhere in the bowels of the building, behind a damp
wall, a kink in a carbonised wire had become a tiny furnace.
Down this half-blocked artery it travelled to a worn Bakelite
socket, and the tenant asleep in the basement – it was past
midnight – never woke. The January night was cold. Far
below, the sea made an angry rasping. Inland the town
showed broken threads of light where it had gone to sleep.*

*The landlord was watching other fires. From his rooftop
terrace the sky was so clear that he – an insomniac muffled in scarves and padded jacket – could write his notes by*

starlight. Hunched in the circle of his makeshift observatory, he watched his breath misting in the night air, and listened to the sea, and wondered if his wife was yet asleep. The tube of the telescope was ice cold under his palms. This refractive model was not like his old one, grown friendly over the years, but a computerised tyrant. In the dark his fingers would blunder uncertainly over its keypad, or jog the ocular as he coupled it with his camera. But after long minutes of fumbling, the focused sky would startle him with a revelation far beyond his ageing naked eyesight. A supernova would appear like a ghost in a zone he had thought empty, or he was transfixed by a nebula whose mist now splintered into a blaze of separated stars.

His gaze had changed over the years. As a younger man the remoteness of these galaxies had swept over him with an icy faintness, as if he were falling upwards. Their voids, their silence, sometimes left him physically trembling. He even wondered about his lapsed belief in God. But little by little this night-time hobby toughened into something more familiar. He observed all the prime objects catalogued by Herschel, and in the hope of making a small contribution to science, he embarked on a fruitless search for undetected dying stars.

Then an old passion for photography surfaced. With a single-lens reflex camera mounted on the telescope, he accessed even distant galaxies. After focusing on nebulae to the south, where light pollution faded over the empty sea, the results of his half-hour aperture exposures shocked him into something close to fear. On his sensitised prints the mammoth hydrogen clouds boiled in great articulated explosions of gas and dust, scattered with blue asterisks where new stars were shining. Each of these lurid turmoils, he knew, was an ungraspable ferment of new creation, often the birthplace of a million suns. The photographs were beautiful and petrifying. Whole galaxies turned like Catherine wheels silently in space. And most spectacularly his camera yielded crimson images that burst and spilled out like intestines on the blackness. He could not look at them without the illusion of some celestial wound. Whole seams of stardust – a hundred thousand light years across – undulated like arteries in space, or blistered up from nowhere. And the constellations shone so dense that scarcely a gap of night showed between.

But tonight, although the sky was full, he ignored his camera. He was expecting the annual meteor shower of the Quadrantids. A sharp wind had got up and was ruffling the sea into faint crests. Once or twice a solitary meteor flared and died across the sky. But the rain of fire he had anticipated – sixty Quadrantids could stream out in less than an hour – was still impending. They would come, he knew, from the radiant of Boötes, where in 1860 an enigmatic new star – a brilliant nova – had blazed and vanished within a week. This star would perhaps reappear – it survived in the charts as the invisible T Boötis – and it had taken on a stubborn significance for him, so that he had returned to its site again and again, like a mourner to a grave. Its void, far beyond the light of Arcturus, seemed to promise some mysterious epiphany. His computer-controlled telescope mount could lock on to its site within a single minute, and he did this obsessively now as if he must personally witness its resurrection. But when he refined the focus on it, there was only a circle of dark. And this deeper void, he knew, was seven hundred million light years from Earth.

Occasionally these numbers trembled out of the meaning-lessness of their charts and lodged in the real sky. The near-infinite speed of light yet travelled so slowly through the firmament that it might reach humans thousands of millennia after its departure, transmitting the image of a star as it had been long ago. Sometimes it dawned on him that everything he witnessed up here was long departed. He was watching only the dead. He saw the Coma cluster as it had existed when creatures on Earth were still confined to the sea; and the light of dim blue galaxies, now invisibly touching him, had started out before the Earth came into being and might replicate for people's eyes, as if in a time warp, the process of Earth's creation. And time itself, of course, was not an absolute; it might be bent by the force of gravity, even reversed within a black hole. Given light and time, he imagined, his own past life could shake back into fragmented being.

The meteor shower stayed desultory, and the wind had hardened. He thought he smelt something burning. He imagined it a neighbour's dying bonfire, and peered down into the garden. But he saw nothing. Another hour would pass before the rain of meteors reached its climax, so he descended the narrow stairs to his studio, pushing between heaped files and film cassettes, and eased open the bedroom door. His wife was sleeping. He could hear the harsh whisper of her lungs – the sound that had first distressed him four years ago – and saw the laboured rise and fall of her upper body under the blankets. She was facing the ceiling from a tangle of auburn-grey hair. Her slanted eyes were closed. He stooped and softly kissed their corners, then went out, shutting the door.

The faint stench of burning rose again. He assumed a tenant overcooking something, but the smell was acrid, unfamiliar. Sometimes the tenants themselves seemed alien to him. Immured in five storeys beneath him, most had been here on old leases almost as long as he could remember. Some rarely left their rooms. Others came and went seemingly at random. He saw them on stairways or in the corridors, where often the timer switch was defunct, and in the gloom he barely recognised them, while they, in turn, might not acknowledge him. One or two looked haggard and frail, as if life had discarded them. But over time his distaste for them had dissipated, and now he felt towards several a remote indulgence, even tenderness. Occasionally he asked them questions in passing (they did not always answer). He had come to think of them as uneasy acquaintances.

He could not sleep. Yesterday, trying to bring coherence to past disorder, he had assembled his old 8mm cine films – many still in their Kodak envelopes, shot over fifty years ago – and started splicing them together with the same thin brush and pungent glue left over from his youth. He began this as a night-time chore, with the feeling – nostalgic and uneasy – of reviving a practice abandoned long ago. He did not know if the lamp would blow on his obsolete projector, or if the acetate glue would still hold.

Tonight, in the darkened room, as he waited for the hour of the meteors, the first film strip bunched on its spool with a brittle crackling. He eased it free, started again and a yellowish light appeared on his screen. In its dust-framed rectangle, the image came up of a young woman on a bare stage. With the film's celluloid flaking away, she seemed to move under black rain. It was a second before he recognised her, that elfin brightness. She was fooling about as usual, gesturing at nobody in sight. The theatre seats were empty.

In a lull between rehearsals, she had lifted an auburn wig from her blonde-streaked hair and was addressing it like Hamlet his skull. The camera strayed playfully, affection-ately, over her. Without cinematic sound, her mouth opened and closed in noiseless exclamations, and her laughter was a silent hiatus. Once she turned to the camera, complaining of its gaze on her. The next minute she was clowning again, mimicking the curtain calls of her fellow actors, curtseying coyly, bowing augustly. Then her hands lifted and splayed, blacking out the screen, and she was gone.

He threaded the reels more nervously now, unsure what they would resurrect. The subjects of old snapshots seemed to occupy a time irretrievably vanished; but in these cine films people moved unnervingly in the present. As they flickered into life, he found himself gazing back at a once-familiar past – his childhood home – that had yet turned strange. Those who were once old to him had grown magic-ally younger, far younger than he was now. But as if he were seeing them bifocally, they harboured like a memory trace his early perspective. His father on the screen was barely fifty, yet sealed in his son's memory now, impreg-nably senior. The woman walking among the fruit trees in the garden seemed vivid and girlish, but she carried the mother's power of his remembrance.

Several film strips snapped inside the projector, or their sprocket holes tore and they jammed around its gate, where the lamp's heat blistered them within seconds. Each time this happened he was touched by momentary panic. He had not viewed these pictures for decades, but now the loss of a few frames produced an incommensurate sadness. Each cassette seemed to enclose its own time capsule, where people continued in a bright-lit parallel existence. Yet like the light departed from a dead star, the life they projected was an illusion from years ago. And their celluloid inhabitants – loved or forgotten – were bitterly mortal. Their world could be destroyed by a pittance of glue, and each breakage was like a death. He noticed how his hands trembled as he repaired them, scraping away the emulsion to hold their cement: hands that he remembered as a child in old men, wondering at the corded delta of their veins, their liver spots, and had at once been repelled and fascinated by what could never, surely, come to him.

For half a minute the camera panned across parched scrubland. In a settlement like an improvised village, a woman is sitting on a rough bench. He feels the hard sun again, the smell of dust, and torpor. It is hard to look at her now. She no longer exists in the context of the refugee camp, alongside others less than herself. She is alone, on his screen, gazing back at him. His throat has gone dry. She does not smile. Maybe it is not the custom (he cannot remember). Her face is young now, of course, although she was older than him. She looks shy and unexpectant. Her black skin is lighter than he remembers, the illusion of dark silk. She remains perfectly still (she does not understand the cinecamera) so that his film has the stasis of a portrait. It carries with it the bitter pathos of something long ago. Aeons, lives, ago. He whispers: 'Forgive me . . .' She goes on staring.

In the cramped studio the smell of burning has intensified. He thinks it comes from the projector now, and switches it off. Then he remembers the Quadrantid meteors predicted after midnight. He climbs the staircase to the rooftop, where their fire is falling from the sky.

2

Priest

How quiet it is here. Sometimes at night you can hear the waves falling and receding on the shingle, like a slow-beating heart. The sound becomes sadder as you listen, and at night, as now, it grows inexorable, as if a cosmic clock were beating out time to its end.

The tenant felt this melancholy while slipping into sleep, and at first, when the smoke began rising through the floorboards, he covered his head obliviously with the duvet. His ground-floor flat should have been simple to escape. But over the last hour the basement below had become a contained furnace, its explosion delayed by an old fire door and fast-disintegrating plaster. In the end his flat could offer little to the flames. He was a lean, rather ascetic man, and he kept things clean and spare. His clothes barely filled one wardrobe, and his books had been pared down to those he remembered having loved. Only that morning his gaze had travelled over the familiar shelves, wondering at their fleeting knowledge. He had put on an old LP record of the *St John Passion*, and was listening with agnostic pleasure when out of its sleeve fell the yellowed photograph of the seminary.

And there they all were. Standing self-consciously on the chapel steps, they looked dated and formal in their jackets and ties, with their hair combed forward or neatly parted. This was not as he remembered them. Their faces looked pale and enclosed, but their different smiles – intent, open, prim – seemed to coalesce in a bland happiness whose secret he had mislaid.

He wondered what had become of them all. After he left, their mutual correspondence had lapsed through a distance that was more than geographical, and they had faded into the past. Except Ross, of course. How embarrassingly innocent he looked, with his sunburst of hair and cherub's cheeks! The child of an infantilising God. Yet his imagined purity had once exerted a quiet moral force on his fellow ordinands. Beside him Vincent looked twice Ross's age: a figure already of lean authority. Even now it was hard to believe that this louring presence, with the caved-in cheeks and the black focus of a Byzantine saint, was then only twenty-seven. Vincent often talked of the unending spiritual journey, but he had already arrived at his changeless convictions.

Alongside Vincent there was a gap where the photographer – himself – had stepped from the group to record it, and he had playfully inscribed 'Stephen' in the empty space. And smiling there beside it was Julian, sporting fashionably wide lapels and a perky bow tie. Among all their chaste smiles, only Julian's looked equivocal. His head was a different shape from everybody else's – it was enough to convince you of phrenology: a triangle dwindling to a little cusped mouth that sometimes emitted qualms of mistrust. Of all of them, Julian was the one he most wondered at. He had never understood him, and even in the snapshot his expression was indefinable: amused, perhaps cynical, in a way ungiven to priests.

The problems and passions in those cramped lecture rooms and seminars, the intellectual ferment around the Gospels, the suppressed doubts, the strained questioning of his foremost teacher – a man huge in rhetoric and learning, but without human sympathy – all these belonged to a civil war from which Stephen had been invalided out. Now he wondered, baffled at his past belief, how he had created God in private prayer. Yet this thought came to him always with the ringing of an alarm bell – faint and harmlessly far away – as if perhaps, after all, he had once been right, and now, in his half-examined life, he had fallen from the grace of self-judgement.

Sometimes in the seminary at night he tried to imagine the prayers that were rising from those darkened rooms: not the communal worship of chapel or even the impromptu petitions at study meetings, but the night fears and confessions of men kneeling alone by their beds.

Often he felt extraordinarily light and happy. It seemed to him that he had discovered the only meaningful life. Sometimes he felt he loved his fellow ordinands, with their earnest smiles and confidences, their reticent ardour in workshops. He imagined compassion even in his teacher, whose rubicund jowls and bursting waistcoat contradicted the implacable rigour of his mind, and identified a discreet sweetness in the seminary principal, who looked like an ancient boy. And he thought gratefully of his chosen friends, with their conflicting integrities. At such times they seemed all to be living in a charmed circle, a brotherhood of revelation and trust. It was easy to pray for them. These were the blessed nights.

But there were other nights when a dark restlessness descended. After struggling with a piece of exegesis or a doctrinal essay, he would find himself rereading Bible texts without faith or consolation, trying to absolve God of everything he found inequitable. Then the surety of Vincent and Ross seemed far away. Obsessively he would alight on those passages that had never featured in the comfortable parish sermons of his childhood, but which were here confronted head-on. Even the fate of the blasted fig tree or the Gadarene swine could surface to unsettle him. Above all he agonised over every Gospel inconsistency, culminating in the differing accounts of the empty tomb, where the holy word seemed to contravene itself at its heart.

Sometimes he wrestled with the texts far into the night. It was as if there was some chamber of divine grace that he could not enter. So he kept building intellectual edifices to resolve his misgivings. He fell into the sin of judging God. Sometimes, for comfort, he remembered the works of faith that had awed him as a youth – Bach's *St Matthew Passion*, the great rose window of Chartres – and felt a fleeting reprieve.

In the end, exhausted, he confronted his God in prayer. He lit a candle to obscure everything but the wooden cross beside his bed, and this shadowy concentration through the cross – the focus of all redemption and love – would start to calm him. He imagined his fellow ordinands kneeling likewise at this hour, and sensed their prayers massing in the night around him. His supplication and thanksgiving felt warm and answered in the candlelight. Often he whispered aloud, and the words took on a free-floating power. God was beating like a drum in his brain. This was the grace beyond which logic crumbled, the ferment of Christ caring for his flock against all reason, the Christ whom arguments could not wound.

But then came confession. Its lonely self-scrutiny filled Stephen with despair. It had settled into a grinding cycle of contrition and repentance in the recurring wake of sin. He repented his scriptural doubts and his failure to love, his too-great sensitivity towards himself, and the vanity of his unfocused ambition. He repented his harsh parting from his former girlfriend. And abjectly he repented that he masturbated remembering her, the lissome smoothness of her legs. He would caress himself in half-sleep, as if the deed were unconscious, and afterwards would fall into drowsy remorse.

Once he dreamt strangely that he was making love to a woman on a summer hillside. Coppery butterflies rose from the shrubs and shimmered above their naked bodies, then alighted on her face, her breasts, as though enacting a private sacrament, and he awoke to wetness and the memory of ecstasy without sin, and the after-scent of asphodel.

Whenever he left the sanctum of the seminary, the world outside barely jarred on him. He detected God at work even in the ordinary country town nearby. The everyday had become the theatre of divine grace. Twice he was allocated weekend chaplaincies in a neighbouring parish, but he took his visions and anxieties with him, and plagued the overworked vicar with questions that went unanswered. For hours one night he walked in the church graveyard, as if the dead might still him, while the winter sky opened in a blaze of stars. It was years since he had seen such a sky. Those tremendous galaxies glittered down in silence on the graves: a fathomless order where trillions of suns and planets spun in their orbits, suspended in an open miracle above him. He was astonished by their colours: golden, silver-white, pale blue. And once a comet flared like Lucifer across the dark.

He went back into the church with wincing eyes. He was shaking. He slotted Sunday's hymn numbers into their place above the pulpit, then subsided into a choir stall. Behind the altar a dark green drapery shifted in the cold air. It stirred in dim columns. He wanted, for some reason, to part it, and got shakily to his feet. It could only conceal a stone wall, he knew; but he hesitated, as though there were another possibility, as though behind the curtain was something unimaginable. Perhaps it would merely open on a memorial plaque; but perhaps – he was feeling faint now – on a landscape he had never known, the door to lost grace. Then he laughed out loud, a clatter of self-deprecation in the silence, and sat down again. He thrust his head between his knees to revive his circulation. The curtain had gone still, as if the mana had departed from it, and he closed his eyes.

A week later, the seminary was shaken to its roots. The principal did not often give addresses, but when he did, the lecture was attended by all staff and eighty students. He spoke with clipped precision on Heidegger's 'primordial thinking', but nobody later could remember a word. What no one forgot was the third-year student, Bradley, who stood up to speak afterwards. Everyone imagined that he was about to ask a question, or even to offer a sycophantic thank-you. Instead he announced that he was quitting the seminary because he had ceased to believe. He thanked his tutors for their care and scholarship, and was sad that their trust in him had been misplaced. His decision was no reflection on them, he added, but was the result of a long inner conflict which had now resolved itself, he said, with a feeling of release and cleansing. This last he spoke with a hint of defiance, and as he looked round at his erstwhile friends, his face seemed tinged disturbingly with pity.

Shock waves of disbelief went through his audience. Most of them froze where they sat. They simply stared back at him with drained faces. Some of their mouths had fallen open, but one or two retained leftover smiles. The effect was only deepened by Bradley's lack of anything distinctive. He was a sallow, slimmish man in a tired cassock: he might have been any of them.

As the meaning of his words sank in, two of the teachers rose to their feet in half-suppressed alarm. The principal, usually aloof, seemed overcome by fatherly concern, as if Bradley were ill, and left his lectern to go to him. But the student was already walking to the door. The dignity of his retreat was marred only by his shoes, which squeaked like mice across the floorboards. Stephen never forgot how he half turned to look back at them all, then disappeared under the Exit sign.

The atmosphere in the seminary changed that evening. Several formerly quiet students became boisterous and voluble, as if to stress their firmness of faith, while others had turned sombre. Two of the teachers moved solicitously among them, speculating that Christ in His mercy would redeem Bradley after this inexplicable crisis. Stephen's group huddled instinctively into his room for privacy.

Vincent was angry. 'Why did he have to do that in front of the whole seminary? Why couldn't he just sneak away? I think he wanted to drag us down with him.'

Ross's eyes were darting between them all, almost in panic, he so rarely clashed with Vincent. But he said: 'There wasn't evil in him. Bradley was eaten up by something. I don't know what it was. Once he asked me: "Can a person walk on water?" He was strange.'

Their dialogue lurched into talk of Hell and the afterlife. It was as if Bradley's exit was a prefiguration of death, as if he had gone out into the dark, leaving them all behind in the wan light of speculation. Nothing seemed stranger to Stephen than the contrast between Vincent and Ross as they talked: the gaunt handsomeness of the one, and the other like his acolyte, frail and shocked. Ross would have seemed comical had he been less distressed. His blond hair lapped around his head like a disordered halo. Several times he murmured to himself: 'I'll stand on the promise of Your word', as if dropping anchor in a storm. Vincent, meanwhile, seemed ever harder and more secure. He spoke with gravelly authority, his bible in his hands. Occasionally he tried to make a joke, but it came out wooden, as if the language was foreign to him, and he was the only one who laughed. And between them sat Julian, suave and apparently unruffled, his triangle of a head registering alternative amusement and objection.

Around the critical doctrine of Hell, the seminary had left unwonted latitude. In trembling tones Ross maintained that the damned were not tormented for ever, but simply fell into extinction.

But Vincent shook his head with a tinge of regret. 'Christ's sense of justice isn't ours, Ross. Punishment isn't evil. It's the cancellation of evil.' He returned remorselessly to the Gospels. There was already a bookmark in the passage, Stephen noticed. *Then shall he say also unto those on the left hand, Depart from me, ye cursed, into everlasting fire . . .*

Ross murmured: 'Let us pray for him.'

A familiar tension had started up in Stephen. Cold air seemed to be blowing through him, and his stomach contracting. He had combed through the New Testament verses on the fate of the lost – there were more than two hundred and fifty such verses. He heard his own voice out of the blue: 'How can evil and good coexist in God's universe for ever, Vincent? That would be divine failure. "Christ remains on the Cross as long as one sinner remains in Hell."' He couldn't remember which Church Father had said that, but he knew Vincent would.

'God permits evil, Stephen. He permitted the greatest cruelty of all, in the Crucifixion.'

'But surely not evil for ever, Vincent.' Stephen was surprised by the harshness in his own voice. 'Not in the hereafter.'

He stopped as suddenly as he had begun. He wondered if he had slipped into heresy. The breath was beating up inside him in a hot, tearful agitation. He knew its cause but was helpless to stop it. He let his head sink down, as if acquiescing in whatever Vincent was saying, but he did not hear a word. He clenched his eyes shut and choked back the pity engulfing him.

Sometimes her hand returned his grip, as it had done since childhood. Each time he felt a rush of hope. But increasingly her fingers stayed lax in his, or – far worse – they twisted away. He knew she was sunk in a sedated dream, and that this repudiation was only the instinct of a wounded brain. But every time, it hit him with new anguish, so that he massaged her fingers tensely in his, willing their grip to return.

There was no hope of real return, he knew. But his mother's face was still her own, fair and high-boned. A massive stroke, at forty-seven, with no time for a coherent thought or prayer. Yet he did not think about her repentance, although fervent from his first year in theology. The chasm between saved and damned had faded before her, who had never pretended Christianity. Some agitation travelled through her in unpredictable waves. She murmured things he could not catch, and imagined visitors who were far away, or dead, or unknown to him. She never called his name.

At night, the nurses allowed him to sit beside her, unable to share her sleep. The ward groaned in the dark. Dim-lit machines purred and beeped by the bedsides, keeping the dying alive. His eyes grew used to no light. Hour after hour, compulsively, she raised a leg as if to climb from the bed, threatening to sever her intravenous tubes and catheter. Gently, again and again, he lifted the leg back to lie beside the other. But he hated himself for resisting her, because he had the idea that she knew where she wanted to go, and was trying to break free.

After two more days she had slipped further away from him (they had injected morphine). Her hands were no longer clasping anything. He held one for comfort, in case it was still feeling something. They drew a curtain round the bed. Near the end he whispered in her ear, 'All will be well.' He had read that hearing was the last of the senses to fade, and perhaps, for a little, survived death.

When he raised his head again, Ross was talking to Vincent. He might have been going on for an hour or a minute, Stephen did not know. The afterlife, Ross imagined, might not be of the body or even of the soul, but in the memory of God. He had been reading Tillich and Hartshorne. The book of life would be closed, but its pages remained perfect for ever in the cosmic mind.

Stephen thought only: What resurrection is that? God's memories are not living people.

Julian, scenting false consolation, asked: 'And will evil still exist?'

'It wasn't my idea.' Ross looked alarmed. 'But the theory says that evil will be forgotten by God.'

Vincent said: 'It sounds like universal salvation to me.' This was a concept he hated. Salvation for all cheapened the severity of sin, he said, and gutted Christ's atonement of its meaning. 'This doctrine is a fallacy of modern humanism. Nothing in scripture supports it.'

Watching the points of colour rise in Vincent's cheeks, and the way his eyes focused unseeing, and his long hands interlace as if for future prayer, Stephen was surprised by an upsurge of anger, an anger that left him unashamed. Who was Vincent to deny her salvation? For the first time, he thought he hated him. Yet nothing Vincent said perturbed him deeply, or marred his mother's decency. In the voice that was still not quite his own, he said: 'Christ died on the cross for all. It was a universal act.'

Vincent began sifting his bible. But Stephen did not wait. He felt a perverse desire to annoy him. He brought up the old riddle of pagan conversion – a subject Vincent disliked – and wandered through its tired questions with feigned naivety: would all those from pre-Christian history be doomed to everlasting torment? And all those who lived and died in distant countries and cultures?

Julian inserted a moment's mischief: 'Rousseau called religion *une affaire de géographie.*'

Or would Vincent agree with the Papal encyclical that ignorant humans may be saved by grace without knowing it?

For once Vincent did not instantly reply. Instead he went to the basin and dabbed water over his eyes. It was odd. He had even laid aside his bible. Perhaps Julian's quip had irritated him; but Stephen felt rather that his austere friend had sensed a particular sorrow in him, and did not know what to do. At last Vincent sat down again and said: 'I know I'm too much sometimes. I'm sorry . . . I've no business to preach. But I've always thought the act of choosing was crucial. That's how I was brought up. But certainties change . . .' He made one of his laboured jokes, and his lonely laughter was echoed by Ross. He looked strangely crestfallen. 'Sometimes I think we've all been here too long. It's time we were out in the world, doing God's work.'

It was at this moment, Stephen remembered, that the idea of the journey to Mount Athos took hold. They had each mentioned it from time to time, but only now did it seem practical. In two weeks' time, at the term's end, they could take the train to Thessaloniki in northern Greece, then reach Athos by ferry. Its other-worldly solitude appealed to them all at this moment. Its high peninsula was a theocracy within the Greek state, an ancient Orthodox precinct confined to monks and a few travellers. For more than ten centuries it had existed in its own sealed authority, like a time warp in Christian faith.

Stephen thought: perhaps its transcendence will revive us all. Yes, we need to leave here for a while. Maybe it will calm Ross, loosen up Vincent. I need this too. I need other voices, other rites. Perhaps the Orthodox way with death is better than ours. They seem to lay less weight on the human agony of Christ. The torment of atonement is swallowed up in triumph and resurrection. We'll forget all this theological turmoil for a while, the endless questioning. Perhaps I'll find some very old monk, and imagine that I'm closer to divinity. (It helps that they have beards.) Perhaps the mountain will even be beautiful, and we will find peace.

That Sunday, the sermon concerned the denial of St Peter. It was delivered trenchantly by Howell, Stephen's tutor, whose chest heaved under his rhetoric, his red jowls quivering with authority. Denial was different from betrayal, he said, as Peter was from Judas. One was the result of momentary terror, the other of premeditated perfidy. One man, of course, would return to sainthood, the other hang himself. Even while invoking the parables of the lost sheep and the prodigal son, Howell made no mention of Bradley; but the ex-student loomed like a ghost in all their minds.

* * *

For thirty miles the spurs of the peninsula receded into haze, repeating themselves in fainter echoes until they fused with the sky. Beyond the ferry's bows the land fell in forested walls, split by ravines where winter torrents had swept down orange scree. To the west the twin peninsula of Sithonia left a shadow on the sea.

A few gulls wheeled in our wake, crying. We had all grown quiet. A brisk wind was in our faces, and we felt its purging. None of us had been in such country before. Julian was humming a song to himself, trying to remember the Greek words, and the rest of us were smiling into the wind. The only other passengers were a group of Orthodox pilgrims, whose language we did not know.

Ahead of us the promontories unfurled ever more steeply. In this unaccustomed brilliance – the rinsed Greek light – a sense of other-worldliness descended before we even set foot on the holy mountain. The only noise was the weak blend of gulls and waves and the guttural murmurs of the crew. And then out of the sky the scarp of Mount Athos emerged in a snow-streaked pyramid – more precipitous and remote than anything we had imagined – streaming with cloud, six thousand feet above the sea.

After a while, some signs of life began. We could make out the landing stages for hermitages invisible in gullies beyond, then monasteries appeared, one by one, along the shores. Above their ancient walls, fortified against piracy, a crowd of pink-stoned cupolas and filigreed crosses jostled against clock towers telling unfamiliar times. Not a soul was in sight. Once bells sounded quaintly over the water, like the tinkle of a musical box. As we neared the promontory's end, the spurs steepened into cliffs. The walls of the monasteries rose in blank escarpments for fifty feet or more, then burst into precarious windows and galleries. We all stared up in astonishment. We forgot even to take photographs.

At last, as the headland's tip slid behind us, there sailed into view the mother monastery of Athos: less a building than a whole fortified settlement crossing the heights in battlements and turrets, dark with cypress trees. By the time the ferry crunched against the jetty, the place had withdrawn five hundred feet above us. We were the only ones to disembark. The pier was empty, and I wondered if the monastery too might be deserted. For twenty minutes we toiled up the track to its gates. Behind us the slopes dropped to grey rocks above the sea. My breathlessness rose more from excitement than strain – the place so alien and silent – and we all seemed curiously small with our rucksacks and improvised pilgrims' staves, which made a lonely clinking on the path.

Ross murmured: 'Are we in the right place? Can this be it?'

Above the entrance gate a frescoed Virgin and Child lifted their hands in faded blessing. The stones underfoot were indented by generations of booted and sandalled feet. Three massive iron-bound doors and a curving ramp steered us into what seemed to be an abandoned village.

The courtyard was filled with chapels and dormitories. We didn't know where to go. Wonky stairways climbed to shut doors, and other, half-timbered buildings sagged under slate roofs like English barns. We gave up searching for anyone, and wandered in mystified peace. I started taking cine film. We passed alcoves which we took to be abbots' tombs, each carved slab resting beneath the gaze of a painted Christ. The silence was touched only by the piping of unseen birds and a faint chanting from somewhere. The place had the feel of a sleepy hamlet, but clouds were streaming off the heights above.

At last a young monk found us and led us to a balcony where the guest master – a genial patriarch who spoke no English – welcomed us with traditional ouzo, coffee and Turkish delight. Other monks were now gathering for vespers below. They looked too few for the spaces round them. In their soft black caps and black cassocks they walked like shadows. Their hair was drawn back and twisted into buns, but gushing grey beards turned everyone over forty-five into a Methuselah. When we descended to join them, the eyes that stared back at us looked guarded and overcast. I wondered what they were seeing, or if these men knew any language but their own.

The sun was setting. The domed church, painted in faded rose, gave no hint of what was inside. In the porch a stately elder asked us: 'Roman Catholic?'

Vincent said: 'Protestant.'

Gently the monk ushered us to seats in the narthex: high, creaking pews where we propped ourselves awkwardly and could glimpse the service only through an archway into the sanctuary. We had, I realised, been relegated to a zone for heretics; but as the rite proceeded, any anger faded. We were spectators of a ceremony utterly mysterious. For hours two bodiless voices in the sanctuary carried a thread of prayer in lonely antiphony. Often the only sound was a thin patter, as if the readers were chattering to God, and we understood no word except an endlessly recurring *Kyrie Eleison*, 'O Lord have mercy'.

Even in this gloom, by the waning light, I saw that every wall and ceiling was covered with frescoes. Unfamiliar saints held up their books and swords in threat or blessing. They filled the dark with their gaze. Inside the sanctuary the giant candlesticks and chandeliers and gilded thrones and icons were fading to glimmers. Among them an old wood-burning stove sent a rusty flue pipe into the cupola. Meanwhile the cowled monks shuffled in and out at random, pausing to light candles, stooping to kiss the icons one by one, or to press their lips to a frescoed foot or hand. Sometimes they murmured together, or fell asleep in their pews.

I could only guess what the others were feeling. Vincent was craned forward in his seat with a concentrated scrutiny, as if to wrench out some meaning; Julian lounged a little, detached but interested; Ross looked scared. The only pilgrims were a pair of Greek pensioners and a violent-looking youth who embraced the icons with shivering fingers.

As the chanting continued, I lapsed into baffled wonderment. A monk in a crimson chasuble strode into our narthex, censing the icons, censing us, in gusts of blue perfume. I stood up to receive this, copying the monks around me. My bewilderment was painless, almost peaceful. This plainsong descended from ancient Byzantium, I knew, and its language had barely changed from that of the New Testament. I heard no Protestant yearning in it, only a timeless monody, as if all the questings of our distant seminary were useless, even arrogant, before some unknowable grace. Here the sacred and the secular had become conflated, and I imagined the monks moving casually in the anteroom of God.

Julian murmured to me: 'Reverence is immaterial here . . .'

In the dying light the painted martyrs and angels were dimming from our sight. But the amber haloes still glowed around their darkening faces, until at last nothing but this disembodied sanctity survived, like so many golden coins scattered over the walls.

I think this was the last time we were happy together. Some spell had enveloped us all. Julian and Vincent even imagined that the monks' vespers reflected the certitude and liturgical austerity of the early Church. Its celebrants might have been revenants from another time. That evening we ate in the refectory – a frescoed chamber built half a millennium ago for several hundred monks. Watched by the gaunt saints limned on the walls, we supped in silence to the drone of a novice's reading, seated with other pilgrims at chunky marble tables. Our fare was a thin vegetable soup – it was the fasting time of Lent – with bread and olives.

Our dormitory was whitewashed bare. An icon of the Virgin hung in one corner, with her oil lamp lit beneath it. The guest master crossed himself in silence, then left us alone. I had brought a camp stove with me, and we lit this for warmth, huddled on the edge of our beds. There, locked in my failing memory, we remain unageing, and are conversing together softly, although there is nobody to overhear. Vincent's hands are outstretched to the gas flame. His hollowed cheeks and dark eyes still look grimly medieval, but he is smiling. Julian has cowled himself in a blanket like a music-hall monk; and Ross, with his odd, reticent sweetness, is passing us cream chocolates from his backpack. We are unmoored from everything familiar, drawn closer by our isolation here, and I sense the mountain silence all around us like an embalmment: for Athos is a closed theocracy, a country without women, where nobody was ever born, but only dies. Even time here is strange. The monks follow the Julian calendar, abandoned elsewhere four centuries ago, and they tell the hours in the old Byzantine mode, starting the day from sunset. In the cells around us they must be praying alone, reading their canon of Church Fathers unknown to us, or perhaps murmuring the Jesus prayer, whose solitary exercise brings them to salvation. We can hear the waves beating on the rocks far below.

As for myself, I looked like a boyish replica of Vincent in those days: lean and strong, but too sensitive for my own peace – and very ignorant. In truth, we all were.

The Revelation of St John the Divine was a mystery never studied in the seminary; but along the muralled arcades of the monastic church its Apocalypse unfurled in meticulous detail. Here were the trumpeting angels and the four destroying horsemen, the nameless Beast of the Sea and the lion-headed horses puffing brimstone; and the monk who showed us round next morning, reviving some half-forgotten English, pointed them out with stentorian authority as if the rolling-up of time were imminent.

We gazed in perplexity. All through the church and refectory the severe and brilliant frescoes seemed to return us to a primitive, purer time, closer to scripture. Gospel episodes – Christ's baptism, the Nativity, the raising of Lazarus – became newly unfamiliar to me. In their bare economy, they took on the force of sublime facts. And a sense of triumph suffused them. The Crucifixion barely featured, and when it did, the agony of Western portraiture was absent. Instead, angels were flying in to collect Christ's blood in a chalice. Even the scenes of martyrdom were not fleshly tragedies but divine celebrations, in which the executioners too were going about the business of salvation. Their expressions were no different from those of their victims, which remained mild and pain-free even as their heads were flying off – with haloes still intact – at the swing of a sword.

As the ranks of alien saints multiplied – St Basil the Great, St Gregory Palamas, St Maximus the Confessor – Vincent became impatient and irritated: the murals were crude, he said, without depth or perspective. But Julian scrutinised them with fascination. Their artists, he guessed, were not inept, but simply had no interest in perspective. Their frescoes did not draw a spectator in, but projected themselves as living presences. They were sacred propaganda.

Our guiding monk spoke of them matter-of-factly. Here, for him, was all the meaningful past and the promised future. He stopped before a huge fresco of the Last Judgement. His face was nested so deep in beard that only a pair of soft hazel eyes shone through, and seemed to contradict the booming majesty of his voice. From the throne of God a river of fire carried the damned into the mouth of Hell, where Satan writhed (a pilgrim had scratched out his eyes). The monk answered Ross's qualms with implacable certainty: no, this was not extinction but eternal torment. 'This is what God has said. There are sheep, there are goats . . .'

Damnation always troubled Ross: he, who seemed least destined for it. Enclosed by the stained glass of the portico, the Judgement was inflamed still further by blocks of reflected purple and green light. As the monk pointed out the figures drowning eternally in fire, Ross said: 'These are only symbols . . .'

It is strange, in retrospect, what power we accorded these aged monks, with their ascetic robes and God-like beards. For our guide, nothing scriptural could be symbolic. He repeated remorselessly: 'This is what will happen.'

Ross turned away. 'I think in Orthodoxy,' he said, 'you don't believe that people inherit Adam's sin. But in the West we follow St Augustine. He said that we're damned from before birth and our passions are turned to one another instead of to God.' He looked oddly wretched. 'We're always in sin.'

The monk frowned back at him, not quite understanding, but repeated: 'We are always in sin.' The next moment he was declaring: 'The Apocalypse is not far now. The world is turning to Lucifer. His agents are warring against Mount Athos. They mean to destroy us.' The hazel eyes still shone mildly out, as if severed from his words. 'But our trust is in the Virgin. You've seen her icon in the church. She has promised to feed and protect us always . . .'

He began to ramble, sometimes talking about world destruction, sometimes about his cats, and his momentary and delusive power leaked away. Only Ross went on seeming troubled. In the painted refectory, reaching the alcove where the high table stood, I found him staring up at the mural of the Last Supper that overarched it. He smiled weakly at me, then asked: 'Who do you think was "the disciple that Jesus loved"?'

'I'm not sure, Ross.' Many think that the unnamed disciple who rested against Christ's breast at the Last Supper was the youthful St John. But why he was singled out as Christ's beloved, nobody knew.

Tensely Ross asked: 'Can it have been different, do you think? I mean, what He felt . . .'

I answered unthinking: 'The Gospel doesn't say.'

We lingered a moment longer. Ross said out of the blue: 'I'm sorry.'

Above us in the dark the fair young head inclined across the chest of Jesus, while Ross went on gazing up. But still I did not understand.

We climbed that day over the wildest spurs of the peninsula, aiming to reach the western shore by noon. The sky had clouded. The monastery dropped from sight below, and we were ascending on one of the ancient paths which undulate for miles in rough-laid stones. A corridor of shrubs and trees enclosed us. On one side rose the sheer curtain of the mountain; on the other, far below, lay a misty sea.

As our way grew overgrown, we found ourselves brushing through purple-red anemones. The track deteriorated from carefully compacted pebbles to stones set down haphazardly, and at last to naked rock. We went in Indian file, Vincent leading. He was used to trekking holidays, and his stride threatened to leave us all behind. Ross followed him in silence, then Julian, complaining. Once we heard the sound of bells. A train of mules weaved past, laden with wood, untended. And once a shy young monk passed us on his way to another monastery, and wished us Godspeed, touching his hand to his heart.

By noon the way had levelled out through forest. The sky had darkened. Gnarled holm oaks and chestnut trees had dropped their twigs and husks underfoot. In this heavy stillness the chirruping of the birds had stopped. We rested on rocks for a while, eating hunks of monastic bread. Somewhere the sea made an odd hush. It was now that Ross, sitting beside Vincent, reached into his backpack and pulled something out. He handed it to Vincent with a look of such naive ardour that I turned away. His gift was an icon of the Virgin of Tenderness, bought in the ferry port where we had embarked. Julian had already made scathing remarks about these commercial icons, produced by some cheap photographic process, and Vincent, in any case, disliked such things.

Vincent took it in his hands with embarrassed surprise and stared at it. For a long minute he did not know what to say. Ross was still gazing at him. 'It's hand-painted,' he said (even I could tell it wasn't). At last Vincent patted the icon in a curious gesture of conciliation, thanked Ross – his voice taut with pretence – and tucked it away.

It was two hours more before we turned north through precipitous foothills. Our sporadic talk seemed strained, often died away. Mountain outcrops loomed through the trees, and cold streams flowed over our path. Soon we were all labouring, no longer speaking at all. The clink of our trekking poles sounded sharp and lost. The clouds came down so low that we were tramping in swirling mist.

Then we crossed a watershed. Within a few steps our path had crested a little rise, and suddenly beneath us the whole western shore unfolded in brilliant sunlight. Behind us, grey crags burst from the forested slopes in slabs of living rock. In front and beyond, the headlands plunged to the sea for three hundred feet or more, before fading in parallel shadows into the haze. I caught my breath, thinking: no wonder the monks chose here.

Ross cried: 'How can people not believe in God!'

But soon afterwards, where someone had raised a wooden cross, our footpath began to teeter along the cliff edge, fringed by stones laid crosswise to firm it up. Glancing down we could see, through clinging shrubs, the turquoise shallows hundreds of feet below. Once or twice our feet dislodged a stone, which disappeared soundlessly over the edge.

For ten minutes, perhaps, we walked gingerly on, Vincent still in front. The air was bright and silent. A buzzard quartered the sky above us. I fell into a drugged stupor, eased by the level pathway and the sun's warmth. Then Ross stopped dead in front of me. His whole body was shaking. He said faintly: 'I can't go on.' His trekking pole clattered to the ground.

I thought he was exhausted, and said: 'It's not far now.'

But he sat down abruptly on the track, clasping his knees, his cap awry on his blond head. His eyes were clenched shut.

Julian said: 'It's the height.'

I crouched behind Ross, touching his shoulder. 'It's safe,' I said. 'The track's safe.'

But his voice sounded drained and high, like a child's. 'I can't.' His face was turned toward the hills, away from the chasm two feet off.

Vincent had turned back and was standing over him. He asked irritably: 'What's wrong?'

Julian said: 'He's faint. It's the height.'

Vincent bent down to Ross, his mouth close to his ear, and said quite tenderly: 'You walk beside me.' He put one arm round Ross's shoulders, and pulled him to his feet. 'Now, first step.'

For a moment Ross did nothing. I thought he might sit down again. Then, like a robot starting up, he took a short, numbed step. Vincent was on his far side, closer to the cliff edge, blocking it from his view. Ross's gait was stiff and unnatural. He might have been sleepwalking. For twenty or thirty paces this mechanical walk continued, while Vincent's arm steadied him; then his movements started to loosen. But the path continued narrow, and the two walked on, crushed together on its constricted thread. Coming behind them, carrying Ross's trekking pole, I sensed his terror draining away, until at last he seemed to go quite easily, with his head resting on Vincent's shoulder. And for a moment I could not remember what I was reminded of – the fair head inclined to the upright body beside it – until I recalled with a start the fresco of the Last Supper.

Then the track widened. Vincent said: 'You'll be all right now,' and he strode ahead again, Ross following shakily, until we were trekking high above the roofs of a scattered hermitage. Chaffinches flittered ahead of us, and the path cast its sun-warmed spell again, as if nothing had happened. It was fringed with violets and euphorbia now, where bumblebees sounded and saffron butterflies were flying over the shrubs.

By sunset even Vincent was flagging, and the rest of us were exhausted. A sharp wind had got up. We had miscalculated our destination on the map, underestimating the steep terrain, and we were all relieved when through the trees, in the mouth of a wild ravine, the fortress walls of St Paulos monastery rose in the darkening sky.

An austere guest master directed us to the dormitory, where we were the only sleepers. We were forbidden, as Protestants, to attend either vespers or matins, he said, and there was no food. The only other monks we saw looked old and oblivious. It had grown suddenly cold. Soon the wind was moaning round our windows, and we could hear the waves throbbing below. We ate biscuits out of our rucksacks, and fell dog-tired into bed. I must have been too strained, at first, to sleep, and instead remained half dreaming, distracted by incoherent thoughts. Later I mistook the breaking of the waves for the roar of passing traffic. But of course no car had ever been here.

Hours later, near to dawn, something jolted me awake. The wind was battering at the windows, but the disturbance was close by. Somebody was sobbing. The sound was like a deep, hollow dread. I eased myself from my bed and padded over to Ross; but he was fast asleep. The trouble was rising from Julian. I could not see his face in the dark, but his weeping had the muffled, internal secrecy of a dream, not of waking sorrow. He would be ashamed, I thought, if I roused him, and I crept back to bed. But for a long time this enigmatic sobbing continued, as if from somewhere inconsolable.

I have lost the habit that I had long ago, of sensitised self-scrutiny, let alone confession. I am no longer grateful to an ungraspable divinity for my blessings, nor feel that my troubles are his purposeful affliction for my good. There is no more personal relationship to the unseen. I am, in a sense, free.

Lying in the dormitory at night, when the oil lamp had died beneath an icon of the Baptist, I had a foretaste of this severance, as though I had left some harbour for the open sea. I had been too self-conscious to kneel by my bed, even before colleagues, and the God that I usually invoked there, the God I felt tingling inside me at prayer, seemed suddenly to have withdrawn. When I tried to speak with Him in the dark, it was as if I had asked a question into silence, and I felt no pain, only a dulled bewilderment. I gazed across at the blanketed shapes of the others, and they were momentarily strangers. I closed my eyes. In the swimming blackness, nothing happened. Only gradually did this alienation ebb away, and God returned, seeping back through the windows with the dawn.

I hoped to slip into the church after matins. In the courtyard, constricted by battlements and multi-tiered dormitories, the wind barely stirred. But I shivered in the cold. The whole monastery seemed thrust violently against the mountain, its keep and belfry jostling for air.

A few monks were returning from matins to their cells, leaving silence.

I sheltered in the church portico, enclosed by stained glass. Above the doorway a pilgrim had hung a faded icon of the Virgin. I was peering up at this, thinking of Ross and Vincent, when Julian's voice behind me said: 'It's odd, isn't it?' He seemed as composed as usual, with no trace of the night's rack. Perhaps he had no memory of it. 'The Virgin's whole cult is based on a mistranslation. St Matthew translates the Hebrew 'young woman' of Isaiah's prophecy into the Greek 'virgin'. An easy slip. And from there, of course, everything flowed.' He gave his impish smile. 'But in those days, of course, anybody who was anybody had to be born of a virgin. Alexander, it was rumoured, even Julius Caesar . . .'

I couldn't help laughing. 'Julian, what on earth *do* you believe?'

He answered sharply: 'I believe Christ died to take away our sins, not our minds.'

Sometimes I felt that his abhorrence of sentimentality arose from conscious self-discipline, a barrier against another, indulgent self. Perhaps there was a Julian somewhere else who dreamt of valid miracles and unconditional forgiveness; but I would never meet him. I may have been remembering my pre-dawn bafflement, because I found myself saying: 'It must be easier to be Vincent . . .'

'I'm not sure. Vincent wants to be his father. It must be a horrible strain. I met his father once, when he visited the seminary, did I tell you? At first I thought Vincent had gone a bit grey and got even taller. His father is huge. He's chairman of something-or-other big. Vincent told me his paternal advice was: 'Never say you're sorry."

Julian sat down on the bench under the stained-glass porch. He too was shivering. His habitual playfulness dropped away. 'I'm not saying Vincent is seeking God because of his father. I don't know why God calls people.' He looked up at me. 'Maybe He called you through your mother's death.'

I said: 'I'd decided before that.'

'Well then, I dare say your calling is as mysterious as mine.' The old levity returned. 'There's nothing in my family to explain anything. My father works for the local council, perfectly boring. I have no desire to mimic him or replace him with a divine patriarch, let alone earn the grace of the Holy Mother' – he glanced up at her icon. 'My mother is rather plain and works in a bank.'

'And Ross . . .' I began, staring at the floor. Its black and white tiles spread away like a giant chessboard. 'Do you think he is replacing his absent father with Vincent?'

'Yes, in a way.'

I marvelled then at how easily we all spoke now that we'd left the seminary. I'd discovered more about my companions during the past few days than in many previous months. In a sense the brotherhood of the seminary levelled us all; but now I realised that Vincent's family was rather grand – he'd been to a small public school, like me – whereas Ross was the only child of a broken home, and his mother took in lodgers.

Julian said: 'With Ross it may be different. I'm not sure. He's a sweet boy.' He glanced at me, unsure what I understood. 'I think he's very ashamed. I don't think he wants to be what he is. His background can't be very understanding . . .'

But the next moment the two of them appeared, Vincent and Ross, stacked with their backpacks and trekking poles, and joking: 'We thought you'd gone!'

Within an hour the wild peninsula had changed again. By the time we reached a ruined watchtower on the shore, a hard, brilliant sun was playing over the sea. We sat in the scrub and munched our iron rations in silence. To our north, a curtain wall of mountains plunged sheer to the waves, appearing to seal us into the cove, before we noticed a goat track vanishing up its rocks. This happened again and again. Some giant spur or declivity would seem to put a full stop to our path, but minutes later an unseen passage would be worming around ravines, or finding a pass between precipitous ridges.

Perhaps it is only in retrospect that I imagine some dynamic changed among our group, because I cannot identify it. Vincent still strode or clambered ahead, his eyes shaded by an old cloth cap, with Ross following, sometimes breathless, and Julian in cavalry twills and a paisley scarf, too dapper for this rough country. In my memory, too, I go light-headed behind them, young even for twenty-two, watching them make their unequal way along the cliffs, while the peninsula has coalesced around us all into a static blaze of rocks and sea. And here the open wound of my mother's death begins to close a little, as if the bottled grief of the seminary were being cleansed in the clear light.

We reached the monastery of Dionysiou by noon. From its plinth of coagulated rock, so steep that no shrub touched it, the sheer glacis of the monastery walls, slit with loopholes, burst into galleries sixty feet in the air. Some monks were tending olive trees on the terrace below; and beyond the entrance ramp, where the iron-bound doors stood ajar under frescoes of girlish archangels, the courtyard was mellow with birdsong and incense. Its gates and passages ended in vistas of mountain or sea, and a decrepit clock tower told the Byzantine hours.

A courteous old monk welcomed us with coffee and Turkish delight, and escorted us to tiny cells with windows on to blankness. That evening we dined in the painted refectory, on pasta and lentils, while readings from the Church Fathers, intoned by a nervous novice, compelled us to silence. Afterwards, in the solitude of my cell, I got down on the cold slabs and prayed to the God who had eluded me the night before, and his feel was familiar again, palpable, so that I lay calm at last in the hard bed.

The monastic semantron was an iron bar which a monk beat with a hammer to summon the brethren to prayer. At four in the morning its call to matins rang plangent in the dark, and I got up, after rare hours of insomnia, remembering how the liturgy had mystified me before, but curious again, and expectant.

As I crossed the deserted courtyard to the church, scattering a mob of cats, I seemed to be the only worshipper. At first I could make out almost nothing. A few oil lamps dangled disembodied lights, and here and there a candle guttered under an icon. At long intervals blackveiled monks filtered into the sanctuary, while the lonely chant of cantor and reader started up its conversation in the dark. Sometimes I got up from my pew, as the monks did, and followed their leisurely itinerary into the side chapels among the grander icons, where they lit their votive tapers.

As the hours wore on, I came to think that the time-less rite, for all its invocations to forgiveness, had already crossed some threshold into the beneficence of God. Julian had mentioned that these churches were a mirror of the celestial world, following a changeless scheme, and I began dimly to discern this. To the shambling and comfortable monks, I realised, the walls opened on to paradise, and the life-size saints and Fathers, unfurling their scrolls or unsheathing swords, were present with us in prayer.

It was a strange realisation, aroused by the hallowing candles that now burned beneath the icons, and awakening the frescoes out of their other world. For a while, three or four late-assembled pilgrims – they looked like farmers – blocked my view into the inner sanctum, but at a ritual climax, as the *Kyrie Eleison* pleaded again for mercy, they knelt and laid their lips to the marble floor. Among them, with a jolt of fear, I saw and heard the sunburst of a blond head striking the marble, and as he withdrew, I glimpsed the glittering eyes of Ross, more distraught than I had ever seen him. His pink cheeks were streaming tears. He knelt again, almost prostrate, while the deep 'O Lord have mercy' re-echoed from the cantor. I felt a shock of sadness. I wanted to go over to him, but did not. I remained rooted to my pew, fearful of his privacy. Sometimes, in retrospect, I despise myself.

When the pilgrims moved away from the sanctuary arch, there was nobody there any more – I even wondered if I had imagined him. The two monks beside me were fast asleep, and the others barely stirring. The church, in this inflamed light, was becoming as they wished: the refraction of God's universe, inhabited less by men – who had grown small in His worship – than by the supernatural populace looming from the walls and columns, ignited by human prayer, and growing minute by minute closer and more alive.

At the end of the service some trestle tables were assembled, and I feared a funeral. But instead three relics from the treasury were displayed for pilgrims' worship. I was glad that Ross was not here, nor Julian, to witness this credulity. In their enamelled frames lay a splinter of the True Cross, a bone of St Paraskeve (sovereign against blindness), and the left arm of John the Baptist, still dangling some skin.

I hung back from these, while the farmers fell on their knees again, and the monk in charge ushered them forward one by one to gaze and kiss, before ordering the relics away. I noticed this monk watching me – a man still young but in some authority (the others kissed his hand) – and before I left he came over and said in grave, deliberate English: 'You understand we do not adore these things for themselves. They are not idols. God's grace is in them.' He had seen me recoil from what was precious to him, and he wanted me to understand. In his sallow face the eyes looked black and anxious, but the mouth spoke donnishly from a silken beard. 'You are one of the Protestant group, are you not?' He murmured a welcome. 'Do you believe in the resurrection of the body?'

'Of a spiritual body . . .'

He looked relieved. He touched my forearm, like a blessing. 'St Paul said the body is the temple of the spirit, and the righteous will rise clothed in it. Even in this world the body is holy. So the relics too are holy.' He was smiling. 'Our bodies wait for redemption. That is why we bury our brothers in the earth. *All things will be freed from the chains of corruption.*'

I heard myself say: 'The earthly body doesn't matter.' My mother had wanted cremation. 'It's gone to ashes . . .' But I still found this hard to say.

He clicked his tongue. 'I think that in Protestantism you are very separate from your dead. I'm told you do not pray for them.'

'No, we don't.' I heard my own regret. Perhaps he heard it too.

'That is very wrong. You do them wrong.'

I didn't know what to say.

'We pray for our departed. We pray for them while they are being purified before the Last Day. And I think they pray for us. That is an important thing.' His eyes flickered to the fresco above us, where Christ was pulling Adam and Eve astonished from their graves. 'Every week we eat the *koliva* cake in memory of our brothers, as a petition for their souls.'

I thought then: how strange. In the seminary we were taught that the dead were beyond our help, and we beyond theirs. The chasm was absolute. But now a cold ache opened in my stomach. Was it only a chance of history or geography – or a theological text – that separated us from the Orthodox belief?

The monk said: 'My father is dead, but we pray for one another. I feel it.' He crossed himself, and lifted his head. 'You may even pray for the Devil if you like!' This brought on a sudden uproarious laugh. It echoed incongruously around the now-empty sanctuary; then his expression recomposed, as if he had regretted his thought.

We walked from the church and into the dawn-lit court-yard. In parting he said: 'I think the dead are sometimes alive among us. There are miracles that have happened.'

I did not want to hear these miracles – they might stain his fleeting authority – and I was glad when he said good-bye. I went out for a while to a little kiosk beyond the gates. It overlooked an empty sea. A narrow stream, swollen by spring rain, was clattering down the ravine behind, and I watched it glimmer in the thin light, feeling a faint sickness.

That night I prayed for my mother's soul.

This was our last day. On our way down to the shore we passed the chapel that the monk had spoken of, where the bones of the dead brethren were heaped in an open-air ossuary. We gazed at them numbly, so impersonal did they seem, reduced almost to mineral: femurs, tibias, pelvic girdles all stacked together in kind, and the skulls in bleached ranks, yet each painted with a name.

By mid-morning, as we climbed the cliffs, the coast unfurled again below, and the sky was blazing. Vincent and I exchanged trousers for shorts in the sudden heat, and Julian put on a jaunty straw hat. We slipped into our accustomed places as though into a natural order: Vincent's lean-muscled legs preceding Ross up the scarp, Julian dabbing at the sweat under his hat, I following dreamily behind.

Toward midday we ate a frugal picnic, bolstered by two bottles of local wine, which Julian had bought from the monks of Dionysiou. On Vincent it had no discernible effect, but Ross gulped down whole cupfuls, as if he had never drunk before, and joked that it might cure his vertigo. After a while Julian pronounced it undrinkably sweet, and poured the second bottle into the rocks.

As we started north again in the noon hush, there was no more birdsong. Even the waves were silenced by distance. Underfoot, white lichen splashed the stones, and unknown flowers grew. The light was so clear that a ship far out to sea was as distinct as the trees beside us.

We reached a pass where a wayside shrine, painted white and blue, sheltered a flame-blackened image and a melted candle. On either side the mountains poured to the sea. I have wondered sometimes what might have been averted had there been no bench there, where we sat for a while, or if Julian had not bought wine. As it was, we propped our rucksacks against a boulder and slumped down, three of us panting a little. The light was dazzling. A hawk circled us in the breathless air. Far below, a red-roofed monastery was nestled above the sea.

I remember now Ross's flush as he sat beside Vincent – the wine, perhaps, mounting to his neck, his cheeks. He seemed in a sort of ecstasy. The land's beauty, the dazing light, the alcohol: I don't know what released him at this moment. But he turned to Vincent beside him and exclaimed at nature's power in a voice turned loud and high in its own rejoicing. The memory of his delusion still tightens my throat when I think of it. One of Vincent's legs was spread carelessly against him – the lean thigh flecked with black hairs – and Vincent's gaze, released by the sun, indulgently met Ross's own.

It seemed such a slight thing, in the end. Wretchedly slight. I cannot remember precisely what Ross said. But his gaze on Vincent was rapt and unflinching. I noticed he had an erection. Then he leant forward and clasped Vincent's thigh with his hand, squeezing its sinew. His mouth had fallen open.

I felt cold with apprehension. Something known but unacknowledged had surfaced into the light. I saw Vincent's cheeks tauten, and his jaw. Very deliberately, he reached down and disengaged Ross's hand. Grasping his wrist, he carried the hand clear across Ross's body and laid it as far away from himself as he could. Then he stood up, hoisted his backpack and walked on.

A terrible shock came over Ross's face. All the joy – the rush of intoxicated ecstasy – had drained from it in an instant. He had turned chalk white. His head sank and his hands were trembling. For a long time nobody made a move. At last he murmured: 'You go on, go on . . .' So Julian and I followed Vincent along the levelled path, and down to the last monastery, in silence, while the heat ebbed out of the sky.

One other memory survives from that journey. In the small port from which a bus would return us to Thessaloniki – Mount Athos now far out of sight – we spent the last hours on a deserted beach. A few gulls were pacing along the tide-line, and grey pebbles shone under the waves. From childhood I had loved to bathe in a cold sea, and that morning the spring heat, and perhaps recent events, nerved me to wade in.

Vincent and Julian remained on the shore, thinking me mad. Then I saw that Ross, standing on a ledge beneath them, had stripped to his underpants. He plunged into the freezing water, crying out: 'It's fine! Come on in!' and revolving his shoulders above the waves in hectic bravado. The damp yellow helmet of his hair turned him for a moment into a different man. But close to, I saw that he was pink and shaky, and the stroke of his crawl was an uncoordinated flailing. Yet he continued to match me stroke for stroke in the icy sea.

It's hard to think of the following days with detachment. And I cannot trust my memory. I know only that an odd depression descended on me. I couldn't locate its precise cause, or slough it off. The seminary now seemed dark, physically dark. I ascribed this to the contrast between an overcast England and the remembered clarity of Athos, but my eyes never again filled the place with light. Our holiday receded in my mind into its own country, and became a little unreal. Few of the other ordinands showed any interest in it. Many were still haunted by Bradley's defection, and the dedication noticeboard was plastered with prayers for his return to the light. My supervisor, I think, felt momentarily wary of us, mistaking my bewitchment at Greece's scenery and my curiosity at its liturgy as a drift towards Orthodoxy, and even Howell, in his bluff way, joked: 'Don't go muttering mystic prayers instead of studying your bible!' When I read about Orthodoxy, trying to understand those distant monks, I imagined that the gulf between West and East was due less to theology than to a profound difference in temperament, which a thousand years had deepened, and I could imagine no bridge across.

Vincent, Julian, Ross and I might have drawn closer, remembering those Athos days. Instead, insensibly, we cooled to one another, as if reluctant to see ourselves transformed out of that sunlight into the drab strictures of the seminary.

In my mind, too, the memory of Ross's blunder faded, and might have grown almost forgotten were it not for his own closure and silence. At lectures and workshops, as usual, he barely spoke; but in prayer services too, where he used to interject a fervent note of praise or wonder, I saw him shut away. He was always seated at the back now, and his face had the pallor of a mask behind which his real features had withdrawn. I think he purposely avoided me. He avoided us all. And my habitual reluctance to intrude on others, along with my own preoccupation with work, reproaches me still.

Vincent too seemed restless. Once he came to my room, more gaunt and intense than usual, and reiterated that it was time to do God's work in the field. The world's people were spiritually perishing out there, he said, while we spent our time pondering the exegetics of the Mosaic covenant. 'In the summer break,' he suddenly asked, 'will you join me abroad? It'll be hot, Tanzania, and getting there expensive. But someone I know is working in a refugee ministry, and they need help.'

I said unthinking: 'What about Julian? I think he could afford it.'

'He wouldn't be able to stand it.' Vincent laughed: his short, dry cough. 'You would.' He thrust out his hand for me to shake. I took it automatically, at once flattered and alarmed: it felt like a sealed promise.

Neither of us mentioned Ross.

Within two weeks the world outside had brightened into late spring. Daffodils appeared along the seminary lawns, and in the nearby streets the girls went in sleeveless dresses, with glimpses of distracting legs as they bicycled to work.

In afternoon seminars we began to study pastoral theology. It was an undemanding course, taught by a sad-faced tutor whose stress on sacred duty was laced with droll jokes. I started to settle once more into an eventless routine, while the journey to Tanzania receded into the future.

Then one morning somebody asked: 'Have you seen Ross?'

I realised that he had not attended morning service, nor breakfast. And now his seat in the lecture hall was empty. Julian motioned me to slip away and joined me outside Ross's room. Its door was locked. We called his name, but our voices rang out unanswered, loud in the silence. I strained my ears for a murmur, a cry of sickness, or even from an overdose. But nothing came. Our knocking on the door became strident, finally weak. I think we both then knew what had happened. I wondered whether to call a teacher, but Julian shouted out once more, 'Ross!' and nudged the door with his shoulder. It didn't give. He looked at me mutely, and the fear in his face chilled my blood. Then he said: 'Shall we?' and we rammed the door together.

The lock snapped and it floated open. We froze in the doorway. For a moment I imagined that Ross was standing on his desk, fixing a light bulb. His head was turned away from us. Then I saw his feet touching nothing. The disturbed air from the open door began to turn his body, and we watched as he revolved to face us, like an accusation. I shut my eyes against his stare. The tip of one finger was caught in the wire noose, as if at the last moment he had changed his mind. We rushed to hold him up, but his body was heavy and cold. The hand that tapped against my cheek was cold too. He must have hanged himself early that night.

This happened, of course, in another time, in a time of secrecy. Several years before I held Ross's body in my arms – we cut him down with a pair of blunt secateurs – the Wolfenden Report had decriminalised the man he might have become. But the stigma of so-called perversion ran fathomlessly deep. Barely a century before, homosexual practice had been punishable by death. In Ross's time, legal same-sex partnerships were still unthinkable, and gay culture not even a glimmer on the horizon. The Church clung to Leviticus, St Paul and the destruction of Sodom, and it would be fifty years before a gay partnership was sealed on consecrated ground. Ross was born too early, and too frail: one of those whom Oscar Wilde lamented when he wrote that the way forward would be red with sacrifice.

In the seminary the shock was steeped in bewilderment. Ross's sweetness and accessibility – people imagined him transparent – bathed him in an aura of innocence. His self-violence was all but inexplicable. Some students even imagined that he had hanged himself by mistake, or was the victim of a dementing disease. Others struggled with the lessons of the early Fathers, with the condemnation of St Augustine and even of Thomas Aquinas, and feared that a suicide, without chance of repentance, dies in sin. But I described to them Ross's uplifted hand, plucking at the noose, and ventured a last-moment contrition for his act, that he continue in a state of grace. I tried vainly to imagine this. But most often I imagined his own terror as he consigned himself to the extinction in which he had said he believed.

I never knew precisely how Vincent and Julian responded to the principal's interrogation, or to that of the police. Julian had returned to his sometimes cryptic self, but was tinged by a new world-weariness, which might have verged on despair. I often wonder what became of him. Vincent continued as stringent and focused as usual, and perhaps only Julian and I recognised an undertone of pensive regret.

For myself, when summoned to the principal's office, I was overcome by a blind loyalty to Ross. I realise that I validated his shame by barely mentioning what happened on Athos. Facing the principal – a man in whom I expected no understanding – I baulked at all hypotheses. My naivety must have been obvious to him, but my resistance went undetected. I even felt sorry for him. But when he asked me: 'Did you notice any change in Ross's behaviour?' I could only say yes. Something was afflicting him, I admitted. Something he found unbearable, that violated his faith. I felt too that he had a profound desire to be like others. Beyond that, I could not tell.

The next question, which I dreaded, never came. Why didn't you talk to him? Why didn't I? Why didn't I even broach it? Because I was young, and embarrassed, of course. People were, in those days. Perhaps I even feared it somewhere in myself. And I neglected Ross, banally, because I was struggling to understand divine command theory, and was falling behind with my essays.

The principal always surprised me when he lapsed into sympathy. Perhaps it was only his appearance – that face of a wizened adolescent – that made me recoil. But suddenly he said: 'This has been hard for you, Stephen. I know you and Ross were good friends. Now Vincent has asked me if he can take early leave this May. He wants to go to Tanzania, to something called the Pentecostal Church of Good Tidings. I don't know this place. We can't help you there. The people will be refugees from Rwanda. War refugees, Tutsis. He says you will go with him. Do you want that?'

'Yes, I think so.' I welcomed this now. I welcomed any-where but here. 'Yes.'

I had never heard of the Tutsis, nor could I know that I was about to enter a region that thirty years later would be laid waste by genocide. For a minute before dismissing me the principal scribbled some notes on a pad. As I stood up to leave, I blurted out: 'Has he gone to Hell, sir?'

The principal looked suddenly very tired. 'I can't say. He didn't give God much chance to forgive him, did he?' Flippancy came unnaturally to the principal, but perhaps he simply wanted me to go. He mumbled without looking up: 'The God you wish for is not necessarily the God that is.'

These were words that rankled for a long time after-wards. I found them vaguely insulting, although I think he meant them kindly. Sometimes they intruded on my prayers.

It was Howell who gave the sermon in chapel that Sunday, his bulk overflowing the pulpit. A month before, his sermon had never directly cited Bradley, but now he met Ross's suicide head-on. His red hands massaged the pulpit's rim. He looked flushed, almost angry. No one had the right to abrogate to themselves the power of God, he said. *'For to God alone belongs the judgement of life and death.'* And the Sixth Commandment was as valid for the killing of the self as it was of others.

Whereas Bradley's defection had aroused anxiety and latent anger, Ross's death filled us all with diffused guilt, and the faces gazing back at Howell looked as tense and young as schoolboys'. They wanted comfort. But as his talk went on, Howell's voice darkened into a different regret. Suicide, he conjectured, was rarely the crime of the grossly worldly. It tempted more delicate psyches, less suited to the world's harshness. Ross, by all accounts, was such a man. There were those, even in the early Church, who took their lives to escape evil. Theirs was, in a way, a purifying act – a deliverance from the sins of others and perhaps of the self. (I wondered then if Howell had sensed more of Ross than he declared.) Nothing in the Gospels condemned suicide, he went on. Christ Himself had gone knowingly to his human death.

What had begun as condemnation smoothed into compassion. God, who knew the death of a sparrow, would surely be careful of Ross. And who were we to judge? To judge him would be to repeat his own sin: to steal the divine prerogative. At the end, exhausted by his own oratory, Howell fell back on quoting Donne, leaning forward and glaring at us all, released at last into the tide of another's words: '*Thou knowest this man's fall, but thou knowest not his wrestling; which perchance were such that almost his very fall is justified and accepted of God.*'

* * *

The road was a ribbon of pink earth laid straight to the horizon. On either side the country undulated in shallow hills, blurred by yellow fescue grass. Here and there a shrub or acacia tree showed still green from the vanished rains, and left a silhouette in the haze. Even in the land's dryness, the air felt humid. Our Land Rover bumped and groaned over the track. The driver sang soft Swahili songs. Whenever we stopped to stretch our legs, the silence crept in on us. There was no wind, and no birdsong. Everything was still.

Neither Vincent nor I had known anything like this. The farthest south I had been was Greece, which had enclosed us in the stark divides of sea and mountain. But here the land might have been limitless. Close at hand it was broken into a low, shapeless confusion: hillocks peeled to a rose-coloured soil under the grass, and speckled with dying shrubs. But beyond, the whole continent appeared to wane into infinity. It was beautiful and alien. Range upon range of huge, static clouds overspread it, and looked as solid and permanent as anything below. It seemed a country that was waiting to become something, or that had long ago been so, then fallen asleep.

We travelled like this for more than a hundred miles, exhausted already by the twenty-four-hour journey from

Dar es Salaam, and by the dazing heat. Our throats were dry with dust. Once a herd of antelope shimmered and stopped in the distance, poised between curiosity and alarm. And once a rust-coloured patch of ground had been cleared before a group of huts, and a lone woman was walking beside the track.

I watched this land with a feeling of detached release. Vincent must have felt the same. He said out of the blue: 'We were right to come here.' The claustrophobia of the seminary was starting to lift, replaced by this heartless and sanitising emptiness in which everything – grief, guilt – became lost and small. Even my remorse over Ross began to shrink into a kernel of shame which has never left me. Because of this guilt, I think, I never purely mourned him.

We saw the refugee camp from a long way away. It swarmed unprotected over a plateau: a whole town of thatched mud dwellings, circled by a no-man's-land of stubbled maize. We drove into it down streets split by gullies of waste water. The compacted ground glared red. Nothing was quite as I had expected. No children rushed to beg from us, and whatever tents had once composed the place had been redeployed to insulate its roofs or hung torn in the doorways. A gang of boys was playing in a clearing among the huts, kicking a football of scuffed rubber, and some women in brilliant skirts queued at a water pump.

The Pentecostal Church of Good Tidings was built of clay like the rest, long and low and washed blue. Powdered in pink dust, we arrived to find the pastor waiting for us in its doorway. He may have been standing there for hours. He was a mahogany-skinned Rwandan, important in a dazzling white jacket, smiling welcome. But Vincent's friend Alan was not here. He was recovering from malaria in another village, the pastor said, and would not return for a week. But we shouldn't worry. In the dry season, malaria was rare.

Our room was a neighbouring hut. Our beds were quilts laid on its clay floor. There was a single window, and no furniture. We would wash from an enamel basin filled from the nearby pump. Vincent was unperturbed, even perversely exhilarated. Later we were to hammer nails into the mud walls and suspend our mosquito net across. Our suitcases became our wardrobes. A huge padlock on the rickety door gave us some security.

Walking in the early evening, we could barely compass the camp. Its alleys were compacted mud underfoot. The dwellings were thatched above lattices of sticks or corrugated iron, and our way was overhung with drying clothes and threadbare blankets. Barely a window showed. Four thousand people lived here, the pastor said, many of them widows and children. But there were young men too. Some remained listless under their makeshift porches, and watched us in calm enigma. Their unsmiling gaze began to unnerve me. They had witnessed unspeakable things. Perhaps they had also committed them. Others were walking in the streets, as if they had somewhere important to go, and sometimes came to clasp the pastor's hands, even the older men calling him Papa. He answered them affectionately, with a tinge of self-importance, his white jacket shining among them like a lodestar.

What were they wanting of him? Vincent asked.

'They want to go home.' The pastor's English was deliberate, newly learnt. 'They ask me for news. But I have no news.' He frowned. 'They wait. They do nothing. There is nothing to do. Maybe a little farming.'

Vincent said: 'But in the end they'll go back?'

'That is in God's will.' The pastor stared at the ground. 'Some of us may never go back.' He pointed behind us. 'You see that building? That is United Nations. They feed us. We have just enough. Twelve kilos of maize per person per month. And cooking oil. No beans now, no sugar. They say we will be here for long haul. The Jesuits have made a primary school also. And there are four other churches. And a clinic, with nurses. But the hospital is three hundred miles away.' He waved to the south. 'God has not decided when we go home.'

The people passing us were of near-uniform poverty. War and flight had all but levelled them out. But the women went in their bright native dress, and a few glittered with salvaged jewellery. Once an elderly man went by – a former civil servant, the pastor said – wearing a linen suit, with a white shirt and frayed tie, and talked to nobody.

We ate in the pastor's home that night. It was grander than most, its courtyard enclosed by a brushwood fence. He owned a Bush transistor radio and a broken sofa. We ate by the light of a paraffin lamp, squatting on the clay floor before a dish of boiled maize and a little spinach, which we scooped in our fingers. His wife served us in smiling silence, and did not eat with us. His adopted daughter – a twelve-year-old war orphan – stood in a corner and watched.

They had inherited French Christian names – the pastor was Olivier – and French words seeped into his English. 'But the Belgians abandoned us five years ago,' he said. 'They turned us against the Hutus, then left us. In my village everyone I know was killed. Even our church there, the Hutus come inside and kill us.'

He did not say how he had escaped, and we did not ask. But he started talking about the camp in a vivid, guttural rush, and often laughed. Their troubles were all of idleness, he said. They had no work here, no future. So they took to adultery and theft. There was no electricity, nothing by night to show up crime and betrayal. Many families were headed by young widows, and some by teenage children. There were murders, which the Tanzanian police could never unravel. The camp would close against them.

'The word "refugee", it is a very ugly word. We are all ashamed. People take refuge when they are weak. But we Tutsis are not slaves, we are *un peuple fier*. You will be with us six weeks, but many of us have been here five years . . .'

That night, too tired to pray, somehow too tired to sleep, I stretched out on the thin quilt and gazed into the dark. Vincent lay a yard away, restless too. The air was cool and no mosquitoes whined around our nets.

I said in the silence: 'I don't understand Olivier. He seems happy.'

Vincent's voice came back: 'I don't know what he is. I asked him how he counselled people wanting to return to Rwanda. And of course he said he counselled patience, that God has a purpose, that we are all part of God's purpose. But I think he was laughing at me.'

Outside, from the quietness of the camp, everyday sounds became unaccountable in the night: the faraway clatter of an enamel dish dropping on to a clay floor; the rustle of something close in the thatch, like a rodent stirring (but none would survive here). In the disembodying dark it was easier to talk to Vincent. I imagined his laser stare dissipating into nothing. After a while I braced myself to ask: 'Do you think about Ross?'

For a long time I thought Vincent would not answer. Then his voice said: 'I worry about where he can be. He died in sin.'

'I think he is with Our Lord,' I said. (Strange to remember these words, after fifty years. Words uttered by another person, even then unsure.)

Vincent said tautly: 'Our Lord will be the judge.' He sounded curiously like Olivier.

I wanted to ask: Do you feel no regret? The way you moved Ross's hand away, so cold, like the judgement of God . . .

But then Vincent said: 'Goodnight, Stephen.'

It was long past midnight when I woke again. Vincent was snoring. I wanted to go to the latrine, and padded outside, barefoot. Then I stopped dead. Above the unlit camp spread the African stars. Nothing familiar shone there. I looked for Venus or Orion, but they were far below the horizon. The whole sky was alight with an infinity of strangers. The heaven of the northern hemisphere had become an ice field of unknown constellations, multiplying their millions into a haze of alien light. I went on gazing up in emptied fascination.

For the first few days I was invited to teach the Bible classes while Vincent squeezed into the church office and coped with English documents from the Tanzanian government.

A cheery junior pastor appeared, speaking only Bantu, and an eager interpreter with fast, grammarless English.

The pastor's courtyard was packed with thirty students of different ages. I could not guess who came out of curiosity, and who with some vocation. They sat on rough benches in the glaring light: the women sleek-faced in their turbaned headgear, the men a cluster of shaven heads, silent at first, nervously respectful. They had only two bibles between them: New Testaments in their Kinyarwanda Bantu, thumbed and torn on their laps. Each sentence that I spoke was followed by the interpreter's vowel-filled torrent of words, giving me time to phrase what I would say next. And the students, I came to realise, wanted stories. That was their tradition. My tentative theology drew only silence – even the interpreter looked bored – but they greeted the parables of Jesus with excited recognition and cried alleluias at His healing miracles. Later I moved to Proverbs, but the faces raised to mine had lived too deep, too painfully, and my thoughts rang out naive and condescending to me, and sometimes died on my lips. I had never felt more young.

'When will God deliver us from evil?' The question came from a burly man. Then: 'Are my ancestors the same as saints?'

A woman asked if the Bible could cure cholera, and what offerings might be made to the Holy Spirit. Another, simply: 'What did we do wrong?'

Two men, in particular, fixed me with blank expressions that never changed, as if their gaze had been frozen by something years before. But the pastor had invested me with priesthood, and I must have carried with me the aura and hope of a wider world, the world outside. Afterwards the women clasped my wrists in gratitude, and some of the men touched their hands to their hearts.

These classes continued all week. Sometimes I suspected the interpreter of invention, since he brought the students to excitement at unexpected moments. But twice he was replaced by a young woman, an ex-teacher, who translated my words with a soft familiarity, as if I were telling secrets, and then an illusion of intimacy arose among us, and their questions multiplied, and I relaxed a little.

On our first Sunday Vincent and I entered the low, mud-built hall of the packed church. Its walls were washed pale blue, and almost windowless, its corrugated ceilings hung with shining cloths and loops of tinsel. There was no altar, no lectern, only a platform where one man plucked a guitar while another tapped a pair of drums. We were ushered to the front, where the pastor sat us on aluminium chairs before a low table and three bottles of Coca-Cola. Other men were circling the walls with uplifted arms, their heads thrown back in prayer, their eyes shut in private ecstasy, and a young woman in scarlet collapsed shaking behind our seats, her fingers splayed over her face, and poured out inchoate cries.

One by one, groups of worshippers – sombre men, brilliantly clad women – climbed on to the dais. They sang hymns of joy and exultation, remembered from their shattered homes, and the drums and guitar throbbed like a promise beneath them. From time to time some part of the congregation would surge to its feet to sing out in euphoria, their hands outstretched or pointing to Heaven. I sensed Vincent simmering with concern, then sitting like steel beside me, while on my other side Olivier sipped at a Coca-Cola and drummed his feet. Frozen in surprise, I hoped he would not call on us to speak. I waited for the familiar service of the seminary – for statements of belief, prayers of intercession – and they did not come. Instead, on and on, the crowded men and women, gaunt from malnutrition, broke into their ecstasy of salvation, while small children wandered in and out, stamping to the music, and the congregation sent up its hosannas and amens, and rocked in unison. But out of this celebration there would sometimes arise a contravening threnody of loss, whose just-composed words yearned for a New Jerusalem where no government or United Nations need exist, only a plenteous peace. Over four hours no prayer of forgiveness or repentance sounded, no *Kyrie Eleison* for elemental sin. I felt utterly bemused. It was as if the people's sufferings had absolved them of all guilt, and they were free.

Then Olivier launched into his sermon. For a full hour he commanded his congregation to seek Jesus. He abandoned the dais for the aisle between their benches, shouting, flailing the air, sometimes whispering. Later he told me what he had preached, but for the moment we could only watch astonished as he danced amongst us, crying out the text from Matthew: '*Ask, and it shall be given you; seek and ye shall find; knock, and it shall be opened unto you.*' His flock replied at first with frightened quietude, then bursts of adulation, springing up to screams of 'O Yesu!' Soon I dared not look at Vincent. Remorselessly Olivier repeated his command as if sheer will and incantation could prevail, hammering the air to shouts of 'Knock! Knock! Knock!', beating his knuckles on the bench ends and wooden dais, then slipping into a theatrical hush, as if the outer world had momentarily prevailed, before his hands cut the air again, and he bent forward in a parodic prance to 'Search! Search! Search!', his teeth flashing, and the people exploded into clapping and alleluias. *'For every one that asketh receiveth . . .'* From time to time he cradled the offertory box, whose gifts would feed the camp's orphans, and a worshipper would come up to drop a coin there; and once a stately woman strode forward and lifted off her gold necklace, saved from her life's wreck, and laid it among the rest.

Vincent murmured: 'Olivier's like a clown . . . these people . . .'

At the end they queued for the pastor's blessing, while on the dais they started singing again, the drummer dancing and beating his drum between his knees. This grave-faced drummer never rose to rejoicing, but went on thudding out his refrain until long after the last troupe had ended. For a while people seemed reluctant to leave, and a chilling sadness descended. The women waited and murmured together, their babies asleep on their laps, and the men stood round the door but did not go. On the platform the drummer continued monotonously, and I started willing him to stop. The relentless undertone was too much like the noise of reality, as if all the furore and exultation were only a delusive release from whatever was waiting outside.

I barely noticed her at first. She stood behind me sometimes to interpret at Bible classes: an immaculately dressed young woman whose hair was swept back uncovered from her face. She spoke with a precision that somehow deflected enquiry. I knew her simply as Chantal. Once, at the end of our third class, she asked if she had correctly understood an expression I had used. The phrase, I remember, was 'memory trace', and I had spoken it doubtfully. Already I was wondering if I had anything to teach these people. What new could I impart that they did not already know in their veins?

A memory trace, I said to her uncertainly, was perhaps the faded remembrance of something long past, even something imagined.

She frowned. 'Can you remember something that never happened?'

'I'm not sure.' I felt stupid now. 'I suppose you imagine an event, then you remember what you imagined. Then you keep remembering your memories.'

'We have no Kinyarwanda word for that,' she said.

I heard my own laugh, short and dry, like Vincent's, meaningless, and then my tentative 'You have enough real memories here . . .'

'Oh yes.' Her look on me was suddenly softer, uncertain.

And at this moment her beauty began to dawn on me. She was touched by the defensive detachment of many women here. I had the illusion that her features – the wide nose and full lips, the high, delicate cheekbones – were swimming seamlessly into one another, to compose a mask of alien serenity, and her uptilted eyes watched me with some thought that I could not guess.

I blundered on: 'It must be very hard . . . Life here is hard enough, but the memories . . . that must . . . Olivier says it is memories that will either drive people away or drive them back to Rwanda.'

'There is no way back to Rwanda. Our homes are not ours no more. If we go back, we be killed.' She broke off. 'Do you really want to know these things?'

'Yes.'

She had backed a little against the brushwood fence. Her words stayed precise, as though she were still interpreting. 'Our leaders already been killed, and there is worse coming.' She gestured at the courtyard, where the last students were filing away. 'Nobody has wish to stay here. The worst thing is despair. We have to hope for something. Maybe the Tanzanians will settle us in the end. But this will never be our home.'

'What will you do?'

'We'll be farmers. Maize farmers.'

'I meant you. What will you do?'

She said: 'I will like to teach again. In my home town I taught English. It is good to hear it from a real Englishman.' The ghost of a smile. 'Perhaps I will start to talk like the BBC.'

I laughed again, then met her strange eyes. Their tapered almonds seemed to tilt back in her head, so wide apart that I imagined her gaze unfocusing into a dreaming privacy.

I asked: 'If you left, where would you go?'

'To Tabora or Dar es Salaam. But you need money for that. And my mother very sick. The journey will kill her.'

I blurted out cruelly: 'And your husband?'

'I do not have a husband.' She was looking past me, at nothing. 'Very much will surprise you here. I think you come from a good country. Ours is not a good country.

My people belonged to a church, but it was Christians killed us. They even hunted for us in the churches. They were people we knew, neighbours.'

I asked: 'Were they poorer than you?'

'We be the same. They all been to my school. My father was a pharmacist, and treated them the same. Tutsis and Hutus intermarried in our town. My people had a few cattle, that the difference. One night the Hutus came and hacked off the legs of our cows. That was when we be afraid.'

Later Olivier told me that hers was a common story. The Hutu had broken into her father's shop and clubbed out his brains, then killed her husband in the road outside. She was found unconscious, her clothes torn from her, cradling her father's head.

There seemed no order to these alleys except the numbers chalked on their doors. Only the scaffold of the United Nations water tank lifted a landmark higher than one storey. Here and there, glimpsed through a window in a wall scrawled *Magasin* or *Coiffeur pour femmes*, somebody was trying to resurrect their old profession; but no customer ever seemed to enter.

I walked these streets for hours while small boys called out, '*Musotho!*' – white man – or '*Bonjour mister!*' and broke off their games in ragged packs to stare at me. One of them, an orphan named Raphael, would slip his hand into mine and follow me, gazing up with uncomprehending eyes, never speaking. But there were faces I came to know. Many of those who greeted me seemed innocently grateful, trusting that the outer world had not forgotten them. We exchanged unchanging greetings – 'How are you? You good?', 'I good!' – and students from the Bible school came up to converse in broken French with diffident smiles. It was easy to forget the tragedies they came from.

On Sundays a rowdy street market gathered, but the only food for sale were tomatoes and cassavas, with some mussels and sprats caught in the local river. A quiet trade went on, I realised, between charcoal-burners and those prepared to barter their paraffin or cooking-oil rations; and a Tanzanian trader arrived to haggle for the women's jewellery at a fraction of its city value. The ratio between time and money had become pitiful. I saw people sit all day in the market with a padlock or a cheap brooch or a handful of fishing hooks, and sell nothing.

But beneath the greetings, the children's games and the faces that broke easily into smiles, I became conscious of a dark undertone: a kind of seething languor that harboured rage and stunned memory, I think, and boredom and a bittersweet homesickness. Young men would sidle up to me as I left my hut and ask if I could procure them a work permit for America or a visa to England. Others watched me in silence from their doorways, and walked in the alleys with averted eyes. There seemed always to be one or two of these men lingering on the fringes of things, even around Bible studies, watching, without interest, or with an interest of their own. From time to time I glimpsed others more enigmatic: purposeful men in shining suits, who must have belonged outside the camp. Yet the nearest town was over a hundred miles away. I had the ugly thought that the Hutu and the Tutsi were in essence the same people, as Chantal had intimated, and that what one had been able to commit, the other might avenge in equal measure.

The nights seemed endless. Sometimes Olivier would invite us to eat with him, but he was often morose for no reason we knew, and I was anxious in case Vincent offended him. Vincent complained of his petty vanities in the church office, his neglect of pastoral care and his overall ignorance. He called him 'the witch doctor'.

But most evenings Vincent and I ate our boiled maize alone. We had one paraffin lamp between us, by which he read into the night. He had brought the whole of Barth's *Church Dogmatics* with him, and I would sometimes wake from a fitful sleep to see him still reading, his gaunt features sharpened and concentrated in the lamplight, and his finger on a text. For myself, by the day's end, I was often worn into a state of odd, jaded suspense. Something was eating my energies from inside. I shrank from kneeling by my quilt in Vincent's presence, and tried to pray in the dark, lying under the canopy of the mosquito net. But my thoughts would always cloud, then wander. It was as if I had forgotten how to speak with God. And when I thought about the seminary, I imagined only schoolrooms far away, dim-lit by an English sun. Yet it was only three weeks since we'd left. I should have felt alarmed, but I was filled instead by a numb bemusement, as though waiting for something to happen.

By the third week I was growing very thin. It seemed to draw me closer to these people. I imagined that the throb of hunger in my stomach, my inner emptiness, was the throb of self-denial, or penance. I tramped the lanes with it as if it were my exoneration, and it was in one of these alleys that I saw people emerging from a tiny hut that I had noticed before. Its doorway was chalked with a faded spiral. At first, peering into its darkness, I thought it empty. Then I saw under my feet a white circle and star inscribed in the clay floor. A ledge along one wall was dotted with offerings: cassava roots, some polished stones, a bowl of water. A red mask lay in one corner. I had entered an ancestral shrine, and these were offerings to the dead. For a long moment the bowl of water disquieted me. I dipped my finger into it. Out of a parched mouth, my mother had cried for water, which I could not give. Liquid can choke those suffering from a stroke. Women's voices sounded near the door, then faded away. My eyes became accustomed to the dark. The water shone on the shelf against the blank wall. There were dead gnats in it; but it was offered to the living past. I left into the dazzling sunlight, my eyes flinching. Foolishly I had to hitch up my trousers from my thinning waist, and Raphael, who was waiting outside, laughed for the first time: a sudden, unpleasant sound, like a tin rattling.

That morning my Bible class overflowed Olivier's courtyard. The faces upturned to mine were more relaxed and vocal than before, and I answered their questions with apparent assurance. But as my voice became more resonant, it seemed to sound out separate from myself, as if another person were speaking – Vincent, perhaps – and I began to despise it. When I spoke to these ravished people about God's purpose or the Lord's goodness, the phrases turned hollow in my throat, and nobody seemed to notice.

But I was conscious of wanting to make a certain impression. Chantal was standing behind me, interpreting in her meticulous voice. Sometimes, as I continued, my words became spoken not for the students, but for her, and they then grew meaningful. Words of compassion, even of love. I read the parable of the Good Samaritan and the opening of the Sermon on the Mount. Whenever I spoke and she turned to me, a little fleur-de-lys of concentration gathered between her eyes, and the illusion of our union – our shared purpose – was like an indefinable healing. 'Blessed are the poor in spirit, for theirs is the kingdom of heaven.' In these exchanges – I thought of them as exchanges – the heaviness lifted from me. My words sounded musical in her voice. I imagined them nesting behind her eyes as I spoke. 'Blessed are they that mourn: for they shall be comforted.'

Afterwards, to my astonishment, she came up to me and said: 'Did I do something wrong?

'No, nothing.'

'You always looking at me.'

'No, you interpret very well.'

She gave her faint smile. 'How can you tell that?'

'By the students' faces.'

She had stopped against the brushwood fence again. 'But you still use some words I don't know. Maybe they are not in our language. And ours are not always in yours.'

I might have replied piously that God speaks all languages, but I said: 'There are always things we can't understand.'

'Yes.' She seemed content with this. 'But we are all glad that you have come, and can teach us about Jesus. And Monsieur Vincent also. Although he is not happy with us.'

I was startled. 'Why do you think not?'

'He don't like Papa Olivier. We all see this. He don't like our service.'

'We're surprised that there is no prayer, only sermons and music.'

She said: 'Music is our prayer.' She touched a hand to my arm. Her fingers were fine and tapered. (You could tell people here by their hands.) 'This church is good for us, you know, especially for women. We are not protected in this camp, women alone, and girls. The old systems have broken up. There are no more elders, and no more *inyang-nmugayo*. Our families are broken. Some of us are afraid.'

'You too?'

'I will leave here when my mother stronger. But we have no money.'

There was no hint of pleading – it did not occur to her. But a momentary dream unfolded in my head. How much would it cost to change her life? Three or four hundred pounds, at most. The sun was hard and near-vertical over-head. She stepped back until her face was shadowed by the fence. She said: 'It is hard for you to understand this place. People hide themselves here. They hide what they know. They hide stolen goods. They even hide their crip-pled children in case they bring bad luck.' She made as if to go, then stopped in the sun's glare. Her *mushanana* left one shoulder bare, with the lift of one breast. Its skin was caramel-smooth, a little paler than her face. She said: 'They hide weapons too.'

'I didn't know.'

'Papa Olivier will not have told you. You don't see them, but this camp is full of guns. Our young men are not patient. Did you hear of the *inyenzi*, the cockroaches? They called that because they go by night. They are our Tutsi, fighting to return. In the camp they still talk of going back, although I think it is hopeless. But they are everywhere . . .'

As she spoke, I lost track of these important things and became conscious only of her eyes' strangeness and the beauty of her rising breast. Her stare gave no hint of whatever it was seeing, so that I could read nothing into it. Sometimes I imagined her becalmed, disappasionate, at others the eyes seemed stricken. They might even have been merciless.

Nothing grew easier. The twelve-hour nights were interminable, and the dry heat turned us dazed and lethargic. Sometimes Vincent and I bolstered our diet with an egg or some river sprats, fried on the paraffin stove. But when I peered into my shaving mirror I saw the febrile glitter of tired eyes, and my hair pink with dust.

This physical depletion, and the hours of idle darkness, had shrunk me into dreaming. My head filled with Chantal. I fantasised about her thoughts, her body. The most beautiful of colours was black: her caramel darkness. I kissed her full lips in my half-sleep. We made love in an imagined night, and I woke to her moist absence on my quilt. Then I dreamt of taking her away. Several times a day I would make a detour from our hut to pass by hers – a hovel like the others, numbered 147c. Usually it was silent, its door shut; but once her mother emerged – a tiny, wizened woman, who greeted me without warmth – and once Chantal herself, immaculate in her crimson *mushanana*; but they did not ask me in. Later I would ruminate over her simplest remarks, hunting for some hidden intimacy. What lay behind her 'Where are you always going?' or 'Please define what is "renunciation"?'

Vincent was oblivious to my moods. He was furious at the work he'd been assigned: dealing with Tanzanian legal requirements for the church's incorporation. That was not what he had come here for, and only the work's approaching end delayed his outright refusal. His cheeks had hollowed under their bones, and his walking, even his eating, had turned jaded and fretful.

One evening, as we finished supper, he said: 'I saw a vile place today', and I knew he had come upon the ancestral shrine. 'There was a woman there offering a bottle of baobab juice to dead spirits, and mumbling things.' We were running low on paraffin, and I could barely see his face in the lamplight, but I could picture its stony glower. 'A place like that should not exist in a Christian community. But when I told that witch doctor Olivier he just said his people were like that. He said they prayed to Christian relatives.'

'I only saw some cassava roots there,' I said, 'and a bowl of water.'

'So you know that place. You didn't tell me. Didn't it disgust you?'

But my reactions to the shrine were incoherent, mystified. And when I asked myself the long-taught question – What would Our Lord have said? – I heard no sure answer. 'A few centuries ago we prayed to the dead too,' I said. 'Remember the monks of Athos . . .' I was thinking of their inscribed and waiting skulls.

'That shrine was not loving towards the dead, Stephen, it was propitiating the ancestors. I hear their spirits get angry; they get fed up unless you give them something.'

'Maybe the people here are missing them,' I said. 'The ancestors are believed to live in their homes, like part of the family.' Chantal had told me that. 'But their homes have been burnt down. Perhaps people don't know where the dead are any more.'

Vincent went silent, then answered: 'They still worship an African God. The Trinity has to be taught them. Today somebody asked me: 'Why was God's son a Jew?' How do you answer such a thing? What is happening in a head like that?'

The African God. When I read the students Old Testament narratives or Christ's miracles, they surged with understanding and delight. They wanted joy and hope. They were like the Children of Israel, longing to return. But when I tried to expound the doctrine of atonement, I heard myself talking into silence about an alien and complicated God. I was starting to hate this. Perhaps they were listening to me, I thought, only because I was white. My God was a white, post-colonial God, whose character had been decided far to their north. Their dead were not in heaven, but were gathered round the family hearth, listening. Sometimes they cried for water. But Vincent was getting irritated. He scented heresy. Back in the seminary he had sometimes guided my thinking with an almost pastoral affection, and I had thought of him as a benchmark of probity. But now I felt refractory and irritable. Perhaps this arose from our isolation here, or from some inner distress, or my obsession with Chantal. But

I heard myself say: 'Shouldn't theirs be an African God? Can't faith include the monks of Athos, and us, and these people?' I checked myself. 'That's a beauty of Christianity, isn't it, Vincent, that it can mould itself to different cultures . . .' But even as I said this, I was starting to recognise a kind of despair.

Vincent said curtly: 'Athos was different. The Orthodox have a creed. They study.' He seemed to have forgotten his exasperation there. 'Each of those monks had a mentor, you know, a personal confessor. Ross discovered that' – he touched the name with warmth. 'But the people here have no concept of repentance or salvation through Christ. Their faith is a narcotic.'

'Maybe they've suffered too much,' I said. 'Perhaps they feel they've already expiated everything.'

'The only expiation is through Christ. You know that. Besides, this place is rife with crime. The witch doctor is always denouncing adultery and rape. The victims come to the church office sometimes. They turn up at the United Nations clinic. Some have committed murder. You mustn't go soft on these people, Stephen. You're betraying them if you do.'

He turned off the lamp as if to silence me. I heard him wrenching off his shirt and trousers a yard away, his legs rasping against the mosquito net. I hoped he had finished, but after a minute he went on: 'We have a duty to save them, Stephen. A loving duty. That's why Alan came here.'

He hadn't mentioned Alan for days, but now this promised figure was touching our conscience: Alan lying with malaria somewhere to the east in a town we couldn't pronounce; Alan, who might have had plans for us here, which we'd never received. For the first few days we were always saying: Alan will explain this when he comes. But we'd been here over four weeks now, and he had not come.

Vincent said: 'Alan knows these people's language. He speaks Kinyarwanda. When he comes we'll know better how they define the key doctrines. Who knows how things are being interpreted? Your Bible classes, for instance?'

I said: 'The woman interprets well.'

'How do you know?' She had asked that too.

'They listen to her.'

Vincent's teacherly voice had returned. 'But I wonder how she understands the remission of sins or the Passion. These people . . .'

'She's not "these people"! She understands suffering better than you or I do. Her father was butchered before her eyes.'

Then came one of those soft retractions which sometimes endeared Vincent to me. 'I'm sorry.' My chagrin must have glared out. 'It's terrible . . .' He fumbled to redeem his condescension. 'The number of lost parents is shocking here . . .' I heard him turn away from me in the dark.

I remembered then what Julian had told me: that Vincent lived in his father's shadow. Once, I recalled, standing with Vincent beneath the dome of a monastery church on Athos, I saw a boyish awe transform his upturned face, as the frescoed Christ Pantocrator gazed down at us from the ceiling: the patriarchal God of all Power, who cradled the Gospel in one hand and raised the other in a stern, conditional blessing.

Soon afterwards, as my Bible classes were assembling, the male interpreter told me: 'Chantal is ill', and all through the lesson a guilty excitement distracted me: the possibility of her need, of something changing.

It was foolish to be taken aback by the poverty of her rooms. They were no different from others. She and her mother slept opposite one another on low brick platforms spread with soiled blankets, and they kept their possessions in two wooden boxes. A few pots and a jar of manioc stood in the kitchen alcove, with a broken stool.

Her mother closed the door behind me. She spoke in a staccato mutter, which I only later realised was French. Her eyes were fixed on the floor. '*Le Papa Anglais est ici.*'

At first I thought that Chantal wasn't there. The light seeped through a side window edged with broken glass. The old woman sat on the stool, saying nothing. Then I saw the blankets stirring, and Chantal turned suddenly to face me, levering her back against the whitewashed brick. She was shivering. She said: 'Why are you here?'

'I heard you were ill.'

She pushed the hair back from her face and pulled her slip against her chin. She seemed confused. 'We have nothing to offer you.'

'I don't want anything. I came to help.'

She let out a long, wavering sigh. 'You are very good.' Her eyes rested on me at last. 'But there is nothing to do. This comes and goes.'

'Is it malaria?'

'Yes.' Under the thin coverlet I saw that her whole body was faintly, continuously shaking.

But the rainy season was over, the mosquitoes almost gone. 'When did you get it?'

'Last year. Malaria come back. I feel cold now. But in a while I will be hot. Then it fade.'

I said: 'Do you want more blankets? Can I get something from the clinic?'

A spasm of cold shook her shoulders, trembled through her sheeted body, subsided. She murmured: 'The clinic has nothing for this.'

I took out a packet of aspirin I had brought – better than nothing, I thought – then pulled another blanket from the old woman's bed and laid it over Chantal's trembling.

'The cold don't mean anything,' she said. 'It's just a feeling.'

I found a bottle of water on the kitchen shelf. 'Aspirin will dull the pain. Are you in pain?'

'My head.' She closed her eyes. 'And my back aches . . . like my mother's.' A slight smile. 'And my shoulders.' She eased herself flat again.

I knelt and cupped my hand behind her head and touched the water to her lips. The sudden intimacy of this – I realised I had never touched her – surged through my body with a hot tenderness, mixed with an irrational fear that she was slipping away. Her hair was rough and crisp against the palm of my hand. I cradled the weight of her head. I laid the aspirin between those full lips, yearning to kiss them, and tilted the bottle until her tongue's tip took the pills in.

I waited until the blanket's flicker showed she had swallowed them. Her eyes stayed shut. She remained rigid on the bed, then another spasm seized her. I whispered: 'What can I do?'

'You are very kind, Papa.'

'I'm not a Papa. I'm not ordained, Chantal. I'm Stephen.'

She repeated: 'Stephen.' It sounded wondering, husky, like somebody else.

Then her mother intruded with a flood of incomprehensible words. I had forgotten she was there. She creaked up from her stool and stood above Chantal. She nudged her. Chantal opened her eyes. 'My mother thinks I have a brain disorder,' she said. 'She says an uncle of mine is causing it . . . She doesn't know anything.'

'How does he cause it?'

'He doesn't. He's dead. She thinks his spirit is evil.'

I wondered if the old woman was demented. Her upper back was so hunched that it thrust her head forward until her face was near-invisible, and her hands – oddly small and delicate – clutched at her breast. Chantal said: 'She says the brain is a journey. It is coiled up like a life, then it uncoils . . .' Meanwhile her mother went on talking above Chantal's bed. Her voice sounded from deep inside her crippled frame. Chantal said: 'She says that some lengths of the brain are dark, others are light. This is what causes sorrow, or relief. The brain uncoils to a destiny. That is a life.'

In the claustrophobia of that room, resounding with the oracular depth of the old woman's voice, I had the apprehension that she might possess some secret knowledge. After all, she had seen her husband's brain threaded across their shop floor, uncoiled from her daughter's hands.

'I will go now,' I said.

To my surprise Chantal said: 'I like you here.'

The old woman wrenched up her face to look at me. She had clouded, kindly eyes. She said: '*L'âme de Nishyimimana va dans un voyage sombre...*'

I asked Chantal; 'What does your mother call you?'

'She calls me Nishyimimana. That is Kinyarwanda name.'

That was hard to pronounce, I said, but she asked me to try. Her father had called her Chantal because as a child she liked to sing, but the name hurt her now. Perhaps I would call her Nishyimimana: it meant 'Glory to God'. This intimacy over her name elated me. I imagined it private to myself. As we spoke, her trembling began to subside. She had heard from someone else, she said – the faint smile returned – that Chantal meant 'a stone'. Her mother shuffled back to her stool where she started, wordlessly, to sing.

I sat by Chantal for what seemed a long time. She appeared to sleep. Her mother's singing tailed away. One of Chantal's hands lay beside mine where I sat on her bed's edge. The hand was fine and narrow, its tendons like lyre strings. Its fingers wore no ring. I imagined clasping it, but did not move. Sitting in the unlit room became very restful. Her crimson *mushanama* hung on the wall above us. Perhaps it was the only dress she had. Outside in the alley the noises seemed far away. I might have got up and left, but instead I remained in this static euphoria, sitting beside her on the rough bricks.

After an hour, perhaps, Chantal became restless, and her breathing quickened. Her eyes flickered open. I imagined shadows moving under her face's skin. Her eyes had the lustrous, swimming darkness of fever. She said: 'This is what happens.'

When I touched her forehead, it felt rough, hot. I poured out the cool water on my loosened sleeve and dabbed it over her face. I didn't know what else to do. Her skin was burning. I read pain in her eyes: a contained, private pain. I heard my own breathing become sharp and fast alongside hers. People could die from this. She began softly to groan. 'You can't stay here.' The words were my own. 'I want to take you away.'

Then the stare of those eyes passed over me. They had lost their ethereal calm, and were vivid and glittering with fear. They filled me with panic when I imagined their extinction. I touched her hand, held it. The hand too was hot, dry. Its fingers curled on mine.

She said: 'How can I go away?'

'I don't know. But you can't stay here.' I looked round at the walls of pocked whitewash, the broken window (who had tried to get in?), the corrugated roof edged with rust, the mud floor. 'I will find somewhere else for you.'

'There is nowhere else.'

'I can't leave you here.' I was imagining reciprocity in her hand, its furling round mine. 'I'll take care of you.'

I am ashamed of these words now, their callow passion, their ignorance. I was caught in the swimming flux of her gaze, and in my panic at her momentary delirium. I had the idea that she was too delicate to survive the camp. I touched the moistened sleeve over her cheeks, her neck. She seemed not to notice. Her eyes were clenched shut now. She had eased the blankets off her chest. Her shoulders shone black against her white slip. Her body poured out heat. But even then I could not take my eyes from the lift of her breasts under the camisole.

Then I became aware that her mother was squatting beside me. She was stroking Chantal's feet. A little later the paroxysm of fever subsided – it went in waves – and Chantal detached her hand from mine.

'Stephen, you go now. Soon I be sweating. It is ugly. I be ashamed.'

'I don't mind.'

'Go now. It's all right.' The faint smile. 'I not dying.'

As I emerged outside her door, which her mother closed behind me, everything was bewilderingly the same: the same sunlight on the rubbish-strewn alley, the same boarded windows, the same washing hung from the thatches. It was as if within ordinary time nothing had occurred at all, and that the door of 147c was the entrance into my imagination, where I had reached out and taken Chantal's hand.

I did not understand all of Olivier's business. He lived a little better than his flock, but still poorly, and shared the same maize diet. I think he was at once self-serving and benign. His church compound included a sty with seven pigs, but I never discovered precisely who owned them. The orphan whom he had adopted seemed little more than a servant. But he had started a sewing school for traumatised girls, who sat at their Singers in a room behind his office, and you sometimes heard their laughter.

He barely knew Chantal. He employed her sometimes, where her English was useful, but his colleagues were all men, and she was a little resented. Even to her own people she was perhaps an enigma. He defined her as a childless widow, as though her life were over.

In these few days I had lost control over what was happening to me. My haggard features repelled me in the mirror. I continued to teach Bible classes, but the faces that confronted me seemed more mysterious than before, as if they understood things that I had forgotten. I walked compulsively, but hoped to meet nobody I knew. Often I went with my eyes on the ground, like those unnerving youths who tramped the streets unsmiling. Sometimes the orphan Raphael tried to accompany me, folding his hand into mine, but he had taken to whispering, 'Papa, Papa!' at me in a mantra that seemed to comfort him, but to mock me.

Only once or twice, during this numbed penance of my walking, something shocked me into fear or pity. One such sight has never left me. Perhaps they were among those whom Chantal said were kept from view, in case they brought a curse on the community. I saw a small girl leading an old woman, whose hand clutched her shoulder. The woman walked with the short steps of a frightened child; the child with the hunched anxiety of the old. Both of them were blind. They groped their way along the street, ignored. Nobody knew why they were blind, or what atrocity their eyes had last witnessed. But I watched them from a well of despair, because I knew that in this darkness they were for ever inconsolable, and that no faith could heal them.

All my life I have been prone to romanticise suffering. It has sometimes led me into impetuousness, then retraction and even betrayal. When I knocked at Chantal's door next day, there was no answer. But I knew that malaria was cyclical – it could fade and return within two or three days. I imagined her in exhausted sleep, and I left. At night my head teemed with plans. After my time here ended, I would hire a driver and take her to Dar es Salaam. Her mother would survive that better than a train journey. I would rent an apartment for her, and she would find work as a teacher, and I . . .

But I wondered where her people were. What was left of them? Was she quietly paralysed here, still hoping to return across the border? It was only twenty miles away. How vulnerable was a single woman in the great city? How much would it cost? And when I imagined her there, any sense of our future failed me. I had only a heady dream of loving her, as if she was an actress on a stage of my own making; and as the night wore on, my imaginings wandered into make-believe, and died beyond the tent of the mosquito net, where Vincent was snoring, and the African stars were shining in through our lone window, and nothing was quite real.

But Vincent's anger had gone. His office work was finished. By daylight he was visiting homes in the way he thought Olivier neglected. He took with him an eager youth who translated his schoolboy French into Bantu, and gave out simple messages of Christ's redeeming love. Sometimes I would see him emerge from the homes of the sick or diseased, holding their children's hands. He heard that many babies born in the camp had never been baptised, and together with the deputy priest he held ceremonies in the church porch, in which an enamel basin served for a font. These people had to be saved, he said, they had to have the clear knowledge of their redemption, otherwise it was better never to have known the Lord. He looked more expansive and purposeful than I had ever seen him. People came to our hut, even late at night, to ask his advice. I think of him still as a mature man, middle-aged almost, for ever senior to me. Yet he was only twenty-seven.

One event emerges from that time whose explanation I have searched for with no answer. Vincent and I were taking our breakfast – a mess of spinach and sweet polenta – when he said: 'There is something I want you to take.' He reached across to his rucksack and unwrapped a thin packet. Then he handed me the icon that Ross had given him on Athos.

He said: 'You know I don't like these things. I don't have the feel for them.'

I held it in confusion: the almond-eyed Virgin of Tenderness, cradling her child. A poor thing, mass-produced. The memory of Ross came back in a tremor of loss and accusation. I blurted out: 'But he gave it to you.' I wondered: did Vincent feel guilty after all?

'Ross made a mistake.'

'Yes.' I was not sure which mistake Vincent meant. I didn't know what more to say. Vincent hated mistakes, of course. Perhaps he was trying to clean away anything from his life that confused or smirched it in his eyes: anything that hindered his project for the world's salvation. He wanted to become pure crystal, perfect for God's work.

In the end I murmured: 'Thank you', and laid the icon aside, awaiting whatever it might do to conscience and memory.

When I tapped at her door, I was surprised that it eased off its latch into darkness. I stepped softly inside. I saw and heard nothing, at first. The quiet and dark of evening seemed to have infiltrated the hut. But there was an acrid smell in the air, of something sulphurous burning. After a moment I made out the rectangle of the broken window hanging in the night, and I heard a voice barely two yards from me. It was a man's voice, but high and strident. It seemed to be asking questions which nobody answered.

I could see him now, a silhouette massed over Chantal's bed. The questions rose again – shrill and incantatory – and again, after each one ended, silence fell. Then the man shifted position. I heard the rustling of something like a snake over the mud floor. As he moved around her bedside, the dim flame of the paraffin stove appeared, with its tin of embers. Its glow illumined her closed eyes. One of her hands was trembling, and a braid of sweat glistened along her hairline. In the shadows above her, replacing the silhouette, there hovered a masked face. So dark was the man's dress that the white circle, with its black mouth and eyeholes, leered there disembodied.

Then I saw the blood trickling from Chantal's forehead. I was suddenly furious. I pushed forward, shouting wildly, and kicked over the stove, which toppled in a spurt of flame. In its glare I saw the mask slip from an old, frightened face, whose owner snatched up some utensils – a deer's horn, a small knife – and ran crouching past me into the night.

I battered about in the dark until I found the lamp. I could hear her mother coughing in the far bed. In the brightened light Chantal was streaming sweat, and the tiny incision across her hairline was still bleeding. I found water again, and a handkerchief. A white paste had been pressed into her cut – it looked like kaolin – and I bathed it clean. I washed her neck and shoulders, feeling a fading alarm. She gave off a hot scent. She went quiet, before another spasm shook her, but each was lighter than the last.

I said: 'Who the hell was that?'

She answered: 'I don't know. My mother asked him in. She knows these people.'

'You shouldn't have let him.'

'I too weak. Then I thought: my mother have her way. It don't matter.'

As I cooled her, she fell into exhausted sleep, but woke up soon afterwards to her mother's hacking cough and desultory talking. The old woman sounded angry.

'What is she saying?'

'She is saying that the Christian God has no power . . . not for this . . .'

'We don't cut people open for malaria.'

'He did that to let out the spirit.' She touched the cut. 'My mother thinks an uncle is stealing my blood. She thinks we forgot to offer him food, and so he has become one of the *abazimu* – I can't translate that. He always liked sorghum beans. But we have none here.' She was staring at the ceiling. She did not smile. 'This is old people's talk.' Her mother's voice started again, then broke down into wheezing. 'She says we have starved our ancestors.'

I wanted to joke about this, to hear her laugh, but I said: 'Who was this uncle?'

'He was my father's brother. A mean man.'

'He wanted to marry you.' I was guessing.

'Yes. But I did not want. He died soon afterwards. He had stomach cancer, but my mother said he died of bitterness. She said that after death he became an *abazimu*, and put a stop to my children.'

I said, not knowing: 'You may still have children.'

'My children never started. There was something wrong. My mother wanted to blame somebody. She chose this dead brother. I should not be telling you this, Stephen. I cannot tell it to anybody else.'

I felt a moment's rush of warmth. But of course I did not belong in her world, I thought, and perhaps I did not count.

She said: 'It is very hard, to give no child. That is unhappy to think of, that my husband left without continuing. He was a river that died in the sand.' Her eyes were moistening. 'I always be ashamed for that.'

'You loved him.'

'He was my husband.'

All this time I was touching the handkerchief to her face and neck, although her sweat was drying and her skin no longer burned. My touch had become a caress. Sometimes I smoothed the cloth over her eyes, for the pleasure of seeing them close and open again, and of stroking their lids.

But it was hard – always – to know what she was thinking. Sometimes, as now, when she turned to me on the stained quilt, her expression sharpened and glittered; but after a minute this would always fade, leaving me momentarily lost. Then she seemed to retreat into indifference, as if whatever had happened to her had turned her vision back into herself, and left those strange, tilted eyes to dream over a world no longer important to her.

At least that is how I romanticised her.

I said: 'You told me you would never go back.'

'Not to my home town. It is Hutu now. And I don't believe in my people no more . . .'

'They weren't your people.'

'Mine been killers too. They imagined new things. Once the Tutsi ruled again, they thought, there would be no more taxes or hunger, and the spirits of the ancestors would return from their graves.' She suddenly laughed, a throaty sound, too much like her mother's. 'Do we seem children to you? Alan, Monsieur Vincent's friend, said once we were children.' I shook my head. 'But here in the camp we cannot grow up.'

I appealed: 'You must go to Dar es Salaam.' She eased herself up and turned to me. All the problems of the night were forgotten in her gaze. I said: 'I'll hire a car and take you. We'll find the Rwandan community there. There must be one. We'll find a flat and a job for you, interpreting.'

She laughed again, quite gaily. 'What can I interpret? The Tanzanians speak Swahili and English. Perhaps I will learn to sew or do hairdressing. I hear that people want their hair straightened now.' She threaded her fingers through her own. 'Africans want to be like Indians who want to be like Europeans.' Her laugh petered out. 'Maybe I make Europeans of us all.'

My handkerchief was still soothing her temples, her cheeks. Tonight, I thought, I will sink my face in it, I will inhale its scent. I whispered, as if her mother might hear and understand – but she was sleeping: 'Do you want to stay here for ever?'

Softly: 'No.'

'In three weeks my time here will be over. I will get you both out.' My promise filled me with tenderness for her. My hands held her shoulders. They no longer pretended. She was staring at the ceiling again. When the white slip began to drop from her arms, she did not return it.

She said: 'Yes, if my mother well enough.'

'We will go gently.'

'You are kind.' She seemed to say this to herself, her tone wondering.

'I'm not kind,' I said. 'I love you.'

Only once before had I said this, on an English summer night. The words carried their intoxication now, like self-fulfilment. My hand was descending the dark slope of her body, easing the slip away, until I held one breast. I bent to kiss her lips, the flared wonder of them, but she tilted her face fractionally away. Then her hand came up and covered my own at her breast, pressing it there, her long fingers enveloping mine, and we remained like this, cradling her like a shared possession, until the wind opened the door where the witch-doctor had gone, and her mother stirred.

How strange it seems now. I did not even know if her people kissed. I went away with my fingers hot from their cradle between her hand and her breast, and the confused memory of her eyes.

Three days later, a United Nations jeep stopped outside the church office, and a man lurched out. It was Alan. He looked like the ghost of himself, Vincent said. Malaria and the aftermath of jaundice had pared him to tendons and bone, and he moved with the stupor of a sleepwalker. But once he had sat down with us, a tired authority surfaced, and we listened to him because every sentence cost him strength. He had returned to gather his few possessions, and some documents. He was not going to stay here, he said, and nor should we. During his journey from the north, the villages had been aswirl with rumours. A Hutu militia had crossed the border thirty miles to our west, and was advancing on the camp. Some of the Tutsi refugees here, everybody knew, had joined armed incursions back into their homeland, and the Hutu were bent on annihilating them.

For a moment we were stunned. Olivier must have known something beforehand, because the meagre office files were stacked for removal, and the walls were now bare except for a yellowed photograph of the Tanzanian president. He said: 'I been talking to a fellow in Tabora. He'll find a truck for us.'

Alan said: 'We should go before nightfall.' His stare took us in almost sorrowfully. His eyeballs were shiny orange. 'They say the Hutu are on foot, but they go fast.'

The assistant pastor, quiet until then, murmured something in Kinyarwanda. It sounded like a meek petition. 'He asks what will we do about our congregation,' Alan said. 'Won't we stay and protect them.'

Olivier seemed visibly to bulk out in his white jacket, and his hands fastened over his knees. We could not protect them, he said. The churches in the past had been sites for massacre. His tongue hung loose between his lips. It was hard to tell how frightened he was. He would find any transport he could, he said, so people could get away, but the nearest town with trucks was a hundred miles off, and there was nothing beyond that at all. He was talking over his Bakelite telephone as we dispersed.

Outside, something had changed. At first a deathly silence had lain over the camp. But now, as if the news had spread telepathically, people were crowding into the streets and doorways, and children were being gathered in by their mothers. On my way to Chantal, I twice encountered young men with rifles and revolvers. Some were riding bicycles. They said they were going to fight the Hutus, but they looked scared. Here and there a family was clustered round a transistor radio, tuned to Radio Rwanda, but there was no news at all, nor hope from the Tanzanian army.

When I entered Chantal's hut, she was not there. Her mother groaned in her bed against the wall, and did not understand my questions. I calculated I had six hours left. In the United Nations compound the workers were locking their storerooms against looters, and preparing to leave in their two jeeps. They were Tutsis, and frightened. The nearby Jesuit school was in darkness. In the camp clinic the three nurses had heard nothing, and ran away to their family huts when I told them. My heart was cold and hammering in my chest. All the islands of security were disappearing. On the western outskirts I stopped to catch my breath, and scan the bush. Several families were grouped here too, gazing out to where the Hutus would appear. The scrub was a yellow underbrush, thinned almost to transparency, and flowed to a skyline of low, irregular hills. A faint haze blurred the land. It looked empty.

On the camp's fringe the Tanzanian flag was flying over the police post, where four officers were usually to be seen lounging outside. But this morning, when I approached, a voice shouted at me to stay back. Two heads moved above the toy parapet, and a rifle glistened. I called up in English, asking did the army know there was a raid imminent? But I was warned away, without answer.

When I returned to our hut, Vincent was sitting on the floor, his knees at his chin and his long arms thrust in front of him. I think he was praying. He had already packed my belongings into a rucksack, but his own were scattered defiantly round the room. An unfocused anger seethed under his wretchedness.

'You know, Stephen, this place could have been these people's salvation. Somewhere far from the city, even with Olivier. There are worse things than maize farming. But now Alan says they'll just go out into the bush and wait, unless the Hutus find them.' Suddenly his hands covered his face. 'They're crowding outside the church now, calling for help. They want us to shelter them. They ask what God's plan is.' He got up and began hurling his clothes into a case. 'I can't face them.'

I asked: 'Are the trucks coming for them?'

'There aren't any yet. The lorries have to come from a hundred miles away, and Olivier says there's a petrol shortage.' He turned to face me. 'I asked Alan if you and I might stay. We're not Tutsis, after all. If the congregation sheltered in the church, if you and I stood guard at the door, I thought . . .'

My blood froze. I sat down on the floor.

He went on: ' . . . But Alan said a church full of Tutsi would be an invitation to slaughter, and that we'd probably be butchered as well. These Hutus aren't even regular soldiers, they're mostly vigilantes with machetes and clubs.'

I could sense in him a deep, shamed relief at his plan's rejection, and a shaky exoneration. He was no longer looking at me. He had proposed this, I thought, under the compulsion of his God and father, but longed for the cup to pass from him. His lips were drawn back tensely from his teeth all the time he spoke.

Just ten minutes ago, he said, a woman had arrived from an outlying farmhouse close to the border, where a few Tutsis had taken their chances as farmers. The Hutus had slaughtered her menfolk before her eyes. For more than twenty miles she had fled headlong to the camp, and her descriptions of their executions did not bear retelling. As Vincent said this, his face drained of its colour, and I felt myself paling too, and faint, and closed my arms around my knees.

I thought: I must find Chantal, wherever she's gone. But when I emerged into the sun, something in the air had changed. An incoherent noise was rising from the camp, like nothing I'd ever heard. It was the noise of thousands of muted voices and movements, of windows being boarded up, of things lifted and discarded, of doors closing. It was the sound of departure.

I ran into Alan as he came towards our hut. Were there any trucks yet? I asked. I felt a coward. Only two had been promised, he answered, enough for the church workers and their families, enough for us. I wanted a place for my interpreter, I said, and her sick mother. He looked sour, uncertain. I demanded: 'What will happen to the women left here?'

'They're usually raped, then abandoned. Sometimes they're killed.' He might have been talking of cattle. He's sick, I thought, he may be dying. I went on staring at him.

At last he said: 'If you insist enough, Olivier will give in.'

'How close are the Hutu now?'

'Ten, fifteen miles, I don't know.' As I turned to go, he said: 'You'd better hurry.'

The alleys were filled with people leaving. They were walking swiftly, in near-silence, their arms lifted to the bundles on their heads. If I run, I thought, I'll start to panic. So I strode fast while the cold fear beat up from my stomach, filling my chest. Women were crowded round the water pumps, filling tins and plastic containers before flight. The armed youths had vanished. Outside one hut three old men sat unmoving. As I passed, wondering at them, one laughed and said simply: *'Nous allons mourir.'* Another man ran up to me, pleading through bloodshot eyes. I must help him leave, he said, he was a good man, God was pleased with him. He clung to my arm down successive alleys, until I shook him off.

As I neared Chantal's door, I looked behind me and saw a toppling cloud of smoke rising to the west. It ascended high above the rooftops, five miles away perhaps, in an ash-grey column against the sky.

She was standing inside, as if waiting for me. Perhaps her mother had, after all, understood my previous coming, or else my mission was written on my face, because she said at once: 'We can't go.'

I stared back at her, suddenly gutted by despair. It was as if something long known, unspoken, had slid into place. Even now I am not sure if she ever truly wanted to leave, or if her mother's frailty was not an excuse. Years later I was still torturing myself with this. Because I never did know. I could read anything into those eyes: her sadness, her contempt, her love, even her emptiness. But when I looked at her now, I knew there would be no appeal. She appeared perfectly calm. But I said: 'I have places for you on the lorry. Your mother too.'

'My mother would die there. She is dying already. I can't leave her.'

I said: 'I will carry her.'

'No.' The old woman was still lying by the wall, retching her tubercular cough.

I said: 'The Hutus may be here in two hours. You know what will happen.'

'We have known them before.' Then she said: 'Stephen, I think you will go.'

I don't want to remember this. My silence lacerates me. People were running in the lanes outside now. Somebody cried out. And the fear surged through me. I must have been visibly shaking. I loathed myself. Perhaps she was helping me, pitying me, when she said: 'You are going to leave us.'

I heard no accusation, only a remote sadness. Even now I am afraid to remember my response. She went on gazing at me steadily, with no trace of surprise: a person I did not understand, vivid in her crimson dress, standing above the old woman, who now slept. In my memory she stands stark but detached, not only from me, but from everything except her mother: the last thread back to her old life.

I don't remember looking at her again. I was staring at the floor – I can still see the hairline cracks in its clay – then at the rotted base of her door as I opened it, then at the emptied street. And I ran.

Eastward beyond the camp stretched four miles of stubbled maize. Then the yellow underfelt of grass began, with a sprinkling of acacia trees and the rise of bare hills. From a distance the land offered cover almost to shoulder height, but closer you could see how thin it was, the grasses almost diaphanous, and the shrubs – mostly prickly euphorbia – too widely spaced. A few of the refugees had gone along the river, but the rest were on the track south, where the nearest settlement was two days' march away.

They walked in silence, with long, quick strides. Their balanced bundles overcast their faces, and appeared too big for the slender necks and heads that bore them. Many women walked with babies slung to their backs, and their free hands carried water canisters or clutched the wrist of another child. Some were barefoot. From far away they resembled a single organism – a long, skeletal body that travelled with the illusion of terrible calm, as if this was the will of God. Behind them, beyond the camp, the smoke had spread and darkened into a towering storm cloud.

The truck carrying Alan had disappeared in front of us, and our own followed, tortuously slow, threading between the refugees. I was seated with Vincent and Olivier in the open back, in people's full view. Olivier perched upright beside me in his white jacket, even now touched by a little vanity – he had commandeered two lorries, after all. On my other side, Vincent's head was bowed in prayer. Above the clank of the truck I heard: '... bless ... save ...' Twice he turned to me, to bolster or comfort me, talking about the seminary and the Lord. Dazed, choked with dust, I wondered: what Lord, what seminary?

On either side of the track the faces raised to mine – some were barely a foot away – looked steeled and old in resignation. One or two lit up with misplaced hope at the sight of us. If they bore resentment, I could not tell. Sometimes the driver honked his horn to clear our way. At first I smiled weakly at these people, then I could bear it no longer. I noticed several of my students. I leant forward against the truck's rail, and covered my face.

I could not know that this was only the beginning, and that thirty years later these people's homeland would be torn again, more terribly. The line of refugees straggled at last, then petered out over the pink savannah. Soon we had crested the first horizon. The track ahead of us was empty now. Our tyres whispered over the dust.

* * *

The fire ate into the timbered bowels of the house. It licked away the plastered ceiling of the basement and reached the joists above. The smoke alarm had been defunct for years, and the flames spread in near-silence. Anyone viewing the house from far away would have mistaken them for the lights of a New Year party.

All at once the smoke was pouring up between his floor-boards. Sleeping beneath the duvet, he inhaled the fumes into his dreams. Then asphyxiation woke him in confusion and pitch darkness. He groped from his bed and slithered to his knees. Some memory set his lips in automatic prayer, which stopped of its own accord, and he clambered to his feet. He found the torch by his bed, but its beam lit a swirling wall of grey. When the fire at last burst through the floor, it opened up below a roaring furnace whose flames leapt ten feet into the room. But by then he was lying unconscious as at the lip of a volcano, and in his fainting mind there was no heat or light at all.

3

Neurosurgeon

The human brain – the seat of memory and consciousness – weighs just three pounds, and has the texture and colour of beige blancmange. It can be held in two cupped hands. But it is the most complex and baffling structure in the known universe. Floating within the skull in their own cerebrospinal fluid, its eighty million cells put out electrical connections that outnumber the stars of the Milky Way. The brain is threaded by a hundred thousand miles of blood vessels. Yet cut it with a knife, and it feels nothing. It has no pain receptors, but it survives in a frenzy of activity. In its structure it holds the history of human evolution, from the reptilian stirrings of the brainstem that regulate breath and heartbeat, to the limbic system of the earliest mammals, to the bulging cortex of the primates. All these strata lie buried in the human brain, like ancient memories.

Its receptors for smell, perhaps the oldest of the human senses, are intricately divided and subtle, and were alerted now by the smoke rising through the corridors of the house. The stench entered Walford's nostrils as he slept, but was dismissed by his forebrain as the harmless aroma of cooking or of a coal fire in some distant apartment. His breathing, for the moment, barely changed. Once he imagined he heard a faint human cry, but this too, muffled by his dreaming, carried no alarm.

In any case, although he had been here many years, the other tenants were barely known to him. He distantly envied the schoolteacher upstairs, who had retired early and taken to travelling; but he seldom spoke with the reclusive woman who shared his landing, and he avoided the anaemic-looking tenant in the basement. As for the owner, Walford glimpsed him so rarely (and paid his rent by standing order) that he sometimes wondered if any landlord existed here at all. Fancifully he imagined the flats as the different cells of a dying brain – its residents seemed mostly frail and old – connected only by these passages where the light bulbs might need replacing and the faded crimson carpets were starting to split along the staircase treads. Months ago he realised he would not be staying. His rooms here were the den of a single man, redolent of his years as a registrar in the county hospital nearby. This was no place for a wife. The garden far beneath his balcony was shorn by salt winds and traversed only by cats. No child would play there. The once-proud building reeked of seclusion, of retirement, not of life's beginnings. He had planned to leave several years ago, but had found no time for buying a place of his own. Now that he was going, he wondered how he had tolerated the house so long. The thick walls smelt damp in winter, and the corridor windows leaked and rattled. He could imagine children growing sick here. This was how he thought nowadays: of marriage, children. He would soon be gone.

*   *   *

They were walking high above the sea. A bitter wind had got up and was beating the waves into silver fish scales far out to the horizon. The path was too narrow for them to hold hands. He marched behind her tensely, angry that this day – of all days – should be fouled in August by a cold wind. But she did not care. Her neck was unbuttoned to the sun, and she went with the loose-limbed stride that had sounded too loud in the hospital wards. Long before he met her, a colleague had described Kate as radiant, a description that alienated him. Kate was a paediatrician, and he imagined an overwrought gaiety enacted to inspirit bedridden children. She, in turn, had been put off by his looks, she later said. She thought they bore a strain of arrogance (she'd never retracted this) and laughed at the hero-worship that neurosurgeons attracted. They were little more than technicians, after all.

Strange, he thought, how mutual distrust had turned to desire. (There was no neurological clue to that.) As Kate walked in front of him, long strands of hair escaped her cap and blew ash-blonde in the wind. On these rare week-end walks along the coastal paths of Dorset or Cornwall, the claustrophobia of the hospital dropped away, and they entered a country of their own whose inhabitants strode past with backpacks and curt greetings, and where the fragility of brains or lungs seemed far away. Beneath the path the limestone cliffs dropped two hundred feet to blackened rocks, and seagulls were crying in the clefts. She turned from time to time to share something: the curious patterns on the sea, a flight of cormorants. She was touched by girl-ish elation. That was her oddness, he thought. There was an innocent vitality about her, and a hint of rebellion, that had survived her professional self-possession. You could not pass lightly through eight years in paediatrics, then specialise in respiratory disease. Children had died in her arms. Sometimes her elan seemed to him a kind of courage. He was in love, after all, at the age of thirty-seven.

They climbed to a coastguard station and to the chapel on St Adhelm's Head. His arm circled her waist. She was flushed and smiling. The chapel was square and plain, ringed by sunken earthworks – a stone tent pitched against the sky. They stood under its sheltering wall, in the high grass. He imagined that these treks honed his mind. That was typical, Kate said: he could do nothing without purpose. His workload in the hospital was so concentrated that the thought of aimless walking took time to catch on. While trekking was to her a kind of ambulatory rest, he would designate an object for their journey: a distant quarry, perhaps, or a lighthouse. It was as if he were making up for some immemorially lost time. He had the idea that before his mother's death his adolescence had been spent adrift, that this surgical commitment was his absolution, and that his teenage dreaminess had been waiting, like protoplasm, to evolve into what Kate saw as an introverted ambition. But sometimes he traced the choice of his career to a time even earlier, when as a nine year old boy he had stumbled on the woman.

He had wandered away from his parents down an aisle of the local supermarket, turned a corner and found her prone and stiffened on the floor. She was ashen, staring. As he gazed, her body began to shake. Then her arm lifted and pointed at him. The pupils of her eyes rolled back in her head. He froze in terror. What had he done? Some liquid flooded out beneath her body. He screamed. From behind, his mother's arms encircled him.

He had never heard of epilepsy, of course. The mystery of it – of the ordinary adult deformed into something else – haunted him for months. He saw her in the street the next day, and she smiled at him. He gaped after her. A demon lived inside her, waiting, lived inside everybody perhaps, lived even in his mother, in him. The horror of it went on in his memory. The woman quivered and pointed in his nightmares, unexplained. He wanted to understand her. He wanted to know why she hated him. His mother explained that she was ill; and then he wanted to cure her. He wanted to cure his fear.

Years later, after his mother's stroke, when for three days she wandered in her own labyrinth, emitting words and cries to people not there, he longed to share the zone she was inhabiting, the fragments of her consciousness, before the relief of death. What had she seen or heard? Where was her pain?

He was already studying medicine, but he knew nothing about this neural twilight. He chose to practise general surgery. For a while, prosthetics and transplants obsessed him. Then, as a junior house officer, he witnessed his first brain operation. In the annexe to the operating theatre, before going under anaesthetic, the patient – a middle-aged bus driver with trigeminal neuralgia – told him through clenched teeth how for the past four years he had scarcely dared shave or brush his teeth for fear of activating this torment. It would recur, he said, like a jackhammer entering his jaw.

Yet five minutes later, nothing seemed simpler, more economical, than the way the surgical needle glided into his unconscious cheek. The surgeon – a gaunt authoritarian – briefly checked the X-ray screen to confirm the needle's position, then released a weak electric current down it. Drowsily the awakened patient confirmed the focus of pain, and was returned to sleep. Then the surgeon passed a high-frequency current to the needle's tip, and somewhere in the forest of sensory nerves the tormenting fibres were cooked and destroyed. Within ten minutes the whole thing was done. The bus driver's four-year agony was over, the surgeon hurrying to another case, and Walford was left with the realisation of his calling, which had slid into place with the ease of something preordained.

Fifteen years later, he felt that the only real frontier of medical knowledge was the brain. By comparison, the make-up and function of a heart or kidney were childishly simple. Even their transplant had become commonplace. But the brain stayed all but unknown: less a composite organ than a labyrinth of electro-chemical activity. Its workings could be most typically guessed only when one area was damaged; and it learnt from itself, and changed. He thought of the brain as he might of an unbreakable cipher. In its memories it held the web of human identity. It was the incarnate self.

The most potent advances in surgery would surely be here. Long before he ended his career – in twenty-five, thirty years' time? – the excision of brain parts would be in decline. Already sub-cranial stimulants were being developed, electrodes implanted to destroy rogue brain cells, nutrient drip-feeders to nourish others, and neuro-pacers that would forestall cortical seizures.

Neurosurgeons, of course, had a reputation for self-importance. They rarely believed in their own inexperience. A senior surgeon once joked to him that you could teach a monkey to operate, but you could not teach it to desist. But after fifteen years in surgery, Walford felt at last that he needed no superior beside him at the operating table, that he could deal with whatever crisis was thrown at him.

Still, but rarely, things went wrong. No two operations were alike. Even the simplest one taught you something, even now. There was no such thing as an easy process. Misguide the knife, and a patient might lose her hearing or his mind. He prided himself on his record in an inexact science. But he was never reconciled to imperfection. The operations he found hardest were those by which a lasting injury had to be inflicted in order to cure an illness or save a life. They carried always a rankling sense of failure. Last year he had excised the malignant tumour of a young woman with acoustic neuropathy; he saved her, but at the expense of a disfigured mouth, and he could not think of it without self-censure.

But there had come a point in his career when he emotionally withdrew. A patient had been referred to him whose frontal lobe tumour had been resected in Switzerland. It was a grade 2 tumour which would surely turn malignant. Lying as it did in the language hemisphere, it had been extracted too cautiously. Fragments remained, and now the cavity was refilling with cancerous growth. After he had operated, excising part of the supplementary motor area, the woman could communicate only in whispers. It had been an acceptable risk; but she would never speak normally again. For months her husband raged at him, sometimes barging into the hospital reception hall or waiting for him outside, and hammered him with abusive emails and solicitors' letters.

It was after this that he willed himself into change. There could be no perfect record. There were patients you damaged, others you lost. He slammed his mind shut on them, because next morning he must be in the theatre again, his mind and hands steady. Now he operated without the relaxing banter or quiet curses or soothing music that some of his colleagues employed. He wanted complete silence. His orders to the registrar or nurse were curt and toneless. He exacted a chilly tension. Colleagues thought him cold, and he took it as praise. Coldness was competence. The secret was to understand the patient, with no confusing empathy. A patient, after all, was more than a person. A patient's response might spell a small medical advance. The successful operation was the one that increased knowledge.

He had enjoyed, at first, the moment after surgery when he could convey good news to relatives, bathing in their gratitude and respect. But he guarded against this now. Sometimes he would speak to them almost harshly, reminding them of essential post-operative care, of the patient's fragility.

At about this time he took to winter sports. He could afford to holiday in Austria and France, and he skied fast. He relished the solitary mastery of it, the rhythmic turning of his body over a difficult piste, the soundless speed. Meanwhile, three successive girlfriends floundered on the nursery slopes below. They each accused him of heartless ambition, of an obliterating obsession with work. And they were right, of course. His practice – bordered always by the risky, the unknown – only goaded him on.

The wind was dying round the chapel on St Adhelm's Head. Out at sea, the racing cumulus of storm cloud was ebbing to the south, isolated in its own tumult. He pushed at the chapel door, assuming it locked, but it swung open on to a stony darkness. Its central pillar upheld a vaulted chamber, arched above a marble altar and a wooden cross. The rough-stoned walls were orientated out of true, and the pillars inscribed with half-decipherable initials and distant dates.

By chance they stood together at the altar, as if at the marriage they had never discussed, and in this instant's awkwardness Kate stepped away. This would have been his moment, he thought, but he did not want to ask her here, in this enclosure sombre with the carved names of others. And neither of them were Christian believers. Kate must have sensed some restless preoccupation in him, because she asked suddenly: 'Was it a hard week?'

'Yes.' This was true (but not the reason for his silence). He was seeking the long-delayed moment for his question, and it was not now. He had imagined turning to her instead on the coast high above the sea: blue waves, alone, a hot sun.

She said: 'Did you have tough cases?'

'Two.' Yes, two. Not surgically tough, not really; but they had left an obscurely troubling aftermath.

They walked on above the calming sea. Beyond the chapel headland they started round the long white curve of coast, pocked with caves and abandoned quarries, that stretched to the lighthouse on Anvil Point. The limestone cliffs yawned beneath them in tiers of champagne-coloured rock, which sometimes dropped their fragments two hundred feet into the waves. Beneath their path the ruins of a wartime radar station lay half invisible under ivy. The way was still too narrow to hold hands.

The candidate for surgery had been a forty-two-year-old secondary school teacher with a mesial temporal lobe tumour. Her reports showed nothing unexpected. At the hospital's multidisciplinary meeting two weeks before, the psychologist had painted the picture of a tense, rather enclosed woman, whose intelligence seemed unimpaired by four years of increasingly severe epileptic seizures. A raft of first-line drugs had failed to alleviate her. The epileptologist had expressed concern about aftercare in her family, but nobody questioned the case for operating.

When he re-examined her file, the records showed an almost classic concordance. The video of the seizures she had suffered under surveillance agreed with the assessment of the normally cautious physiologist, and with the results of the MRI scans. Even her cognitive assessment – in which she performed near-perfectly – supported the diagnosis of hippocampal sclerosis and a low-grade tumour in the right temporal hemisphere. The operation would be delicate, but he had been performing it successfully for three years.

She arrived for interview dressed with austere formality. Instead of sitting indulgently beside his patients, Walford preferred the distance and authority of his desk. It was important that a patient have confidence in him. Whether she liked him was irrelevant. Besides, the third chair was now taken by the woman's husband, Richard Greene, a big man, running to fat, whose face was a mask of foreboding.

Walford knew the value of consulting relatives, but Claudia Greene, according to the neuropsychologist's report, was perfectly clear-headed. She said at once, in a quiet, metallic voice: 'I don't know if I want this operation.'

'I'm not here to persuade you either way.' Walford anticipated complications. 'I can describe the procedure to you, and the risks involved. Then it will be your decision.' There was silence. 'I hope you understand me.'

'She understands,' her husband said. He wanted this over quickly, Walford could tell. His fingers were drumming on his knees.

Walford said: 'You need to think about the quality of your life now. How badly you want to change it, how much you want to risk.'

Her husband said: 'She wants to risk it.'

'No two people feel alike about this,' Walford said. 'But your seizures have increased. Does this frighten you?'

Her husband said: 'Yes, she's scared. She can't teach any more.'

'Mr Greene, your wife must answer the questions herself.'

Walford thought he saw the ghost of a smile cross her face. She had once been pretty, he felt, but now looked much older than forty-two. Her face showed a papery dryness and was webbed by shallow lines. Her grey-blonde hair was pulled back to the nape in a spinsterly sheath.

'The seizures frighten my husband,' she said drily.

'But you?'

'They're getting more violent. You've seen the videos.' Her voice filled with distaste. 'At first I feel air rising in my stomach, then I try to fix my eyes on something nearby, to steady myself, and I swallow to make the air go away, but it doesn't work. Then I see my hands picking at my dress.' She looked down at herself, her thin chest. 'Then this fear comes. A kind of terror. I smell burning.'

'Burning?'

'Yes, burning. And I feel it's all happened before, in a life I've forgotten, that's the strange thing. It's perfectly familiar, but I'm very frightened. There's fire passing over my head, my skull. I can feel it searing in, and everything in my head is pouring away . . . I can't describe it. I'm pouring away . . .'

She stopped, as if she had said too much. It was odd. He had the impression of an intensely private woman, contemplating her own psyche. He said: 'The feeling of déjà vu is common for your condition, and some olfactory sensations too.' But he hadn't heard of burning.

The woman said: 'My husband tells me that I then stare at him, just stare, before collapsing. I don't remember this. Sometimes I wake up in the street with people round me.' She gave a terse laugh. 'I don't wear dresses any more . . . I have an epileptic friend who remembers nothing about her seizures at all. I'd rather be her.'

Her husband said: 'You don't want to be her. She's going stupid.' His mouth set. 'So what happens now, Dr Walford? When can she go in?'

'She must decide in her own time.' He asked her: 'How much do you know about the surgery?'

'I know very little. Only that the tumour is very deep inside, and that it has low malignancy, at least for now.' She added with clipped irony: 'Can you really take off the top of my head, doctor, and peer in there?'

'It's not quite like that.' For certain patients, he said, a more delicate approach was better suited than entering directly through the temporal lobe. He outlined this simply, as he always did with surgery candidates, while trying to assess her, to sense any impediment or loss in understanding. He needed to be sure of her capacity to decide. But he was aware too that she was assessing him, listening with some reservation that he could not identify; and once, of course, her attention went to his hands resting on the desktop, the hands that might recreate her. They were not the sensitised instruments that he would have liked, but wide and heavy-veined, with blunt fingertips.

The process was like extracting tissue through a keyhole, he said. It should do minimal damage to surrounding areas of the brain, to speech or memory or eyesight. The operation itself was more fine-tuned than entry through the temporal lobe, more prone to error. She would go under total anaesthetic, of course. Yes, she would be held in a head clamp. He would cut in a curve above the ear, deflecting the skin, then drill out the bone and fold back a little of the cranial membrane. This way he would have a window into the brain. He would intrude a surgical microscope, and from there the micro-instruments must find the ventricle leading to the hippocampus and the tumour. That was the crucial stage, with a small danger of inflicting haemorrhage.

She asked: 'But this way preserves memory?'

'There will always be memory loss. In your case the surgery must excise not only the tumour, but the surrounding organs. They would be vaporised, then sucked out. You would lose most of the hippocampus, which might make for memory deficit, together with the nucleic cluster called the amygdala, where the tumour is pressing. This is the area that colours memory with emotions.'

Claudia glanced at her husband, then away again. Her laugh was sudden, high and ugly. For the first time Walford wondered about her mental balance. He said: 'The point is this. It will become harder to lay down memory in the future. It will affect your profession, I'm afraid.'

She said in her quiet, tense voice: 'My profession is over.' For some reason she looked relieved.

Walford was always rigorous in laying out the dangers. He knew colleagues who had minimised them, then suffered afterwards from furious relatives. Despite the sophisticated technology now in use – image guidance systems, volumetric sterotaxis – the end depended on the human hand. It must steer a way through a maze of fragile fibres and blood vessels. He cited the risk of impaired vision and of outcomes peculiar to the left hemisphere, even loss of language. She went on watching him intently. In her pinched face the eyes were curiously uptilted, and might have been beautiful in somebody less ravaged. He thought of Darwin's awe at the exquisite perfection of the eye. But their glitter seemed incongruous in her, touched with obsession.

At the end she asked matter-of-factly: 'Could I die?'

'There is a tiny risk. But if you leave this tumour untreated and your seizures worsen, you are more likely to die within the next three years than you ever would be from surgery.' He thought: something private is troubling her. But it was not death, or anything he could trace. She was gazing at the floor.

Her husband broke in: 'What are the statistics, then?'

Walford was expecting this. 'After operating, the chances of being seizure-free are about seventy per cent. There's a twenty per cent chance that the seizures will somewhat decrease, a ten per cent chance of no change at all, and a one per cent possibility that the operation will miscarry. But in the end this is not a statistical decision. It's an emotional one.'

Claudia smiled faintly, and asked: 'What would you do?'

He said: 'It's not me, it's you. This is your body, your life. So it doesn't matter what I'd do.' She nodded. 'If it wasn't sensible to be entertaining surgery, you wouldn't be sitting here. The question is: are you prepared to take the risk?' Even to himself he sounded too brusque, too cold. He added: 'You don't have to decide now. And you can withdraw at any time, even at the last moment.'

She turned away and stared out of the window. Across the street the plane trees were shining in the late sun. Her husband looked mystified by her indecision, and suddenly crestfallen. Then she stood up and shook her head, as if brushing off a trance, and said: 'I need to think about it.'

That night he dreamt perplexedly: a dream without incident, with nothing to account for the intensity it carried.

He was a child again, crouching by the water tank in his parents' garden: a rusted cylinder of rainwater, whose tap dribbled greenly at its base. His brother was standing beside it, older and taller than him, smiling. Somewhere nearby he sensed the orchard's mellow tangle of pear and apple trees. And that was all. He remembered from boyhood how toads and a grass snake – the familiars of those years – had sometimes hunched or slithered beneath the water butt. But in this dream-instant there was only the sheen of smeared water, and the tap, and his brother saying something inaudible, and the resonance of forgotten days before and after.

He woke with a maddening sense of loss, of something that had been almost in his grasp. He believed dreams to flow from agitated long-term memory, so this saturated fragment had been salvaged (he supposed) from a far longer story that had slipped away.

The man looked like a startled hare. 'What a wonder it is!' His eyes jerked and dithered as if the nondescript surroundings – the styleless furniture, Walford's desk, the clinic pictures – held alternate threat and fascination for him, and his coxcomb of chestnut hair wobbled above a face that seemed famished.

'Nobody sees it, Doctor! There must be a fog in people's heads. The glory is all around them and they're blind! It's burning in every moment of our lives, all around us, and . . .'

This had been going on for twenty minutes now, and Walford could find no way of stopping it. He had been confronted by such epileptic personalities before, but in Roy Peters the prototype had arrived in troublesome force. God was pulsing through all human events, even the most trivial. Ordinary objects overflowed with mana, and certain places around them – hadn't Walford noticed? – emanated a celestial power. You could feel it brush against your face. And God had spoken to Peters in confidences that others did not know, often before the onset of an epileptic fit. The joy of this was indescribable. Sometimes Peters noticed daylight stars which loosened from the sky to balloon into dazzling light. He had seen the face of Jesus. 'Do you understand, Doc? Do you see what I'm saying? Do you realise how God is moving in the world?'

'What I realise is irrelevant to this interview, Mr Peters.' Walford was growing tired, irritable. He forced himself into a purposeful calm. 'What is important is that you understand the implications of the operation. You say you want to have it, but I think you . . .'

Peters broke in: 'I'll be in God's hands!'

You won't, Walford thought; you'll be in my hands. But he said: 'If you're to be free of seizures, I'll need to extract part of an area called your limbic system. There is a structure there named the hippocampus, shaped like a sea horse . . .' But he could see that Peters's gaze – the eyes that had glistened over him a moment before – had detached itself to enter some dream of his own. The man was already suffering from some anterograde memory deficit, Walford knew. Four times in the past year he had split his head open in sudden falls. A lesion in his right temporal lobe had been spreading since puberty – Peters was now thirty-three – and his focal seizures had grown longer and more frequent, deteriorating into bouts of status epilepticus.

The case for surgery was absolute. Walford would resect a part of the amygdala and the whole sclerotic right hip-pocampus, the ancient controllers of learning and emo-tion, and return Peters to something like normality. The strangeness was that Peters was not alarmed by his seizures. He even welcomed them. His pale eyes swivelled round to Walford again and glittered into his. 'First I hear this music, Doc, this chanting, and I know He is calling me, He is breaking through, and then the curtain between us is torn aside, like the veil of the Temple at His crucifixion. But when I hear His voice, the Devil can't bear it. The Devil knocks me unconscious. But I wake up in my rooms or on the street, because the Devil can't kill me, and I will go on carrying Jesus's message.'

Walford said: 'If we get the operation right, Mr Peters, these events will stop.'

'Yes, yes. We will destroy Satan together. You will be the agent of God too.'

Walford was jotting down notes for the rehabilitation therapist. 'We can't know for sure what the results will be. Every patient is different.' He came from behind his desk and stood above Peters, who thought he had come to embrace him and stretched up his arms like a child. But Walford looked down dourly at the sprout of boyish hair and the trembling knees in their split jeans. 'I want you to understand this. After the operation you will not feel the same. It may be that these visions and voices will disappear.'

'They will never disappear . . .'

'The brain is very complicated, Mr Peters. It is through the brain that we understand the world. Touch it, and the world changes.'

Peters stared up at him. His voice came high and tense with angry alarm. Walford was trampling on holy ground. 'Are you saying that you can cut God out of me with your knife?'

'I am saying that you suffer from a lesion, a piece of your brain that is abnormally formed. It has been explained to you already that you run the risk of early death. But whether to operate or not is your decision, and first you must understand that the procedure will change you.'

Peters's cheeks flushed red. 'You haven't understood anything, Doctor. Nothing at all.' He started to cross himself, again and again, with a smile of secret self-replenishment. 'Do you think that God lives in the brain?' His hands were clutched at his chest, shaking. 'No, God is battering outside us, asking to be let in. Let Him in, Doc! How can you say the brain can change Him?'

Walford answered with stony clarity: 'Rational ideas of God evolve in the frontal cortex, Mr Peters. The occipital lobe may anthropomorphise God, and the limbic region supply emotional experience of Him. Suppressed activity in the parietal area can induce the conviction of unity with the divine.' He pronounced this grim parody knowing it would not be understood or even heard, but he felt a cruel exoneration in the words. What troubled him was the question of informed consent. How could you perform an operation on a patient who did not understand what it might usher in? The person Peters would become might well forget or laugh at this whole discussion later. But he would be a person recreated by Walford.

With chilly courtesy he told Peters that he would see him again after a week. Peters had a week to consider what Walford had explained. But Walford knew that nothing would change the man's mind.

The excision of any part of the limbic system was a delicate and uncertain process. The hippocampus still preoccupied and amazed him. It received a meteor shower of sensory information every second, processed the information, arranged it in sequence, coloured it from a vast palette of emotions, then filed it away in the cortex for the demands of instant memory. To resect the hippocampus or amygdala was, in its way, to reorder nature.

Yes, you might cut out God with a knife.

One night, while Kate's arm was draped round him in sleep, he had measured her marriage finger with a piece of string. The engagement ring he secretly bought held a single diamond – small but very pure and finely cut – set in platinum. Its discreet brilliance, he thought, was right for her, and from time to time he fondled its hard shape, wrapped in tissue in his anorak pocket, and awaited his place and moment. But nowhere on the cliffside path was perfect: here a bay was occupied by others, there the view disappointed, here the wind had started up again. So he marched behind her in frustration, his heartbeat a little faster than the walk exacted, while she went blithely ahead, interpreting his quietness as preoccupation with the past week. She could not know at what moment he found himself thinking· when I ask, might she refuse? The question had barely occurred to him before (yet it was she who sometimes accused him of arrogance). She wasn't one of the nurses whose wide eyes gazed at him from their surgical masks; and for marriage, she once said, her exemplars were hardly promising. Her father was often absent, her mother alcoholic. To him, whose home had been stable, hers was a source of grim wonder, and she herself a little miraculous.

Around them the chalk grasslands flowed gently seaward, while below, the waves boiled in and out of shoreline caves, and flocks of guillemots shrilled from the cliffs. Here and there a dry-stone wall meandered down to their path, overgrown by brambles.

She began playfully to probe him. His abstractedness was not usually silent, but would surface in speculations (as far as she could follow them) on whatever brains he had been resecting that week. But today, if he momentarily emptied his mind of her, it was occupied not by neural science but by two oddly troubling patients. The woman, Claudia Greene, he said, had been opaque to him at first, her interview gaping with things unspoken, but her neuropsychiatric report stressed her lucidity. Then there was the fanatical Peters, for whom the concept of informed consent was futile: a man too engulfed by his condition to be informed by anything but a hallucinatory God.

For a while the two lovers carried these strangers with them along the coastal path, she teasing him that his self-trained detachment had faltered before two complex human beings. Had he fallen in love – she bantered – with Claudia Greene?

Yes, he was in love, he answered, enjoying the adolescent words. He was in love with Kate. As for Peters, what would be left of him if God was gone, he did not know. Ahead of them the long white wall of cliffs curled to the lighthouse headland three miles away, and the sea had calmed to a grey plain under a watery sun. He walked beside her now. A windless peace descended. Once he found her quietly laughing at the beauty of the country: her laughter not a release of tension, but a curious, sweet tinkle of inner exultation, like the involuntary gurgle of a baby. He loved her for it.

But soon afterwards, she said: 'Poor Mr Peters. Can the temporal lobes really be responsible for God?'

'In his case, they may be.' He touched her cheek.

'So who knows?' she laughed. 'The brain may simply be our means of apprehending God.'

He said: 'In which case I'll be destroying someone's salvation.'

'Oh, so you are God. I was wondering where . . .'

He cuffed her gently. He might have asked her then and there to marry him, but they had argued before about his view of patients as neural specimens – as though detachment had turned him heartless – while he sometimes tried to distance her from her children's sickness, which often racked her dreams.

The death of the past had grown only slowly to trouble him. It was memory in the present – the capacity for efficient day-to-day recall – that surgery could most crucially destroy. For the sake of patients' survival, mental acuity might be irreversibly dimmed, careers broken, relationships wrecked. As for retrograde memory, the unique history buried in the individual brain, its loss was less easily assessed. In the altered mind of the post-operative patient, the past could slip away unnoticed. Whole stories remained buried alive, inaccessible in the labyrinth of the cortex.

For her second and last consultation, Claudia Greene arrived alone. She was dressed as sombrely as before, and in the harsh light of his consulting room the tension in her face, with its fragile bones and ghostly web of lines, deepened her look of premature age. She sat opposite him, on her seat's edge, her small, gaunt body held very upright, and her hands fidgeting over a tight-rolled umbrella. She asked in her faintly ironic way precisely what parts of herself he planned to remove, then turned at last to her dread of lost memory. How much of her past would be gone? What periods of her life were most threatened? Did memories vanish wholesale, or leave themselves behind in fragments?

His answers, he knew, would be insufficient. Neuroscience was young and imprecise, he admitted. Each human brain was different. The brain was best imagined not as a cluster of discrete regions, but as a traffic network of information. When one road became impassable, another might open. What was it, in particular, that she feared?

She went silent. He wondered how long this would last. Then she said: 'There is a period of my life, four years ago, that I don't want to lose.' She turned her oddly brilliant eyes on him. 'It was a love affair.'

He had not expected this. Her pared appearance had deceived him – but after all, she was little older than him – and her aura of propriety. He found himself nodding at her, frowning. 'I understand.' But he was not sure he did.

She was looking at him now with bizarrely mixed pride and shame. 'The memories are very strong. I can't imagine myself without them. I don't know who I would be. It must sound feeble – it sounds feeble to me – to feel your identity so wrapped up in somebody else's, and years ago now. And the man is dead.'

'I'm sorry.' Walford was wondering why no other patient had confronted him with such apprehensions: fear for the continuity of the self. Had others imagined memory to be so intrinsic that its loss did not occur to them? Or perhaps, given the depletion of so many patients, they had not thought at all.

The woman said: 'Will all this disappear, Mr Walford, as if it had never happened?'

For a moment he wondered why she did not want this: to be returned to the illusion of fidelity to her marriage. But she went on: 'I want to know what happens here.' She touched her head, then added in a voice beginning to tremble: 'If you can, preserve it.'

He realised that she had already read and understood something of her condition. He said: 'As you know, the tumour is in the brain's right hemisphere. But the hemispheres are not discrete. They learn from one another.'

'Where do memories reside, then?'

'They are processed by an organ in the limbic system – that's a region deep inside the brain – called the hippocampus. It assigns some memories for long-term storage in the cortex – the upper, rational brain, if you like – while the more trivial memories drop from our consciousness.' She was watching him with a fierce, sad stare. 'It was recently thought that after some years the long-term memories remained solely in the upper brain. But now we are not so sure. For all we know, the whole limbic system is awash with memories. That's why your question is hard to answer, Mrs Greene.'

But he had always resisted false consolation, and he added clearly, deliberately: 'What I would expect you to lose is part of your so-called "autonoetic consciousness", the ability to travel back into the past and recall it in detail. This may affect time over all periods of your life. It may be that only a simple memory trace will be left of some events, just a sense of familiarity . . .'

As often before, he knew that he had been harsh. He added that he expected her semantic memory – the ability to read, speak – to be spared, as well as any procedural skills: ex-patients went on riding bicycles and dancing.

But her gaze had dropped from his and he knew she was not listening. She said tightly: 'Perhaps it's better to go on enduring seizures.'

'That way your memory will deteriorate anyway, worse than anything surgery can do. You've been unusually free of damage so far, but it cannot last.'

She said: 'I have not forgotten a single hour of those years yet.' The words, even in her clipped, metallic voice, sounded oddly girlish. 'Nothing of him at all. I still speak to him, listen to him. Even the epileptic fits are filled with him.' She was suddenly blushing; he concluded that her seizures were accompanied by orgasm.

Guessing, he said: 'That is quite frequent for women in epileptic spasm.'

'I didn't know.'

'Patients rarely speak of it, of course, but the statistics are there.' She was silent again. 'As I explained in our first interview, Mrs Greene, this is a very delicate operation, which will remove as little as possible of the outer brain, the cortex. This is the best we can do to preserve language, and memory.'

She stood up and went over to the window. She was still carrying her umbrella. All her life, he imagined, she had kept this self-control, like a pure flame, and now it was passing from her. He could sense her fear. But at last she said, still staring through the pane: 'I've decided to have this operation.'

'I think you've made the right choice.'

'But there's something I need from you.' She reached into her handbag and laid on his desk a slim packet of letters. He saw by their stamps that they came from Spain. 'How long after the operation will you see me?'

'I see patients within half an hour, in intensive care, then twice daily in hospital.'

She said almost vehemently: 'I want you to show me these letters as soon as the operation is over. I want to remember at once. You say my semantic memory will survive. These will make me remember. Will you do this, Mr Walford?'

'Does your husband know?'

'My husband knows nothing. He is too busy with himself.'

But Walford felt his irritation rising, anger at this imposition, and impatience with her subterfuge. No one had ever asked him such a thing. He could not know what memories – fractured or dimmed or whole – would reassemble around her. Even now, after so many seizures, her past might be corrupt. Memories were not static. With every re-remembering, their neural structure changed, so the most dwelt-upon past might be the most impure. Even an imagined event, if vivid enough, could leave its print on the brain as permanently as a truth. He said: 'I don't think I can do this.'

But Claudia had leant across his desk and placed a photo on the sheaf of letters. Her voice was breaking. 'Perhaps

I won't remember anything. But before you operate, I want to know I've done all I can. If the letters don't mean anything, perhaps the photo will.' Her face was close to his now, its eyes filled and shining. He glanced down at the photo and saw a small, sallow man, with a dark beard. The margin was inscribed simply 'Joaquim'. Beside him, her hand in his, was a woman he did not recognise at once, young for her years then, and lit by wonderful eyes. He did not know if the shock he felt was one of admiration or pity. She followed his gaze and turned the photo over, as if it were still secret.

'He was Spanish. He was a Roman Catholic . . . but I've always found God a little ridiculous.' The metal of her laugh softened. She was recalling something affectionate. 'We met in Salamanca, at a conference, and then in England. Those boarding houses . . . years of subterfuge . . .' Her voice found its coolness again. 'You will do it, won't you?'

This is maudlin self-indulgence, he thought. He kept the irritation from his voice, but said: 'I'm sorry.'

Some days were long and unpredictably demanding, and intensified in him the concentrated energy that he relished. After his ward rounds next morning, during five hours in the operating theatre, he resected a construction worker's high-grade glioma, clearing the residual tissue under an MRI scanner. His half-hour break was spent consulting with the oncologist. In the afternoon, with the senior registrar away sick, he operated on a fifty-year-old solicitor, excising a tumour pressing on the inner ear.

In intensive care the man responded satisfactorily to his voice.

By early evening he was interviewing the parents of a sixteen-year-old girl with subdural haematoma, and anticipating a final consultation with Roy Peters. Peters was more subdued than before. He gave a distracted wave from the doorway as he entered, as if Walford was far away, and sat down gingerly. His eyes had a cloudless fixity. During the past five days he had suffered two seizures. Once his brother had found him unconscious in the hallway of their shared flat. His arm was bandaged to the elbow. He had decided to quit his part-time job as a packager, he said, in order to write. He was writing about the purifying power of everyday phenomena. He had knelt in prayer each afternoon for over an hour, and Jesus had come to him in the sunlight. Jesus was the Word, and Peters would write it. Jesus had explained to him the order of things, and that there was nothing to fear. He had even told him the purpose of his seizures, and where his daughter had gone.

'You have a daughter?'

'She passed away.'

'I didn't know that.' There had been no mention of this child in Peters's clinical reports, nor in interview with his relatives. And he had never been married.

'She is with God now,' Peters said. 'She is His angel.' So how could Peters be sad? There were times, he said, when he felt a profound detachment from the material world, as if everything inside him were at last resting, and the edges of himself bleeding into the infinite beneficence of God. 'And when I kneel by the window I can see across the rooftops and the satellite dishes, and there is the church spire with its cross. Then I fix my eyes on it and I can feel Him coming, and after a bit I close my eyes in the sunlight, and He speaks. At night the cross is lit up, a kind of reflected light, and God is still there. You said that God is in the brain, Dr Walford, but it is the Devil who is in the brain, in the dark, indoors, and God is in the light, asking to come in . . . Isn't this very beautiful?'

It was now that Walford felt an unaccustomed misgiving. He would operate, of course, there was nothing else to be done. Peters's lesion was sub-acute, and spreading. But he wondered how much the post-operative Peters would lose of his divine comfort. In his dimmed world, would nothing any longer be explained? And would his angel daughter be a corpse? Then quickly these questions curbed themselves. He wondered if this daughter might not be a fantasy. But when he looked at the patient now, at his hare's eyes staring and his gawky perch on the chair – Peters seemed about to leave at any moment – Walford felt a stab of something like pity.

Now Peters was saying: 'After the op, the Devil won't pull me down again?'

'No, I hope not.'

A minute later Peters jumped up to go, elated by Walford's agreement to operate, and seized both his hands, and blessed him, and walked backwards to the doorway, waving.

Walford felt suddenly very tired. He remained in his chair for a long two minutes, staring at the doorway as if Peters had absconded with his energy, bequeathing only his little hand wave and his childish convictions. Walford thumbed half-heartedly through a dossier of referrals and a radiologist's report, then prepared to go home. Peters was a little mad, of course, and might remain so. There was no knowing if the operation would blur his faith or unravel it altogether.

Some brain studies claimed that repeated contemplation of a concept could render it as real as any sense perception. A function of the thalamus, Walford thought. So Peters's invocations could enforce belief as intensely, say, as the candlelit prayers of a seminarist addressing God. The brain created its own idols. It did not always separate fact from fantasy. It had evolved to promote its owner's survival. And Peters needed his God.

The sea has gone dead now, and the air still. They walk hand in hand. In front of them the coast curls in a level wall of cliffs under green hills, and the waves make only a light froth below. The richer limestone seams lie here, and abandoned excavations gape in serried caves high along the shoreline. Once the path descends into the canyon of a derelict quarry, where they emerge on to a natural terrace above the sea. The slope of a ramp remains, and a concrete slipway where timber derricks once swung the stone on to barges fifty feet below.

He feels the sun on his face and the warmth of the encircling rock. As Kate explores the ruined quarry, he sits apart and watches her with a tinge of apprehension, nursing his delayed proposal, consciously loving her. She is sometimes still mysterious to him. Perhaps she will always be. He can never quite predict her: what will upset her, what she will love or laugh at. She has taken off her anorak and cap in the sun, and her fair hair drifts back from her forehead. After so many years, so many other loves, harsh indecisions, he thinks with wonder: this is the woman I want to marry. He leans on the empty ramp while she wanders through workrooms where a few brick piers still stand, their iron beams rusted and broken. The quarrymen have been gone for a century. The square mouths of their excavated caves yawn beside her. She vanishes inside one, and he follows her.

Its chasm extends deep into the rock face. Huge, misshapen columns of living stone uphold the ceilings. Kate calls out to him: 'There are bats. Little ones.' Now his eyes accommodate to the dark. He stands beside her under a ceiling blackened and shifting with pipistrelles. A stench of urine rises. Around them the rock walls are split laterally in regular seams, as if the stone foreshadowed its own cutting. Their footfalls scrunch in the silence. They wonder aloud at the cavernous vastness of these works, at how many stoneworkers died of silicosis and TB, how many churches and city squares were created from its emptiness.

When they emerge, his arm around her against the dankness, the noon sunlight is refracting from the rocks in a warm brilliance. They lie down in a patch of sheltered grass. His hand finds her cheek and touches her mouth to his. They look up at the sky and the stone beauty of the cliff. Her body is supple and alive beside him. When he loosens her jeans at the waist, she helps him. He is fierce in his longing for her, in his imminent proposal, and hears her low laughter, and feels at last the bloom of the full, athletic body that furls nakedly into his. A Tortoiseshell butterfly flutters from the grass and settles on her shoulder. He brushes it away. In the long intensity of his desire, of his lips smothered in her neck, of her own whispering orgasm, his words of marriage are momentarily forgotten. As they drift into calm, he wonders how she will greet this irony, then falls asleep on her breast.

Later she murmurs teasingly, waking him: 'Why did we make love here? Did you plan this all along?'

But his mind goes perfectly blank. 'I don't know why.'

'But you know everything!' She often says that, with a mocking complaint that he explains everything through the brain. Now she announces that it was not they who were making love, of course, but only his amygdala and her anterior cingulate, and she bends over to kiss his forehead, and playfully massages his heart.

It was an easy walk from the flat to the hospital. You went through a public park and a small cemetery, and in the early morning it was so tranquil that you heard little but the pipe of waking birds. This interlude between breakfast and the surgery gave him a cleansing momentum. He enjoyed his own energy while others were barely stirring. His footsteps fell sharp and purposeful on the gravel paths. The near silence, the brightening sky and the sea air concentrated him for the day ahead.

In the churchyard the faded flowers and repeated epitaphs passed by, today, with a faint dissonance: 'in loving memory', 'forever remembered'. This morning's patient would be Claudia Greene, whose memory's fragility obsessed her. In the afternoon he would operate on a pensioner whose memory would be impaired with the excision of his astrocytoma. He thought: there are things we cannot afford to dwell on, and the sacrificed past is among them.

He construed 'forever remembered' not as reality, but as an extravagance of grief. The remembering brain was as corruptible as any other flesh. By the time he reached the hospital, all thought of these delusive consolations had vanished. The receptionists were as sleepy as usual, and the passageways empty. Familiar antiseptic smells hung in the air. He put on his loose-fitting scrubs and disposable gown in a darkened locker room.

At this early hour, before the clamour and fussing of others intruded, he liked to take ownership of the operating theatre. It was a reassuring ritual: the checking of instruments and screens. He wanted nothing superfluous here. He needed the surgeon's stool precisely calibrated beforehand, its arms adjusted. He checked that the guidance system was loaded (this morning it wasn't) and that the patient's scans were up on the screen. The marking pen for incision and the tapes and razor for the hair should be in place.

At 7.30, he went up to Mrs Greene's ward. She was awake, with her husband beside her, and an anxious teenage son whom she'd never mentioned. She looked newly taut and pale. The metallic control of her questions jarred on the silence. Her husband shifted in his seat and kept clearing his throat as if to say something, but did not. How soon would her anaesthetic fade, she asked, would she wake with a headache, how long afterwards would he see her? A few minutes later his anaesthetist arrived and explained her procedure with chatty assurance. Then Walford left them.

He was conscious of Claudia wanting to say things that she could not. He disliked such irregularities, but he waited in the doorway of the anaesthetic room beside the theatre, until the porter wheeled her close. Then he gave her the encouragement that sounded so stereotyped to him, but which often elicited in patients a pleading gratitude, and sometimes a shaky hand would rise to grasp his.

But Claudia Greene only licked her dry lips for a moment. Her slanted eyes stared up at him from the trolley. Then she pulled out the same packet of letters – she had smuggled it beneath her gown – and pressed it against his chest. Forced to accept it, he expected to be struck by anger, but instead felt a mixture of pity and curiosity, as if her forgetting or recollection might, after all, have some clinical value.

His team was in the theatre. It was almost a routine morning. He had a reputation for punctiliousness, he knew, and they were waiting a little edgily: his registrar, Salim Gupta, talented but young, together with an experienced scrub nurse and her runner. The patient's MRI scans were up on screen, showing sections of the diseased left hemisphere. He and Salim studied these cursorily, already familiar with them. There were two linked sites of operation: the amygdala and beside it the sclerotic hippocampus. Just on the basal nucleus of the amygdala hung the cloudy blister of a low-grade tumour. There was no immediate telling how deeply and invisibly this penetrated. The attached hippocampus showed sclerosis over half its body – in the enhanced images it shone brilliant white, then faded towards the structure's tail – and it was twenty-two per cent smaller than that in the right hemisphere.

Claudia Greene was wheeled in unconscious, accompanied by the anaesthetist with her registrar and operating assistant. Although the patient's eyes were taped over, and her mouth stopped with oxygen and gas tubes, her face, to Walford, seemed younger, smoothed out, and her hands were interlaced like a child's on her stomach. He undertook himself the shaving of hair from the area of operation, and marked with a surgical pen the line of cranial incision. It circled out in a wide question mark above the ear. He gave to Salim the task of pivoting the patient's head in the clamp, holding it rigid for the computer guidance system, and supervised the placement of its pins into the skull cosmetically, just behind the hairline. The fiducial markers on the patient's head were correlated with the navigation system on screen. Then the scrub nurse veiled off Claudia's face.

Now, with the operative site isolated, he felt his focus sharpen. It was a familiar moment. His attention converged on a single depersonalised segment of the head. The patient became a surgical field. He felt the tight exhilaration of his own control. His murmur and lifted hand would automatically receive the right grade of scalpel or retractor. And he regulated the tension purposefully, like ventilation, with a pressure never dropping to casualness or rising to panic.

He started to open up the cranium with customary swiftness, slicing the muscle over it, folding back the facial nerve. The bleeding was minimal. Then came the drilling of the burr holes into the skull and the circling incision of the craniotomy saw. For long minutes its shrill whine filled the silence, and there was a stench of singed bone. Then he cauterised the flap of loosened cranium, and lifted it off.

Around the cavity, and the sheltering membrane of the dura below, he and Salim packed in oxidised cellulose until the operational field was defined in a bright circle.

Less than thirty minutes had elapsed, and there might be four hours to go. But his sense of time would disappear now. These operations happened in a temporal vacuum, insulated under the artificial day of the surgical lights. After he had perforated and sliced it, the dura began almost of its own accord to ease away from the white folds of the brain itself, and so much bleeding followed that he sutured the site swiftly, stitching back and weighting the clips around it.

Now, with quickened concentration, he lowered the theatre microscope and began the long, deep probe into the inner brain. Experience lent him a familiar calm, almost elation: the practised delicacy that guided his retractor and forceps to the sylvian fissure and opened his way at last to the threshold of the amygdala, the anciently formed organ whose removal could destroy emotional recollection. Its detection was the most challenging part of the procedure. The jagged navigation lines, superimposed on his microscope field, warned him off the optical regions, and highlighted his target. From screens around the theatre his team could scrutinise his progress, but to his naked eye the amygdala and hippocampus were still invisible. Probe too far back and you might damage the patient's language strip. Go too high and you would cut the optical radiation fibres, wrecking the right-side vision. All the while, he and Salim were cauterising the surrounding vessels: vessels whose precise function nobody knew. He said to Salim beside him: 'Watch closely.'

He was discreetly proud of his abilities in this hardest of regions. Now, after only twenty minutes probing a path through the temporal lobe, his aspirator entered the ventricle itself, betrayed by a flood of cerebrospinal fluid, and he knew he was on track. On the MRI scan the tumour showed in a solid nucleus, ringed by magnified light. As he began to debulk it, the cancer came hard and fibrous against the instrument's tip. He could not yet know how deeply it had intruded. For a long time the lesion's resistance continued – he could sense it through his fingertips – then its texture loosened, and the pure amygdala's tiny arteries splashed against the aspirator's head and rose through the tube in a soft flow, the consistency of redcurrant jelly.

Meticulously now he started to disconnect the amygdala from surrounding organs. He needed to sever it, in particular, from the sclerotic hippocampus – the channel and storehouse of memory itself – which lay half exposed beyond it. During this rigorous process his hands continued to do what they had been trained to do, but his mind started strangely to detach, as if inured to what he was performing. The amygdala, the seat of primal feeling, was deeply embedded. As he started to separate it from the hippocampus – as if from the bedrock of memory – he was struck by the irreversibility of what he was doing. He even imagined his hands hesitating – but they were not – because he had become aware of this woman's past, and the years he might be gutting of their meaning. He was doing what he had trained himself never to do: identify with a patient; and he was glad that his vision was confined within the microscope and that he could not see on the surrounding screens, as the others could, the crimson exodus of Claudia's memories.

For a moment he paused, adjusting his mask, and glanced at his team in case they had noticed something. But the anaesthetist was scrutinising the monitor on her machine, and Salim was glancing at him for more instructions as they prepared to shave down the hippocampus. He drew up the surgical chair. After three hours his arms were aching. For a minute he waited, settling his elbows on the armrests, until his hands hung free above the patient's head. He focused his gaze on neutral objects – the newly installed humidifier, the gleaming scrub basin, the endoscopy ceiling pendant.

It was clear what must be done to render the patient seizure-free. He had performed this operation often. The MRI scan and the oncologist's report showed sclerosis over half the hippocampus. This organ looked less like its sea horse namesake than a long white tadpole, netted in red veins. When he ran the mouth of the aspirator over it, its surface barely shivered. It seemed like ancient skin. Even when he maximised the tissue selector, nothing crumbled; so he turned the vibrating tip to dissect the tissue from the brain's lining, and cut it into segments, lifting them out piecemeal. At first the residue massed and coagulated round the aspirator's head; then it started to lurch up the tube in a thick, resistant waste that quivered through his fingers. He was easing it away from the brainstem, which loomed below, and at last reached an area where on the scan the sclerosis faded away.

As his aspirator touched Claudia's living tissue, his mind flinched. Every fragment that he removed now might be abrading her memory. His breath inside his mask felt stifled and heavy. Again he imagined his hands shaking above the rasp of the aspirator, though in fact they were perfectly assured. There was no way to know precisely what he was doing. Every human brain was different. Perhaps years ago her right hemisphere had begun to compensate for the other; or maybe even now he was severing the bridge between her consciousness and memories. He could not know. Only the feeling persisted – almost the knowledge – that with every second, as his aspirator went on ingesting, he was no longer sucking up flesh, as he sometimes told himself, but the memory of a woman's self-esteem, the man's voice returning to her. The incarnate flow of her past was vanishing up the aspirator's tube to end in the hospital incinerator.

Perhaps he left her with a millimetre more of the hippocampus than he had intended, he did not know. His working hands and brain had performed unerringly. He irrigated the cavity, watching for blood leaking into the water, then staunched more vessels with diathermy. At last he returned the dura to its sheltering place, and allowed Salim to close up the skull and stitch the temporal muscle. When they unclamped Claudia's head, he peeled the tapes from her eyes and checked their pupils for dilation; then he and a nurse bandaged her tightly against haemorrhage.

Only Salim, who normally regarded him with spaniel hero-worship, had sensed that anything was wrong. While the anaesthetists and porters were wheeling the patient out to the adjacent recovery ward, he asked quizzically: 'It went all right, Steven, didn't it?'

*　　*　　*

In the muted light of the recovery room, an hour later, the only other patient was awake, staring through his oxygen mask. Four staff nurses were moving about softly, adjusting equipment. It was almost silent. These were the anxious moments after operation, waiting for patients' responses. Nothing was quite predictable. Several of Walford's colleagues had been confronted by paralysis of limbs, speech, sight. He walked down an avenue of empty beds. Claudia was at the end. Her head looked white and shrunken under its turban of bandages, but he saw that she was already testing herself, curling her fingers, feeling her thighs. A nurse was seated at the monitor behind her. Claudia turned on her pillows at his approach and her eyes opened. He asked her how she felt, and her words seemed to surface from a great distance, but they were clear and careful. 'I'm all right. But my head is numb.' Her free hand lifted, dragging the cuff of her pressure gauge with it, and touched her bandaged forehead.

'You've had local anaesthetic. It will fade in a couple of hours.'

Above her head the screen showed normal ECG and respiration, and lowered blood pressure. He asked her to move her right leg, her right arm – the control side of the left hemisphere – and she did so without trouble.

Faintly smiling, she asked: 'What did you find inside my head?'

He laughed. It was a good sign. Weakness and anaesthesia normally eliminated humour. He said: 'The operation went to plan. I don't expect you to have more seizures. And we excised the tumour.'

'Good.' A pause, then: 'I know they can come back.'

Strange, he thought, how he had delved into the private depths of this woman's brain, yet how impersonal that seemed, as if human character and consciousness lay somewhere else. These were returned to him instead by her thin-lipped mouth and the pale slant of her eyes. She asked about her tumour again, its extent and prognosis. He was able to reassure her. She enquired about time in intensive care, and her referral to a new neurologist.

Perhaps it was the anaesthesia, he thought, or a deepened sense of privacy, that prevented her from asking after the packet of letters. But he pulled them from the pocket under his gown. He was clinically curious about her response. 'You asked me to show you these.'

She looked momentarily, drowsily, surprised, then said: 'Oh yes. I do remember.' Her free hand emerged from the blankets to take them. She stared at the photo for a long time.

He asked: 'Do you remember?'

'Yes. That's Joaquim Gonzales.' But she said this without colour, as if she were identifying an unfamiliar object. 'He died three years ago.' Again, no tone at all. Just a fact. 'Poor fellow.'

The staff nurse hovered a moment longer by Claudia's monitor, then moved away, sensing a plea for privacy. Walford said: 'Can you read those letters?'

She fumbled a sheet from its envelope, and examined it. He wondered if she had forgotten Spanish. But she took out another and read that too, her face knotted with a slight frown, like brackets gathered between her eyes. She said: 'They're very sweet.' The words held a baffled distance, tinged with condescension.

He insisted softly: 'Mrs Greene, you asked me to show you these letters so you would be reminded of somebody you still loved.'

She looked down at them again, and shuffled them in her hands, like playing-cards. He regretted his words, too insistent for a weakened patient. He said: 'I didn't mean to intrude.'

'You didn't intrude, Doctor.'

'You said that after his death you used to listen to him.'

'Did I?' She stared at the foot of the bed as if baffled. He thought: why would she bother to access a voice that she has forgotten to love?

He wondered now, with his own chill of puzzlement, why he demanded so strenuously that she remember. Professional pride, of course: he wanted an operation unmarred by any deficit. But he was thinking too of the frailness of memory itself, and of Claudia's affair – the love of strangers – surviving somewhere, even as an inaccessible memory trace. He began thinking involuntarily of Kate.

He drew back from Claudia's bedside. He realised that he had been craning over her. It was a medically interesting case, after all. But it was more important, he knew, that her capacities survive. Patients like her would notice, above all, the failure of short-term memory in the future: the frustration of small things forgotten, the compensating accumulation of lists and memoranda. Her rehabilitation therapist would not care about an affair buried in her past.

He envisaged her living a restricted but competent life. But as he looked at her, he felt a reluctant disquiet at what he had created. She smiled at him wanly as he started to leave. The letters lay under her inert hand, beside the cannulae that snaked out of her forearm.

He found himself clasping her shoulders in farewell.

He said: 'Rest now.'

The day is almost gone. We are far inland. Our path moves along a shallow spine of hills, a highway in prehistoric times. To one side the sea is out of sight: there are only downlands quartered into fields; on the other, the bays and woods of Poole harbour look interfused in the twilight. This has continued too long. Our daylight will end on a windy tableland in semi-darkness. She walks beside me, flushed and carelessly beautiful, and sometimes turns to me, as though to question something. She thinks my silence has to do with work – it usually does – and asks outright: 'What happened to that woman? And the man with religious mania?'

'Roy Peters?'

I tell her. His temporal lobe procedure went well, impersonally, as any such operation should: a process that concentrates on resecting not a human mind, but an impaired physical structure. Apart from problems with equipment (the irrigation system seized up), there were no hitches. By the time of his discharge two days later, Peters was shaky but lucid. He sat calmly in my office, wearing a jauntily tilted fedora hat to hide his bandages. We talked about his home, and his brother's ability to look after him; about the probability of future work, and about the existence of God, or otherwise. He supposed that God existed all right, he was pretty sure of it, but that He hadn't much time for Peters. His indifference seemed to be reciprocated.

'My people were Methodists, you know. But my mother gave up going to chapel after they divorced. She was ashamed, like. We didn't have much God after that . . .'

His talk was weakened and sombre, but from time to time a note of frustration sounded, as if, before his epilepsy, he had been a confident, rather cocky youth. He said: 'If you ask me, God's a bit of a joker. He doesn't trouble himself much with the likes of us.' Here a twinge of irritation. 'Did you tell me that God lived in the brain, Doc?'

'I said no such thing.'

'Well, there's nothing important in the brain, is there? What did you find there? You just got rid of my hippo . . . hippo . . .'

'. . . campus.'

'Whatever . . . and I don't feel any different.'

'You are different.'

Kate, what was I to say? That once the world had burned with meaning, that Jesus came down and spoke to him?

'You are calmer, Mr Peters. I think your seizures won't return. You may even be able to hold down a job now.'

'A job?' He frowned. 'I don't know what I'll do. I wanted to write . . .' He rummaged in the rucksack at his feet, and pulled out a cloth-bound manuscript tied with blue ribbon. 'I started writing this in July. It was amazing, it just poured out of me like I can't describe, like it was being dictated . . .' He opened and closed it again, bewildered. 'But now . . . I can't read it. I thought it was beautiful, but something's happened to it. It makes no sense.' He got up and laid it open on my desk, like a precious relic. It was titled 'God's Plan for the World', and its pages were covered in cabbalistic symbols interspersed with paragraphs where half the words were underlined or indecipherable. 'Would you read it, Doc? Maybe you can explain these things.'

But I won't read this man's rubbish, Kate. We have only one life.

Peters got up abruptly and took back the manuscript, clasping it like a body. 'Tell you what, Doc. I don't give a shit about the brain. I read that after you're dead, the brain rattles about in your skull, the size of a walnut. And you know what happened to Einstein's brain? Somebody kept it in a mayonnaise jar and . . . something . . . You can do what you like inside my head, Doc, and it won't make any difference.'

He slumped down again, still cradling his book. Suddenly he seemed close to tears. He whispered: 'My brain is not me. I'm me!'

Without knowing it, Kate, he was illustrating the deepest mystery of neuroscience. How does the brain, a lump of meat, convert into the great theatre of human consciousness? Neither Peters nor Stephen Hawking knows. There's a theory that the sequential narrative which the brain offers up to us, giving the impression of a coherent self, emerges from a babble of competing soliloquies in our neural channels. These voices are constantly supplanting and interrupting one another. Hence the haphazard way we think. So the self is an illusion. The greatest illusion of all. It emerges only from the raw material of our speech and perceptions. We are, in a sense, these materials: the product of electro-chemical tumult.

Kate gives a blithe laugh. 'Speaking as an illusion, I have my doubts.'

Yes, this theory too will pass. They all do. But walking like this, with her engagement ring tingling in my anorak pocket, I've grown absurdly sensitive. I realise I am afraid. My mind diverges and goes adrift, throws up a smoke-screen before my asking her. Flint stones grate underfoot. A late mountain-biker strains by. It is almost dark. If I had left one extra centimetre of Peters's hippocampus, he might have kept more of his God. The lights of Poole are starting up to our north. To our left, Bronze Age burial mounds appear. But the hippocampus was totally sclerotic, and my business is to heal people, not preserve their fantasies. Four-thousand-year-old skeletons beneath the grass with bronze implements for their afterlife. And then there is Kate. The miracle child of an alcoholic and a serial adulterer. (Of course I am in love.) Sometimes she turns and smiles at me: lemony skin over wide, high-boned features, the trace of a Polish mother . . .

I must soon. Very soon. It is nearly night. I glimpse the scarlet fruit of a low shrub, and bend to pluck it. I will present it to her, like a quaint emissary. It will prepare her for what I will ask. The fruit is not growing, but fallen, and when I bend down to gather it, the odour is over-powering. A pear, perhaps, overripe or rotten. A wild pear. In itself the smell may be slight, I don't know. But it carries a shock of the past – heady with undivulged promise – like the passage into a forgotten room. How curious. Anxious now, faintly sick, the aroma of damp orchards.

Nothing inexplicable, of course: smells are paired with memories by the entorhinal cortex. Yet I feel something precious slipping away. It escapes as I think about it, as I straighten up empty-handed from the shrub, and my head swims.

Foolish, this. If I go on, I'll become as brainless as Peters. I throw back my head to the salt wind. Kate is in front of me, surveying the burial mounds in the deepening dark. They are barely higher than we are, rounded and shaven by rain and wind. A light grass covers them. They look like outsize craniums. I move behind her, hold her shoulders. I never meant to ask her this here, but it doesn't matter. The stars are coming out, and the land beyond Poole harbour is ablaze with lights. And we are standing, shivering in the night wind, above where the Bronze Age dead lie in their foetal sleep, their brains filling with dust, and I take her hand and I ask her to marry me.

She is staring at the ground. I can't see her expression. I squeeze her gloved hand and hold it for what seems a long time. I think she is sobbing. Alarmed, I say: 'You haven't answered me.'

She looks up. Her eyes are wet, but she is softly laughing. She says with an odd, choked whisper: 'Of course I will, you fool.'

She used to joke that I understood the brain, but nothing at all about the heart. It is suddenly very cold. She is in my arms now, fondling the engagement ring, then slips it mischievously on to the wrong finger. As we disengage, the jewelled hand lingers in mine. We must descend in the dark now.

*　　*　　*

If the house had been less solidly built, the fire would have burst through timber and plaster in a single, furious conflagration. As it was, each closed room became for a while a noxious chamber of bluish gases, where the flames lived a stifled half-life, licking at paint or munching curtains and clothes, before a window or ceiling joist cracked apart, and fresh oxygen sucked up a violent torrent of fire and light.

He woke with a start, imagining naked flames, hugging the duvet around his body as he lurched to the telephone. But the line was dead, and his mobile phone was in the car. He found a light switch, but the electricity was gone too. His lungs were heaving and retching. From his bedroom window he saw the flames pouring from the casement below, and could not glimpse the ground. He clenched his eyes shut. He fumbled for a bathroom tap – the water, at least, was still running – and wrapped a wet flannel round his mouth and nose. He must warn the woman across the landing, the frail-looking woman. He crashed into the packing cases heaped beside his doorway. He was leaving next week, he remembered, and it gave him irrational hope. When he opened his door, he was hit by a wall of smoke. A window exploded somewhere below. The stairways and landings were drawing up the fire faster than the sealed flats, blanketing the mezzanine fire escape. For a moment he stopped, blind, disorientated. Then he became aware of a deep, visceral shuddering in the building's foundations, the groan of shifting timber, and a near-silent roar as from the furnace of a ship's engine. Some instinct from school fire practice dropped him to his knees – oxygen rose between the floorboard cracks, he was taught – but now, through the damp flannel, he inhaled the suffocating stench of melting steel, and a gasping faintness.

He backed away on all fours and closed his door, where the smoke was pouring in. In his ears sounded the deep, level roar of settled flames. He lay with his head against the floorboards, imagining air there, then realised he could not stand. He had time for a spasm of relief. Kate was not here. Then, attempting to get up, failing, he felt a bitter, transient anger: anger at what would not be, as the future fell away.

Long after he was unconscious, he was spared the heat of the flames over his body, the terror of flames passing over Claudia Greene before her seizures. In this last paralysis he envisaged his own cremation, his skull spilling out its brains, and feebly curled his hands over his head, until the fire crescendoed in his ears and into silence.

4

Naturalist

She lived beside the others in her own privacy. The building was heavy and austere – it was the overgrown garden that had enchanted her years ago – and she maintained only a guarded acquaintance with its ageing tenants, and was grateful for their self-effacement. Perhaps it was Stephanie's increasing myopia, or the intermittent gloom of the stairs and passageways, but she would often mistake one occupant for another, and could imagine them all to be distantly related. The haggard young man in the basement, who was usually out of work, might have been the son of the gaunt bachelor in the flat above, or of the retired schoolteacher who had taken to travelling, or was perhaps related to the landlord himself, who was kindly enough, and would accept her monthly rent by hand with the distant smile of a long and tired acquaintance. As for the surgeon across the landing, her old hesitancy with men resurfaced: he was handsome in his way. In her insomniac wakefulness she would hear the vigour of his footsteps on the stair, departing early for the county hospital.

That last night it was the choked shriek of her pet lori-keet, and the thrashing of its wings against the cage, that alerted her to a strange, deep trembling in the wall beside her head. The lorikeet could mimic human speech, and although she knew that this was a meaningless sound, she imagined the bird's guttural cry rising from a knowing intelligence: 'Well here we are. Well here we are. Well here we are . . .'

Long after infancy she had projected human feelings on to even inanimate objects. Most people thought her a soft little girl. For years she could not dispel the notion that the stone tortoise in her parents' garden was alive, and she was distraught when her father sometimes chipped its shell with the motor mower. In fact the whole garden, which petered into wilderness, possessed for her a wild and sometimes eerie magic. Nobody tended it much. It was big for a three-bedroom house in suburbia, but its rockery and straggling borders had once been planted with knowledge – groups of fragrant mahonia and daphne survived – and in autumn the overgrown orchard beyond the water butt was heavy with pears and apples, so many that they fell rotting and ungathered into the grass.

Nearby, miraculous and solitary, as if wind-sown, stood a purple-flowering butterfly bush. Years later she wondered what life she would have led if someone had not planted it there, or if a chance breeze, blowing from another garden, had not dropped its seed into the orchard's undergrowth. It was the most common of buddleias, she later realised, but in high summer she would watch in disbelief as its conical flowers grew jewelled with butterflies: Red Admirals, Tortoiseshells, Commas, Silver-washed Fritillaries. They shifted above her with the hypnotic scent of honey, and opened their wings on a delicate brilliance that she imagined had arrived from another world.

The Peacock butterfly, in particular, mesmerised her. The counterfeit eyes that shone from its forewings in a wash of crimson and indigo, and flashed half concealed on its hindwings, unfurled from a body of brownest velvet. In its head, where a pair of feelers stuck out like needles, two bulging compound eyes shone back at her, and an impossibly elongated tongue curved from its mouth into the flowers below.

She was twelve years old when a distant cousin of her mother – an old man, he seemed – visited them from Sussex. Cousin Arthur called himself an entomologist, but her parents seemed ignorant about his strange profession, and even joked about it. Instinctively she despised them for this. At first glance Arthur looked too big and ungainly to be concerned with insects. He smoked a pipe – the only person she ever knew to do so – and his grey moustache was smudged with an orange bib of nicotine. He wore frayed pullovers with leather elbow patches stitched on years before by his wife – he was a widower – and these smelt of nicotine too. But Stephanie noticed with fascination how long and high-veined his hands were, and his voice sounded oddly broken and fragile, lodged far back in his head, as if another, more delicate man were speaking deep inside him.

Within a day she loved him. He described to her the swarms of Monarch butterflies that migrated two thousand miles from Canada to Mexico in autumn, and how the Morpho Blues and Malachites lit up the Amazon rainforest. Then he was gone. It was years before she saw him again, but a week after his visit there arrived in the post a book titled *The World of Butterflies*, inscribed 'From Arthur, to my fellow lepidopterist, Stephanie'.

Her house agent father spoke of insects only as pests and intruders. The part of the garden he nurtured was his mown front lawn (the stone tortoise soon disappeared) and its two beds of regimented tea roses. He had dressed up the house with a colonnaded porch flanked by carriage lamps, and a gravel drive leading to a double garage. Later the lamps were joined by security lights, but Stephanie could not guess what was so valuable in the house – the grandfather clock, perhaps, or the Rockingham china teapot? – that had to be protected.

In summer, occasionally, her mother came to marvel with her at the butterfly bush, but her wonder quickly faded – Stephanie knew she was frail from a disease called leukaemia – and she would retire quickly, palely, into household routine or to rest. Years later Stephanie wondered if the faint reverie that sometimes overcame her in autumn orchards – like a passing sickness or nostalgia – had something to do with her mother. The recollected smell of rotting pears could still sicken in her nostrils.

She could not think of her mother now without regret. Stephanie had understood almost nothing of her. All through her childhood her mother was fading, and Stephanie resented the love her mother received from her father. This affection distantly extended to her elder sister too, yet to herself never. But then her sister Louisa was sensible. Louisa you could rely on. She was sunny and ready for anything. If you asked her to do something, she did it. Stephanie, on the other hand, was dreamy, lived in her own world, and sometimes sulked. Her girlhood seemed filled with her own shortcomings, and with the accusing refrain: 'Watch how Louisa does it' or 'Copy Louisa!' or worst of all: 'Why can't you be like Louisa?'

And Stephanie loved Louisa too. With Louisa began her intermittent desire to be somebody else. She loved her exuberance. She envied her long fair hair and her wide-set grey eyes. Hair was a woman's crowning glory, her father would quote, and touch Louisa's approvingly. But Stephanie's was brown and lustreless. Her mother kept it bobbed, as if there should not be much of it. Only once she murmured: 'Yours is nice too.' From time to time Stephanie inherited skirts and coats that Louisa had outgrown. Then she felt she was catching up, and that the approval of Louisa might one day devolve upon herself.

Louisa, two years older, indulged her and sometimes involved her in her dreams. When Stephanie was thirteen Louisa presented her with her old record player, and she listened to country singles that Louisa had enjoyed. Louisa, meanwhile, had a new-fangled cassette player, and was besotted with Queen and Whitney Houston. She would recruit Stephanie to dance with her. In Louisa's bedroom they writhed and twisted to funk and techno, laughing and occasionally intertwining, until their father, returned from work, would catch the twang and thump of 'Crazy Little Thing Called Love' or 'Fat Bottomed Girls', and burst in to reprimand them for disturbing their mother. Stephanie relished these half-secret sessions, although her father frightened her. She was unconsciously aware that Louisa, in the reverberation of 'I Want It All', might be imagining another partner altogether, but Stephanie was happy dancing with her.

When not obsessed with his business, with evaluating property or supervising brochures, her father would regale his family with funny stories about his clients. But often Stephanie did not understand. His saturnine looks (she had inherited them) seemed to contradict any humour. She felt excluded and foolish. His world was filled with the stupidity of other people. Half his sentences started with: 'People don't realise that . . .' or 'What people don't understand is . . .', and Stephanie feared that she belonged among these ignoramuses. Sometimes, too, he would begin: 'Louisa will understand this one . . .' and Stephanie would strain to unravel what was so funny or idiotic about a surveyor's report or a vendor's asking price. Louisa's laughter sounded like betrayal.

To Stephanie it seemed that her father regarded her sister with forbearance, even occasional affection, but that herself he appraised with remote distaste, something crueller than indifference. She felt he found her ugly. It even occurred to her, with dismay, that she looked like him, whereas Louisa was a full-blooded version of her mother, the woman in young health whom her father had married.

Towards his wife the stout, irascible businessman showed a protective tenderness. 'You mustn't tire your mother' was a cardinal rule of the house. Sometimes, when her mother relapsed from some infection, the girls whispered and tiptoed about the passages or were ordered out into the garden. This afflicted Louisa with foreboding, Stephanie with bewilderment. Their mother herself seemed lost to them. She appeared to be fading inward, as though she were in constant, quiet mourning. They could not realise that the bereavement she anticipated was her own, and occasionally, when they were boisterous, an exasperated bitterness would escape her. But sometimes, too, a lilting peal of laughter surfaced, as if from somebody else, some-body young. Although this grew less and less.

Dimly Stephanie sensed that there was a whole imagin-ative world preoccupying her mother's head: memories, meditations, perhaps longings, to which Stephanie could have no access. Adults dreamed differently, of course. Her mother read novels with enigmatic titles, and played LPs of Mahler and Wolf songs, which her father called 'that gloomy German stuff'. Once too, her mother read to her from a long poem, a passage she thought would please her, and her hand arrived lightly on Stephanie's arm, alarming in its unexpectedness.

'*Do ye not comprehend that we are worms*
Born to bring forth the angelic butterfly . . .'

After a while her mother began breathing strangely, and closed the book, and her hand trembled back to her breast.

In a story told to Stephanie by Cousin Arthur, a Chinese philosopher dreamed he was a butterfly, then wondered, awake, if he might not be a butterfly dreaming itself a man. This at first perplexed, then engrossed her. She imagined iden-tities shared and persons interchangeable. One day she might break out of a chrysalis, or wake up to find she was Louisa.

Years later, as a young woman, she wondered about her own abstractedness – her childhood seemed to have been dreamed away – and about the neural censor that dictated what she remembered and what she forgot. Hurtful events were too easily retained, of course, but why should she so minutely remember climbing into a hollow tree – she must have been five years old – and pretending to be an owl? Recollection shed a curious lustre on ordinary experiences.

The scent of hollowed tree bark and the roof of sunlit leaves seemed invested now with a thick, impenetrable meaning.

There were memories that left her sad or bitter for reasons she only later understood. On holiday in Cornwall, after wading with Louisa into a shallow sea, she had swum far out of her depth, then panicked. She heard her own shriek of alarm, and saw her parents stand up on the shore. Louisa called out: 'Take my hand!' and guided her back to where her father had waded in to the waist, fully clothed.

Stumbling against him, she longed for his relief, any sign of affection. But he was only furious. 'Your mother was beside herself!' She felt anger shaking his whole body. 'You stupid little girl!' She could not pretend even now that this was displaced tenderness. She was merely the agent of her mother's distress.

She stood up to her father once, blurting carelessly. Her primary school music teacher – a formidable woman – visited their home to discuss Louisa's progress, and suggested they buy an upright piano. Finally she asked: 'And what about you, Stephanie, wouldn't you like to play?'

Her father said at once: 'Stephanie's not interested.'

Then she heard herself: 'I am. I am interested. I like the piano.'

She saw his face dumbfounded. He said: 'She thinks she can play without practising.'

But she went recklessly on: 'I don't think that. No I don't. I know what I think.'

Her father turned away. He said to the teacher: 'We'll consider buying a piano', in a tone that said he wouldn't, and Stephanie recalled with satisfaction his fury after the woman left.

Another memory: her first grown-up dance, aged thirteen. It was given by the daughter of a family friend, in a rather grand house. Stephanie is wearing her birthday earrings. They are tiny golden butterflies. She waits in the hall for Louisa to descend, Louisa with her long-planned party dress, and looks forward to dancing with her. But Louisa does not come down. Her mother grows impatient, then alarmed. Her father pushes upstairs. There are noises then, sounds of sobbing.

Stephanie cannot remember the dance at all: only Louisa's faltering footsteps as she descends at last, and her father muttering to Stephanie's astonishment: 'Louisa needs encouragement. Keep her company, Stephanie, won't you? And dance with her.'

And another, stranger recollection. She hears an unknown man talking in her mother's bedroom, and peers hesitantly in. Her mother's back is turned to her. She is listening to an old Grundig tape recorder, and her shoulders are shaking. The man's voice on the tape is slow and intimate. Stephanie cannot catch his words. It is her mother's reaction to her that strikes her now. Her face, when she glances round, looks paler than usual, suddenly agitated, and she quickly turns away. The tape reel slurs to a halt. Her mother's voice sounds like someone else's. 'Please leave me.'

Stephanie did not want to lead this life. She imagined another one. Her best friend Sally thought they should open a hairdressing salon when they left school, but Stephanie wasn't interested in people's hair. That summer immense clouds of Painted Lady butterflies streamed over the Channel to England. They drifted through the orchards like falling leaves, and set the roadsides on fire with the massed shimmering of their wings. To Stephanie this was like a visitation. They were more intricate than any flowers – even their folded underwings translucent with eyes and veins – and the Peacocks and Red Admirals mingled in with them. Her fantasy intensified that butterflies overflowed into ordinary life from somewhere more resplendent and meaningful. Yet the sheer multitude of Painted Ladies carried a frisson of alarm. Something was going on in the parallel world from which they came: some organic disturbance she could not imagine. Their hordes seemed faintly threatening, even verminous. But within a week they had vanished – or left their tragic bodies in the grass – and she ached for their return. They had come from – and had disappeared to – nowhere she could conceive. She might have dreamt them.

The disclosure of their mystery in Cousin Arthur's book only deepened her wonder. In early spring the parents of her Painted Ladies had set off from North Africa and alighted to breed in southern Europe. Two months later their offspring in turn had taken to the air – moving north on a mysteriously set compass – reaching even Iceland. There might be twenty million of them. Then, as the summer cooled, they would instinctively turn back south, flying invisibly high – but too far and late to survive – and pass out of human knowledge.

The swarming that Stephanie had witnessed was common a century ago, she read, when the Victorian skies would be darkened by unpredictable migrations. Multitudes of invading whites might cover the night-time trees like snowflakes, before taking off at dawn, eclipsing the sun. Clouded Yellows crossed the unmown fields in a golden mist, and Great Southern Whites still flowed along the coasts of Florida in aerial rivers forty-five feet wide.

There were lone migrants too, which she longed one day to see: the Camberwell Beauty and the Queen of Spain Fritillary. How did they navigate across the seas? (There were different answers.) Why did some butterflies have eyes on their wings? Why did others fly by night? And what was the Morpho caterpillar up to, as it combed and washed its hair?

That September she found three speckled caterpillars in the next-door cauliflower patch, and placed them with their stolen leaves in a perforated jam jar. Feverishly she imagined what they might hatch into. Her father said she was obsessive, and it sounded like a disease. Even Louisa thought she was too old for such a hobby. But Stephanie fed the worms with shamed excitement. They ate voraciously. Their purpose, she knew, was to become butterflies. They grew plump and sometimes shed their skins. They looked pathetically vulnerable. She pored through *The World of Butterflies* to discover how caterpillars protected themselves. The bright-hued ones like hers, it seemed, might be poisonous to predators. Other caterpillars exuded acid or spurted venom. Still others, she read – and this was a wonder of the creature – took on near-perfect camouflage. They aligned their bodies with the veins of leaves, replicating even mould and leaf decay. Some looked like twigs or bird droppings. The American Tiger Swallowtail dissembled as a noxious tree frog, with bright eyes and gaping mouth. Their cunning was inexhaustible. There were caterpillars that escaped enemy insects by dangling from a self-spun thread (although hungry wasps might reel them in).

Within a week her caterpillars were hanging from their cauliflower stems in silk-swathed chrysalids. All that winter they hung apparently inert, transformed from green to beige. She read that even naked caterpillars and butterflies hibernated. Walking with Louisa at Christmas over the snow-bound heath beyond the house, she could hardly picture this. While Louisa was talking about a boy she fancied at school – did Stephanie think him good-looking? Had he said anything about her? – Stephanie's eyes roamed over the hardened ground and leafless hedges. Concealed in this frozen landscape, sheltering in their silken tents and leaf huts, disguised as tree bark or dead foliage, millions of sleeping insects were awaiting spring.

In January, to her dismay, two of her tame chrysalises turned black and dropped from their stems. But a month afterwards she thought she saw the final chrysalis twitch on its perch. She stared harder. Now she was certain. Imperceptibly its casing had reshaped around the bulge of wings inside, and the shadow of an abdomen. She hunted through *The World of Butterflies* again. What was happening was not quite as she had expected – the slow transformation of one organism into another. Rather this heralded a total metamorphosis. Inside its carapace, over the winter, the caterpillar had all but liquefied, and out of this larval sludge would be born a miraculous new creature.

Early next morning she noticed a rent in the upright end of the chrysalis. As she gazed, it began to pull apart of its own accord. Out of the slit emerged ridges of green hair followed by a staring opaline eye. A minute later a pair of bent green legs unsheathed themselves and started to prise their body out. Two antennae unfurled and overswept the hair, and wings of greenish white shook themselves out like bedsheets. It was not an Admiral or a Peacock, still less a Painted Lady, but the common Small Cabbage White. She watched it, hypnotised. Its compound eyes gazed back at her. Now six exquisitely thin legs were gaining purchase on the overhanging stalk and levering the butterfly into the light. The shaken wings looked bridal white to her. It was beautiful. The whole process had taken barely five minutes. She and Louisa had often watched the evolution of tadpoles in a neighbour's pond: a slow, visible transition. But the butterfly's resurrection was different: the winged angel risen from a worm. Its cerements were left behind in the jam jar to prove it, like Jesus's shroud, she thought. It showed that anything could become anything. Yet it was somehow heartbreaking. She only had to look at those science-fiction eyes to realise that the creature was indifferent to her. Perhaps it did not even discern her. She unscrewed the lid of the jar, and watched it shuffle its wings. A day later it had flown away into the sunlight.

Soon after Stephanie's fourteenth birthday her mother went into hospital, and never came back. For months beforehand she had remained in a ground-floor bedroom, too weak to climb the stairs. Stephanie's father told her not to enter the room without permission. Two or three times a week she and Louisa would creep in to tell their mother about school. They never knew how much she listened, although sometimes she let out her tinkle of weak laughter. During these months she seemed little more than a cosseted ghost, so that Stephanie unconsciously disowned her, imagining that she would be there always. Whatever world her mother inhabited did not meaningfully include her. Her mother gave up even reading. Words, she said, tired out her eyes. Later, when Stephanie wondered about her, there often came to mind only her closed door: a heavy-panelled door, scored with the claw marks of a long-dead spaniel, beyond which sounded the faint strain of lieder. Her father told Stephanie always to knock, and to stay away if her mother didn't respond. More often than not, she and Louisa would stand outside the door for a dutiful two minutes, their raps unheard beneath the music perhaps, then trip away with relief. Later Stephanie imagined that her mother wanted to die to Schubert's *Winterreise*.

For over a year, while her mother ebbed, a boisterous local woman arrived each day to cook and clean. Theresa wore pale blue dungarees that lent her, in Stephanie's eyes, a comic glamour. In their father's absence the house filled with the clashing of plates and cutlery, the grumbling dishwasher, the clattering legs of the ironing board. Theresa cooked huge, wholesome meals – beef stews and cottage pies – and carried slivers of these in to their mother. If their father was there, she would emerge from cleaning disused shelves and cupboards with her hands splayed in front of her, and declare: 'Look! Look at the dirt! Did you ever see such . . .' announcing her indispensability.

Louisa took against her. Theresa had designs, she said. She wasn't all she seemed. Just look at her shrewd, cheerless little eyes. Stephanie disagreed. Theresa treated everyone the same. She told Stephanie she was too thin. 'Your mother says you should fatten up!' Stephanie knew that her mother could have said no such thing, but Theresa, in borrowing maternal authority, reanimated her mother at second hand. 'Your mother says you mustn't go through the gate on to the heath . . .' 'You should cover your mouth when you cough. What would your mother say?' 'Your mother thinks . . .' So Theresa, like a ventriloquist, gave her mother a presence in which Stephanie liked to believe: a clamorous voice, but rudely caring.

Her father did not allow Stephanie to attend the funeral. She was too young, he said. She spent the afternoon playing Monopoly with Sally, while Theresa cut them lettuce sandwiches and made a sponge cake, singing, 'A girl is brave as she can be . . .' But Stephanie was not brave. She felt excluded and resentful. The thought of the coffin frightened her, but she had wanted to be at her own mother's funeral. Sally treated her with tentative concern, almost respect. She even let her win at Monopoly.

Stephanie went alone into the garden. It was a soft, bright evening. Beyond the orchard the butterfly bush was not yet in flower, but as she stood there a Small Cabbage White came tumbling out of the trees. Her own Cabbage White would have died long ago, and this one – she could tell by its black spots – was a female. It flopped around the shrubs as if only just woken, and alighted here and there, as the whites do, with closed wings. Stephanie tried to take her eyes from it, but could not. She imagined it was her mother. She even followed it, knowing her own foolishness, and felt angry when it drifted away.

Louisa returned from the funeral a little smugly. She was feeling adult. The vicar had preached a nice eulogy, and they had sung 'Abide with Me' and 'Lo! He comes with Clouds Descending', but she had stayed inside the church during the interment. Stephanie, who was suspicious of God, said nothing.

A week later, they went to their mother's grave. It was covered in dying wreaths. Stephanie did not understand why the earth was mounded so high above the grave, and did not believe it would ever subside. The smell of rotting lilies remained in her nostrils for days. She said she did not want to come here again, and her father thought this sprang from grief, and humoured it. She was in shock, he said. Stephanie was in shock.

It was true, there was a kind of numbness; but it did not arise from grief. Sometimes she tried to pinch herself into feeling. My mother is dead, she said aloud. My mother is dead. But the words produced only bewilderment, and a pang of shame. Her mother had died a little long ago. Now she had only taken another step away.

Stephanie dreaded the visits of family friends. She had to dress more demurely than usual. These visitors were self-consciously sombre, or they laughed too loud, and their words were all predictable.

'She was a wonderful woman.'

'We know you'll miss her terribly.'

'You'll be a great comfort to your father . . .'

Louisa was subjected to this too, with an extra plea to look after Stephanie. Sometimes Louisa covertly sighed and rolled her eyes. There was a secret between the sisters now, something they shared but never openly acknowledged. They mutely recognised it in one another: the shame of their indifference. They went through the decorum of mourning.

Once only, as if something in Stephanie was being wrenched apart, she started to weep. Tangled in the underfelt of the drawing room carpet, one of her mother's earrings caught her eye. She remembered how her mother, the year before, had lamented its loss. Now she held it in her hands while her tears fell, and she was glad.

As spring wore on, the house became increasingly oppressive to her, and she took more and more to the garden. Her father had locked the downstairs bedroom, but she sometimes peered in through the outside window, as if her mother might still be there. Inside its darkness the sofa was still heaped with its patchwork cushions, and summer dresses were hanging in a half-open cupboard. She could just discern the bedside record player with its pile of old LPs, and the Grundig on its bow-legged table. But out in the orchard, as the days lengthened, she was expecting the early butterflies – the golden Comma, the Orange-tip and the ethereal Holly Blue – and they came on time, in the bustle of their nectar-hunting, and she photographed them with her Brownie 127.

Meanwhile Louisa took over the house. She was enjoying a new importance. She returned from school with bags of food shopping, and was learning to cook. On weekends the place resounded not with the clash of cutlery – Theresa had given in her notice – but with the purr of the vacuum cleaner and with Louisa's newly adult voice announcing her next domestic duty. Her father, in a rare moment of joking, called her his second wife.

But his funny stories petered out now, or they did not begin. Stephanie never knew what he was thinking. At table there were long, frightening silences. Sometimes he would say: 'Well, girls . . .' but his sentence never finished.

Louisa told Stephanie darkly: 'He's drinking, you know.' His moroseness with Stephanie seemed to deepen, while he had fits of anger even with Louisa. 'His house agency business isn't going well.'

'I didn't know.' Stephanie felt a twinge of alarm: might they have to leave the garden?

'You don't notice anything, Stef' – this was Louisa's new maternal voice. 'You live in wonderland.'

'So what? It's better than here.'

Sometimes she felt she was suffocating. There were moments at night when she had to breathe very calmly, very slowly, because the air in the room seemed too thin to sustain her.

Louisa was laughing, and kissed her. 'Don't worry. We're going to be all right . . .'

Louisa, she thought, was her mother now. Perhaps she always had been. At school Louisa's popularity protected Stephanie from bullying. But both girls now were surrounded with awe and a whispering distance. 'Their mother is dead.' Stephanie's teacher was newly solicitous, and she secretly cherished this. She had become, for the first time, somebody special. Nobody else had no mother. Sally gained reflected prestige, imagining she had privileged access to Stephanie's mourning. She was always taking

Stephanie's arm and whispering intimacies, and she relayed to her the sympathy or puzzlement of the others. 'They wonder what you're feeling . . .' Stephanie sensed that if she expressed anything openly, or even cried, some spell would be broken. Bereavement had become her identity.

That autumn Stephanie's class was to study biology and physics. Louisa said the science laboratory was like a dis-used toolshed, and the teacher – a French woman hard to understand – set too much homework. But then Louisa was more interested in going to dances with a moody youth in the class above hers, sporting her suede pirate boots and a denim jacket bought on sale behind her father's back.

Stephanie, meanwhile, became fascinated by biology, by the make-up and behaviour of different creatures. One after-noon she wandered alone into the laboratory, and while toy-ing with its dusty filter unit, cluttered with bleary test tubes and pipettes, she came by chance upon the microscope.

The science mistress had described this as the doorway into another world, but had then forgotten it in favour of teaching the laws of linear motion. Stephanie had no idea how to operate it, but some faded instructions hung on the wall nearby. There was a book showing magnified insects and flowers, inscribed in the science teacher's hand with the words of Victor Hugo: 'Where the telescope ends, the microscope begins. A nebula is an anthill of stars.' She lis-tened for footsteps in the passage outside, but there were none. Most of the others were in the dining hall. Tentatively she took a sliver of lettuce from her lunch box and pressed a fragment of it on to a slide. Peering into the eyepiece, she at first saw only the white moon of the aperture below. The lines that wavered there were merely those that trembled under her closed eyelids in sunlight. Slowly, hesitantly, she turned the focusing knob. She expected to see a fan of fragile green veins, but instead found herself gazing astonished at what might have been the pencil sketch of an enormous tree: a colourless thicket of interlacing branches, intricate and strange. Next she tried sugar, then salt. The sun came out, flooding the laboratory table as she focused the sugar crystals, and they lit up like a scatter of icebergs, every one different. When the sun went in, they turned to opaque metal, while the salt grains shone in near-uniform cubes, each one edged with black, like tiny blank-faced televisions.

As she continued, rifling her lunch for specimens, nothing was as she expected. This was paradoxically comforting. Her own saliva resembled a city map complete with roads and side streets. Apple peel became a skyburst of turquoise-fronded flowers. The blood pricked from her thumb was a broken necklace of orange. Even the single cotton thread that she pulled from her blouse splintered into a complicated vine.

She finished her lunch delicately, in the laboratory silence, wondering what precisely she was eating. All matter was moving, the biology teacher had told them, trying to explain elementary particles: stasis was an illusion. To Stephanie everything seemed interchangeable, and could blur into something else. Sprinkle sugar and you might create an ice floe. When an ant scuttled across the table, she shocked herself by squeezing it between her fingers. Under the lens it looked armoured in polished bronze. She could make out its tangle of crushed legs, and a bowed head.

As she walked back to the bus station that afternoon, the brick walls and tarmac streets seemed to be creating only a deceptive solidness, while all the time shuddering with inner life. She had the idea that if she concentrated enough on anything – a fallen petal, say, or a paving stone – she might enter this other, microscopic universe, the real universe, the elements from which the illusion of everyday was built.

Sally joined her, eager to talk about her collie having puppies, and wondering if Stephanie would like one. Her father would not allow it, Stephanie said, and realised with secret sadness that Sally would never understand her. 'They'll be adorable,' Sally said, then glanced behind her at the pudgy youth following them. 'Did you know,' she added, 'that Thomas has a crush on you?'

Sally must be mistaken.

'Haven't you noticed?' Sally gave her conspiratorial smile. She had full, woman's lips. 'He can't take his eyes off you.'

'He's probably feeling sorry for me.'

'No he's not. People forget. And they aren't that nice.' She glanced behind again. 'He even asked me where you live.'

'What did you say?'

'I told him you lived in a world of your own.' Sally laughed. 'It's true. You do. Nobody knows what you're thinking. Thomas may think you're dreaming about him.'

The idea confused Stephanie. Why would anyone have a crush on her? Maybe Thomas was following Sally. Sally had outgrown Stephanie by three inches, and had taken to wearing tasselled cowboy jackets. Stephanie had not grown for a year. Sometimes she imagined that Sally's friendship for her was waning, and this frightened her. She loved Sally's self-assurance, her humour, even the way she moved. As for herself, she could see in the mirror that she was delicate, prettier than she used to be, in a starved-looking way. She would never have Louisa's voluptuous bloom. Perhaps she did not want to become a woman at all. But her periods had started five months ago, and later she learnt that the map-like pattern of her saliva under the microscope was a monthly sign of ovulation.

But boys were another tribe to her. Half of her school contemporaries seemed like men already, in their coarse jokes and swagger. Even Thomas, with his gangling mouth and hedgehog hair, sported a vestigial moustache, although his trousers always crumpled endearingly round his shoes, as if they were falling.

Next lunchtime Stephanie found him lingering round her classroom, but she slipped away to the laboratory. Her lunch box included two envelopes of butterfly wings. She had picked up the Red Admiral, dead but still pristine, in her father's garage. Its wings had covered her fingers in a rainbow dust. The Comma's wings she had found side by side on the front lawn, the body eaten by a bird.

She edged the fragment of Red Admiral's wing on to a slide and focused its orange-black divide. She saw that what appeared seamless was in fact the impingement of thousands of scales, overlapping like the successive pelmets of a curtain, their colours melting from midnight blue into coral, then into blue again. And the underwing was stranger still: a russet tapestry – its weave was clearly visible – scattered with snow-white flecks. As she gazed, Cousin Arthur surfaced in her mind. How strangely wonderful his world must be! In some butterflies, he had said all those years ago, the wing scales were raised or angled, creating an iridescence that lit up the rainforests. Her microscope, she knew, was too weak to discern these, even if they were there. But on the underwing of the Comma she located, with a tingle of discovery, the white hook that gave the creature its name, curled in the hairy fabric as in a cornfield.

She closed the laboratory door carefully behind her, as on somewhere forbidden, and ran straight into Thomas. He was hovering in the corridor. 'I was waiting for you,' he said.

Her 'Oh!' hung in the passageway: hapless, dead.

'I was wondering if you'd go out with me.' His face had a puppyish ardour. 'Robert is giving a party . . .'

She stared back dumbly at him. She had been to several of these parties, with Sally. Indulgent parents went out for the evening while everyone gyrated through 'I'm Coming Out' and 'You're the One for Me'. Some of her schoolmates, conscious of the envy of the others, would be snogging on the sofas. She supposed they were being grown up. A few others – and this was mysterious to her – would retreat to some darker room, and she would see them passionately kissing, lost in the fascinated dream of one another. At some of the more daring parties there was a whiff of cannabis (Sally could detect it) and cans of lager appeared. As for Stephanie, she was happy that the music drowned all chance of conversation, since she had nothing to say, and felt abashed and solitary.

Now she repeated: 'A party?' The word became bleak as she spoke it. 'My father wouldn't like it.' But even to her this sounded idiotic.

'But you're fifteen, Stephanie.' He was looking at her bright-eyed, pleading.

'I'm sorry . . .'

Thomas was running his hands through his hedgehog hair, as if something might be out of place there. 'I'm splitting up with Vicky, you know.'

Vicky was in Stephanie's form: one of the spiteful ones. Stephanie realised she might hurt Vicky. For a moment she imagined herself in that subworld of jealousies and charades that whispered round the school and that she found at once frightening and ridiculous. Thomas followed her to the end of the corridor. In the sudden sunlight she noticed he had covered his pimples with women's blusher.

'So you have somebody already. Of course you do . . .' He was starting to look wretched. 'Is it Jim?'

'Who on earth's Jim?' But she remembered a tall boy in Thomas's class, an athlete. She said: 'No, I don't have anybody. I don't want anybody.' This became clear as she said it. 'You can ask anyone in my form. They'll tell you. They probably think I'm retarded.'

'You're not retarded. You're bright. You win prizes . . .'

Now she tried to squeeze past him through the doorway, but it was narrow and he didn't budge. She could feel his chest brushing against her breasts, then his hands lifted helplessly to her face and he tried to kiss her.

She felt a spasm of alarm. 'No!' She pushed him back, but already the look of wounded pathos had resurfaced on his face.

He murmured: 'Maybe another time.' He walked backwards through the doorway, still gazing at her, and out into the sun. 'Another time . . .'

Angrily she brushed down her blouse, and noticed on her fingers, already glazed with the Comma's wing dust, the pink make-up from his neck. She leant against the wall, trying to catch her breath, deflecting the sense of suffocation. She closed her eyes, waiting until he had gone. In a day or two he would probably be telling everyone she was a prude.

Suddenly she wanted to cry. What was she meant to do? What was she supposed to feel?

The ultraviolet light that may flash from the wings of butterflies is invisible to vertebrates, including humans. There is a species of Swallowtail whose female variations, confusing to the human eye, vanish and converge in the ultraviolet forms that butterflies see. Although their kaleidoscopic wings are part of their sex appeal, the mating of every butterfly genus is complex and different.

Stephanie now read these things in books other than Cousin Arthur's. The courtship of the butterfly, she thought, was often beautiful. The male would envelop the female's antennae with his forewings and dust her with odours exuded by hair-pencils in his body. These scents were infinitely varied – so strong that even humans could detect them – and a pair of primitive secondary eyes on the genitals could tell the male when to close on her. In some species the pair would ascend together in nuptial flight, one seeming to carry the other. They would remain clasped for hours or even days, and occasionally, if their organs stayed locked, they would stay together in coital embrace until they died.

Louisa, in the year she learnt to drive, often dropped Stephanie off on the way to a rendezvous of her own, and returned to meet her on the edge of some promising wood or marshland. For Stephanie these brief hours held a solitary intoxication. Sometimes, if the sky was overcast, she would see no butterflies at all. Their seasons were short and variable. But she began to understand their habitats – how the Black Hairstreak barely wandered from its hatching place, or its purple cousin sailed in the treetops – and recognise their different flight patterns.

But they always brought with them a touch of melancholy. Their lives were poignantly short. Most would be on the wing for only two weeks before they died, some for less than three days. Compared to the months they spent as eggs, caterpillars and chrysalids, their transfiguration seemed tragically brief. The Purple Emperor might take a whole year to mature, then live for barely fifteen days in its glory. More than half the butterfly species were endangered, she read, and she grew to love the less flashy kinds: the Small Blues and the tiny skippers that fluttered in the grassland like dappled leaves. Once, while walking on chalk downland, she watched a host of little Brown Arguses descend on to a patch of rock roses, alighting so close that she could see the drumming of their legs by which they tasted the plant, and the twirl of the antennae that smelt it.

And there were moments of miracle. She realised she had fallen into the collector's habit of cherishing what was rare, whatever its appearance. Once, in a flowering meadow, while looking out for a quite different species, she glimpsed a Wood White, close to extinction: a tiny, weak ghost of an insect, floundering along so erratically that she thought it already the last of its kind. Once too, on a July afternoon, while she was ambling back to her meeting point with Louisa, a White Admiral glided into her path. Serene, implacable, it sailed down the glade ahead of her before lifting with unearthly grace into the woodland canopy.

Then she understood how a famous naturalist had suffered all day from an ecstatic headache on seeing Queen Alexandra's Birdwing, the largest butterfly in the world, and how, despite the heartbreak of their transience, another naturalist described butterflies as a solace for the pain of living.

She cannot now remember where it was, or even the precise year: a hotel room somewhere, while travelling with her father and sister. The night air was warm and salty. There was a sound of far-off thunder. She lay restlessly under her sheet, as though there was something she must do.

Her body felt febrile, with a hot self-awareness. She wondered if her period was starting. She imagined her skin flushed. Her hands travelled down herself tentatively, in nascent exploration, holding the small, new breasts a little wonderingly, as if estranged from her own flesh. She was starting to sweat, and eased off her nightdress. The wind blew soft from the open window across her body. She felt the heat and tingling of her skin under its breath. She kneaded her thighs, touched her nipples. Submissively she spread out her arms, still feeling the salt air, and the emergence of her own beauty, beautiful not because some other felt her so, but from a sensation more intimate, as if she had become her own lover.

Later she thought of this night as her young epiphany, her becoming a woman, although she could not say exactly why; but it seemed nearer to her than her first kiss – with a kind, gauche youth she did not like to disappoint – or her virginity lost at eighteen, when she felt nothing beyond fear and the need to catch up with Louisa and Sally, and dabbed off the blood – there was surprisingly little – and refused to see the man again.

When Sally left their school at the age of seventeen, Stephanie felt bereft. Louisa had left two years before and was working for a London advertising agency, returning on occasional weekends to confide the mysteries of brand awareness and guerrilla marketing, and a switchback of emotional dramas. For another two terms at school Stephanie was the clever, friendless outsider, who might have gone to university; but her father said she would have to pay her own way. Besides, university seemed too much a prolongation of school, while she longed instead for an imagined freedom.

She replied to an advertisement for a 'customer relations officer' at a wildlife trust in the neighbouring town, and to her surprise she was accepted. At first she found herself answering the telephone and booking travel arrangements, but she was soon entrusted with the reception of donors and volunteers, and became aware of a quiet respect in the office. Yet her weekends, if Louisa was not home, were becoming unbearable. She only realised later why her father, at the age of barely fifty, was losing energy. Whole mealtimes passed in which he said nothing. His skin had taken on a greenish pallor. She noticed trembling in his hands. His dislike of her had mellowed into indifference now. He had no use for her – Theresa had returned to manage the house – and in the evenings he was continuing to drink.

That summer she took refuge in work for a wildlife conservation charity, recording the changes in a transect of chalky downland. Every Saturday she walked its two miles and noted down the species she recognised, reporting back their prevalence or scarcity. The path meandered over a grassland thick with knapweed and harebells. The scent of crushed thyme rose under her feet. On sunlit days a pale dust of butterflies drifted everywhere.

It was during a visit to the local conservation headquarters that she heard a familiar name. Somebody was quoting from an article by Cousin Arthur. She had imagined him old, perhaps dead. But no, she was told, he was still writing about endangered butterfly species. She found his address, and wrote him a humorous message that produced an invitation to visit him in Sussex.

She drove her third-hand Citroën to the outskirts of a village near Petworth. On the passenger seat was her inscribed copy of *The World of Butterflies*, so thumbed and reread that it had disintegrated into a sheaf of separated pages. Although the day was overcast and there were no butterflies, she could have guessed Arthur's house by the buddleia and verbena crowding its porch.

The doorbell sounded deep inside the house, just as she remembered his voice had sounded, as if from someone far away inside him. She felt suddenly nervous, wondering how old he had become, and how she would appear to him. But the door opened on a man unchanged from her memory; his pale eyes looked down from a foot above her and his moustache was no whiter, and still smudged with its disconcerting orange fleck beneath the nostrils. He said at once: 'What a fine young woman you've become!'

He brought tea and some stale Petit Beurre biscuits into the conservatory, and they sat and talked hesitantly, while she grew used to the faraway rasping of his voice, and looked out at a garden different from any she had seen. Instead of a mown lawn there was a small flowering meadow, surrounded by the different shrubs and flowers that nourished butterflies: buddleia, honeysuckle and mock orange, with swathes of phlox and marigolds. Later she felt ashamed of how much she had eventually talked, of her enthusiasm for experiences surely banal to him: her first sighting of a Swallowtail, and her memories of the Painted Lady year. But he watched her with a kind of remote sweetness, and the distant voice seemed less an impediment than some inborn restraint.

All round his sitting room, beneath the bookshelves, were waist-high cabinets labelled 'Papua New Guinea: western islands', 'Peru: Huallaga river' or 'Ivory Coast: Great Nimba rainforest'. She knew they contained butterflies. She felt as if butterflies electrified and possessed the whole house. In her own home the bookshelves were monopolised by her father's middlebrow thrillers, and the pictures were framed watercolours of scenes she never noticed. But here the volumes on wildlife, entomology and travel were ranked two deep on the shelves, and nineteenth-century prints of the Blue Morpho and Owl butterfly shone on the walls.

When she asked him about those labelled drawers, he pulled out at random 'Costa Rica: Osa peninsula'. She gazed down. Outspread on their trays, sealed in glass, were the lovely winged insects of Central America. They were as exquisite and strange as any she had imagined. Their wings were luminous sapphire, leaf green, scarlet or miniature tapestries of overlapping black and aquamarine scales. There were butterflies with lacquered gold forewings or bat-like tails edged in crimson, others whose wing veins surged black between a blizzard of white spots, still others whose hindwings were enamelled with brilliant eyes.

For a second she wanted to break the glass and set them free. But they were scrupulously labelled with location, family, genus. Some of the labels were starting to yellow and curl. These creatures were, in their way, more dead than anything she had known, the shimmer of their flight unim- aginable now. There were more than a hundred trays of them. She noticed Arthur's hands as he opened and slid back their drawers, how lean and delicately veined they were. She imagined them killing. She said: 'You caught all these.'

He must have heard the sadness in her voice. 'People rarely do this now,' he said. 'These were netted for science, for teaching. It's not collectors that have driven butterflies towards extinction, you know, but the destruction of habitat . . . everywhere . . .'

She said bleakly: 'Yes, of course.' He was a scientist, after all. Lepidoptery was a science.

'But specimens are not enough. They can't tell you the insect's feeding or flight pattern or mating habits, let alone its host plants. That's all in the field notes. Each exhibit has a history.' As he walked back into the conservatory, he suddenly asked: 'Do you know how to type?'

'Yes.' She had learnt in the past few months.

Fifty years of collecting and research notes, inscribed in his erratic handwriting, lay in boxes upstairs, he said. Some survived in the indelible ink of a rapidograph drafting pen; but in the tropics, where ink could clog or dissolve, he had preferred pencil; and he feared these records were fading. Before he donated the collection to his old university, he needed all his field notes typed up. He could only offer her 'pocket money'. But instantly she said yes.

'Shall I take some home with me?'

He hesitated. His voice sounded even farther away. 'Well . . . they are my life's work . . .'

'Then I'll come to you. I'll bring my computer.' She was rather proud of this.

Now the sun had come out over the garden. Relaxed again, he said: 'Let's see what's out there.'

They were walking through the spent meadow grass. The air was heady with lavender. Now, among the phlox and flowering shrubs, she noticed asters and an undergrowth of morning glory. They were fluttering with familiar life. A bed of nettles – a favourite plant of the Peacock caterpillar – flourished hidden behind ranks of zinnias. He said: 'I give them larval plants in the hope of colonising them. But you can't contain butterflies. They're wanderers.'

The sixty or so species in Britain, Stephanie thought, were nothing beside the eighteen thousand flying in the world; but she felt she understood why he nurtured them here. They were a penance for the pinned and cabineted dead. Their short, intense days – nectaring, mating, laying eggs – burned with concentrated life. In a week or two they would leave their bodies behind in the long grass, under the honeysuckle, in the potting shed, but only after their vibrant and obsessive cycle was over.

She and Arthur watched the clustered insects without speaking. She felt curiously at peace. This collusive silence was for themselves – butterflies could hear nothing – and she copied the rapt discernment with which he watched. Once he leant over a bush with his slight, gangling stoop and transferred a Red Admiral on to the back of his hand. This intimacy intrigued her. How did he know it would stay? At last he blew it softly into flight. She caught a look of impish pleasure. She wondered if he was perhaps lonely, but imagined that like her he cherished solitude. When two Small Whites appeared – they still reminded her of her mother – she asked him: 'How exactly are we related, Cousin Arthur?'

'I'm not sure.' He gave a light, rasping laugh. 'Your mother said it was through a great-uncle on her father's side. I think that's right. But her family was complicated.'

'How?' She was asking him the things she would have asked her mother. 'She said so little.'

'That was very hard on you, Stephanie, she declining for so long.' He was looking down on her with something like concern. 'I never knew her parents. But they were cultivated people, musical. I believe there was Austrian blood. I saw your mother most before her marriage. She was enchanting then, a very quick mind, very sensitive, although she was always pale and somehow weak.'

'Why did she marry my father?'

'I don't know . . .' He let the question drift. 'These things are mysterious.'

It crossed Stephanie's mind that Arthur might have been a little in love with her himself.

Louisa had come back early that weekend, and greeted Stephanie in a dark flurry. Their father had cancer of the liver, she said. It was probably inoperable. He was too angry to talk about it. He had been drinking all day. So what could you do?

Stephanie did not know how to talk to him. She had never known. He had never taught her. Next evening, after he had returned from work as usual, she found him hunched at the kitchen table, consuming Theresa's seed cake and a tumbler of whisky. Now that she focused on him – she so rarely did – he appeared vulnerable to her. His stoutness looked hollow. Then she felt a surge of alarm at that brute strength failing. She had imagined him all but immortal. For years their eyes had been averted from one another. Now she saw how his hair thinned back still dark from his temples but had lost its sheen. She had always hated his bull neck, how it defined him. But she noticed its skin was loosening. It was with a feeling of cold strangeness, as if crossing into a foreign country, that she asked him if what Louisa said was true.

He stared at her. He seemed to be reassessing her. He had never asked her for anything, nor given it. For a moment she thought he would bark that this was none of her business. But instead he said: 'It depends what Louisa said.'

'She said you had cancer.'

He gave a grunt of contempt. 'They want to give me that bloody chemotherapy' – this swearing was new – 'so I suppose I'll have it.' He went on staring at her. 'And where've you been anyway? Did you go to that Arthur again?' He made it sound like a tryst.

'Yes. He wants me to type out his research.'

'Well, whatever suits.' He swallowed the last of the seed cake, and said more gently: 'He's an odd fellow. Your mother liked him.'

'I like him.'

He got to his feet. 'What else did Louisa say?'

'She said it might not be operable.' Her voice sounded small, detached.

'Well she's talking rot. I'm fighting this bastard. It'll get cleaned up.'

Then Stephanie stretched out her hand to touch him. She had not touched him since childhood, and rarely then. Her hand was trembling.

But he said: 'Don't bother with that', and barged past her into the sitting room. Now she no longer knew whether he was talking to himself or to her or to nobody. 'I just need time to wind up the fucking company. Put it on the market. Maybe this place too.'

'You said . . .' But when she met his eyes, their glance had unfocused.

'I said I'm fighting the bastard.' He was addressing the whisky glass shaking in his hand. 'Where's Louisa?'

'She's gone back to London.'

'Where's Theresa?'

'She'll be here tomorrow.'

'All right then.' She heard the clink of his glass. Then he turned his back. And this was the image she was later left of him: not his face, with its pugnacious vitality, but this repudiating back, still broad in its tweed jacket, its shoulders closed in on the privacy of his obliteration.

Later, walking in the garden, she peered through her mother's window again. But nothing had changed. The room remained sealed: less a shrine than somewhere forsaken or unconfronted. The cupboard was still half open on its summer dresses; the pile of records undisturbed, the shadow of a bed. It was six years since her death, and Stephanie no longer had to stand on tiptoe to look in. She wished that even for a day she had known her mother through adult eyes. However much she tried to recall her, to reinterpret who she had been, the memories remained elusive, and strangely few. She had bought a pair of binoculars for studying the downland butterfly transect, and now trained them through the window at her mother's books and music. The names on the record covers – Lotte Lehman, Elena Gerhardt – meant nothing at all to her, but here and there the disparate book spines – Robert Musil, Marguerite Yourcenar, Elias Canetti – gave out the scent of a Europe she might one day touch on. After her father had died and they opened the room, she thought, she would take these books for herself and experience the world and time they recreated.

'Inambar river, Puno, Peru. 13.4 degrees S 70.3 degrees W c.18m south of Puerto Leguia. Elev. 740ft. Habitat coverage: tropical lowland rainforest. V. diverse, inc. kapok, cedar, tornillo, mahogany (*Swietania macrophylla*), pona palm, ficus, invasive bamboos. Canopy c.110ft. Date: 3 June 1949, 8.30–17.00. Mid-level humidity. 81 degrees Fahrenheit. Wind 0–2m/hr. Threat to habitat: low-yield agriculture in vicinity of Puerto San Carlos. Species: *Morpho helenor, Morpho Menelaus, Caligo eurilochus, Heliconius numata, Heliconius pardalinus, Perides neophilus*, Glasswing *Greta oto, Hamadryas feronia . . .*'

Every Saturday she typed out Arthur's field notes with dogged care. The handwriting that he had called erratic was in fact quite clear, although very small; occasionally a soiled or crinkled page betrayed some tropical downpour, or the shudder and slope of the entries had been inscribed, she imagined, by failing gas lamp. At first, when he read over what she had typed, he alighted unfailingly on her small mistakes, but as she became accustomed to his script these strictures dwindled away, until he was reading only for the pleasure of remembrance. Two or three times a day he would interrupt her with a cup of weak coffee or a snack, and she would elicit the stories his notes condensed or hid, his eyes nearly closing while he retrieved memories unshared for years. Sometimes he went over to his cabinets to show her some prized creature captured four or five decades earlier.

These tales mesmerised her. He had seen whole river-banks and valley sides swarming with now-protected species. In Papua New Guinea, the Queen Alexandra Birdwing drifted over its dwindling habitat on wings a foot in span. He had watched Rajah Brooke's Birdwings cover a sodden clearing of the Malayan jungle in a near-solid carpet of emerald and vermilion, and whole troupes of flame-coloured Cymothoes flying through the Congolese rainforest. He had known all the great lepidopterists, from Edmund Brisco Ford to Frederick Frohawk. One year he had watched Alexandra Sulphurs streaming down the Fraser river valley in a cavalcade of yellow and lime green; the next he had been studying the African Swallowtail, whose harem ran through more than fourteen variations of female (including a male disguise) and who protected themselves by mimicking the flight and colouring of toxic species.

The butterflies' survival tactics fascinated and sometimes puzzled him. In the evening, after Stephanie's work was over, he would light his charred pipe and delay her leaving, sitting alert on a high-backed chair or tinkering with his specimen trays. Sometimes he forgot her ignorance and ruminated on taxonomies obscure to her, before pulling himself up short with a muted laugh of apology. But the wonders of butterfly camouflage deepened to a quiet drama in his narrative. Once, in the Amazon, he had seen a Hamadryas pursued by a manakin bird. So perfectly did the butterfly simulate the bark of a certain tree that on landing there it vanished before his eyes, leaving the baffled bird to strike at the trunk again and again.

There were poisonous butterflies in violent, protective hues, whose steady, disdainful flight signalled their venom, and edible ones that had evolved to fly under the same false colours, copying even their flight pattern. Other species, like the Owl butterfly, had underwings inscribed with frightening eyes, which they opened and shut by flickering their wings, and still others were marked with a false face, close to the tail, so that predators would misdirect their attack, leaving the vital parts to fly away. (Arthur had seen specimens with perfect holes where the eyespots had been.) So some species, Stephanie thought (and perhaps humans were among them), preserved their core by pretending it lay elsewhere than it did.

The strangest of these tacticians, to her, was the Glasswing Greta, which spread in pathetic series on Arthur's trays: a creature whose transparent wings, edged only thinly with scarlet, turned it into a flying window pane, barely visible. But most beautiful of all, in Arthur's words, were the Morpho Blues. His first sight of one, in the Upper Amazon, had moved him like a late epiphany. In the dim forest its iridescent sapphire wings and dull underwings, alternating as it flew, flashed on and off with an unearthly, discontinuous light, to the confusion of all predators, like a glint of ectoplasm.

The rigor of Arthur's discipline – the obsession with taxonomy and insect behaviour – seemed to have left undimmed a childlike pleasure in the creatures themselves. Instead of Stephanie's enthusiasm being met by condescension – she had long ago given up voicing it at home – she felt his lopsided smile and his grey eyes warm on her. He made her feel normal, and intelligent. She even came to enjoy his specimen trays, and cherished the strange intimacy of mutually loving the green-armoured thorax of *Siproeta stelenes* or – under his magnifying glass – the tiny hairs on the forefeet of Swallowtails, by which they tasted.

And she wondered about him. You could not look at the world (or at him) with such sweetness, she thought romantically, if you had not known some kind of sorrow. (Somehow she had always paired gentleness with suffering.) But she did not know how to ask him personal things. On his sideboard stood a photograph of himself ten years younger, perhaps, hand in hand with a stout, soft-eyed woman in a sunhat. In their other hands they cradled butterfly nets, and the country behind them was lusher and more forested than England. The woman looked aglow with health, and sturdier than the man beside her. She was smiling up at him. There were no photographs of children.

Stephanie, as she typed, always hoped for those rare passages that suddenly broke into story. Then she knew why he understood her. The pursuit of something splendid and evanescent, even the tabulating passion of the collector – the thrill of capturing rarity – she felt she shared. She thought she recognised how you might risk your health and even your life in pursuing that flickering ectoplasm in the forest.

Once she came upon: 'De Osa peninsula, Costa Rica. Elev. 170ft. Date: 5 Sept. 1948. Habitat coverage: primary rainforest. Arrive with rotting plantain fruit to attract species of pierid: but no need. Whole forest teeming. Some eighty species flying in a single glade. Different families intermingling, impossible to separate by eye. Flash of malachites, Crimson-patched Longwings, iridescent preponas, Swallowtail perides, and ghostly, transparent Ithomiini. Pools fringed with coral-red heliconids, marpesias, daggerwings. Owl butterflies cover the tree trunks. *Thecla damos*, *Oryas lulia*, *Morpho amathonte*. The whole forest ablaze. I forget to raise my net. Can I call myself a scientist? Not here. Science is why I do this. But you can't kill in paradise.'

Another time, just as her day was finishing, and Arthur brewing coffee in the kitchen, she read: 'I can't always love them. Again the Pala nymphalid targets my eyes. The most aggressive species in the Ivory Coast. I duck, he crashes into my net, swerving away, returns to his territorial perch. There must be a female nearby. He flies very fast from high up. As he goes for my eyes again, I net him. I pinch his thorax without pity. It isn't usually so. There's always a twinge of guilt . . .'

When she asked him about this, he replied, uniquely, that he could not remember it at all. Soon afterwards he had gone down with malaria, and later read his notes with astonishment, written as though by someone else, in his own hand.

'Cordillera de Vilcanota, dep. Cuzco, Peru. Can no longer fix position by grid. Elev. c. 8,500ft. Date: 17 July 1966. The farmers say I mustn't go on. Armed men are on the track below. I circumvent them at dusk, and camp in cloud forest. Why am I risking this for *Pedaliodes niveonota*? But only one specimen, to my knowledge, ever collected. It is chocolate brown, lustrous. I may die for it. The ventral surface of the forewings is suffused with magenta: this stretches from its costa to vein $M2$. It grows rarer and more luminous in my head. Perhaps I am going mad . . .'

But he had never found *Pedaliodes niveonota*, he said, and even now the memory chafed. She squeezed his cold hand. In these weeks of her typing, she had grown at ease with him. He had collected enough, she laughed. He could leave the rest to others. He smiled down at her. She loved him, as she had when a child. She could safely clasp his hand, or embrace him in parting, because he seemed barely to notice. If she teased him, he would answer with his affectionate smile, and occasionally patted her hand, as if in conciliation, and murmured in his far-off voice: 'You're very dear.' If he sensed her subtle release of feeling, he withheld any showing of it. And when he said near the end, 'You've made me happy', she knew his meaning: that his field notes were now legible before his death.

Towards her last Saturday with him, he mentioned that he had a place on a butterfly expedition in Normandy – he wanted to walk along those forest rides again – but he did not feel up to it now. Would she like to go instead? She suspected this was a covert gift, and longed to accept. But she said: 'I can see my father's declining. The chemotherapy didn't work. It's only a matter of time.'

Arthur said: 'This group won't leave until July.' It was February now.

'I see. Yes.' She didn't meet his eyes 'I'd love to go.'

She sensed that behind his distant smile and buried voice, Arthur was concerned about her. Perhaps he felt he was standing in for her father, or even, obscurely, giving something to her mother (but she was guessing). She could tell he thought her vulnerable, too soft. She mustn't idealise the world of butterflies, he said. They were, in many ways, creatures like us. And sometimes, when she waxed too enthusiastic, he would sound a warning note of science. In their least attractive habits, he said, lay their survival. Their beauty was a gorgeous irrelevance. Much of their brief lives was spent at war. In many species the males patrolled and battled remorselessly for their territory, often perching high in a position of command. They could even attack humans, as he knew. As larvae they might eat their own siblings. One fascinating genus changed from herbivore to carnivore overnight.

He asked her: 'Did you read about the larva of the Large Blue? It attracts meadow ants by secreting a sweet liquid. They carry it into their nest, where they come to believe it's their queen. It even sings softly to them. They feed on its honeydew, while the caterpillar feeds on their grubs. Basically it's eating their children. Then its chrysalis hibernates among them underground, until the butterfly starts to emerge months later. By now the ants are angry. But as they attack it, it sprays out a sticky fluid which clogs their feet and feelers, so it has time to dry its wings and fly away. It is a repellent and yet rather wonderful story . . .'

Quite useless to anthropomorphise insects, Arthur said. This was simply the way continuance was organised. Even butterflies' mating, sometimes so delicate, could be furiously rivalrous and violent. Sex was the chief purpose of the male's brief span. Few females remained virgin beyond their first morning. Many carried the scars of needle-sharp penises that misdirected. In some Heliconids the males gathered around the female chrysalis and impregnated her even before she emerged. Occasionally this killed her. In a small proportion of species, they sealed their ownership by plugging their mate's vagina with a monstrous sphragis, which she carried to the end of her life. Rivals might try to unhook it with ingeniously developed augers, and the females themselves had evolved increasingly external genitalia in defiance. The Russian writer Nabokov, a passionate lepidopterist, imagined these chastity belts as almost beautiful, shaped like helical shells or tiny lyres. As for pupal rape, Arthur said, the female was exuding sexual scents even in her chrysalis.

When he, with a quaint paternalism, said that the outside world could be very cruel, Stephanie imagined, for some reason, that he was regretting something in his past, as well as trying to shield her. When he parted from her that evening, his touch on her shoulder was more tentative than usual, and she kissed a cheek that was almost turned away.

Stephanie's father went into hospital to die. Neither she nor Theresa had been able to lift him on and off the surgical bed installed in the sitting-room, and morphine was turning him confused, so that his anger drained away. He now took Stephanie's hand. He was barely recognisable to her. His skin was putty grey and his hair scattered to strange blond curls by chemotherapy. His old concerns had disappeared, his business forgotten, its sale still incomplete. Whenever he surfaced from delirium, his eyes wandered the room in bafflement. He seemed to be hunting for some visual reference point. Sometimes he fixed on his wife's photo on the table beside him and scrutinised it in perplexity a while, before calming. And sometimes his gaze alighted on Stephanie seated beside him. Each time, she dreaded seeing his features contort in distaste, but instead he would only nod faintly, as though reassured.

She took it in turns with Louisa to watch him. At first she wanted to feel something, anything. She thought it might be easier to warm to this gaunt, balding stranger than to the memory of her father. His fingers were stick-like in hers. She was distantly appalled by herself. She wanted him to hurry up and die. She wanted to go to Normandy and find butterflies. Louisa was more distressed than she: but it was the distress of somebody long ago released from him. Louisa wore smart business suits even in the hospital, and her blonde locks were tied back with a crystal hairpin. Stephanie, waiting in the bedside chair, listening to her father's fitful breathing, let her thoughts stray into a different future. Now she would go to university, become someone else.

Behind her, in the hushed privacy of the corridor, an old man started to weep, shedding the tears that they could not.

Towards the end, while Stephanie sat half asleep beside her father, he jerked awake and murmured: 'You've been a wonderful daughter.' She stared back at his white, unrecognisable profile. She thought: Why do you tell me now? She felt furious. Why only now?

After his death, she asked Louisa if he had had any last words for her, but there was nothing. She thought: Have I then imagined his favouritism? (Louisa says I have.) Am I so sensitive and self-deprecating? (She says I am.) If he had cared for either of them, Louisa said, it was too late to tell. 'You know, he wanted sons.'

7 July. Saint-Aubin-sur-Mer. The sea is calm, steel blue. There is a faint mist. The cliffs and islands scatter to the north. Will the seagulls follow us to Cherbourg? Below deck, you might think we were not moving, it is so still. But I write this near the prow, in the sun. Nobody else here at all. Louisa says only schoolgirls keep diaries. Poor

Louisa. She drives me to the dockside and bursts into tears as I leave. She in her business suit. And I'll only be gone five days. Then I start to cry too. What's wrong with us? We're alone now, she says. But it's better alone, I tell her. We were alone anyway. We dab each other's tears. Our laughter sounds hysterical.

My group assembles at the arrivals depot in Cherbourg. Feel nervous. There are nine of us. A middle-aged couple from Yorkshire; two stout elderly ladies; a tall woman in her early thirties, I'd guess, a bit aloof; another married couple, he huge and crippled-looking; and our French leader, a delicate young man, fidgeting, wonderfully like a butterfly.

Our minibus carries us for an hour over country I don't know. Villages of black-tiled roofs above stuccoed walls and shuttered windows. Apple orchards and fields of sunflowers. Our hotel is on the edge of Saint-Aubin above the sea, and my balcony looks along the cliffs. This thrill of isolation. Nobody I know here. No one for miles. Only wild butterflies, tomorrow.

At supper we eat 'Normandy cuisine', but I don't know precisely what this is. The fish tastes sweet. Opposite me a bouncy woman asks: 'And who are you, then?'

For a moment I long to be anyone else. Samantha, perhaps (she's the tall one), or Mrs Gilbert (married to the giant) or Fiona somebody. But of course I answer: 'I'm Stephanie', and my voice emerges so bleak and girlish it makes me angry. The name sounds stupid too.

But the woman nods and smiles in a protective way, and the Gilberts smile too, and it occurs to me that I'm happier with older people. Yet I don't feel I exist as these others do. They seem so solid, so comfortable. They have gardens and grown-up children back at home. They pay extra for the local wine. Jean-Paul, our leader, shares his demi-bouteille with me. He talks in agitated bursts, in English more mellifluous than ours. His hands flutter. When he asks about my parents, my answer sends him into convulsions of embarrassment and regret. He even clasps my hand. Oh dear.

It is night now. From my balcony the waves fall in near-silence. The sky is awash with stars. They make me feel faint, because their peace and order are an illusion. I've read all about that. Up there is a graveyard of black holes and dead galaxies. Plus millions of planets flung out of their gravitational field, or whatever it's called, wandering in emptiness. The sky is full of them, apparently, frozen and alone. It's easy to believe. It reminds me of something I saw under a microscope – was it a butterfly's eye? – a mass of roving particles. And the whole universe dispersing into nowhere after the Big Bang. Everything thinning into the dark, like a ghastly mistake: a final refutation of God. Maybe the beams that fall on me now went out from stars that died long ago. All the same, I can write this diary by their light. What a fluke that I'm alive at this moment, out of all the other moments before and after! Impossible to think about tonight. My brain goes blank. These hotel walls are so flimsy I can hear Mr Gilbert snoring. Unless it's Mrs Gilbert.

I must sleep now.

8 July. The foothills of Les Monts d'Eraines are covered by chalky meadows. Alongside crops of dying rape the grass is thick with mallow and poppies. There is wild thyme, and basil too, and pink vervain. Butterfly heaven. We fan out with our cameras and binoculars. Only Jean-Paul carries a net, but this is to capture creatures for our momentary inspection, he says, before he lets them fly again. Only scientific expeditions keep specimens now.

A tingle of excitement. Tiny moths shift about our feet. A honey buzzard cruises overhead. From time to time one of us – usually Jean-Paul – calls out a species sighted: Marbled White, Brown Argus, Dark Green Fritillary. We all unite to concentrate on these tiny things in the grass and shrubs. The world that goes unnoticed. The Yorkshire couple identify birdsong, and one of the older women is engrossed by chalkland wild flowers, and presses specimens into her notebook. If arguments break out, they only concern the audibility of the bush cricket or how far the White-legged Damselfly strays from its riverine habitat. Everyone moves quietly, even though butterflies are deaf. Perhaps people in later age revert to caring for the small, wild things they loved as children. I wonder if I will.

But the butterflies obsess us. There are hosts of tiny, flashing blues that settle to show gorgeous underwings. How restful it is! Just a little pulse of anticipation as we wade forward through the grass. There are species here unknown to England. I am the first to sight a rare Pearly Heath, and to notice the long, wavering flutter of the Berger's Clouded Yellow.

At noon we settle for a picnic where the hillside overlooks misty fields. Jean-Paul unwraps local fruit and cheeses from his backpack. I sit between the married couples. Mr Gilbert squats like a giant crab beside his small, dreamy wife. His pate sprouts ginger tufts. He has bought us all bottles of Normandy cider. The Yorkshires (I've forgotten their real name) share the photos in their expensive cameras. Everyone is indulgent to me, and playfully respectful since my sighting of the Berger's Yellow. (But I wish they wouldn't call me 'our young friend'.) They treat me as a kind of mascot. As for Jean-Paul, he keeps plying me with chunks of baguette and different cheeses: Camembert, Pont-l'Évêque . . . His eyes flicker on and off me. I think he may feel sorry for me.

Only Samantha sits apart, reading a journal. I have a feeling she despises us all. She is a handsome woman, with fiercely arched eyebrows. A bit scary. When I get up to pour myself cider, she comes and stands beside me, and I feel absurdly flattered. She is a university biologist. I find myself babbling about butterflies and host plants that I've never seen.

I must have sounded naively idealistic, because she reminds me that plants and caterpillars are engaged in an everlasting war. Perhaps she teaches in these graphic images: how the leaves of every forest are armoured in protective spines and saw-toothed rims. Some plants, she says, tempt butterflies to lay their eggs on outlying fronds, which are then discarded. The sacs and veins of innocent-looking foliage are brimming with protective poison, and sometimes unpalatable juices are rushed straight to the site of the caterpillars' munching. She tells me this in a voice of detached amusement, and smiles faintly. Her lips remind me of Sally's.

She is the only scientist among us, I think, and I'm not sure why she's here. Perhaps to complement some specialist research. I have no time to ask. Our picnic is packed away, and we are off. But nobody like her or my cousin, I realise, would be invited on such an amateur trip. It is simply Arthur's sly way of giving me a holiday.

I'm sitting in the hotel lounge after supper, just now, and a voice says: 'Stephanie.' It is Jean-Paul. He sits beside me with a look so sweet and tentative that I want to ask him what's wrong.

Then he says that his own father is dying, too young, like mine. Am I a Christian? 'How is it possible to believe, when . . .' But his mother is pious. He has to comfort her. He amuses her by talking about butterflies. How people from ancient Greece to Japan imagined them the spirits of the departed. How an early Irish law forbade the killing of white butterflies because they were the souls of children. Sometimes he breaks into soft, self-deprecating laughter. He is full of quaint lore and stories. Several times he strokes my hand. Perhaps I have drunk too much Calvados, but I don't recoil. He is so quick and funny. Like an elf. Before I go upstairs he tells me that butterflies bring night dreams. But I'd rather know what makes us dream by day. Such silliness.

9 July. This morning a light rain falls. We arrive at the forest of Cerisy. Broad avenues move among beech. When the rain lifts we find Weaver's Fritillary, Large Tortoiseshell (vanished from Britain), various skippers. But Jean-Paul is dissatisfied, and we drive on to somewhere I lose on the map. Here a waist-high meadow is ablaze with poppies and ox-eye daisies. We have a first sighting of the Large Chequered Skipper.

Two small boys emerge from the woods to stare at us. I think how outlandish we must seem as we comb the verges in our waterproofs and clumping boots, clutching tripods and trekking poles. I too, in my baggy trousers and floppy hat, with a rucksack full of suncream and useless things. The cry goes up: 'An Ilex Hairstreak!' and the boys follow us open-mouthed as we converge with cameras and binoculars on an oak leaf where a tiny brown insect sits. Even to me, we sometimes seem absurd. Familiar beauties flap by – Peacocks and Red Admirals – and we ignore them for this chip of brown. It is all about rarity, of course, collector's mania. I feel it myself. I tick off the Ilex Hairstreak in my mind, and it may never be so exciting again.

But for the moment the creature sits for our cameras, until only Samantha and I are left. I am fumbling to focus it with my Leica when she takes out a hand lens and holds it to my eye. The insect is transformed. Now the closed brown wings are suffused with pale orange, splashed by apricot spots and fringed with white like a carpet. Its head and thorax are furred in blue. Facing us, and very strange, two polished ebony eyes are angled back over the entire head. It seems to be assessing me.

'Does it know we're here?' I say.

'Of course. But it doesn't want to fly yet. It's nectaring.' At last it flies. 'They're not stupid. They have good memories. There's even some evidence that butterflies remember what they learnt as caterpillars.'

'I thought they turned to sludge in the chrysalis.'

'It seems that something survives.'

So memory, I begin – why does she make me babble? – may not lie in the hippo-whatsit, but is swishing about everywhere.

She laughs and doesn't answer. When she looks at me, I have the same sensation as if I were gazing at the butterfly. I wonder why I have not noticed this before. Her eyes are dark and slanted far back into the shadow of her sunhat. Beautiful in their way. A little frightening. I blurt out that she looks like the Ilex Hairstreak.

She answers: 'And you're the Arctic Clouded Yellow', which momentarily pleases me (it's the prettiest of the yellows). But now I wonder what she meant.

This diary is growing silly.

This evening Jean-Paul tells me he'll drive some of us into Arromanches, twelve kilometres to the west. But when I climb into the minibus, there's only him and me. He talks all the way, and gazes at me too often for safe steering. He is playful and effervescent. Do I know the sounds and odours of butterflies? Their chrysalids rasp and squeak in need or warning, their caterpillars sing. The Peacock butterfly hisses like a snake. And yes, they give out sexual perfumes: musk, verbena, vanilla, stale Gauloises . . . His hands dance on the steering wheel. His father is dying. In an old people's home in Cherbourg, among people twice his age. His grandfather was wounded in the Normandy landings, at a place where we are going. His eyes flash on and off me in expectation. His laughter sounds a little manic. But he is sweet and fragile, I know. I try to smile. His voice is touched with pleading.

Walking along the beach at Arromanches. On the horizon the remnant of the wartime harbour, towed over the

Channel from England, looks like a discontinuous railway train strung across the sky. The sand is hard under our feet, and runnelled by receding waves. I stuff my hands into my jeans to deter Jean-Paul from holding one. His talk is slowing down. Every time it peters out he mutters, '*Alors*', the only French he uses to me. 'So you will be going back to England on Tuesday. *Alors* . . . I think the tide is coming in now . . .' *Alors* throws a bridge of fading hope over our silence. It says: We are not yet finished.

He asks about my life and future, and my orphaned state elicits pity again. His eyes are watering. I tell him I hated my father.

The lights are coming on along the esplanade above us. War memorials, and leftover anti-aircraft guns and jeeps intermingle with crêperies, ice-cream parlours, and a carousel where children are riding painted horses and giraffes.

Jean-Paul slips his arm around mine, so we walk, linked like lovers, across the sand. Black-headed gulls march in front of us. When I try to detach my arm, he finds my hand. I'm starting to hate this. Can't he feel it? My fingers freeze in his. Iron caissons from the disintegrated bridge lie beached along the tideline, hung with seaweed. They are painted *Accès Interdit. Danger*. I wish this was written on me. Children are playing hide-and-seek inside them. And Jean-Paul starts his feverish talk again. He says I must begin a new life. Do I plan to attend university? That's good. He himself went to Dijon, studying literature. He loves literature. *Alors* . . .

Poor Jean-Paul. There is nothing you can do. Let's go back. Because it doesn't work: not pity, not talk of butterflies. I hear myself saying that I have a boyfriend back in England. His hand goes clammy in mine. You skunk, Stephanie. Why don't I just tell him I don't care? Not like that. Instead I secretly turn to steel. I start to despise him. He makes me hate myself.

'Let's go back.'

10 July. I dreamt about my mother last night. She was standing at her window looking out into the garden. I waved to her – I was the height of a small child – but she gazed through me at the orchard or at something else, and her eyes were clouded. They did not contain anything, only reflections. I even saw my figure in them, very small, as if I were translucent. Just a reflection in my mother's eyes. Then I heard my father's voice, loud and rasping: Do not disturb her.

The weather changed today. The waves are crashing in against the grey shore. Gulls flying inland. We go to the broad forest rides around Lessay. Heavy, sunless air. The pine trees grow out of the bog and marsh of the Ay watershed. Silver-studded Blues are fluttering above the heathers, but other butterflies have gone to ground.

Our group is easing apart. The two older women have taken against Mr Gilbert, whose massive ginger head obliterates any view of a butterfly as he clambers to photograph it. One of them has offended Jean-Paul by disputing his identification of a Mallow Skipper, and the Yorkshires, for some reason, have stopped speaking to one another.

I follow an Alcon Blue among the pines, but the forest floor is stubbled with hummocks and hidden marsh, and I have to go back. A weak sun glimmers out. For a while

Samantha comes and walks beside me. The ride is shining with brackish water, and there are swathes of orchids unknown to Britain.

Suddenly Samantha asks: 'Why are you so angry, Stephanie?'

Why what? 'I'm not angry.' Does she mean now, or always? 'Sometimes I think the world's angry with me.' The things that come out of my mouth. 'No, I'm not angry at all.' I don't know. No.

We go in silence. I feel a surprised perplexity. I imagine I normally convey reserve or diffidence. Samantha slows her pace to mine. I find nothing to say. Then all at once she points. 'I think that's a Purple Emperor.'

It is sailing high up along the treeline, like a bird. The first time I've ever seen one. 'It's settled.' I stare up, but I've lost it now. 'There.' I follow her pointing finger. It has perched on an oak branch, wings outspread. A shimmer of dark purple. My binoculars find it, and we gaze up together. 'It's moving . . . wonderful . . . no, it's staying . . .' and our shared pleasure creates this unforeseen intimacy, as it was with Cousin Arthur. But of course she is not Arthur. There seems no frailty in her. She looks very lithe and strong.

I say childishly: 'How can I be angry in the same world as that?'

'Even a great naturalist, Henry Walter Bates,' she answers, 'wrote that the contemplation of nature was insufficient to fill the human heart.'

'And you,' I say, 'a biologist!'

'We biologists are human too.' She laughs. 'Some of us.'

The others have caught up with us now, and we pinpoint the Emperor high in the trees. But our first intimacy has gone, as though the butterfly had lost some magic by being shared. Samantha walks away.

At supper all is conciliatory. Mr Gilbert buys us cider again; he says there are no good Normandy wines. The Yorkshires are talking too, thanks to the Purple Emperor, and revelling over their photographs. The extension tubes and telephoto lenses on their Nikons make mine look puny. But their close-ups seem intrusive to me, capturing the creature unaware a hundred feet above, its wings unfurled in privacy.

We have one day left. I wonder if I will see a Swallowtail, or a passing Painted Lady. Mrs Gilbert has set her heart on sighting a peregrine.

We part for sleep more cordially than usual. In the passageway by my room, Samantha says goodnight. Then, drawing me lightly to her, she kisses me on the lips.

Nothing I write can understand this. I doubt if I will sleep. It seems so natural. As if these are the lips I have always longed for.

11 July. On the Britanny ferry Barfleur. I'll never know where we went today. Nowhere on any map I can imagine. As our group fans out among the beech trees, the sun emerges and a cloud of butterflies hovers over the bracken. The air fills with the nervous chatter of blackcaps, while a sparrowhawk patrols overhead.

Samantha and I take a higher path than the others, going through silver birches and hazel. She is telling me about butterflies in Mexican belief: not the fairy tales of Jean-Paul, but stranger things. To the Aztecs, she says, butterflies were the returned souls of the slain, and in promise of resurrection the love goddess slept with young warriors on the battlefield, a butterfly between her lips. Butterflies are more versatile than humans, she says, their self-sufficiency prodigious. There are butterflies born half-male, half-female, their wings on each side different. There are even females that never mate, but lay eggs, unfertilised, which hatch out other females.

These miracles drop lightly from her. She no longer talks like a teacher. I know she is wooing me, in her dark way. We wander through knee-high grasses and flowering broom, sprinkles of pink germander. I answer the grip of her hand. A secluded glade is shining with asphodel, the flower of the dead. She lays down a waterproof coat. The ground is very soft. Clover and mauve rampion. I thought this only happened in folk tales, or perhaps in Aztec make-believe. Her kisses release something deep and long-waiting. My lips pour back her fervour. As she peels off my clothes, I am amazed to be easing away hers. Her eyes are fiercely tender on me. Her shoulders beautiful in my hands. I can only say her name. Her lips understand everything: on my breasts, between my thighs. Her fingertips also. Her dark hair unloosens over me, as if to keep secret the enchantment she is performing. After we are over, she teasingly relates my body parts to those of a butterfly. And out of the asphodel the tiny brown creatures of the glade – the Ringlets and Meadow Browns – alight on our entwined bodies, on her back, my breasts, sucking our sweat and dappling us like fallen leaves.

I do not know what you have done, Samantha. But whatever else happens, I will have understood this – it seems a kind of understanding – this consummation in my flesh, saying that I may be released from my childhood, and become a woman, even.

* * *

In the dark she imagined that an earthquake was breaking not far away. Beside her head the wall tingled and hummed. She sat up, shaking. An acrid stench was growing in the room. A bottle of mouthwash was clinking on the bathroom shelf, and all the window panes were rattling. By the night light that she kept burning – a sentimental leftover from another time – she saw that nothing around her apparently had changed. Then an explosion reverberated below, as if a great beam had cracked apart, and a second later she heard a glass smash on to the kitchen floor.

When she stumbled into the sitting room she saw that the lorikeet had dropped into the sawdust of its cage. The thrashing of its wings had died to a rustle and its cry of 'Well here we are' had become a hoarse whisper.

The smoke seemed thin at first. It was only when she opened the door on to the landing that she realised. Then the heat hit her like a molten wave, and the pouring smoke snuffed out her light. She thought she heard something falling in the corridor, but she could not reach the door again, even to close it. Beneath her the deep inferno roar was broken by crackling like rifle shots, and through the smoke a dull orange glow lit up the door frame.

Frantically she hunted for her coat, a blanket. Anything. By her relit night light, as she reached the sitting room, the air was thickening black, and her gaze swept over everything she might save, not realising that this was useless now: the stacked files of her biology students, the photographs in their tortoiseshell frames: Louisa's smiling family, Samantha haggard and brave in her last year. In the kitchen she pulled the fire blanket from its place on the wall, and for a moment held it like an apron in front of her, then tossed it away. When she opened the window, the smoke was sucked after her – she imagined flames behind – and she scooped the lorikeet from its cage and threw it crying into the night.

Then, with its release, a satiated calm came over her. She was fleetingly amazed at herself. Perhaps it was lack of oxygen, she thought, or because this unreality belonged most certainly in a nightmare. Was she dreaming? She peered down from the window into pure smoke. She knew the ground was seventy feet below, and that it would kill her. The fumes and heat were banking up behind. But this unearthly clarity continued, as if her consciousness had separated from her body. When she climbed on to the windowsill, there came into her mind no future that she longed for. She imagined stepping on to solid cloud. It would not be like dying at all.

She spread her arms.

5

Photographer

You cannot enter the basement rooms at will. Such flats are all but buried out of sight. Even the landlord can barely remember the layout. The tenant has changed the locks and does not answer the door. Yet dry rot or rising damp can undermine the whole building, and a musty fetor sometimes leaks into the house, seeping out of this underground obscurity into the upper storeys.

Occasionally the tenant's music percolated up to the ground floor, but thinned to a faint throb of drums. Listen to such sounds under the spell of cannabis, and the individual notes become a hypnotic parade of dissociated chords and instruments. After the music from his old CD player stopped – cut off with the severed electricity – the tenant went on hearing the sounds of the sea. Infused by five smoked joints and a bottle of vodka diluted with Diet Coke, each fall and pull of the waves became a constellation of scattered water drops, endless and transfixing, so that he lay in the darkness for what seemed many hours, listening.

If he gave up smoking dope for more than a few days, an inchoate anxiety surfaced: the fear of some visceral loss, in which his whole body seemed to be drifting apart from him. But after four or five joints this no longer mattered.

Nor did the smoke now drifting in his nostrils from another room. The vodka separated his head from his body, and hallucinations arose – images whose origins he could not have traced – beyond any control, into half-sleep.

But towards midnight the fear of some nameless deprivation returned. Steve dreamed that his memories were being extracted by forceps, one by one, from his surgically opened head, until he saw his own emptied body suspended, as if through a doorway, rotating to gaze back at him. Whatever experience this travestied might have been attributed to the impact of cannabinoids. But he never woke to explain it. When the flames entered the sitting room they found it full of inflammable furniture, old and now illegal. This fatal stuff – the landlord had never replaced it – had lain for years in the dimness, as if waiting.

The smoke was denser now than the stench from the spliffs that lay discarded by his head. Soon afterwards, his anxiety settled to memories so diffused and ungraspable that they would have eluded him altogether, had he woken. There swam into his mind's eye images from early childhood: a forgotten beloved, more potent than any he would know as a man.

When he saw her again, he recognised her by her eyes: Cleo, the care worker who had helped his mother. It was from her that he had learnt of his mother's death. She had thought at first that his mother was sleeping. But she had died sitting upright in her chair, with the arm of her record player oscillating at the disc's end, where Elizabeth Harwood had been singing 'How Beautifully Blue the Sky'.

But his mother could not really be gone, Steve knew. She was somewhere close, she was listening. She wasn't dead at all. She was sitting in her orchard, under the pear trees, or standing behind his shoulder. Why then this old terror of dismemberment? How thin he was without her! He could no longer hear even her accusation: the intolerance that would surface out of nowhere, her anger a dark contralto. She had sung for two seasons with the revived Carl Rosa Opera, and her voice would remain to him indelibly beautiful and angry. Pull yourself together, Steve. Stop dreaming. You're like your father . . . Now she had gone away, but he was still here. She too must then be here. Her low voice, after all, was his own, her soliloquy inside him, a voice that strived to root him in reality.

The seance medium is thin, with a greying beard. His washed-out pallor might come from the strain of accessing other worlds. His eyes are smoke blue. He sits before his clients without ceremony. Steve is at the back, nervous now. He hears the medium shuffling some papers before he stands up for a moment and says formally: 'My friends, all life survives death. We survive in all our faculties: our personality, our intelligence, our memory. Take heart. We are all joined in the Infinite Intelligence. If you do not recognise what follows, I can only say I'm sorry. I can make no guarantees. I simply relay to you what I see and hear . . .'

How strange. These are Christian people filling the tall room, people who believe in a just heaven. Like him, they want to talk with the dead, but their dead are in some communal paradise, while his stands in her pear orchard, trying to speak. 'When I'm gone,' she had said, 'will you still hear my voice?' These people probably go to such a seance every week. He knows she would despise him for coming here. She is close, so close, yet not there, not there at all. Two months gone now, and nothing. Her voice just out of hearing, sounding in his mind, but weak, too far. Now even her anger would come as a relief.

The medium pauses, his eyes closed. There is silence. Then he gestures to a woman sitting in the front. He says: 'I have someone for you. He has asked to come forward and speak to you. I think it is your husband . . .'

The woman hunches forward. She is elderly, clutching a pair of gloves. 'Yes . . . yes . . .'

'Your husband is a sturdy man . . . I see . . . he loved the countryside . . .'

'Yes . . . yes . . .'

The medium goes on to touch on her husband's appearance, his hobbies, while the woman rocks a little, and nods. Sometimes the medium asks: 'Would you understand?' and she goes on nodding slightly, and sometimes breathes, 'Yes', and sometimes does not respond.

The medium's eyes are closed again. He says: 'I feel fluid in my mind . . . Now I am with another presence from the spirit world . . . She is very strong . . .' His eyes open on Steve. 'Is this your mother?'

'Yes!' He meets the man's stare now. Cold air is beating up from his stomach, into his mouth.

'I hear singing . . .' The medium's words have turned light and wondering. 'I think she is singing. Would you understand?'

'Yes!'

'Her voice is very pleasing.'

'Yes.' Suddenly the banked waters of a lifetime are over-flowing, flooding through him with unbearable relief. He aches to embrace her, even if she turns her back. He half stands.

'Your mother is sending you encouragement. This is a difficult time for you. She wants you to know that she is holding your hand. There is no need to fear . . .'

Steve stares down at his hands, clutched at his chest. He opens them to receive her. He is weeping. He feels something glide over one hand, he is sure of it, like a breeze or a wing. He closes his fist. She is there. He tries to speak but chokes, in an ecstasy of relief, and sits down again, sobbing. He is aware of others watching him, intrigued but tender, not as surprised as he. He only says: 'Yes . . .'

The medium goes on: 'She is singing folk songs, nursery rhymes to you years ago . . .'

He nods, breathes, 'Yes', because he wants to believe, he is caught up in the truth of the medium's vision, which can recreate anything. Perhaps his mother had sung nursery rhymes to him. He did not know. Perhaps she'd been a gentler woman before he could remember. 'Yes . . .'

'She wants to take you in her arms.' Steve wonders who this woman is. Is it somebody else? Can the words be for somebody else in the room? 'Would you understand?'

He cannot answer.

Desolation is spreading through him. His mother is sliding away, becoming another. She had never wanted to take him in her arms.

'She is smiling at you. I think she is remembering driving you to school.'

'No, no, no!' He shakes his head. His mother had not driven him to school.

'It is she speaking now, not me. She is saying: "Go on with your life. Don't look back. I'm here with you. Don't regret the change called death . . ."'

But a cold sadness has opened up in him. He no longer meets the medium's gaze, or responds at all. He does not hear his mother's voice in the man's words. It is not how she spoke or felt. He has lost her, she was never there.

And now the medium's eyes have closed again, and he selects another. Steve hears everything that follows with exhausted indifference. Some clients nod and sigh and give back fulsome answers to 'Would you understand?' Others remain mute, or shake their heads. The medium seems locked in some trance of his own. Sometimes he smiles. His eyes are cold and guileless. His imperial beard gives him a look of old-fashioned charm, and of access to the past.

When Steve leaves the building his footsteps sound noiseless to him, even the traffic far away. He feels a perfect, terrible blankness in his head, as if he were walking into oblivion. There is so little of him.

The chief neurosis of photography, his father had said (before bunking off to Canada) was to stop time in its tracks. For months now, on weekly visits to his mother, Steve had wanted to bring his camera and record her as he might last remember her. He had wanted a bulwark against the delusions of re-remembering. He was anticipating grief. He photographed her at random under her orchard's sunlit trees, but she suspected he was seeking to memorialise her, and baulked at the camera. So he pretended technical preoccupations – photography was his profession after all – and captured at last the gaunt force and irritation in her face, and a rare, flashing smile. Even now, a few days before her death, her exasperation with him surfaced. Why couldn't he follow Richard into some sensible profession? His elder brother had come to terms with the world, but Steve was twenty-three and still dreaming like an adolescent. There was no future in photography. His brother worried about him.

'Richard worries about me? Why on earth?'

'He says you're too solitary, he thinks you're going off the rails. Even your photography. He says you pose your sitters like goddesses.' Her voice thins to gasping. 'Never idolise women, Steve.'

I don't, he thought, I don't. He supported her indoors and settled her into an armchair. He brewed her lemon tea. She hated this dependence, but she could no longer walk unaided. She began talking about his childhood, as if there was something there she had not grasped, or else some hidden affliction between that time and this. Did he still have his childhood fear of being lost, she wondered, or his recurring nightmare when he was torn into bits yet went on living? She spoke of these with irritation, as if he should have stopped them. Why were you such a haunted boy? Meanwhile the care worker – a young black woman – was making up the bed that he and Richard had lugged downstairs, and checking the pill dispenser before filling in a report form. Steve wondered if she was listening.

When he got up to leave, his mother struggled from her chair to say farewell. As he reached the door, she tried to follow, but halted, her hands clenched on her chairback. Her breath was a whistling rush. She said: 'I'm all right.' He gentled her back into the chair, while the care worker took her other arm. She repeated peevishly: 'I'm perfectly all right.'

But he had the illusion, as he opened her front door, that it gave on to emptiness. He was stepping into mist. Everything that lent him substance or meaning was being left behind in the figure of his mother, still solid, but soon no longer. Then he felt the cold, hard surface of the camera against his chest. It was like a nugget of hope. He felt for a moment as if it physically contained her, absorbed and living, and that through it he had saved himself.

Before the door closed behind him, the care worker appeared. She said: 'You're worried, aren't you?'

He looked back at her. Perhaps it was his faintness, he later thought, or something delusive in his head, but she was looking at him with familiar eyes: the hypnotic slant upward, a deep hazel, and soft.

'If anything concerns you,' she said, 'I live just a few streets from here.' She gestured beyond the road. 'You can call me.' She had written her mobile number on a slip of paper. When he took it he noticed his fingers quivering, and her own tapering to polished nails. Beautiful hands.

He took to walking along the coast near the town: not the spectacular cliffs to the east, but more enclosed, sombre places. These beaches appeared to him shorn and primordial: low chalk cliffs and dark pebbles against a fretted hem of sea. Often, even in summer, they were deserted. No buildings, no shrubs, no sound but the water. The moment his feet clashed on their grey stones, the solitude elated him. For hours he photographed the waves where they broke on the stone shore and retired in dissolving rivulets of foam. Often he awaited the right sunlight for half a morning. But whatever it was that his eye or brain experienced was sometimes lost to his camera, and he returned again and again. As he walked, the ebbing tide yielded up a melancholy detritus: plastic toys, old sandals, glass worn to turquoise pebbles, seagull feathers, bones.

It was here that he took his mother's care worker, Cleo, on a solitary stroll from his flat. The March afternoon had turned blustery, and a cold sea was storming in. But she seemed to relish the harsh wind. He loved her long, athletic stride over the stones, and she had a knack of spotting curiously marked shells and pebbles, whose strangeness she shared with him. After her initial uncertainty when he telephoned ('You mean . . . Why? . . . Well, yes . . .'), he felt her relax with him into a hesitant trust. She seemed oblivious of her wave-soaked ankles and wind-torn hair, which was tied back at the nape from the high ridge of her cheekbones. The waves were cascading over the ruined slipways and jetties beside them in a turmoil he would usually have longed to photograph. But he was listening to Cleo, to the reverberant softness of her voice.

She had visited his mother for only a few days, she said, replacing more regular carers, but she'd admired her defiant refusal to rest, and noticed her dark, still opulent voice. She had noticed too how his mother had scowled when another care worker patted her hands and addressed her as 'we'.

He wondered later precisely when he started to fall in love with her. Perhaps it was the moment when she picked a plastic doll from the sea wrack, and looked at it with a mixture of distaste for its tackiness (it blinked with coy blue eyes) and compassion for the child who had lost it.

By the time they returned to his flat – Richard was away – the excitement of her presence extended to everything she touched: even how her eyes scanned his bookcase and DVDs, and her delight at the view from his windows – a wedge of silvered sea. The miracle of her was compounded and complicated by her colour. He had not known any black women, and now this consciousness intensified everything she did, and touched her with enigma. The way she sat on the sofa with her long legs crossed and her hands smoothing her hair seemed at once familiar and exotic. And there were qualities that he imagined to be purely hers: the purl of her speech which cushioned each syllable with the next, the impossibly slender and sensitised beauty of her hands – he could imagine no white hands like these – and those feline eyes which crinkled upwards when she smiled, and in their hazel softness suggested to him some undefined peace.

He poured her wine, which she barely drank, while he gulped his down to still his nerves. He tried to ask her delicately how she came to be here, alone in a white seaside town, but his words blundered, and she laughed. 'Oh, there are others besides me, a few. Down in the club scene it's quite hip to be black. But I don't go there much.' And no, she was not Caribbean, although everyone assumed she was. Her people had never been slaves.

He caught an edgy note of pride, and asked: 'Where then?'

Nigeria, she said. Almost fifty years ago, aged only ten, her father had left his home town in a line of refugees, holding his mother's hand. The dead or exiled leaders she cited – Ironsi, Gowon, Ojukwu – meant nothing to him, and little even to her. Now her father rarely spoke of them. They were the ogres or saviours of a childhood that had gone missing. The son of a newspaper editor, her father had become a porter in a London hospital and married a nurse from Lancashire. Hence, she said, her pale skin. But Steve could see no English in her. Her skin glowed, to him, a deep, burnished bronze.

'My grandparents confused me when I was small. My father's parents were lonely, I think. They wanted to go back to Nigeria, but they never did. My mother's parents would have thought: good riddance. They still hate immigrants.' He imagined he caught every nuance in her talking, and sensed a transient anger. 'But my father's mother was my best friend. When she got ill, that's when I became a care worker. Those girls looked after her like they were her daughters, and earned next to nothing.'

'So you thought: that's the job for me . . .'

'Well, I didn't go to much of a school.' She laughed, remembering something. 'Care worker isn't a posh job, not like your photography.'

'Photography isn't posh.' It seemed, at this moment, pure self-indulgence. 'And I don't deal with the dying, like you do.' He was thinking of his mother. 'Weren't you afraid that one day you'd arrive and find a client . . . like her . . .'

'That's happened to several of us. Of course you worry about some like that.' She was looking at him in a way that he read as profound sadness. Her gaze lapped against his eyes. How could he not love her? he thought. He imagined her calm to be the outcome of her care for those ageing close to death. Her lips started faintly to smile. She said: 'We get fond even of the crazy ones. There's one who greets me every morning as Eileen. She thinks I'm her sister, who's been dead for years. Others get anxious, and worry about losing their possessions – clocks and handbags – even in bed. Another asks me all the time, "Where is everybody?" And you have to wash them, even the men. Some of the girls won't do the men. But you get used to it. It kind of makes you understand old age, everything, how we're all on the same track for that. We ask the men to sponge their own private parts. Except some of the old ones are past it. Anyway, I'm black. They may not think of me in the same way.' She left this undefined. 'One old guy always wants to kiss me, but its sexless, like he kisses his dog – he's got a pet spaniel that stinks . . .'

He felt his desire for her now, imagining himself old, she washing him, her blackness only an allure. She said: 'The worst is when you don't really care any more, the care workers, I mean, when you wonder what's the point . . .'

She stopped there. But he imagined her going on: *When you think: they're degraded. And they're dying.*

He had wanted his mother to die at home. He had wanted this more than ever for her. To die in her own bed in the familiar room, facing the window with its climbing roses. Sunlight, perhaps.

He relished taking Cleo to places she could not have afforded: to intimate restaurants, to the theatre, to sights in London. He bought a second-hand Fiat and drove her to seaside towns that neither of them knew. They walked the cliffs beyond Dover, and along the South Downs to Chanctonbury Ring. Sometimes she broke into vivid excitement, but an innate reserve – it struck him as a quiet dignity – never quite left her, and she was often silent, absorbing whatever was around her with an unruffled and rather solemn attention.

When he took her to the theatre that spring, he basked in the spectacle of her transformation. Her appearance became dramatically at odds with her shyness. Crimson and vivid green set off her neck and shoulders, and the gold discs that dangled from her ears lent her a witching glamour. They saw comedies and a thriller that brought her hands clasped to her mouth, while in the auditorium's dark he could not help secretly watching her, taking in the amused twitching of her lips, or the intensity of her gaze.

Once she said: 'I don't understand how people go on stage. I'd die. How can they do it?'

For her twenty-third birthday she asked to go to a bal-let – neither of them had seen one before – and they found themselves watching *Giselle*, the fairy tale of a peasant girl betrayed in love. Nothing they had seen had moved her so palpably. In the last act, as the corps of spirits drives the faithless lover toward his end, her hand crept into his. The dancers moved in a moonlit whiteness: the ghosts of abandoned brides, their diaphanous dresses and blanched faces the antithesis of Cleo's own, and she was starting to weep.

But there was a second Cleo whom he understood less than he did this one: the sudden dynamo he once took clubbing, who lost or found herself in dancing of her own. It was as if in the enclosed dimness of the nightclub, half invisible, she became someone else. He liked to suppose that her furious gyrations, her long arms flying above her head, her eyes closed, arose from her African unconscious, but she only laughed at this.

His brother Richard dismissed Cleo as 'another of your infatuations'. Steve gave up inviting her to their mutual flat; but she shared hers with three others, and they went instead to seaside hotels. Then an illicit excitement brewed up: the arousal of entering a pristine room, a room without memory, private and prepared for them. The clean linen and small bathroom luxuries (she would take them away), their window overlooking the sea or some street where others walked unknowing, created an intoxication of their own.

At first he could scarcely believe that she would sleep with him. When she slipped off her crimson dress and he took her body in his arms, the skin he had imagined copper-smooth came rough and tingling to his touch, and her pinned-back hair loosed itself in a black aureole around her head. Her flared lips had unnerved him when he first kissed them, but now he found his mouth consuming hers, and he opened his eyes to see the glitter of metallic eyeshadow over her closed lids, so that he imagined she might love him.

Yet to the last there was something resistant in her, something that seemed subtly to confine him even as she softened, and he never knew if she experienced orgasm, only this mounting, fierce breathing and crying that relaxed when he did. But sometimes she sighed thank you, and seemed at peace, and her eyes opened on his with their look of consolation.

He could never separate the wonder of her ancestry from the veneer of common Englishness. Once she showed him photographs her father had inherited, of the Igbo refugees streaming southwards, he among them, in a blurred procession of white bundles and small children. Some, she said, had died along the way. He even imagined her walking in their midst. At other times, especially when drinking with her care worker friends, she seemed very English, almost ordinary. She shared their jargon, laughed at the same jokes. Then he found himself wanting to extract her back into the marvel of her strangeness.

In May the weather was warm enough for them to picnic on Camber Sands, and he photographed her all afternoon while she swam or paddled in a blue bikini. To him she was a different species from the raw white bodies around them. His camera explored her as it might have traversed a bronze statue, burnished and unchangeable. But when he arranged her for his lens, dropping her shielding forearms from her breasts, directing her eyes at the Leica, an old frustration crept in. The darkness of her skin seemed resistant to discovery, and she would shy away, telling him it was all too much, and to put away that stupid camera.

Soon afterwards the first of his friends to become engaged sent a wedding invitation from London. His schoolmates had dispersed these past few years, and had frozen in his memory. He had not kept up. He would go to the wedding with Cleo, he thought. She would be amused by his re-assembled past.

But Cleo said: 'I can't go.'

They were sitting on a bench above the sea. 'Why on earth not?'

'I just can't.' He imagined she had turned pale. 'I wouldn't know . . . I wouldn't know what to say. I have nothing to say.'

'They're no different from your friends.'

'You don't understand. I can't do those kinds of things.' She looked taut and suddenly lost. 'Three years ago I couldn't even go alone into a shop or the post office. I'd start to shake. I've always been like that.'

'But you look after the old and sick. You wash and dress them. You risk finding them dead!'

'That's different. They need me.'

He said gently: 'You mean you have to feel in control?'

'Something like that. I don't know. Yes, I suppose so.' She added unsmiling: 'I'm happiest with children.'

She passed a hand across her face, as if to obliterate her self. A sudden tic was quivering beneath one eye. He felt bitterly bewildered. He did not want to listen to this. He wanted the mask returned to her face: perfect, invulnerable. He said: 'It's not because you're black?'

'No. If people dislike me it's because I come over surly when I'm scared. Like in shops. I can't say anything right.'

He asked: 'Are you ever scared with me?'

'You're different, Steve. When I saw you with your mother you looked terrible . . . so sad. I just wanted to help you. I wouldn't normally have given you my number.'

'You felt sorry for me.'

'Yes.'

He did not know what to make of this. But later the things she'd said began to fall into place, and his past with her to reassemble. Her reserve, even her gentleness, became something else. Everything had its roots in her fear. Once by her bedside he had glimpsed a photograph of her with an ex-boyfriend – Steve supposed him at first to be one of her younger clients – the man leaning awkwardly against her, while she inclined to him protectively, one of her hands clasping both of his. When Steve's own photographs returned from the laboratory, he had expected Cleo to look high-spirited, even proud, standing on Camber Sands. But instead he saw a woman whose expression was subtly withdrawn, somehow bereft, as if the camera had caught something to which he had been blind.

Photographs do not heal. Examine the portrait photo long enough, and the familiar face becomes unknown. As he leafs through his mother's albums, his own face empties into boyhood, and he becomes baffling to himself, while Richard grows blander, his mother smooth-skinned, and his father a stranger. In his own work the hunt for essence becomes a fool's errand, and every face, in the end, an enigma.

He reverts to his cine films – moments filmed without thought, even humorously – and they often capture something precious and unintended. For a brief minute their people live in the present. But he dare not play the films or look at any photograph too often. They die with repetition.

He wonders bitterly if it is too late to take up another profession. He is already twenty-four. During his months with Cleo he has forgotten his passion for image, except for images of her. He has missed crucial work assignments, and his savings are draining away. And now, facing her in his sitting room, where Richard will not be returning for the day, he cannot meet her gaze. She is frightened, he knows. She has always been frightened. His own withdrawal freezes him. But the light has gone out of her eyes, and he cannot restore it.

For a while they talk about the week's trivia: her care work for an old diabetic, his own assignment photographing a racing stable. The silence grows too quickly for their voices to fill. And all the time she is looking at him with the conviction of what is to come, her face tense and pale. He has the idea that she has been anticipating this for a long time, perhaps from the beginning, as if it is her destiny to be betrayed. Even while this realisation numbs him – her dashed self-worth – he feels relief that she may meet him halfway, that there will be no surprise.

Into one of their yawning silences she says: 'You've lost me, haven't you? I don't think I exist for you any more.'

He says: 'Of course you do.' But his mind and body feel like lead. He cannot lift his eyes. His speech falters and mumbles. He tells her she is beautiful and hard-working and kind, but these epithets sound small in the room's quiet, like a roll call for people who are missing. He does not believe them, even though they are true.

She says: 'I don't feel any of that, now that you don't.'

A door slams downstairs, and he wonders if Richard is returning early. For once, he hopes so. But nobody comes.

She says: 'I guess I'm a refugee, like my father.'

He does not understand her, but recalls her old photographs; the long, weary line of fugitives. 'What do you mean?'

'He says that everyone's an immigrant really, that we all come from somewhere else. He's religious. He comforts himself that way. My mother disagrees. She says she's from Lancashire.' She smiles ruefully. 'Maybe I'll go back to them now, to London.'

He says: 'I never met them. You never took me there.' He pulls this tiny grievance forward in self-defence, despising himself. He imagines she is ashamed of them: the hospital porter and his comfortable wife.

She says: 'No, I never did.'

'Why not?'

'They might not understand. They were angry before, when I brought a boyfriend home. They said I just picked up casualties.'

He says: 'I'm not a casualty.'

'No, Steve. But you're not . . . like . . . normal.' Something in his expression – some self-righteous disbelief – triggers the bitterness of her rejection: a quiet, desolate anger. Her voice's softness disappears. 'You live in your own fantasies, Steve. You have a strange look sometimes. I can't describe it. But my friends noticed it. My parents wouldn't think you stable. They want me to find someone stable.'

'So you're ashamed of me.'

'I hoped things would change. I should have known they wouldn't. Even your love . . . I think you loved me . . . was frightening sometimes. Like you're a bit crazy. All that about a bronze statue. You should see someone, Steve. You should get professional help.' Her hands are fists on her lap. 'And now you're smoking dope. I can smell that stuff a mile off. I've heard some guys go straight from that to coke. My parents were right. My old boyfriend's a smack-head now. You could go the same way.'

He meets her gaze at last, appalled. He has taken to cannabis since his mother's death. It is harmless enough, surely. 'I never knew you thought these things . . .'

'I didn't always.' The rush of her words seems to have emptied her. She hangs her head. When she looks up again it is with a strained pity, more disturbing than her anger. 'Often I enjoyed your view of me.' In the long silence she is starting, softly, to weep. For a few more minutes their talk dribbles miserably on. There have always been silences between them, but now these gape like realisations. Once she says sadly: 'I thought I loved you.'

When another door slams, she stands up. 'I'm going now.' But her walk to the door is unsteady, as if hoping he will stop her.

He hears himself say: 'I'll call you.' But he knows he will not. He hates his own voice. The days will slip by, and he will do nothing. He goes to the window and watches her disappearing along the street below. She does not look back.

*   *   *

The Internet is the theatre of seductive women. You can travel there for days. Even the advertisements that fringe the roundabout near Steve confront him with vivid and elusive eyes and opened lips and breasts. While reading magazines, he finds from time to time a movie star whose gaze meets his own with a hallucinatory gentleness or violence.

When he at last saw her, she seemed refracted from a forgotten past. She was entering the stage door of a theatre near the seafront, carrying a duffel bag. Only twice before had Steve encountered a woman with those eyes that can see sideways, like a bird: eyes that may look at you full-face with an other-worldly tenderness or even a kind of luminous indifference. Their upward slant in the head, narrowing to that last unearthly tilt, may be a subtle illusion, of course, the sleight of mascara or artfully plucked eyebrows, but even then the effect remains beautifully strange, as if their owner gazes out from an alien world. Sometimes children have these eyes, still unaware of their power, and once he had seen an old woman from whose wrinkles they blazed like unrelinquished fire.

He could not dispel the idea that such eyes were conduits of light. Since boyhood he had tried to grasp the spell of trees, water, eyes, sunbeams, by anchoring it, at first in childish paintings, then in photographs. Even now he was striving for some photographic breakthrough in insight or technique – his heroes were Karsh and Avadon – and did not know how this would happen. He had grown obsessed by the singularity of people's faces. Even those most familiar to him became foreign when intently observed. Even his own. And in their alienation they became exciting.

Increasingly he devoted his camera to portraits, hoping this feeling of newness might transfer to his lens, and sometimes, rarely, he thought he had achieved a kind of magic.

But the woman who had vanished through the stage door made him forget the camera altogether. Afterwards he read the playbill hanging nearby. It meant nothing to him. But he felt sure that the leading actress must be her, and rolled the name's enchantment round his tongue: Helena Palmer. Instantly he was dreaming of ways to meet her. What would he say? He became aware not only of this outlandish longing but of a light, tingling fear: fear because she was beautiful. The feeling was familiar. He was comfortable with plain women, but their attractive sisters – it was often hard to look into their eyes. He envied the men who targeted them, suave with flattery. His brother Richard had no qualms about seducing them. In the past, at dim-lit discos, Steve had always dithered round whatever girl most attracted him. He would covertly watch her, admire her movements, the way she smiled or held her glass, and in this tremulous interval somebody else – probably Richard – would take her away to dance or into the night to kiss. Richard, sleek and streamlined at twenty-six, was more self-assured than Steve could imagine ever feeling. Richard drove a black BMW (bought on hire purchase). He wore skin-tight jeans and seersucker jackets – not what girls expected of a budding chartered accountant. Steve, struggling to become a photographer, should have evolved a dress sense of his own. But he had none at all.

As he returned to his flat, he felt himself drowning in a sweet, terrible excitement. Who was Helena Palmer? A passing astonishment, her cheeks dipping under their fragile-seeming bones. The face lit to distraction by those oblique powder-grey eyes: he knew nothing more. When he reached his door – the entrance to a renovated apartment – Richard was already back, listening to financial news on television, and lifted his hand in a distracted salute, reminding him that they were going out with friends that evening.

They went to a disco called Le Petit Club des Artistes, tantalisingly close to the theatre. It was packed with dancing bodies. They writhed in and out of strobe lighting, orchestrated by a white DJ with platinum dreadlocks. Richard ordered vodka and wine. But to Steve their friends seemed suddenly boring, and bored with one another. They talked in platitudes until the techno music drowned them out. He knocked back drinks to kill the time. Then he danced with a girl called Vera, a colleague of Richard's. She began to sweat. She asked him about his photography with mystified condescension, then went silent. The drums and the amplified singing filled all the space between them. The air was touched with forbidden smoke. Steve felt himself go vacant, waiting for the moment to leave. The drumbeats moved his limbs robotically. In the midst of this pulsing human closeness, he had a sensation of utter solitude, and that the singer's plangent voice and the scuttling drums resounded from a vacuum.

Then, to his astonishment, he saw her. Even before her eyes flashed blindly over his face, he knew it was her. She was wearing a black halter-neck dress and dancing opposite a red-headed girl with bare feet. He felt as if she had floated unbidden into his hands, and that she must be conscious already of his gaze. She was dancing with carnival energy, her face crossed by a slight, self-mocking smile, while her arms made long, elastic sweeps around her head and body. During the past few hours her blonde-streaked hair and those unsettling eyes had occurred so obsessively to him that their memory was already diverging from its origin, and now he stared at her across the darkness in nervous wonder. As he moved closer to her, he saw how delicate she was. Her slender neck and narrow, dimpled shoulders seemed to contradict her ebullience, and her skin looked almost translucent.

It was while she danced there in oblivion, her head momentarily turning to him, that he called out: 'Helena!' But there was no Helena to turn around. Vera smiled vacantly across at him, her arms lifted. Then the misnamed Helena came gyrating closer, smiling at nothing. As her head turned to him again, he exclaimed: 'I thought you'd be on stage!'

Her eyes focused him. 'No, we're still rehearsing!' He thought she asked how he'd recognised her, but her voice vanished under the music. As the drums pattered to a halt she said: 'We start next week', but he could not tell if this held any invitation.

When she returned to her table, he was drawn helplessly after her. He heard himself say: 'I'll come and see you.'

'Yes, do!' Her gaze flooded over him. 'Bring all your friends!' She laughed. God, she was beautiful. She laughed again at his mistaking her for Helena Palmer. Her laughter was silvery and musical, as if she had practised it. Helena, she said, was a middle-aged celebrity, whereas she – well, she was in a lesser role, somewhere down the cast list. Her name was Linda Spalva. (He tucked this strangeness away, to savour later.) They would play for two weeks here, she said, then on to Peterborough, then on to Sheffield, then into unemployment. Steve had found a chair by now, and was perched between them. The redhead gave her name too – he heard Diana – and for a minute he was alone with them, and the music had stopped. Out of their talk there surfaced precious fragments of Linda's life. She lived in London, sharing with two others. No marriage ring. No mention of a partner.

Then Richard's voice behind him said: 'Did I overhear you were actresses?'

At that moment, for that oiled voice, Steve hated him. Now his brother loomed over the table, owning it. In Steve's head numerous past humiliations – stillborn opportunities, thwarted desires – brewed up in a sickening miasma. Yet here, here was Linda, who still gazed opposite him, golden earrings shining through her backswept hair, and her presence was a fragile, miraculous thing, but one he was terrified was doomed to evanescence. Richard was the harbinger of failure. Richard would overshadow him without even noticing. And now, instantly, typically, he supplied what Steve had neglected. 'Can I buy you girls a drink?'

Their table was bare except for two drained disco lemonades. Diana wanted a daiquiri. Linda asked for wine. Steve found himself sinking into frustrated silence. The apt words always came effortlessly to Richard's lips, while they deserted his own. Richard's stare circled the pair with equal flattery. 'What's the play about, then?'

Diana said: 'It's a murder mystery.'

'Which of you gets killed?'

Linda smiled thinly. 'Perhaps we do the killing.'

Later Steve realised with astonishment that they talked for barely ten minutes; yet theirs was not a conversation, but a timeless ritual. While speaking about the theatre, the disco, the girls' musical tastes (Diana for Europop, Linda for jazz), they were exploring the sexual and personal possibilities of one another, playing, assessing, discarding.

In the mirror that covered the nearby wall, Steve glimpsed them round their table as if in another, unidentifiable world; there, to his surprise, he saw himself not wretchedly less than his brother. The same hair that curled crisply round Richard's head flew dark and loose around his own irregular features, so that he looked sensitised and even poetic in this dim light. That was what girls always said of him: he appeared romantically maverick.

Diana smiled and laughed at whatever Richard said. She was voluptuous, yet oddly shy. Her breasts cuddled in the cleft of her blouse. But Steve remained caged in an old expectation that the evening would escape him. He felt himself freezing, growing stupid. And he was seething with resentment. He was afraid to meet Linda's eyes. It took him long minutes to realise that she was not responding to Richard at all. She was uninterested in him. She was looking at Steve. Through the din of techno he heard her words only in isolation. 'So after Peterborough . . . What kind of photography? . . . Can you do portraits? . . . Acting unmasks you, it's funny . . . You really want to? . . . It's actually a shitty play . . . Monday at the stage door, then . . .' and he could not later remember the words he had responded with. By now the DJ was mixing in more soulful sounds, and the dance floor thinning out, while Linda's eyes went on drowning him.

There's a groove in my soul
And you're turning there, turning,
Turning to me again . . .

Richard had thrown one arm around Diana's shoulder, like a scarf. He was grinning at Steve. 'I thought you said you were going to leave early.'

'I got stuck.'

They both laughed. Steve saw a change in Richard's face, as if, belatedly, his brother had noticed his excitement. For long minutes Richard had backed away from speaking with Linda, and before they left, he touched Steve's forearm in passing collusion.

Steve reached the stage door an hour before the play ended. He had tried to postpone an appointment eighty miles away, but failed, and had raced back after borrowing Richard's car, his eyes darting between the road and the dashboard clock.

It seemed a narrow, secret door compared to the public entrance. Linda had called it the door of disillusion. The people who went in and out, she'd said, were like everybody else, only smaller than you'd expect.

At nine o'clock the sky was still pale with early summer. There was nobody much about. Sometimes a coldness stirred in his chest. And waiting here turned him furtive. When he peered through the stage door's glass panel, he saw a porter at a desk. Then he read the playbill again, but only the two stars were billed there, and the playwright's name was unknown to him. For a long time nobody emerged from the door or went in. The street lights came on. Towards ten o'clock the audience flooded on to the neighbouring street. There were sounds of cars, laughter. A group of students gathered at the stage door, and a tall young man whom Steve feared might have something to do with Linda. He stood back in the shadows, suddenly wretched. It was the old, engulfing fear quickening his breath like a physical sickness. But when she appeared, she hesitated, alone, in the doorway, her duffel bag dropped at her feet, until she saw him.

'I thought you might have forgotten!' she said.

He had booked at an Italian restaurant nearby: an old-fashioned bistro, candlelit. As they entered, he imagined every customer turning to stare at her. The flush of acting was still on her, a vivid afterglow. Although the evening was warm, she was wearing a white blouse buttoned close at the neck, and this obscurely pleased him. He remembered the shimmer of her breasts as she had danced. Only while she read the menu did he dare gaze at her. Her face, as its faint blush ebbed away, took on an opalescent pallor. The long slant of her lowered eyes made dark-lashed crescents which fixed him helplessly when they lifted. She said: 'Why are you staring at me? Am I looking strange?'

He averted his gaze and fumbled with the menu, but for a moment could not read it, as if his eyes' focus was still fixed across the table. Awkwardly he asked: 'How was the premiere?' He remembered the audience pouring on to the street: shouting, laughter.

She said: 'There was no real response. Just the kind of clapping people do to convince themselves they've enjoyed something. And now we have two weeks of acting a failure.' She shivered. 'I'll have the lasagne. What will you have? The audience laughed a bit, sometimes in the wrong places. But it's a lousy play. We've gone round telling each other "Isn't it great? Isn't it ingenious?" but at heart we knew it was crap. Sometimes I think it would be better just to step aside and announce to the audience: Go home! Money back!'

She said this with a kind of hardy vivacity, at once amused and a little stricken.

He asked: 'Who do you play?'

'A betrayed wife.' She opened her hands as if to release something. They were slender and fine-boned, unadorned. 'But I can't find her.'

'What do you mean?'

'Her words are dead. There's no person in there. I need a way into her character. But I can't find one.'

He'd meant to joke, but the words came out tense: 'Perhaps you've never been betrayed.'

She laughed: a quick, low sound that told him nothing. 'Usually you start to understand a role in rehearsal. Your character takes shape alongside the others. But our director's lost his way. He's tired, I think. So the actors start hamming it up. It's a kind of insecurity. Then the play falls apart. Of course it was never together in the first place . . .'

Later, in the quiet of his bedroom, he would realise how inextricably this fascination for her was bound up with what she did, with a stage presence that he could already imagine. Even the way she lifted her fork to her lips seemed delicate and extraordinary to him, as did the pursed mobility of her mouth when she spoke, with a darting intensity that might haunt an audience.

Photographer

When she asked him about his work, he was relieved that he need not pretend. Alongside more humble assignments, he was starting to receive commissions for photographic portraits. Compulsively he set himself to reflect his subjects' inner life. The challenge, he told her, was less a matter of manipulated light or photographic angle than of some unconscious disclosure in his sitters, some essence unique to them. He wanted his sitters to confront the camera head-on.

'Perhaps you'd prefer them naked.' She was laughing. 'And what do they think of the results?'

Those could be unsettling and occasionally cruel, he admitted. Sometimes his sitters' relatives were more pleased than they were, as if something unrecognised had been revealed. Often he was asked to revert to more conventional portraiture, to create flattery.

Linda asked suddenly, still laughing a little: 'Do you believe people have essences?'

Yes, he hunted for something like that. Even in landscape. Recently, he said, he had taken to walking along the South Downs. There were places there that tantalised him, where the view extended beyond the copses and hedges that sliced up the fields, until the fields themselves became foreshortened and then disappeared, and it looked as though a seamless forest was flowing to the hills. Obsessively he would descend to wander among these scattered woods. He could not photograph without this experience of them. Because the woods had become a visual forest, and the forest must have a heart. Perhaps, he said, it was like trying to fathom a theatrical character. He reached across and touched her fingers where they rested on the table: they did not recoil. What did she think?

She said: 'I think you're a fruitcake.'

'What?

'You're nuts. Your forests are an illusion. Illusions don't have hearts.' Then she saw she'd disconcerted him, and burst into husky laughter. 'Well, I guess I just don't get it. I had a camera once and I dropped it in a river. It had shots of my old boyfriend on it and I thought: that's the end of him!'

He smiled at her, but said with sudden pleading: 'I'll show you, Linda. I'll show you what the camera can do. Let me photograph you.' He thought instantly: but where? Not back at his flat, with Richard. 'I'll come to your place, on Sunday.'

'But will you find my essence? I can't.' Her mockery at once ravished and maddened him. 'I look inside me and there's a blur. Maybe that's why I'm an actor. I think I can be anybody. We can all change places.' She went quiet, and toyed with the wine bottle. He had ordered a vintage Chianti Classico, pricier than he could afford, and emptied it into their glasses. She said: 'My parents knew a brain surgeon once who said there's no real heart to us, just synapses firing at one another, or something.' Her eyes shone on and off his face. 'And my father's a vicar!'

'What does he think of your going on stage?'

'He wants to love it, but my changes of character upset him.' She snapped off the dripping candle wax, and aligned its fragments like people. 'He thinks I have a soul.'

'Of course. Who wouldn't? You're so . . .' I must stop this, he thought, she'll guess I'm falling hopelessly in love with her. 'You're very defined.'

'Am I? Well I believe in other people's reality. They may even have souls, for all I know.' He remembered this moment months later, but wondered at the time only if the drink had gone to her head. 'Other people may exist.'

He did not know what to say. She seemed half serious. He murmured: 'I'll photograph you on Sunday. Then you'll be unmistakable.'

'Why don't I come to your place?'

'That's hard. I share it with Richard, my brother.'

'Oh, was he your brother? I didn't realise.'

'We're not much alike.' He heard the distaste in his own voice. 'He's much more mature.'

'Sorry.' She put down her wine glass. 'I thought he was a jerk.'

'That's okay.' He was pleased, of course, relieved.

'Then you come to me. I'm sharing digs with Diana. So you can photograph me in the right setting. Squalid bed-sheets, worn-out carpets. The glamour of theatre life.'

The auditorium was almost full. He looked down the cast list and found her as the lights dimmed. Linda Spalva. The name fitted her. Her paternal grandfather had been Latvian, she'd said, a refugee from the Second World War. Hence, perhaps, her wide-set gentian-blue eyes. He had drunk himself to death in Glasgow.

The curtain rose on an empty Edwardian drawing room. He felt nervous for her. Might she forget her lines?

Or freeze, or trip up? But when she came on – the last to do so – he scarcely recognised her. Her ground-length skirt flared down from a sashed waist, and her hair was swept up beneath a huge sloping hat. During her few scenes, she barely spoke. She suffered. All her animation, her febrile, birdlike intensity, was corseted in a poised tension. He could not take his eyes from her. In her stillness, it seemed, she projected a terrible pent-up sorrow, and when she spoke the words that she had found meaningless, they came with devastation. '*There is nothing . . . nothing that you can do for me now. I have no more love for you. Was there anything worth loving in Judas?*'

Each evening until Sunday he returned to the stalls to watch her. He forgot what the play was about, if he had ever known, and experienced only the astonishment of her presence: the carved beauty of her features, the fragile figure in its cream lace gown, the surprising low voice. Even when she did nothing, and the stage around her teemed with action, he saw only her.

On the fourth day her place was taken by an understudy – nobody explained why – and his gaze widened to take in the whole stage. Then he realised that an entire play had been going on around her: other actors, other emotions. There were movements and speeches that he had never registered. They creaked with cliché. But on Saturday she returned, and once more he was sitting in the dark like a voyeur, elated and faintly guilty, and her intensity suffused the stage again. *There is nothing . . . nothing that you can do for me now . . .* As he gazed at her – he had bought opera glasses – he saw close up her ravaged face and the still blaze of her eyes and the bitterness of her full lips, and her breast heaving, and could not believe that he might be with her next morning; nor did he understand that when the actors took their curtain call the applause for her was not tumultuously louder than for the others, and he did not dare wait for her at the stage door, in case she could not meet him tomorrow after all, and he saw indifference in her eyes.

He took a taxi to her rented rooms, piling his equipment beside him. He had dressed with careful casualness, but he glimpsed his face in the taxi mirror. It was too pale. He had barely slept. When he did, she had entered his dreams. He thought: her enigma will be dispelled by the morning light. A thin rain was falling. The streets were empty. Within ten minutes he was standing with his lamps and cameras on her doorstep.

Her rooms were run-down, she was right: two bedsits with a shared bathroom. He set up his lights and reflectors in cramped corners. She sat on the edge of the bed. Fastidiously, almost reverently, he positioned and lit her. She was very still. He was hypnotised by her changes of expression, even in this stillness. Sometimes she looked starkly inconsolable, her eyes downcast into long almonds. At others a perennial mischief surfaced, and her torso – he was starting to photograph her body too – arched teasingly, and her smile turned ironic. At last she grew impatient. Hadn't he had enough of her? No, he hadn't. There were only so many lights and camera angles, weren't there? There seemed no limit, he said.

Finally she rebelled and lay back on the bed, pretending to snore. He switched off the lamps and leant over her.

She opened her eyes. For a second the air between them was a vacuum of suspense, then her gaze pulled him down. Fearfully, helplessly, he stooped and kissed her lips.

Later he would remember the room in intimate detail: the lopsided curtain rail, the tarnished wardrobe mirror, the pattern of the wallpaper (a trellis of blue roses) behind her head as he lay beside her afterwards for a sated eternity, dazed by the gentian eyes that seemed now part of himself, or nearly, the life of him poured out into her, and she laughing a soft laugh of contentment.

Towards noon they fell asleep in one another's arms. Diana looked in, and tiptoed away. He woke to the hardening rain outside. He stretched out, as if released from something, and held Linda's hand under the sheets. The sky was darkening beyond the window. In the room's dimness the tripods and spectral lamps were still standing around them. Awake, naked, they exchanged random intimacies. He breathed out his anger at his father, and his intermittent solitude – now dispelled by her – and listened to her childhood, which he had started to romanticise, imagining an only child brought up by pious parents in a windy vicarage. But she cut him short. Her father was a hot-headed, faintly ludicrous figure, she said, whose sermons were full of Latin idioms inherited from her grandfather. As for herself, she had been an ungrateful, rebellious daughter. She disliked everything she learnt about God. At the age of seventeen she had an abortion, arranged by her distraught mother. Her father went on loving her, to her mind absurdly.

As for Steve, his boyhood, when he spoke of it, sounded constrained and colourless. But he was afraid to admit to her his inner shaking, how parts of himself were torn away from him, especially at night, so that when his father left – coldly, without warning – it only confirmed an apprehension that had tormented his childhood: nothing was stable, or lasted.

Linda asked gently: 'Did you ever dream of another life?'

Yes, he said. As a boy he thought he might become a surgeon or even a priest: anyone devoted to what he conceived as human essence, whatever did not disintegrate. But his mother had favoured the law or banking.

'Not photography?'

'She said I'd become as useless as my father.' But his mother had not been dead a year, and he could not talk of her. He asked abruptly: 'And what else would you have done?'

Nothing else, she said. She ached to play the complex, meaty women of Ibsen and Strindberg, but her appearance was dead against it. She smiled a little bitterly. 'Why was I born with these stupid looks? I've got the character of Lady Macbeth in the body of Ophelia.'

'Stupid?' He was able to tell her now, without constraint, how heart-rendingly beautiful she was.

She drummed her fingers on his chest, and gave her self-mocking laugh. 'You have funny taste in women.' But she was smiling.

When his photographic prints arrived back from the laboratory the following week, he was baffled. He had been beguiled by her looks. They had tempted him to employ the flattering clichés that he despised, and of which she had no need: the classic turn of the shoulder, the elbows free from her waistline, the placement of her hands. He had angled her face two-thirds from the camera, and had deployed a broad, near-frontal light source that crept illumination round her whole face and blurred its shadows into softened highlights. The delicate translucence of her skin was lost. She looked beautiful, of course, but no longer unique, curiously like others.

But his chief failure was elsewhere. He had also posed her facing his lens full-on. It was an unflattering practice, sometimes heartlessly revelatory, always in black and white. His wide-aperture lens gave a shallow depth of field that misted away the cheap wallpaper and everything else behind her. She emerged from this fog in violent chiaroscuro. He had risked a higher reflector light on her astonishing eyes, which now slanted out of darkness. Eyes that sloped backwards, he realised, were impenetrably difficult to encompass. Some part of hers seemed always to elude the camera, as if they should be shot from many angles at once. Above all he had asked her not to smile, and perhaps it was this that emptied her of any expression he recognised. Her face had taken on the stark definition of a mask. He wondered if the diffuser had slipped from one of his lamps or if he should have used a texture screen to soften her. She was stonily enigmatic. He even blamed the processing laboratory.

He may have imagined that in photographs he could possess her. Just as when abroad he never thought he had experienced a place unless he had framed and shot it, so now the feeling that she had eluded him, that he might never grasp her, rankled miserably. His lens had lost her in a collage of ungiving surfaces.

To distract himself, he dusted down his old Canon cine camera and shot impromptu sequences of his flat, of the seafront, and of her. Filming might not distil a subject's psyche as a photographic portrait could, but it was harder to coerce. Nobody in film could preserve for long the rictus of a photographic smile. They walked in the illusion of the present, grounded in voice and movement. Yet they too were transient and ungraspable. And they were never quite themselves. Before the cine camera they simpered and buffooned or simply walked off as if into reality.

Linda watched herself on screen with indifference, but she leafed happily through the still photographs that he hated. She murmured: 'Yes, that's me all right . . . Why are you so upset? . . . That one's quite good . . . and this one's me . . .' She did not seem to realise how the photos reduced her.

He followed her despised play to Manchester and on to Sheffield. She found new digs, and they shared a narrow bed. He motored half the night between her venues and his work. Her life backstage held a rarefied novelty for him. Its warren of dressing rooms and lavatories seemed extemporised and spartan compared to the affluence of the auditorium, and her fellow actors were like an alien clan to him.

But she did not go into the unemployment she had feared. Instead she was cast at once in a new play, which she admired: an exacting and uneven piece, she said, but her role was real. Several times he inveigled himself into the studio rehearsals, but the action was so often interrupted by the director – a nervous, elfin woman – that he never heard its language flow. Her part was larger than before. To his surprise she was playing a woman older than herself: a biologist whom she described as austere, and lesbian. He wondered how she could encompass such a woman. She was surely too mercurial, too fragile. He was afraid she'd been miscast.

In the evening, in the cramped London flat that she shared with two absent actresses, she appeared to struggle over the words. She was not trying to memorise them, she said, but to hear a tone of voice. She was hunting for a way into the character. Over three weeks of rehearsal she hoped that interplay with the cast would internalise the role for her. She drank many mugs of coffee, even late at night, and dropped into nervous study or effervescent banter. They made obliterating love. After two weeks she could reel off her part verbatim – the words of a mature woman in love with a dreamy girl – but the role had not yet inhabited her, and she was afraid it never would.

Then one evening he arrived late to the flat to find her calmly transformed. This melding with a scripted character, mysterious to him, had happened to her while rereading the play on the underground returning home. The key had been staring her in the face, she said, in a stage direction for her role:

'SAMANTHA [*regretfully*]: There are things you'll come to understand.'

The girl who beguiles Samantha is young and idealistic. In her, the older woman is looking on innocence. It attracts and saddens her. That is the clue to her: she is falling in love with the girl she used to be.

Photographer

Three days before the premiere, he drove Linda up to Peterborough, where they rented a garret opposite the theatre, near the cathedral square. The director, she said, refused to allow any outsider to watch dress rehearsals, so Steve strolled with a camera around the old town, marooned in modern development, and cooked simple suppers for her return. Now she apologised for her mental absence: the role was eating her wholesale. She had become more sombre and authoritative, he noticed. Her sudden smile had disappeared, and her voice had darkened.

One day she said she would go shopping alone, but returned from wandering round the supermarket having bought nothing. She had followed teenage girls there, conjuring in the mind of her protagonist the lure of their innocence, imagining being in love with one, in love with a self she had lost.

For some reason this disturbed him. He exclaimed: 'Loss of innocence! You're too young to feel that!' Then he wondered about her age. He'd imagined her a year or two older than him, but had never asked.

A woman sits in a darkened laboratory, staring at her hands. For a long time she does not move. Behind her head a wall map of South America is superscribed with butterfly species, according to region. But this is a stage designer's pedantry, too intricate for the audience to read, and the footlights are dim.

He imagines, after the curtain lifts, that the woman is Linda, obscured by a greying wig and glasses. But no, this is the leading actress, reflecting on her past as the lights fade. He feels his whole body tingling. He has no idea what will come. Once again, when Linda walks on set, he does not recognise her. A stately woman, perhaps thirty years old, is crossing the stage to conduct a seminar. She seems in sharper, more vivid focus than everybody else. Her hair has turned auburn. She moves with athletic ease. She even gives an illusion of height.

Again, within a minute, he sees nobody but her. There are other characters, of course – a father, a sister, an older man – but her darkly spoken intelligence and the frozen blaze of her eyes consume the theatre. He watches her with reignited love. Is her script so much finer than the others'? And her intuition was right. Her young beloved hardens from enchantment with the intricate beauty of insects to their classification and behavioural analysis, and her personal life goes in parallel: from idealistic delight to adult knowledge and sorrow. Linda's premonitory 'There are things you'll come to understand', which he has heard her rehearsing in the bathroom, is suddenly heartbreaking. She is both foreseeing and remembering. This, it seems, is the play's core: a kind of lyrical and necessary disillusion.

Towards the end, when their first embrace brings a gasp from the packed house, he is amazed by the plausibility of her love for her partner – a petite and faintly insipid actress, he thinks. And the curtain comes down on the play's only sentimental lapse, as they walk away from the audience across a field of asphodel.

That evening, after a restaurant supper with a subdued cast – the audience response had been mistrustful – they walked back to their garret in silence. He imagined her disappointed, but she was not, she said. She was walking with the supple stride of her stage persona, and her close-cropped hair, cut to accommodate the auburn wig, lent her an odd, chiselled boyishness.

That night, when he took her in his arms, he knew he was embracing a different woman. Her habitual vivacity had stilled to a new, purposive control. She twisted on top of him and applied her lips to his chest, his throat. He felt bemused for a minute, then compliant, excited. She stared down at him with a kind of triumphant tenderness. His grip came to rest on her thighs. His gaze reached up to hers, saw someone he barely knew. He felt her hands over him, kneading him like earth: she who had seemed so frail.

Over the next weeks he succumbed to this changed lovemaking. His body grew sensitised and self-aware. Under her hands and mouth, beneath the new strength of her arms, he sometimes felt himself diffusing, as if his body's limits were no longer his. When he breathed 'I love you', he was less sure whom he meant. He felt an inchoate gratitude. He was dissolving at her touch, becoming less known to himself, her tongue deep in his mouth. He dreamt he opened to her like a woman.

After the play closed, and the theatre reverted to its routine roster of musicals and melodramas, and Linda returned to her London flat, there was no more work. She took a job as a temping secretary, while Steve's assignments for a provincial newspaper queued up in a humdrum procession of subjects that bored him: sitters characterised only by their function, shot against background offices, council chambers or sports venues.

When she received work again, the part was light and clownish, created for a slapstick comedy. But now he was wary of saying she had been miscast. He could not tell. She said she could become anybody, given time. She had spent all her childhood in self-created pantomime, pretending to be others. Anyone but her.

She travelled with her play for eight weeks, while he sporadically followed. She had returned to her impetuous self. They made love in the wings of empty theatres, in dressing rooms, under a seaside pier at night. By the year's end he had followed her through three more roles. And always there was the struggle to inhabit her new character. She achieved this once by recalling a cousin eerily similar to the woman she was playing. Her cousin's fluttering gestures and facial tic gave Linda her entry into the role's psyche. Another time, when some final understanding eluded her, she stepped before dress rehearsal into her costume – a skimpy cocktail dress – and the last clue fell into place.

Steve wondered how deep these transformations went. Were they ever quite abandoned? 'No,' she answered. 'They become extensions of you. Like a bad haircut. It's you and not you.' She primped up her hair comically. 'After the show's over, you think they're gone. But no. Once they're created, they stick around, waiting. Angry nurse, comedienne, gay biologist. They're like ghosts inside you. You can summon them back.'

As if to free her from such alter egos, he redeveloped the negatives of the photographs he had taken months before. They seemed now less shamefully mute than he had thought. She appeared decently herself in them, spirited and pretty, a little older than he had expected. Often he had strained too hard in lighting her, or posed her pretentiously. They were portraits in the image of his desire. No wonder she sometimes looked uneasy. It was in his cine films that she seemed most artlessly real. Their sequences were spontaneous. She was often fooling around. Sometimes she even looked ordinary, and this bewildered him. He was growing tired, he thought, he had studied her too often. He filed the films away.

It was at a theatre in the West Country, somewhere he later forgot. He had driven half the day to attend her first night. But the play was poor; and on stage, for the first time, she seemed no different from the rest. He found himself no longer focusing on her, but following the drama's facile development. She was playing an overworked nurse, and her words were as dead as the others'. Some radiance had gone. He blamed the play for this. It had surely deprived her of any motivation. But her recent roles – a teacher, a housewife – were of women without stature or allure, and she had not been able to quicken them. In the interval he was surprised at the audience's applause. He must be jaded, he thought. He went to the washroom and doused his head in its basin. But the play's second half seemed no better.

He found her at her dressing room counter with her head sunk on her arms. The mirror's opal lights shone harsh on her white neck. She said: 'That fucking director cut half my lines. I must have sounded idiotic.'

'You didn't . . .'

'He thought I got it wrong in rehearsal. I didn't, I had my own interpretation. Or maybe I did get it wrong. I don't know. He's a prick.' Her voice came muffled from her buried head. 'I don't know.'

He stood behind her, touched her shoulders. They were shaking. Her skin looked sallow. Her head jerked up and she stared into the glass. Her cheeks were blotched with mascara. She said: 'And that side lighting . . . they should ban it. They did some publicity shots on stage and I looked a hundred.'

Somebody knocked on the door and she swivelled round. She was hoping, he could tell, that a fellow actor was looking in to praise her. But it was a stage hand, trying the wrong room.

She said: 'Maybe I should give this thing up.'

He saw himself standing behind her in the mirror, a shadow. He could find nothing to say. In her anger she looked soured and ordinary. On her dressing table her scattered powders and deodorants appeared sordid to him, and he could not understand her eyes. They had grown unsettled, almost ugly. She said: 'Why the hell can't you say anything? I can tell you didn't like the show, but why . . .'

'I may be wrong. The audience liked it.'

'The audience! This audience are idiots.' She started to change into her daytime dress, throwing her costume into a basin. This stripping of her dress over her breasts and shoulders used to arouse him. Now he felt only frozen apprehension. He stared at the floor. She would not focus on him, only on his reflection in the mirror. She said: 'I don't want to be looked at.' He tried to find words that would not hurt. Her eyes looked wild and lost. 'You can't say anything, can you? Except that I can't act and I look like shit.' He watched her struggling into a rain-coat, stretching a woollen cap over her head. Then she said: 'You'd better drive back.'

It died as suddenly as it had begun. Something vital in her had faded. It seemed to have left her overnight. She appeared immersed in the deadness of her recent roles, as if they had subsumed or inhabited her. Perhaps, after all, it was true that she existed most brightly in the characters of others: she who believed in their existence more than in her own.

The café was not one he had chosen. There were too many other customers. The window beside them side-lit her face in the way she hated on stage. She looked taut and pale. Their hands lay inert on the table.

'Why did you want to see me?' she asked, as if this was a business meeting. Two days had gone by before he had returned. 'I have to be back in the theatre by noon.' Her hands came up to her face, cradling her cup. He sensed her pent-up anger. At last she said: 'You want to end us, don't you?' She made it sound like a suicide pact.

He felt this frozen silence coming over him, but he said hoarsely: 'I can't tell . . .' Then the words choked on his guilt.

She said in the same formal voice: 'What has changed, then?'

He wanted to say: You have. Even her eyes no longer seemed extraordinary. They were dull grey. But he only answered: 'I don't know. Something has.'

'You don't know much, do you?' Now she was set implacably on a course of her own. She could not stop herself. She said: 'Do you even know how old I am?'

Softly: 'No.'

'That's because you don't notice a damn thing. You live in a dream of your own. Do you realise you've never understood anything about me? Nothing. You've just fantasised about me. Gawping from the theatre dark, that's you. Admiring a fantasy.' She made a noise like spitting. 'Well I'm not a goddam fantasy. I'm real. Does that shock you? And I'm thirty-one years old.'

He stared at her. She stared defiantly back. Now that he knew her age, he had the illusion that she was altering before his eyes. But he said: 'I don't care about your age. To me you were beautiful.'

'Were.' She lifted the coffee cup to her face again. For a second he thought she was choking: a sound between coughing and a sob. He reached awkwardly to touch her arm, but it flinched away. When she recovered her voice, it was stone hard. 'Has it occurred to you, Steve, that you're a bit of a phoney?'

'What do you mean?'

'All this gawking at faces and landscapes like they were hiding something! Your drivel about essences! No, it's appearances that obsess you. Just looks.'

He started to blush: a reaction since childhood. Whenever accused, however falsely, he blushed. But he was glad to avenge himself: 'I'm just doing what you do. Trying to discover a centre, a character. It's no different, Linda' – but her name sounded alien now – 'except that what you do doesn't last, does it? It's gone in a week or two. What's left is just publicity shots of it. Photographs. They may be lousy, but they're all that's left.'

He saw her teeth clench, but did not know whether from anger or wretchedness. She stood up abruptly. 'I have to go now.'

He knew she did not. It was barely eleven o'clock. Her voice sounded throaty and distant. His rancour vanished as he thought: so she's leaving. He would not see her again. He heard himself say: 'What will you do now?' He meant in future months, in years.

She thought a moment, suddenly laughed. 'I'll go back to Act One. That's what actors do. Every night.'

He stood too, as if to embrace her, but her hands deflected him, palms outwards, trembling in the air between them. 'Don't.' She was looking at him suddenly with a brimming sadness. Then she pushed past him to the door.

He made as if to stop her. He could resist her anger, but not her tears. But she did not see. He would have asked her back. Yet he was glad, in the end, that he did not.

Browsing the Internet's disordered dreams, you come upon advice about the make-up for slanted eyes: how eyeliner can extend the lower lid until it almost meets the artfully tilted eyebrow above. There are misguided sites for plastic surgery to reduce eye slant; others that expose how the look may be mistakenly created through a facelift. There are Chinese blessed with a canthic tilt at the eye's outer edge, and beautiful black women who look like cats.

He scrolled through images with a hypnotised weariness. It was like a sickness, in which days could go by. He missed five work assignments. He gazed on these faces as if they were fictions (and some of them were). And he walked the streets. For months his mind had pictured only her, blinding him to anyone else around him. Now, with distant fascination, he noticed women passing in the shops, women in advertisements, women on magazine covers.

He trawled the web for Linda's reflection, and found Korean actresses and narrow-eyed Finns and even bird-like cartoon figures. Only once did he come upon her as he first remembered her, or almost, but he never located the website again. Her photographs made him long for her too much, and he burned them. Her attack on him still ached from time to time, like an embedded splinter. She was wrong, of course, appearances were more than surfaces. The smallest facial feature might betray the character. Even the first, faint start of flesh beneath the breastbone – he had captured hers on his Leica – disclosed something uniquely personal and inward. He saw a woman on television – a svelte dancer – in whom this intimation was so unbearably eloquent that he wanted to meet her; but she danced only in the show's background, and it was impossible to tell, from the credits, who she was.

He discovered a computer game called Quest for the Grail. Its hero had to navigate labyrinthine castles, scaling battlements and forcing gates, then entered passageways whose doors succeeded one another into near-infinity. He unlocked chambers whose curtained walls must be parted to reveal something else, and something beyond that, in ever-delayed promise. And all this he could play from a keypad. He took mistaken byways and dead ends, of course – his hero was only human – but returned to penetrate farther and deeper, until the game closed because of his banked-up mistakes.

The hero then returned to the start. Scroll down beneath him and the legend read: 'I will never surrender'. He knew this was a ploy of the game's manufacturer, to make him try again. But he thought: this time . . .

This time the last curtain will part. It may be days before I reach the end, but the doors will open one by one. I know them better now. At certain points you may announce your decision aloud, so that my hero's voice intones: 'I choose the second door on the left, to enter the green chamber . . .' If you are adroit, your appointed route will reach a perfect end. But I can't tell what this end is. I make too many mistakes. I go into the wrong halls, or wander down corridors to nowhere.

It is hard to wrench myself from this fantasy back into sunlit life. But today I have to photograph a church wedding. It's a long time since I did that. The groom, a young businessman, stands a foot taller than his bride, who walks up the aisle on her father's arm with a look of terror under her veil. She is fair and plump. I shoot some close-ups near the altar, but the couple's disparity in height turns these ludicrous, and the priest's bald head wobbles between them like a light bulb. As the congregation stands to sing 'Love Divine, All Loves Excelling' one of the small bridesmaids drops her bouquet and starts to walk out. The congregation splits into laughter or alarm. But the senior bridesmaid – a beautiful young woman – shepherds the child into her arms, and holds her there.

I struggle to find light readings from the chiaroscuro of the chancel, but I capture the moment of their vows, she inaudible, he booming like a major-domo. Their return down the aisle, her veil thrown back from a face now smiling, and their exit in a snowfall of confetti are ideal to the camera, and behind them the small bridesmaid is toying with her coronet of honeysuckle, as if for my lens. The couple's parents join them for a photo shoot in the porch, and for a while I see nothing but faces shining in the June heat, garnished with wide hats and buttonholes. The bridesmaids stand brilliant in shell-pink satin, while the bride and groom gaze at one another as though surprised at what they've done. Then, as I pan for close-ups, there swims into my viewfinder the unearthly radiance of two oblique green eyes. For a moment they are looking straight into the lens, as if into my own, then they veer away and are lost among the others.

In the ballroom of a neighbouring hotel, where the canapés and champagne circulate among a throng of unphotogenic guests, I concentrate on whoever looks important. I know this now. There are people who carry with them a petty aura of prestige, and when my photos are at last submitted to the bride's parents, they are sure to grumble: 'But there aren't any of . . .' and 'But where is Lady . . .?' I do my best. The groom's father, at least, is a handsome man, and I manage some canny shots of guests laughing at the best man's fatuous speech.

Then I find her. She is standing alone, not laughing, and the satin that looks pretty on the smaller bridesmaids falls from her bare shoulders in a coral-coloured sheen, shaping itself to a tall figure with high breasts. She looks, at this moment, very young. Those strange, vivid eyes meet the probing of my camera with a wide, innocent stare.

When the speeches end, the bride's father bustles over and gathers the couple for another photo shoot. My lights are already set up in a nearby room, but the bridal pair and their officious parents take up such unnatural poses that I have constantly to realign them, even while I fear that next door some guests, perhaps she, are filtering away.

And when I return, she is gone. The groom offers me a champagne glass, but it shakes uncontrollably in my hand and I have to set it down. Less than twenty minutes, and she is gone. I search the corridors and the car park. My stomach aches. When the couple reunite to cut the wedding cake, she still does not appear, and I photograph the stilted ceremony from every angle, while the Leica quivers in my fingers and my eyes wander. As soon as it is over, I stack away my cameras and make for the lavatories. I think I will be sick. My legs judder over the carpets. I retch into the basin, but nothing comes. A throbbing starts up in my head. Two guests come in to pee, laughing together. I glimpse my face in the mirror, smooth back my hair.

Out in the passageway, from the opposite door, the entrance to the women's washrooms, the small bridesmaid emerges with drying tears, and turns to hug her as she follows behind, then runs back to the party. I stare stupidly into her eyes. She has her back to the passage wall. She says: 'Oh, you're the photographer.'

The photographer. How did she say it? I can't recall. But I read a kind of contempt. I am not one of the guests. I am just the photographer, an employee. I hear my voice detached, saying things I do not mean to say, separate. 'Oh I'm not the photographer. I'm just helping somebody. Sort of . . .'

She is looking at me with that terrible innocence. My words fade. What am I saying? She asks: 'What do you do, then?'

Is she really interested? She looks like a Raphael Madonna. A coil of auburn hair, twisted with gardenias, falls down her back. And the same voice, my own, answers: 'I'm training to be a priest.' How does this happen? It must be her face, its unworldly gaze. Perhaps it's the flowers in her hair, or the marriage service. The moment the words leave me, I regret them, but I cannot take them back. I say: 'What do you do?'

'I work for a house agent.' She adds the name, as if I might know it.

I ask: 'Who are you, then?' This is gauche, blatant. I want to choke myself.

'I'm Rebecca Ryan. Who are you?'

Oh God. I'm not the photographer. Who am I? 'I'm David Sykes,' I say. Where did he come from? I am falling down a black hole, deeper with every word. I will never reach the bottom. Do I think David Sykes sounds grand? My smile is a wavering plea, a plea for forgiveness for something unadmitted. Her eyes are still on me, and I do not know if their purity sees right through me, or if innocence sees nothing at all.

Then she says: 'I have to follow that little urchin.' She gestures to where the small bridesmaid has disappeared. 'She's grazed her knee.'

Then she's gone.

I clutch her name to me. Haunting alliteration. I even know where to find her. That is miracle enough. I cushion my lamps and cameras back inside the car. I must reverse the lie I've set in motion. I must become myself again.

Richard has left. He has gone to a new job in Glasgow, where his fiancée will follow him: a sourly pretty girl named Sheila. It is our mother's death, I think, that spurred his change. I do not know what it has done to me. I talk to her in the night sometimes. Of course the flat is emptier without Richard. I miss our rivalry. I miss talking about our mother, which keeps her alive. We scattered her ashes under Telscombe cliffs. I don't know why it feels so cold here, in June. Often I cannot feel my legs at all. I should stop taking dope.

When my mother's legacy comes through, I'll buy a place of my own. But it's not for this that I scan a list of local house agents and recognise the name of Rebecca's. It's in the town centre, and when I walk past, keeping to the far side of the street, I see her sitting at a computer almost in the window. She is dressed in jeans and a white blouse. I open the door on an avenue of desks. She is seated at its end, her head lowered. Before I can reach her, a young man calls out, 'Can I help you?' and motions me to a chair. He hands me a form to fill in: accommodation requirements, price range, mortgage position. I dare not look at her. I imagine her scrutiny on the side of my face. Those astonishing eyes could read everything I write. So I fill in my name as David Sykes, but I add the right address and calculate a higher price than I can pay.

The man is eager and puppyish. 'I'll assign you to somebody,' he says.

'Thank you.' I don't meet his eyes. I walk over without waiting and sit down on the chair in front of her.

She looks up coolly. No trace of recognition. I offer a hesitant smile. She reads my completed form, and no flicker of familiarity crosses her face. I might have dreamed our meeting. She reaches behind her for an assortment of particulars, and wonders if I would prefer a period property or something more modern. How important is a garage? Off-street parking is an increasing asset. Do I need a garden? Oh, so I'd prefer something out of town, somewhere secluded. Not too easy to find nowadays. Her laugh is a distant tinkle. She alights on the brochure of a cottage beyond the north-east suburbs. 'It would need modernising,' she says. I imagine it a wreck. 'I can arrange for somebody to meet you there.'

So I could have used my real name after all. She does not know me. I could have started anew. But I can find no excuse for writing down a false name. An inexplicable mistake? A joke? Now she is waiting for me to reply about the cottage, and I am staring into those slanted eyes. They are a beautiful, opaline green. I mumble at last: 'Yes, that's fine.'

Then, with no change of expression, she says: 'And how is God?'

'What?'

'You're studying for the priesthood.'

So she had remembered all along. I feel a rush of mixed relief and horror. She has burst into laughter.

Photographer

The cottage lies down a stony track on the edge of chalk pastures. I don't know if it is she who will meet me. The day is sultry, but I imagine the winter winds flailing over these fields. I can see through the windows that no one is here. In the derelict garden a concrete pool has filled with reeds, and a ginger cat vanishes into a flower bed overgrown with hollyhocks.

I could not live here. There is nothing to hold you in. No comfort in these open skies. You shiver beneath them. There is too much nothing already. I want an enclosed house, private, somewhere that embraces.

From a long way away I see a silver car on the track. It flashes like a warning in the sun. She emerges alone, holding a folder. She comes towards me smiling. I long to tell her my name, and what I do.

She says at once: 'Did you get time off from your seminary?'

'Yes, we're on holiday now.' The lie comes so easily.

She unlocks the cottage door, which jars open on a slur of junk mail. The smell of damp is overpowering. We walk through rooms that might have been abandoned years ago. But the beds are still made up, and half-empty jars of coffee stand coagulated on the kitchen shelves. When I pull a lace curtain, it falls to pieces in my hand. A dead sparrow lies on a window ledge. She says: 'The owner lives in Canada. He wants a quick sale. I'm sorry about the smell.'

Strange to linger with her at the foot of the double bed. Its blankets are pocked with moth holes. A tube of hand lotion still lies on the woman's table. His is bare. She says: 'I don't know why they left.' Her shoulder brushes against mine. I imagine a ghostly intimacy: theirs or ours. She says:

'I know it's pretty creepy. You have to imagine it empty, David.'

I feel light enough already, wandering in the lives of others. And now I have no name. And I've lost my profession. I say quickly: 'I can't imagine living here.'

'Frankly, nor can I. It must be grim in winter.' She goes into the bathroom.

I check my face in the bedroom mirror. I wonder who last looked in it. I'd imagined myself gaunt, white, perhaps not there at all. But instead I see a wild, ardent-looking face, lapped in chestnut hair.

We go outside with relief, and stand in the sun. She enjoys these encounters, she says. She likes to dovetail people and places. Sometimes buyers seem to know their houses in advance, and recognise them. Others are shocked by the discovery of what they love or what they can do without. She likes the dawning certainty in people's faces. She laughs about the downside: the drastic surveys, the gazumping, the office jealousies. She slips easily into mischief. She seems to trust me. Perhaps she trusts everyone. If her face were not lit by those magnetic eyes, she might appear naive. She says she knows what I want now. She has other properties. She'll be in touch. And all the time I am listening to the rhythm of her talking, slightly rasping and formal, then trickling into laughter. She has opened her car door before I say: 'Perhaps you'll have supper with me one evening?'

She looks startled for the first time, her eyes reassessing me. Then she says: 'I'd like that.'

I watch the silver car bumping and flashing back down the track. Her acceptance nestles warm inside me. I tell myself: I'm David Sykes. I'm a Christian believer. I'm studying in a London seminary. At least for now, until I know what to do. Perhaps I will one day live in a house of her choosing. But not here, not on a cold hillside. The silence is frightening. You need the sounds of others (but not too close). And the sky not infinite.

Before she comes to supper, I wipe out all traces of my previous identity: even the name on the doorbell. The absence of theological books is easily explained – the flat is Richard's, after all – but my photographer's lights and reflectors have to be stacked away in cupboards.

She sips my gazpacho soup and eats the overcooked cutlets with apparent pleasure, and is curious about everything: my vocation, my passions, my fractured background. I seem somehow wondrous to her. She comes from a solid home and private schooling. She glows with surety. Some bitterness surfaces in me, I know, when I think of my father's desertion and my own disrupted schooldays, and of Richard who escaped it all unscathed, and this jarring void of my mother's absence, even of her anger. Rebecca listens to me with her bright intensity. All evening I yearn for her lips, which are full and wide in her softly tapered face. And in the doorway, as she starts to leave, our formal embrace grows suddenly different, and we are kissing, and I feel her tautness against me, and her eyes piercing me before they close. We start talking there incongruously in the hall of the communal house, until I pull her back into the flat. A minute later we are entwined on the sofa, her blouse loosened, her back supple against my hands. She whispers that she is more confused by me than by anyone she's ever known – and she's already twenty-two.

'I can't be the first!'

Well, there was one other, she says, a mistake. She laughs. She is 'not quite' a virgin. And I? When I tell her about Linda and Cleo, they transform in my mind less as betrayals than as quiet preludes to herself. It is wrong, I know: lovers as stepping stones to one another. But that's how it feels. Later, lying on my bed, her auburn hair unlooses and flows over her shoulders. In loving, she becomes suddenly childlike and unsure. She stifles her cries of pleasure, as if apologising. She never opens her eyes. It is dawn when she wakes with a start and says she has to go. She is living with her parents, and must tiptoe in.

I feel old with her sometimes. She is impatient of any sadness or misgivings. Yet everything about me is deep and strange to her, she says. She thought so even at the wedding. I was so obsessed with what I was doing, I turned everyone else grey.

'I only felt obsessed when I was photographing you.'

It's true still. Our holidays last one day each, but I capture her in different lights and dress. Here she is in a garden by a wall of white roses, her own white beauty in regal profile, flushed by sunlight. And here standing in dappled woods, wearing a shirt I have opened on her breasts. Her eyes blaze green into the camera. And here she sits on a pier by the sea, muffled in pullovers against the louring sky, pretending to be drunk. And here statuesque on my balcony, in her black dress, her lips pursed in an uncompleted kiss.

But at times she grows gravely serious. Then she starts to ask about my future, about the seminary, and my faith. God has meant so little to her, I think, that she's neglected to disbelieve in Him. I wince inwardly at her questions. A month has gone by, and in theory I return to the seminary, and I start to invent again. I dread these times. I talk evasively, I know. She imagines I'm very private, and I am, oh hell, I am. When I'm with her, I fear meeting anyone I know. She thinks I'm friendless: a stubborn hermit. When she takes me to meet her parents, I can tell they don't like me. Her father questions me too closely. Rebecca says later that they're conservative and stuffy, explaining to herself whatever they've said about me. Impossible to go on with this, or end it.

Sometimes I accompany her to the houses she is selling. I see her infectious optimism. She ignites her duller clients by painting pictures of redecorated rooms and restored gardens, and conjures the magic of a cornice or a redesigned staircase. There is a luminous candour about her. Often she will blatantly point out some defect or eyesore, as if she were not really trying to sell the place. This frankness is not tactical. It is just what she thinks. But it elicits trust, of course, and occasional astonishment. Sometimes I try to imagine our house together.

I grow used to her calling me David. Steve is fading into a stranger. Last week I walked the grounds of a seminary in London, and mentally adopted it as mine. I've even read works of theology – Barth and Tillich – which were boring at first, but no longer. I think I understand the beauty of a belief I cannot hold. I people the seminary with friends, to satisfy her, and they take on deepening lives: an austere one, an innocent, an enigma. I create problems of doubt and conscience; I imagine a suicide. Are they so far from me? Sometimes, as before, I stare at my face in the mirror and it grows strange. Look long enough, and the reflection becomes someone else. I'm frightened, a little. My rooms here are now very dark and still.

It had to happen. It comes as we return from a peaceful day by the sea, the last one, I know now, the last peace. The moment I open my door I realise something is wrong. Rebecca says: 'Oh, I think your brother must be back.'

I should have retreated then, made some excuse, taken her home. But instead my mind goes numb. I sleep-walk behind her into the sitting room. And there he is, Richard, suave and boorish as usual, standing hands on hips, and all my photographic equipment – lights, tri-pods, battery packs, flash diffusers – piled up outside his bedroom door.

'Hullo, Steve, I got home early.' He thrusts out his hand to Rebecca. 'I'm Richard, Steve's brother.'

'Steve?'

Her hand extends woodenly to his. I glare at him hopelessly, signalling him to shut up, but he does not see, and if he did, he might not stop. How I hate him. He says: 'What the hell's all your photographer's stuff doing in my cupboards, Steve? Haven't you had any more commissions?'

Bewildered, Rebecca says: 'He's been at the seminary.'

'Seminary? Steve! What seminary?' He adds: 'Steve's an atheist.'

She stares at me. I will never forget her face. My own is burning, paralysed. I can't utter. Then the blood drains out of me.

Richard senses something at last. He says: 'I have a feeling I'm superfluous here', and picks up his car keys and leaves. Rebecca goes on gazing at me with a look of deep, frozen confusion. Then she whispers: 'Say something.'

'I don't know what to say.' Except that I feel I'm dying now.

'You're not David Sykes.' Her confusion is turning to horror. She asks: 'Who is David Sykes?' as if she might find him again.

'I don't know.'

'And the seminary . . . you're not at one at all. You don't even . . .'

I whisper: 'No.'

'So it was all lies. All the people you told me about. The one who hanged himself. Just lies.'

'It was a story.' Even now, I believe it a little. It's become another truth. Because I created it, it seemed to happen. But she can't know that.

Now her bewilderment has turned to a speechless revulsion. Her eyes are steel. She is staring at me as if I were not quite human, a reptile. At last she says: 'Why? Why?'

'I wanted to appeal to you . . .' How abject that sounds.

'You're mad,' she says. 'You must be.'

I gaze back into another face. I know she has gone from me. She belonged to David Sykes, and he never existed. She cannot bear to look at me any longer. Her bag had dropped to the floor at Richard's words, but now she hitches it on to her shoulder and shakes back her hair. She says: 'You can go back to being yourself . . . if you know who that is. But you go back without me.'

This building is starting to crumble, and the windows that face the shore leak and rattle in the wind. Bits of fallen plaster speckle the basement steps, and the flower box by my door sprouts dead geraniums. Richard has gone from our old flat, and I could not afford to pay double rent or bear to share the place again. I feel safer here, although it is suffused by damp. The other tenants mostly avert their eyes, afraid of conversation. Who the landlord is, I don't know. I pay my rent to an agent. Maybe there isn't a landlord at all.

Richard is unmoved by my anguish, of course. ('What d'you expect if you give your bird all that crap?') He tells me I'm finished if I start taking coke; but I don't do it much, and it restores a vibrant world to me, at least for now. He says I exist in hallucination, but he doesn't understand. He's okay living in deadness. Anyway, he's gone to Scotland.

I've almost cracked Quest for the Grail. A secret passageway leads from the dungeon up into the keep. I haven't far to go. And the Internet is mesmerising. I find a website peopled by slant-eyed women, three or four of them, beautiful; but tonight I can't access them, my computer so slow, and instead, again and again, I see this image of a masked head in firelight. My skin tingles, especially at night, and I can't sleep. I pluck the mask away, and somebody says: 'Why are you staring at me?' Sometimes it's hard to breathe. The oxygen drains out of the air. But I have her photographs, all their photographs, everything there is of them. These are mine: an actress on stage, and a black woman in a crimson dress. She stares into the lens, and says nothing. A dark line of fugitives is wending to the horizon. Often my heart beats too much. Something is my fault. The doctor warned me, but he doesn't understand either. And now it starts up again, and the knowledge of Rebecca nearby. I hold her to me. Rebecca, you can't leave, not really. You are tight against me, and my arms around you. You die quite gently in my arms. You don't struggle much. I lay you down.

I keep her close here, now, just under the floorboards. The landlord won't know, or if he does he won't admit it. So she can't leave me again. People say there's no space to hide a body between the floorboards and the concrete, but she's slender, and I can sense her eyes just beneath me, whenever I walk to the kitchen, the bathroom . . .

*　　*　　*

In time he fell for other women: an all-seeing goddess and a blue-skinned alien screened at the local cinema. He bought DVDs of them later, then grew tired with their repetition. For a while he could not forget a mannequin in the window of a nearby shopping mall. He kept returning to gaze at her. People might say that such figures have no interior, no independent life, he thought, but they have the life we bestow on them, which is no different from how we love humans.

His idols remained lonely fixations. He bought a life-size silicone sex doll with a Japanese gaze, which was lying beside him on the night the fire broke out. He was laughing before he choked into unconsciousness, the hysteria of someone high on cannabis. And the flames melted his photographic files and disused equipment long before they reached him, and peeled away the floorboards where her imagined body lay.

6

Schoolboy

In summer, when sunlight flows through the upper windows of the house, and bathes the faded plush of the stair carpets, a tenant might pause in the landing's silence and imagine an old age of healed memories and a forgiven past. But in winter the seagulls, pristine and a little threatening, alight on the fire escape railings, adding their guano to the rust and peeling paint. The cold seeps through the window cracks, and damp patches appear on the passage walls. Even at night the gulls come mewing and wailing on to the rooftops, and you can hear their hooked feet scratching the tiles, and the droning of the wind. Then a feeling of siege descends: of things pulling slowly, irreversibly apart.

The oldest tenant, barely younger than the landlord, would hear from his bed the gulls' crying, and imagine them in sleep to be the screech of cats or children. He had been bedridden for a week. His right knee had swollen to twice the size of the other. He listened to classical music on the radio, and slept away his pain. When he hobbled to the lavatory, his knee threatened to buckle, and he waited for its surgical replacement with the nostalgic relief of parting from an old enemy.

As a boy he had seemed harmlessly accident-prone. A fall from tree-climbing twisted his lower back, but he appeared to recover almost overnight. And he remembered his knee cartilage slipping in and out on the football field: an event so routine and painless that he paid it no attention. But fifty years later the weakness returned like a ghost, and ached, and grew frailer with more years, while his thigh and calf muscles shrank. Half amused, half appalled, he imagined his whole body filled with memory traces from that time before adolescence when his parents sent him to boarding school. While walking too briskly on winter nights years ago, a chill would start up in his windpipe from a rugby collision, seventy years before, with the biggest boy in the class, and a morning ache now rankled in the base of his spine. If he examined his arms he could see that their skin had never quite absorbed the spattered burns from a prankish campfire, and the scar from a slipped penknife still creased his knuckles.

Perhaps it was some returning wound that put him in mind of school that night, the preparatory school like others on the edge of Berkshire heaths, where his boyhood years were spent in alternating triumph and misery. Or perhaps the wisp of smoke that seeped beneath the bedroom door resurrected for a moment the ceremony in the woods, by the rhododendron lake at night, when he was eight.

He found it hard, even now, to realise how crude it all was: that the Wizard's throne was only a wobbly scaffold of sticks tied together with frayed string, and the sacred fire no more than a foot-high pyramid of smouldering twigs. Yet it was astonishing that they had dared assemble there at all, he thought, climbing through a classroom window near midnight, to crouch in the shelter of the trees where any master might have found them. And Matron, checking the dormitories, would have come upon six empty beds. It was this shared peril – rather than the passwords or titled hierarchy – that knitted the Serpent Society together.

Nothing in later life equalled the thrill and terror of his own initiation. After they took off his blindfold, he did not know which face was whose behind their masks, only recognised the bulk of Fatboy grasping his stick like a sceptre. And enthroned above him hovered the firelit apparition of the Wizard. His death-white mask dangled tawny hairs and sprouted bull horns, while the voice behind it was no longer that of Tansley, but a hollowed incantation. 'You will say the secret words of the Serpent Society after me . . . Step forward now, raise your left hand . . .' And the prick of the ceremonial pin sealed him to them all for ever.

Springdown was less like a boarding school than a run-down country house, whose grounds beyond the playing fields descended to a wooded lake and thickets hollow with boys' dens. Its self-containment was near-complete. Beyond the lake, if you climbed a wooden fence, you might glimpse a high road, and the mystery of the adult world passing. And sometimes, trespassing down the school drive, he would slip through a hedge and find himself staring on to a cemetery, where once, appalled, transfixed, he saw a coffin lowered into the ground.

Tansley the Wizard, his best friend, told him that bodies did not rot in the ground. 'You know, Squit, they stay the same for centuries. I've seen them.'

Sometimes Squit (everyone called him that) only half believed what Tansley said, but would nevertheless sink hypnotised into his vision, because Tansley had access to worlds that Squit could not imagine. Tansley was cleverer than him; he was cleverer than everybody. His high, retreating forehead, and long, receding chin gave him the look of some prehistoric bird, supernaturally gifted. In fact Tansley the Wizard was so clever that he had been moved to a form one year higher than his age. But he shared Squit's dormitory, and told strange stories at night, and only Fatboy dared occasionally to contradict him, or challenge his infallibility in the secret society. But then Fatboy was stupid.

Theirs was a world without women. A pretty art mistress beguiled the boys for a term, but never came back, and the middle-aged matron they nicknamed Cabbage White, who wore the starched headdress of a district nurse, did not count. Twice a term, on Sunday afternoons, the boys' parents took them away to drive in the countryside and eat cream teas; but Squit's parents lived in Cyprus, where his father was an engineer, and his visitors – dutiful aunts and family friends – seemed pallid replicas of his mother and father. His holidays, spent on the beaches of Limassol or in the Troodos Mountains, would end at Nicosia airport, where his anguish at walking out of his mother's arms across the airstrip continued that night in private tears beneath the bedclothes at Springdown. To Squit, his devastation seemed unique. It marked him as different. His elder brother Dick, who went to a school nearby, sneered at him as a crybaby, and increased Squit's sense that there was something wrong about himself. He was in love with his mother.

To his schoolmates he found himself pretending that his parents were dead. They were two thousand miles away, and it was easier to imagine them no longer living. Perhaps he was avenging himself for their desertion. But at morning service in the school chapel – a darkened chamber near the headmaster's rooms – he asked God for their return. Sometimes he slipped in here alone. Inside the entrance, inscribed in silver letters, were the names of ex-pupils killed in two world wars. He knew them by heart. And beyond them the silent sanctuary stretched into dimness: seven rows of boys' pews, the facing stalls of the choir, and the altar with its golden cross. He knew he was not meant to be here. Yet he imagined its protection round him, as if the school rules ended at the threshold of the silver names. Fearfully once, he stepped up to the altar. A dead butterfly lay in its dust. He eased this on to his palm and tossed it into the air, where it fell into the darkness. Then he laid beneath the cross a snapshot of his mother sunbathing in Limassol. For weeks afterwards, at morning service, he noticed it still lying undetected under the golden cross.

Tansley the Wizard said he could resurrect Squit's parents, if only he knew the spells. He would work on discovering them. Squit was touched by a fear as to what effect these spells might have on those still living, but he said nothing, and sometimes he believed his own fantasy: yes, his parents were dead. This inspired a sadness in his other friend Wynne, which he guiltily cherished. Wynne was beautiful, with blond curls and a slight stammer. Often they sat together in the long grass by the playing fields – grasses shifting with butterflies in summer – and Squit had a familiar sensation that he had been here before, among these musky scents and flickering wings, while other people were only far-off voices. Wynne was delicate. The other boys were warned not to be rough with him, because he had a hole in the heart. He was let off games, and even Fatboy did not push him around. The mystery of his heart separated him. He was studious and quiet, and they never enrolled him in the Serpent Society. It must be his frailness, Squit thought, that turned him so sensitive. He was most like a girl. When Wynne said: 'I'm sorry they're dead . . . I'm v-very sorry', and his eyes watered as they gazed at Squit, imagining his orphanhood, Squit would stare back at him, transfixed by his sympathy, and worried that Wynne might soon die instead. Squit did not understand this hole in the heart, since Wynne's heart seemed more complete than anyone's.

Tansley the Wizard, on the other hand, killed butterflies to scrutinise under a classroom microscope. The science master was benign and often absent, and Tansley and Squit would sneak into his room and peer at fantastical magnifications of whatever the Wizard had collected. This was the heart of everything, Tansley said, this was what things were made of. You thought them solid, didn't you, stupid Squit? But no, they were continually charging around. A drop of fluid is a whirlpool of tiny cells.

For Squit there was a magical collusion about these stolen minutes, when the Wizard's head bent over the eyepiece and announced a new miracle. The butterfly's skull was a gush of dishevelled feathers and sprouted feelers like trees, and its eyes were as huge as melons. The texture of its silken wings resembled overlapping roof tiles, and a mountain ridge blistered with hairy craters turned out to be the abdomen of a caterpillar. Squit sometimes felt his head swimming. Nothing was as it appeared. Flies and ants shone in burnished armour, like the Black

Prince in *Our Island Story*, and flower petals turned into intricate textiles. At any moment the puny might become enormous, the beautiful grotesque, and insects transform into malevolent robots.

But the most amazing moments arose when the Wizard brought along bottles of liquid. After he splashed a drop of pond water on to the microscope slide, Squit gazed into a seething universe of unknown creatures that jittered and darted across his vision, scuttling back and forth with revolving arms, or moving through their green world with ghostly precision. There were organisms with embryonic heads and transparent tentacles, pale emerald; others with revolving hands or predatory spears for antennae; still others like serrated trumpets. Squit remembered how once, on a thirsty woodland walk, he had gulped down a mouthful of just such water.

One evening, when the science room was dark, lit only by the microscope's bulb, Tansley moved successive slides of milk and pond scum on to the microscope's stage. Then a shimmering mass of protozoa hung in space: orbs and globules that moved about one another in slow procession, and seemed to turn in their orbits. It made Squit dizzy to look at them, as if he was pitching forward into space.

'They're like the stars,' he said.

The Wizard was suddenly grinning. "That's the secret, Squit. They're called cells. The stars and the ants and you and me and Wynne and Fatboy . . . we're all made of the same cells. And when we're dead we'll all be swimming around together, you and your mum and me, and Cabbage White. Did you know that human beings are mostly made of water? I read that.'

Squit was confused now. 'How can my mum be the same as Cabbage White, and swimming around?' Anyway, Squit knew his parents were in Cyprus.

Tansley made a gesture of despair. 'How did I come to have such a stupid best friend? They're not the same at this exact minute, see. But we could change at any moment . . .'

Squit thought: so we might become another person, and not even realise. This was his and Tansley's secret. Even the sixth-form boys, the only ones allowed to do science, might not realise it. He might even become a priest, and talk to God. But if he ever got the spell right, he thought, he would choose to be a scientist who knew about these things.

Squit wanted to see everything of beauty and strangeness that existed. Across his classroom wall, behind the teacher's desk, a huge map of the world distracted him through many lessons. During maths class, bored by trying to multiply fractions, he would gaze instead at the different-coloured countries, and imagine a journey from the pink speck of Cyprus down the length of Africa, or eastward through those lands of impossible yearning – Persia, India, China, Japan. The maths master might mistake his dreamy stare for an attention to decimal fractions, but Squit only became conscious of him at all when the teacher stood up to write on the blackboard. Then his enormous bulk would interrupt Squit's journey along some pagoda-haunted river by obliterating Burma or Siam.

But Squit's reveries, as he scanned the map, were shadowed by a nagging foreboding. Distorted by Mercator's projection, the pale green immensity of the Soviet Union was advancing like a glacier out of Asia. It might overrun western Europe in its sleep. That year the Cold War was settling into the classrooms of Springdown. Beyond Russia the haunting presence of a multitudinous Red China was coloured violent yellow, and a terrible war had broken out in Korea.

Springdown stood on the edge of heathland that had once been a military training ground. When school walks snaked over it on Sundays, they were following the tracks of tanks. Tansley the Wizard reckoned the army still trained there in secret, and Fatboy said he had heard the tank treads churning at night. Yet when the Wizard called an emergency meeting of the Serpent Society, they all guessed what it was about. On these summer nights, peering from the dormitory windows, they had seen a figure silhouetted on the parapet above the masters' quarters. They could not make out who he was, but sometimes they saw the flash of a torchlight, as if he were signalling to someone, and glimpsed his stooped back as he dropped from view. By day you could just discern on the roof a pair of radio antennae, one upright, one aslant, and the bulk of something concealed alongside.

The rooms below, they knew, belonged to Jarrold, the history master, whom nobody liked. He was a slight, pallid figure of unguessable age, who seemed to favour one or two boys at random, and victimise others, including Tansley.

On the night of the Serpent Society meeting, Fatboy got stuck in the ground-floor window. Two of the members – the beanpole McMorris and ginger-haired Hamilton – panicked and wanted to go back; but Tansley and Squit pulled out the broken sash cord and levered up the window frame another two inches. On the far side, by a flower bed of damp lupins, they swore themselves to silence again, and stole to the ritual trees. It was a June night glittering with stars. As the ceremonial fire flickered into life and they fitted their masks, a fearfulness arose. No lights showed in the school windows. They heard the hooting of an owl. Above them the Milky Way stretched in a wash of silver. The Wizard, who had found the constellation Serpens in a star atlas, pointed in silence to its zigzag in the sky, as to divine protection. His voice rose muffled and hollow. They all realised, he said, that one of the masters was a traitor. Every night he was signalling to someone out on the heath, probably during army man-oeuvres, and he kept a secret radio transmitter on the roof. The Wizard leant towards the firelight, and his eye sockets gleamed. What were they to do?

For a moment the only sound was the spluttering of the fire. Then Fatboy said: 'Let's go in and bash him up. I bet we can do it. The six of us. He's a weed.'

But Squit reckoned Fatboy was a coward. He'd prob-ably run. He said: 'I think we should tell the Head.'

The Wizard's bull horns wavered from one to the other. He said: 'But the Head wouldn't believe us. He'd just joke about it to Mr Jarrold, who'd cover his tracks.'

McMorris piped up: 'Maybe he's signalling the Russians to invade.' His voice was shaking. 'Maybe any minute.'

The masked faces tilted in unison to the sky, as if it might rain down parachutes, and Squit felt his blood run cold. 'We have to get him quick.'

The Wizard said: 'What we need is evidence.'

'How do we get that?' demanded Fatboy. It was less a question than a challenge. He was the only one who dared dispute with Tansley, which he did in habitual frustration at being merely Deputy Wizard. 'What do you mean, evidence?'

'I was in his rooms last week,' the Wizard said. 'I went in with Wynne to get exercise books. He's got a coding machine there. I saw it.' As he leant back from the firelight, his voice seemed to rise from darkness. 'They're called cipher machines. They make a secret language. All the Communists use them.'

Squit marvelled at Tansley's knowledge. How did he know what one of those things looked like? Somehow they would have to steal it and take it to the Head. Then Jarrold's code would be deciphered, and they would all be in the newspapers.

The Wizard went on: 'He goes away every Sunday. That's when we move. One of us will stand guard on his door, and the rest will go in.' He stared round at them, and nobody spoke. 'I know where that coding machine is. We could get the radio too. And all his papers and messages.'

'Everything,' said Squit.

The night had turned cold. The constellation Serpens was edging westward over the sky. For a minute the semicircle of white masks stayed mute and unmoving, but the fire had died to ash, and now the Wizard descended his creaking throne, and they crept back at last to the half-open window, and to their restless sleep.

Squit could never manage the idea of for ever. Everlasting bliss or torment made his mind split apart, just as the multiplication of fractions did. Perhaps Tansley was right that heaven and hell did not exist, but that everybody ended up in a kind of soup, and became each other. Yet at morning service in the school chapel he sang, 'O Paradise! O Paradise! Who doth not crave for rest?' and thought paradise a beautiful word, like Persia, and that he would like to see it. That Sunday he was relieved to notice that in the procession of masters into chapel Mr Jarrold was absent, his place taken by the visiting chaplain.

The chaplain seemed immensely old. Grey whiskers crept down his cheeks and his eyes were watery gold. As the boys left chapel he would be waiting by the door, a pectoral cross shining against his cassock, and he would nod and smile at each boy in turn, so that when he touched Squit's elbow and asked, 'Would you like a word with me?', it carried no alarm.

They sat in wicker chairs on the nearby landing, while the passageway emptied. Somewhere Squit had seen photos of Victorian clergymen – men of huge whiskers and sanctity – and the chaplain must be one, he thought. His voice was very deep and soft. 'Wynne tells me you've lost your parents.'

Squit examined his feet, suddenly afraid. 'Yes.' It was nearly true. They were gone into their own time and space. Cyprus was a distant figment on the classroom map, and he had lost count of the weeks before he would ever see them.

The chaplain creaked forward in his chair. His hands were huge on its arms, flecked with grey hairs. He said: 'Perhaps there's something you'd like to ask me?'

Squit blurted out: 'Why are they so far away?'

'Well, they didn't mean to be.'

'Everyone else's are closer.'

'Yours are close too. You just can't see them.'

'They're not close, sir.' Squit realised this sounded rude, but he did not know how to alter it.

'I'm sure they were good people.' The priest touched his arm. 'They have gone to Heaven.'

Squit said: 'Yes, sir.' But Heaven sounded even farther away than Cyprus.

'It's not in the sky, you know.' The priest was smiling, but sadly. 'It's hard to say where it is.'

'But they can't speak to me.' Squit felt he might cry. 'And I can't speak to them.'

'That's right, in this life we can't communicate with the departed.'

'Why not, sir?' Squit often spoke to his mother in his head. It was something like prayer. 'Don't they hear us?'

'I'm not sure about that. Perhaps they do. Because they're living with God, anything's possible.'

Living with God. The words jerked Squit awake, as from a self-created dream. He felt suddenly ashamed. Would he be found out? His eyes stayed fixed on his feet, where his socks and garters had crumpled at the ankles. He realised: no, my parents are not living with God. They're probably at a cocktail party in Nicosia. He said suddenly, bleakly: 'I'll be all right now.' And then: 'Thank you, sir.'

The chaplain got to his feet. He touched Squit's head. 'Be happy for them.' Squit nodded, and remained with lowered eyes while the old man's footsteps echoed down the stairs to the masters' front door, and a car engine started up.

Squit stayed a long time staring at the carpet under his feet, wondering what he was going to feel. Then he turned back into the chapel. He sat down at his place among the pews and closed his palms together as he had been taught. He noticed his hands trembling. He apologised to Jesus for lying, yet felt it was not such a big lie. He found it hard to picture his parents now. He could not fix their faces in any one remembered place or moment, then wondered if they could picture him. He felt a pang of alarm. Surely his mother – whose beautiful eyes could see all round her like a bird's – could still imagine him?

He tiptoed to the altar, but the photograph was gone. Beside him the panelled walls disappeared behind dark green curtains, which hung in thick folds from ceiling to floor. Even during services these curtains moved him with half-suppressed fascination and fear. Now he found the parting in them, but his grip froze there. He did not know what lay beyond; but he imagined them opening on to a country of terrible beauty or holiness. For a moment his hands recoiled and fell to his sides. Then, on a near-hysterical impulse, he pulled the draperies apart, and there was the panelled wall only, pale wood, lightly carved, impermeable. He stared at it. The curtains rustled back from his fingers and into place. He returned to his pew and covered his face. And when he looked up again, the strangeness had returned, the sense of another country just beyond reach, and he went on scrutinising the jade-green draperies, baffled and obscurely angry.

A voice in the chapel entrance whispered: 'Squit?'

'Yes.' He did not turn round.

'I thought you might be here.' Wynne crept into the pew beside him. 'Are you angry with me?'

Squit said, 'No', but he was, in a way. He looked at Wynne through splayed fingers. 'Of course not.' He was amazed at what Wynne had dared do for him.

'Did he help you?'

'He said my parents were living in Heaven.' Squit felt suffocated here now: choked by the curtains, by his lying. He got up and they tiptoed to the door, where the names of the war dead were lit in silver, and Wynne stopped, staring up at them. Often to Squit there was something other-worldly about Wynne. Now they gazed up at the roll together, as if its names were a discovery. Nobody ever spoke about them.

Wynne said: 'Do you sometimes think about being dead?'

Squit had once decided that he was never going to die. He said: 'No', but he felt a stab of alarm. Wynne looked vulnerable, bewitchingly so, with his tumble of yellow curls and his fair, girl's skin. Squit watched his gaze travelling down the silver names as if he might find his own there.

When Wynne came to the end, his stare transferred to Squit, very wide and candid. He said: 'Why are you always looking at me?'

Squit felt his face burning. He wanted to answer: because you're beautiful. But it sounded soppy. His eyes were trapped by Wynne's. 'I don't, do I?'

Wynne said: 'Is it because you think I'm going to die?'

'You're not going to die, Wynne. You can't. I won't let you.' He reached out and hugged Wynne's narrow shoulders. 'I'll die instead.' Sometimes he didn't know why he said things. 'Where do you think you'd go?'

He expected Wynne to say he'd go to Heaven with Jesus. Wynne already resembled an angel. Instead his face clouded oddly. 'People in India think you just disappear with your corpse,' he said. 'Then there's no more you.'

Squit felt afraid that Wynne thought this too. He was just going into the ground, like the coffin Squit had seen in the cemetery.

'Let's get out of here, Wynne,' he said. 'Tell you a secret. The Serpents are getting into Mr Jarrold's rooms this afternoon. Guess what? He's a spy. He's spying for the Russians.'

They were clustered at the door long before the appointed time. McMorris held his cap pistol with the ivory butt, and Squit had brought along a screwdriver, he didn't know why. The Wizard was exultant. He had suspected Jarrold all along, he said. If they couldn't steal the cipher machine – its cables might pin it to the wall – they could bring down the radio transmitter. It would be a special kind, he'd recognise it. His talk of tubes and crystals dazzled Squit and left the others flummoxed. Now the Wizard ordered Hamilton to watch the door, while he eased it softly open, and the rest of them crept in.

There was no one in the room. Its air reeked of tobacco. There was a small sofa with two easy chairs, some bookshelves, and a radiogram piled with Benny Goodman records. They peered around them, afraid at first to touch anything. The desk was strewn with papers and drained coffee cups. Their own essays on the Hundred Years War lay still unmarked in a heap of open exercise books.

Tansley the Wizard made for an alcove behind the desk, where the cipher machine lay half concealed in a wooden frame. Its lines of spindly keys were all that showed. With tense care he pulled it clear of its case, and on to the desk. Then Squit heard a sad, throaty cry. Tansley was staring at it, stony-faced. Its carriage carried the royal coat of arms and an inscribed 'Imperial 55'. In its roller was a half-typed letter which began: 'Dear Sirs, in view of my mother's wish to move house in September, I would request . . .'

McMorris said: 'That's just a typewriter. My dad has one of those . . .'

'Yup', said Fatboy. 'That's a typewriter all right.'

They gazed at it in silence. Squit didn't dare look at Tansley. He gently turned the carriage knob as if it might change something, but it only eased the letter out. Now he was afraid that Mr Jarrold would return and find his desk disturbed. Fatboy was starting to snigger. 'A typewriter . . .' Then he grabbed Squit's arm and they peered into the bedroom beyond. The history master's suits hung disembodied in an open cupboard, and made Squit even more frightened. On the bedside table a framed photograph showed a pretty woman and a young boy. 'That's him,' Fatboy said. 'That's his conk all right.' Squit felt surprised that Mr Jarrold had a mother.

A deadness now weighed on the master's study. It seemed to have grown darker, although the sun was still bright on the playing fields outside the window. They were all looking to Tansley, yet he had not stirred from the typewriter, and his face was white. But a shallow step beneath a low window led to the fire escape and the roof, and Squit cried out: 'Let's get the radio!' And the spell was broken.

They clambered through the window and on to the clashing iron. A warm breeze met them, and a swallow flew out from under the eaves. Squit turned back to beckon Tansley up. But Tansley looked as if he were staring into nothing. He only said: 'You go', and remained where he was.

They climbed over a parapet and on to the flat roof. The windows of their dormitory shone fifty yards away across a void. Squit stepped out gingerly. The roof felt soft and hollow. Here and there the lead beneath his feet had cracked into spidery veins. A solitary deckchair stood open, facing the playing fields below, its canvas wet with recent rain. Beside it an ashtray was heaped with cigarette butts.

At first they could see no sign of any radio. 'He may have hidden it,' Squit said. He hunted round the water tank and behind the chimney stacks, and tried to see under the parapet, feeling dizzy. Then he realised. An empty packing trunk was lying abandoned near the deckchair, and behind it the rods of some leftover construction work stuck out of cement. From their dormitory this assemblage had created the silhouette of the radio he remembered.

Squit realized this with an ache of disappointment. He did not tell the others. But after a minute McMorris kicked at the rusted rods and said: 'Hey, these are Tansley's aerials!' He was laughing.

Fatboy came to gawp at them too and exclaimed: 'So this is Tansley's secret radio! Tansley the genius! Tansley the thick-head!'

Then they glimpsed a man walking along the cricket pitch beneath them. They ducked below the parapet and crawled back on all fours to the fire escape. It shook and clanged at their descent, and their fingers slid on pigeon droppings. Squit let the others go ahead of him. He did not want to be the one to tell Tansley that nothing was there. Although he felt sure that Tansley knew already.

It was from this moment that Squit's life began to unravel. Jarrold returned and seemed to have noticed nothing, although Squit imagined he looked newly furtive. But the gossamer web of Squit's friendships started to tremble and tear apart. Tansley struggled to reassert his prestige, but Fatboy and McMorris laughed behind his back, and Squit was disconcerted to feel sorry for him. Tansley said: 'I still think Jarrold's a spy', and Squit suggested wanly that the master might have known what they were planning, exchanged the cipher machine for a typewriter and hidden the radio somewhere; and Tansley was glad of Squit's arm around him.

Then two days later came the cricket match. Springdown was to play Cottendale, the nearest prep school, where Squit's elder brother, thirteen years old, had been named team captain. By the time Springdown's juniors settled as spectators round the pitch, Squit was seething with confused excitement. It was an afternoon that threatened rain, and Springdown went in to bat under a louring sky. Sitting between Tansley and Wynne, Squit could easily make out the tall figure of Dick fielding at mid-on. Somehow everyone seemed to know he was Squit's brother, and captain of Cottendale. Even Fatboy came lurching up to Squit, grinning. 'Who do you hope'll win, us or them?'

Squit murmured: 'Us, of course.' But he was not sure.

Fatboy said: 'I bet you don't.'

But Squit felt a loyal dismay as one after another Springdown's top batsmen were bowled out. He gave up filling in his scorebook. In little more than an hour the home team was dismissed for only forty-eight runs, and came out to field in faded sunlight. But then things started to look up. Cottendale's opening batsmen were both caught in the slips for a mere two runs, and a ripple of cheers went round the watching juniors. The third batsman was Dick. He came out from the pavilion, his bat casually cradled, and his team set up a hopeful squib of clapping. When Squit saw him walking on to the field, he felt his own heart lurching. One of the spectators cried out: 'That's Squit's brother!'

Squit alternately hero-worshipped and hated Dick. Dick's lifetime stance was to find Squit dreamy and stupid. But now, as his brother walked toward the batsman's crease, Squit wanted him to slog the Springdown bowlers for six. He wanted to be proud of him. And to Squit, Dick carried with him an anguished memory of home. He seemed to walk in from that gentler world and time, drenched in the warmth of their mother and the Cypriot sun, so that Squit's eyes watered as he watched him, and yes, he prayed he would do well.

Dick was faced by a damp pitch and a fast bowler, but he survived the first over, and in the second he hit a loose leg-break for a graceful four. Squit clapped furiously, then noticed hostile glances around him, and Tansley nudged him in warning. But slowly Dick imposed himself on the field. He began to hit the ball with lordly composure. Sometimes, just before the bowler's delivery, he would look about him with studied ease, noting where the deep fielders were, before finding the gap between them, or slicing the ball fast through the slips. The Springdown spectators clapped weakly, sportingly, as they had been told. They could tell their side was descending to defeat.

But Squit was no longer applauding his brother. He was drowning in a confused sea of dislike and nostalgia. Dick might carry with him the memory of their mother, but he was also, overwhelmingly now, himself. He was flaunting a familiar authority. Squit hated the nonchalant athleticism with which he stroked balls to the boundary, the way he gazed about him after clouting another four, the arrogance with which he acknowledged his team's cheering with a peremptory nod to the pavilion. Squit imagined him thinking: this is my brother's school, so it can't be much use. And when at last Dick was bowled by a flukey off-spin, Squit clapped so loudly that Tansley frowned and Wynne smiled at him for a good sport.

But a few minutes later the match was over, Cottendale triumphant, and the players mingling in the pavilion for cream buns and lemonade. The games master came up to tell Squit he might join his brother as a special favour. 'He's a real W. G with the bat,' he said.

'Yes, sir,' said Squit, with no idea what he meant.

Squit was both longing and scared to meet his brother. The cricket team were all seniors, and he did not know if Dick would even speak with him. It was strange. He wanted to hug him as they used to. But when Dick noticed him, he merely extended his hand, as if Squit were some chance acquaintance, and this gave Squit a pang of loneliness deeper than if he'd been ignored. Within a minute

Dick had turned away to talk with the Springdown captain, and Squit resorted to raids on the cream buns. He managed to pocket one for Wynne, another for Tansley, then joined the juniors lingering nearby.

It was an hour before the games master found him and told him his brother wanted to say goodbye. Then Squit felt a gush of sad warmth. Away from the others, Dick might embrace him in their parents' world. There was a coach in the front drive, already filling with his teammates.

Squit found his brother alone in the headmaster's hall. He looked taller than Squit remembered, alien and important in his cricket whites and blue-fringed blazer. He wore a look that Squit had hated ever since he could remember: taut and sneering. He said: 'You little squirt, why did you tell everyone that Mum and Dad were dead?'

Squit stood speechless. His cheeks were burning. He glanced desperately behind him, as though somebody might help. A rooted habit of bluff-calling made him whisper: 'Who did I tell?'

'You told everyone. The whole school, apparently. Some ginger-headed pipsqueak came up for me to autograph his scorebook and said he was sorry about my parents. I nearly socked him.'

That must have been Hamilton, Squit thought, who couldn't keep a secret if he tried. 'Did you tell him?'

'Of course I did. I told everyone, you lousy spud. Why do you want Dad and Mum dead? What's wrong with you? Dad will be furious.'

The coach started honking outside in the drive. Dick picked up his cricket bat and strode to the door. 'You can tell Dad I made forty-four runs against Springdown,' he said.

'Tell him yourself,' Squit muttered. But Dick was gone.

Squit stayed in the hall a long time, because nobody came there. It was hung with mounted trophies: the heads of antlered samburs and a moulting leopard. He sat down on a leather chair. The only noises were far away. He thought: How could Dick say I want Mum and Dad dead? No, I don't know why I invented it. It just happened, and then I couldn't go back. Tansley says you can kill people by imagining them dead. Tribes in Africa do that. But I've never wanted to kill anybody, except Dick. If Mum died, I'd die too, like with Wynne. Now how will I face them all, Tansley and Wynne and the others? They'll all think I've betrayed my parents, that I've wanted them dead. I must have, or I wouldn't have pretended. Why did I do it? Because I enjoyed the way the Serpents went quiet around it, I suppose, thinking me special. And Wynne, of course, how he gazed with those blue eyes, as if he loved me.

I went out and lay in the long grass that evening, hoping Wynne might join me, but knowing he would not. The undergrowth was whispering with butterflies. I imagined them to be the same as those that fluttered round our cottage in the Troodos Mountains, and that my family were sending them as messengers. One had eyes on its wings, like the butterfly I found on the chapel altar. For all I know, it had seen my mother, and I even imagined it was her. It settled on my hand.

I heard the voices then. A whole crowd of them, boys running. There were even some seniors. 'Where's Squit? Let's get Squit!' I saw them through the grass. Hamilton was among them, but he was the only Serpent. One of them shouted,

'He pretends his mother's dead!', and my heart went cold. I flattened my face against the ground. I wondered if I would ever talk to Tansley again, or to Wynne, who had found the chaplain for me. I thought I should stay in the grass for ever, but at last the bell went for supper, and I had to go in.

Nobody was speaking to me. Wynne never met my eyes. Tansley talked instead to Fatboy, whom he despises. I thought I might sick up the semolina pudding. McMorris, sitting beside me, whispered: 'Tansley's in a whopping bate with you. He says you tricked us all.' I said: 'So did he', although I still think Mr. Jarrold is odd.

In the dormitory I pretended to sleep. The others were sniggering. I wanted to wake up far away, in another country, perhaps in Persia. For the first time I didn't think about going home to Cyprus. I was afraid of what my father would say when Dick told him. I'm not the son he wanted. I'm not Dick. I'm too small, although I'm definitely not stupid.

I dreamt about my mother. Her eyes, which slope upwards, were full of tears, tears of anger. She wondered why I wanted her to die.

I've always been afraid of growing up. There are things that unnerve me: things peculiar to men, like smoking and shaving. My mother once told me that childhood was a long dream. But last week in the changing rooms I saw that a boy had hair between his legs. I thought that was for adults, but he was only thirteen. Just four years older than me. It made me sick and confused.

And then there is what happened yesterday. One day I will ask someone what it means. I wanted to help Tansley.

To be honest, I wanted to get back in his favour. After all, he is my best friend.

I never could believe that Tansley was wrong. There must be something that I did not understand. Perhaps Mr Jarrold tricked us, or we just weren't thorough enough. But if I slipped into his rooms alone, I thought, I would find documents to incriminate him. Maybe the cipher machine would be back. Then I would be the one to prove Tansley right after all. I would be the hero. I wanted to think of him as the Wizard again, and to believe in him.

Sunday, I remembered, was when Mr Jarrold was away, and I waited until four o'clock, the same time as last week, when the corridor was empty and the others playing round the lake. I was scared all right. If anybody found me, I could think of no excuse for being there. And just as I prepared to enter, and knelt to peer through the keyhole, my knee cartilage twinged like an omen. The keyhole, in any case was shut on the inside.

The door opened without a sound. I was so intent on closing it behind me that for a moment I did not see what was in front of me. Mr Jarrold was sitting on the sofa. His face as he turned to me was ashen, his eyes bulging like a hare's. Beside him was Wynne. His shorts and belt lay crumpled on the floor. He was sitting in his pants. And Mr Jarrold's hand was on his thigh. We were all frozen there. Wynne's hair was dishevelled, his mouth open as he stared at me, and his eyes strange. I thought he had been blubbing.

I don't know how long I stood there. After a second or a minute I heard myself say: 'I'm sorry, sir . . . very sorry.' And I opened the door and left.

As I walked away down the corridor, I thought Jarrold's voice would yell at me to come back, or I would hear Wynne's feet running up to me. But nothing happened. I had walked halfway across the cricket pitch towards the lake before I remembered that nobody wanted to play with me any more.

Rain transforms this place. When it sheets across the lake and blurs the playing fields to mist, everyone gets excited, and thunderclaps bring squeals of terror from the juniors. The rain drips into our hollowed rhododendron dens around the lake, and pours through the lairs under the oak branches. My own den is hidden high up in a tree, where I fell last term, and its platform becomes too soggy to sit on. Rain falls on the cemetery too, of course, and makes me afraid: it seems to turn the dead more dead. I hope it will drench the cricket pitch so badly that the next match will be cancelled.

Today my only refuge is the dormitories. Mine looks very bare. The first-year juniors are permitted to sleep with their soft toys, but the second year decided this was wet, and we took ours home. My bed is between Hamilton's, who snores, and Wynne's, which has a mackintosh under the bottom sheet, because he sometimes wets his bed. On the shelves above we are allowed our favourite books. Hamilton owns all the Bulldog Drummond stories; Wynne keeps the bible his father gave him; I have Charles Kingsley's *The Heroes* and Rudyard Kipling's *Jungle Book*, a leftover from India when I was little.

I lay on my back a long time. I didn't know what else to do. The only person I might have asked about Wynne

was Tansley, because although he may not know everything, he knows a lot. But it might be too late for that. It
already seems an age since we raided Mr Jarrold's rooms.
Now when I looked out of the window through the rain,
the secret rooftop radio had become an old trunk and two
construction rods.

Then the door opened, and I turned away. I pretended
to be asleep. Even in the dorm, I thought, nobody leaves
you alone. It was the way he walked – rolling on the balls
of his feet – that made me realise it was Tansley. When I
opened my eyes he was standing close, staring into my
face. He said: 'I know you're shamming.'

I said: 'So what?'

'You're sulking.'

'I'm not sulking. I feel horrible.'

'It's your own fault. You shouldn't have pretended.
Everyone used to feel sorry for you, so you got away with
bags. You even asked me to think up spells to get your
mother back . . .'

'That was stupid.'

' . . . and all the time she was alive. Your brother told
Hamilton they were living in Cyprus.'

'Yes.'

'Wynne says you lied all the time to him. He even asked
old Holy-chops to talk to you. That was pretty wizard of
him. He wonders what other lies you've told.'

'I haven't told any,' I said, but I imagined this was a lie
too.

'He says he doesn't like you any more.'

I felt a pang of hurt, like a gripe in the stomach, one
of those pains you know will get worse later, when you

stop to think. But at this moment I wanted to ask why Mr Jarrold was punishing Wynne, if that was what he was doing. Wynne used to be one of his favourites.

Tansley went on: 'Wynne says anything you say about him is a lie too.'

'I haven't said anything about him.'

'Anyway, if you do, he says it's a lie.'

I pulled a blanket over my shoulders, although the air was warm, and turned away. My heart was beating senselessly. I looked into the light, at the great window pane where the rain was slithering down. After a while I felt Tansley's hand on my arm. He said: 'We're still friends, Squit.' He ruffled my hair. 'You're my second-best friend. After Wynne.'

I held his hand against my chest. I was lost in a tangle of gratitude and sadness. I could not think straight at all. I had only wanted him to talk to me again, and now he had. I went on staring at the beads of rain manoeuvring down the window, while he closed the door behind him.

On midsummer night the school would hold its yearly fire practice. The games master would set light to buckets of newspaper that spread smoke along the dormitory corridors. Then an alarm bell would ring. For some reason we were meant to crawl down the passages on all fours, which was fun anyway, so that Fatboy knocked over one of the buckets and nearly started a real fire. Then we assembled outside, where Cabbage White fussed round us, and the Head read a roll call. That night two boys were missing. They'd just gone on sleeping, so they were officially cinders, and they each got a black mark on the noticeboard next day. But I reckon it was all stupid, since if there was a real fire it would be much worse, and the Head and Cabbage White would be cinders too. But it meant that we were all wide awake for the Serpents' council two hours later.

It was a night without stars. A watery half-moon pushed through the clouds, then went away. I felt afraid. Fatboy, McMorris and Hamilton were whispering together as we went. In our council chamber among the trees we set light to a pile of twigs and an old copy of *Kennedy's Latin Primer*, and the sacred fire burnt so high that I thought we'd be discovered. The night was silent round us. The Wizard's throne wobbled and creaked as he climbed it, and Fatboy's breathing sounded hoarse at its foot. Then, for a long time, there was almost no sound at all, just the crackling of the fire and the owls hooting by the lake.

The moment we put on our masks, something eerie happens. None of us looks like himself any more, or like anybody. The masks are only small, like the Lone Ranger's, but we've painted them white and they turn us ghostly, like skulls, our eyes just black holes. Only the Wizard's covers his whole face, and muffles his voice inside it, so he seems to speak from underground. He says he got the mask from Africa, but McMorris thinks he's seen them in fancy dress shops. At any rate, because we were silent at first, nobody speaking at all, I got more and more scared. I thought they were going to expel me for all my lying, or do something even worse to me. I planned to run back to the school – its windows were dark – but I did not know if my legs would work. They were shaking. Then I remembered – and I suddenly felt a different kind of sadness – that the Wizard had kept me as second-best friend; and now the heads in the firelight were not looking at me but at him, waiting for someone to say something, and he was staring at the sky to see if the Serpens stars were shining, and they weren't.

At last he leant forward above the flames and his eyes glittered inside the sockets of his bull mask. 'I declare the Serpents' meeting open,' he said, 'and I propose a new member.' He left a silence. Maybe he expected one of us to ask who. But nobody did.

Eventually somebody mumbled: 'We're already seven. If we're more, we won't be so secret.'

The Wizard threw back his head. 'Eight is a lucky number.' Then he proclaimed: 'I say we elect Wynne!'

I stared up at him. Wynne: his new best friend. I felt too lonely to speak.

But Fatboy cried at once: 'He's a sissy.'

'He couldn't join us anyway,' Hamilton said. 'He's got that thing in his heart.'

'He'll join,' the Wizard said. 'I asked him.'

'You're not allowed to do that,' Fatboy said.

The Wizard glared round at them, his horns swivelling from one to the next. Then he raised his arms and let them fall again, silently crushing revolt. 'I'm Chief Serpent! I make the rules.' His head lifted again to gaze over us. He crossed his arms. 'What's next?'

Out of nowhere I felt a surge of hatred. The Wizard was sitting there so superior, lording it over us, his stupid skinny legs monopolising the throne. I hated the way his horned head tilted back in the firelight, so certain of himself, dismissing us all, and how smugly he folded his arms.

I heard McMorris mutter: 'We're all allowed a vote. Wynne's too wet. I don't vote for him.'

The Wizard said: 'It's too late. I've voted him in.' He pointed upwards, then said in his unearthly voice: 'I elect him by the power of the Serpens star!'

I thought it was all over then. The silence returned. The fire was dying to red ash, and I was trembling, maybe from the cold. A low wind had risen in the trees. We looked so feeble, all of us, I thought, with our skull faces lowered to the embers and the Wizard preening over us. He was grinning behind his mask, I was sure, perched there in his vanity.

Then somebody whispered: 'But the Serpens star isn't there.'

'It will return,' the Wizard answered.

Suddenly Fatboy said: 'How do you know?' He was leaning grossly against the throne. 'Maybe it's gone for ever. You don't know anything.'

A cold excitement went through me. Something was changing. I sensed that anything might happen. It was like the way fog lifts, or the bursting of a bubble. The others must have felt it too. They no longer sat cross-legged, but were crouched on their ankles, like frogs. McMorris the beanpole stood up, his head almost level with the Wizard's, and said: 'We don't want you any more.'

The Wizard waved him away.

Fatboy almost shouted: 'You told us whoppers about Mr Jarrold, Tansley. Busting into his room like that, you might have got us all expelled.'

Someone else piped up: 'We could have been caned.'

The Wizard didn't budge. 'I still think Jarrold's a spy.'

'He's not. He's too drippy.' Hamilton got to his feet and turned to the others. 'I vote Fatboy for Chief Serpent.'

Three more chorused: 'We vote for Fatboy too.'

And now Fatboy, standing under the throne, had raised his sceptre stick. 'You can get down off that now.' He was suddenly scary, I must say, his buttocks swelling out of his shorts, his thick legs apart. He grabbed the frame of the throne and shook it. Then he brought his sceptre down on the Wizard's naked thigh. It made a noise like a handclap. McMorris started pushing at Tansley's chest. But still the Wizard remained erect and gazing through us all, we were so beneath him. I imagined him still smiling with contempt, thinking how stupid we all were.

I don't know what happened in me then. Something terrible. I came to the bottom of the throne. The Wizard took no notice of me, of course, he was so busy despising us all. Then I couldn't help myself. Someone else was waking in me. Someone I didn't know. I reached up and hit him across the face. It brought a thrill of freedom, like hitting Dick. I hit him again, full on the forehead. The others were urging me on. I was letting go of everything, all my anger, and a bitterness I couldn't name. I heard myself say: 'You're not much of a Wizard, are you?' I pulled at his collar, ripped it. Fatboy was pushing at his legs. I reached up, my feet on the crossbar of the throne. I closed my fingers round his mask – it felt quite flimsy – and yanked it off. One of the horns broke away in my hands.

Then I stopped dead. The others went quiet too. Behind the mask, Tansley's whole face was ashen and pinched inwards. He was staring back at me, his eyes awash with tears. Slowly he slid down the throne and remained slumped against it. He refused his mask from my hands. Fatboy tried to climb up in his place, but the throne shuddered and cracked under him, and he clambered down again, muttering: 'All the same, I'm Chief Serpent,' while Tansley began crying in sobs that shook his whole body.

I closed my eyes. It was the first of my betrayals. And I am still not sure why I did it.

He imagined a long journey, a road that would take him away from here, to Cyprus or even further. If you climbed on to the fence beyond the lake, the highway stretched to Wales, or to London, one on either side. Hurry a short way through the graveyard (although he had never done this) and you might find a path going anywhere, and he could imagine entering the classroom map and making for Persia.

He dreamt of running away, but never did. He was not unhappy. Yet he lived most fully in his head. He was frightened of the future, so he clouded it in dreams. It was easier to live fantasies in those days. He used to imagine himself a great surgeon who restored the dying, or a missionary leading whole peoples to God. Nothing was too hard for him. He became a photographer whose creations outshone real life, and an explorer or naturalist who disappeared into the unknown and returned with butterflies as huge as eagles. At one time he had imagined collaborating with Wynne in these discoveries, or exploring the East with Tansley, but later he pictured himself going alone, and thought this a sign of growing up.

Years later, as an old man, he wondered about the veracity of even long-established memories. Once he ran into

Tansley in a London pub. The man was unmistakable, his face pure bone. Tansley's eyes strayed pleasantly over his old friend. He recalled their looking at pond water under the microscope, and their secret that all elements were one, and like the stars, or the dead. He laughed a lot. No, he did not remember anything called the Serpents. He had become a successful barrister.

That last night it was the seeping of smoke under his bedroom door that reminded the invalid, half asleep, of the ritual fire. He had only once gone back to Springdown, and had experienced it two-dimensionally, seeing again the fields and the rhododendron lake and the panelled corridors. But the masters were mostly younger than him, and callow, and the place touched him with the pathos of its imperfection, and a faint, dreamy nausea. When he looked for the Serpents' clearing among the oak trees, he could not find it. He kicked at the earth there, half expecting some charred remnant to emerge. His knee cartilage jarred him then, as it ached now in his bed, waiting for its replacement and wondering why the seagulls were crying about the house so late at night.

7

Traveller

The uppermost tenant awoke with a presentiment of what was coming; but for a minute he imagined that the danger was not yet his. Stumbling out of bed, he took from his walls and shelves the mementoes of fifty years of travelling: an Indian leopard skin, Tanzanian wood-carvings, a Nepalese Buddha, the granite head of a Tang dynasty goddess (a fake), enamelled Persian vases. After casting these through the sitting room windows, he waited long seconds before he heard them crunch in the sodden flower beds below, and only then wondered whether the same fall might kill him, or whether he should risk the passage to the fire escape beyond.

Craning from the open window, he thought he saw the lights of a fire engine flashing in the thickened smoke clouds below. He even anticipated a ladder rising through the growing mass of smoke and flames, and a fireman balanced there, and the silver steps to earth. But the engine lights were only sparks from the ruined basement, and waves of heat were blowing him back from the aperture and into his room.

He felt dizzy, suddenly sick, and lay down on his sofa, as if it were a place of safety. He stared in perplexity at the new bareness of his walls, forgetting how they came to be that way. To his dimming gaze they intimated that he must begin travelling again, that the world waited outside still untouched beyond where he lay. Had he brought nothing back after all? Or even dreamt his travels? Ever since the excision of a brain glioma late in life, he had not trusted his memory. He even imagined things that never happened, or had happened in some hinterland to which he no longer had access.

* * *

The road, on this last journey, was very long. Time spread wonderfully before him. Nothing any longer called him back. Even in retirement, his longing to experience everything of the world's beauty and strangeness throbbed and agitated. His ex-wife had joked acidly that he never saw a horizon without aching to surmount it. He was still a child, she said. Travel was his vice, his addiction. Or else he was trying to escape something. If he kept moving, that inner demon could not keep pace with him, or have time to breathe.

But to him it felt different. To stay at home was to escape. To travel was to undergo reality. After his marriage ended, he filled his free time with intense, sometimes spartan journeys. He took early retirement from schoolteaching. Travel became a compulsion, a subtle liberation. Nothing exceeded the intoxication of his solitude and anonymity in a place far away from anything familiar, or the sense that just out of reach, beyond the next frontier, waited something revelatory. The encounter with ways not his own still touched him with the excitement of human exchange. There were the women, too. For a short, unhappy time he consorted with the fierce, laughing prostitutes of Dar es Salaam and Mombasa, whom he abandoned without guilt because they did not care, but with a curious regret too, as from some deeper attachment.

But then solitude would return. He moved on, and left no trace. The past banked up glittering in his memories, and hung on his walls. It might even be a kind of understanding.

This time he had meant to visit only Jerusalem and Bethlehem. But the garish delusion of the holy places moved him unexpectedly. He stood in the Church of the Holy Sepulchre, at the false Tomb of Christ, and was overcome by bitterness. In this spurious cave of gilt and marble, the long-disowned Christian in him rose in revulsion. He pushed aside the tendered offertory dish, and backed away. Obsessively he hunted in the city for the few slabs of pavement – all but ignored – over which the feet of disciples and future saints must authentically have trod. He bent down to touch them, like a believer. He even gained access to the underground passage of the Hulda Gate, where in the gloom and dust of long neglect he stroked the huge pillars beneath which Jesus must have climbed to the vanished Temple.

Surprised by his own disquiet, he did not return home. He flew to Istanbul, which he had visited forty years ago with the woman who became his wife. He was afraid of forgetting. Three years ago, according to his doctors, the excision of the brain tumour had left his powers of recollection almost unimpaired. But he was not sure. Cancerous tissue had been removed from vital organs of memory, whose names he had forgotten, and he had been troubled ever since by a fear that whole events, even relationships, had gone from his consciousness.

Sometimes, wandering the streets and mosques of Istanbul, the images in his old cine films returned to him, but often film had taken the place of memory, and he could not recall walking here. He knew that the city had radically changed, and that nothing was more natural than these forty years' forgetting. Yet he imagined a physical aching in his head, the dull pain of tissue closing round a void, and the feeling persisted that he was traversing a metropolis of vanished memories.

Near the ancient ramparts that sealed off the city's peninsula for three miles, he came upon a leftover church whose sheltering walls, rising in tiers of brick and stone, struck him with the eerie sense of déjà vu that he experienced quite often now. He associated the feeling with tiredness, perhaps with age. He had not seen this church before, he was sure, yet he expected it at any moment to quicken into recognition.

In the funerary chapel, just short of the apse, an ominous Last Judgement overspread the dome. Beneath the feet of Christ, where Adam and Eve implored forgiveness for the sins of humankind, a river of fire carried the damned into Hell. It flowed down like a sea of blood, and in it he imagined that discolorations in the plaster were the faces of drowning sinners, who would never know the peace of death. He gazed up at them, and at the banked figures of the saved, with an old nausea, and wondered how many millions had died in terror at this morbid fiction, and whether he had seen it before.

There was nothing to call him home. He applied for visas at a string of foreign embassies. He took trains and buses across the Anatolian plateau beyond Lake Van to the eastern borders of Turkey. The sculptural barrenness of these hills elated him. Once over the frontier into Iran, he entered an embargoed country where tourism had vanished, and even in the cities of Isfahan and Shiraz he was almost a lone foreigner. The concept of home was becoming strange to him. He was feeling an inner lightness. He imagined the country sucking him in, and time softening and expanding before him. He wandered through Persepolis, Pasagardae, and the cliff tombs of the ancient Persian kings. He had never travelled this country before. He stayed in cheap hotels and lived on chicken and rice. He could speak no Farsi, but savoured chance conversations in broken English and French. Because of the way he travelled, people thought him poor. His boots and backpack were fraying. When he glanced in the mirror, he was surprised by a face more gaunt and intense than his own.

Weeks later he reached the old Zoroastrian towns of Yazd and Kerman, and walked beneath the Towers of Silence; then he turned north towards the Caspian Sea. It was pilgrimage time in the holy city of Meshed: the greatest concentration of Islamic shrines on earth. His hoteliers warned him against entering its inner sanctuaries. But fancifully he imagined a nest of passageways and curtained rooms, closing on some unique mystery, and felt the fearful impulse to penetrate them.

At evening, swathed in local shawls, he stooped past the door guardians and into the resplendent courts, until at last, swept up in a slipstream of worshippers, he came along chanting corridors into the tomb chamber of a martyred Shia imam. Trembling, guilty, he stood crushed among a roaring mass of mourners, who clutched and wept at the tomb's bars in inexplicable grief. Even in his fear he wondered: Who were they really mourning? The imam had been dead twelve hundred years, his character occluded in pious eulogy. No feat of memory could restore him. Yet grief was rising up like some immemorial sorrow, and anger too. It was as if grief, rapture, God Himself were waiting to be ignited in the labyrinth of the shrine or of the brain. Then the crowd swept him out again into the cold dusk.

Three weeks later, from a hotel in Lahore, he made some dutiful telephone calls. Back in England, nothing had changed. Only in his brother Ricky's voice – usually so patronising – did he detect an unwonted tension. What was Steven doing? Why had he been away so long? Longer than usual . . . When Steven said he planned to go to Simla, the old British summer capital where their father had once worked, he heard down the crackling line a sharp, aroused interest, as if Ricky were grasping for something – anything, perhaps – that might carry force or meaning. And when at last Ricky said: 'I'll fly to Delhi to join you!' Steven felt a time-worn resentment. Across the pulsing distance the words carried a familiar assumption. Ricky made decisions; his younger brother fell in line. But then Steven heard an undercurrent of pleading, and of a gratitude for Steven that Ricky had never shown before. 'I don't want to muck up your plans . . .' Perversely, the breakdown of that old condescension began to alarm him. He found himself agreeing to meet, just as he would have as a boy, but now from perplexed anxiety.

For a week longer he journeyed in the shadow of Ricky's arrival. The solitude he cherished intensified with the imminence of its end. He camped for two nights in the Himalayan foothills, and at dawn watched the snow peaks light up one by one in the night sky, kindled by an invisible hand, and knew why the Hindus sanctified them. When he entered the smog and pollution of Delhi, this magic still clung to him, so that he shrank from the prospect of Ricky. Ricky would bring England along with him, and the horizon would lower and dim.

At the airport, Steven's irritation sparked the moment he glimpsed him. In the stream of other travellers, dressed in their dark anoraks, shawls and modest saris, Ricky appeared in a tropical suit and loafers, trailing a big suitcase. He must have imagined India perennially hot. But closer to, Steven softened. His brother looked oddly haggard and alone. His hair was swept back thinner and greying from his temples. When they awkwardly embraced, as they always had, Steven was reminded that he stood taller than Ricky, although the moment they disengaged this would seem an illusion. But now, standing in the wan arrivals hall, he felt his brother's body narrower than he recalled, and thought he even shook a little. Perversely he recoiled from this. In the end he wanted things to remain as they had always been: even Ricky's authority.

Outside, the smog had thickened. They took the metro to the city centre, then an auto-rickshaw through the shock of traffic to Old Delhi station. Steven was used to this now, but he momentarily found himself looking out through Ricky's tired eyes: at the press of squealing scooters and rickshaws, the dust-clogged pipal and eucalyptus trees, the pavement sewage and shit, and beyond them the ghostly rise of tower blocks in the smog.

Their train was five hours late. Fog poured through the long vaults of the station, where people slept oblivious under strip lights on the cracked marble floors, their children and baggage around them. Ricky found a lavatory, where he changed into corduroy trousers, sweater and a raincoat. The waiting rooms were overflowing. They walked up and down the cold concourse while Steven wondered at their being here, and what might have happened to Ricky. They had not travelled together since their father took them on holiday as teenagers to Scotland.

'Why now?' he wondered aloud. 'Why here?'

Ricky grimaced. 'I had to leave England. Even for a few weeks.' He ignored Steven's stare. 'And India is the place I first remember. I thought: so why not go back? Stupid, really.' Perhaps he was regretting it already. He was hugging his shoulders against the cold. 'But you, why did you want to go to Simla, Steven? You don't even remember it.'

Simla lived in Steven's mind through his mother's evocation of it, even through his father's quiet. He said: 'I wanted to remember them.'

Ricky gave a curt laugh. 'I think Dad wanted to forget. He hardly ever talked about India.'

Steven remembered his father's silence too. It was his mother who had eulogised Simla: its mountain wonder, the scent of pine woods. But to his father, India had signified lost opportunity. He had passed the Colonial Service exams, then for five years worked in some administrative office before India's looming independence brought them all home.

Ricky said: 'He had ideas about his future. He dreamed of becoming a district officer in the Punjab, administering justice to the natives. Then it was all over . . .'

'Did he tell you that?' Steven felt a twinge of bitterness at how little was ever vouchsafed to him. Ricky had always been his father's favourite. India, to Steven, hovered only on the edge of recall. He said at last: 'Ricky, do you really remember Simla?'

As a boy, Ricky used to torment him with tales of monkeys and elephants, whereas Steven could remember almost nothing of India at all. He was only four years old when they returned to England, sailing on the HMT *Dilwara*. But Ricky was already seven, and his store of exotic tales increased with the years.

As they walked, Steven fantasised that something around him might sharpen into memory. It was easy to imagine. The loudspeaker announcements – in Hindi and stilted English – resounded in his head like ancient trumpets. Each was punctuated by the notes of an organ, which infused its proclamations with baleful divinity. And at the station's heart, beneath its display board, a line of *sanyassin* renunciates slept, stretched out on newspapers in their saffron robes and turbans, their features retracted in thickets of hair. Couldn't he have remembered such things? But Ricky too stared at them in wonder.

It was late evening before they boarded their sleeping car. Lying under its stained blankets, in a cubicle shielded by frayed curtains, Steven closed his eyes with relief against the deepening night. The train rumbled northward through the fog, and Ricky receded into a disembodied voice three feet away. The only other sound was the muffled laughter of passengers from a distant cubicle. In the fading orange glow of Delhi beyond their window, Ricky said: 'Judith has left me.'

Steven felt no jolt of surprise. Ricky and his wife had lived in mutual infidelity for years, and there seemed nothing left to bind them. Their daughters were married and gone. Steven murmured his condolence into the dark. Then he heard himself say: 'I never liked her.'

But Ricky's voice had turned soft and baffled. 'I told her it was too late, Steve. Divorce is something people do when they're young, like you did. But we're old. I'm sixty-nine, we've got used to one another, and forgiven most things. God knows, it's too late to start again.' He left a moment's silence, in case Steven might fill it. 'And she chose the wrong moment to leave.'

'What moment?'

Another silence, then: 'I've been fired from my board.'

'Oh hell, Ricky, why?' Steven expected a saga of takeovers or boardroom treachery, but instead Ricky said: 'There was a misappropriation of assets.'

Steven did not understand what followed. Ricky's words took on a confessional tension in the dark, yet they sounded empty, as if he had spoken them too often. They concerned bank debenture trading and misrepresentation in company records. It seemed his brother had trodden a tightrope between irregular practice and outright fraud. Steven gave up trying to understand his arguments, and listened instead to their tone: by turns guilty, aggrieved, reconciled.

In the end, they lay in silence. Steven stared up at nothing. The air was thick with smells of cumin, sweat, disinfectant. In the past, Steven might have experienced secret triumph. Ricky, the successful one, the suave career role model: his life exposed as a crude charade. But now he waited to feel anything at all. He said at last: 'I never understood business, Ricky.'

'Nor did Judith.'

'Did she leave you because of that?'

'She said she would have left anyway. She said unforgivable things.'

Judith – small, eager, ingratiating – had always irritated Steven. He did not see the point of her. He said: 'It would help if you were angry.'

But Ricky was not angry. He sounded bereft. Some fearsome void was engulfing him in her absence. 'You must think I still love her.'

Steven leant across and touched his brother's hand, where it covered his face. The upsurge of his own compassion took him by surprise, and was followed at once by a fleeting thrill of closeness, then by an old embarrassment. And when Ricky muttered, 'Bloody woman', it was said to close the subject off.

Steven did not sleep, but the train fell silent with the sleep of others. Sometimes it stopped at wan-lit stations, where nobody got in or out. Restlessly awake, Steven felt glad that his mother would never know of Ricky's fall. She, whose affections were spread equally, would have been racked by mystified sadness, and would have strained to disbelieve whatever she was told. But she had died two years before, with her illusions intact. Only at the end did the passionate, big-boned woman sink under a massive stroke. Then, for a week, she had sought the clasp of Steven's hand over the hospital sheet, and his voice correcting her confusions and hopes. Yes, Ricky is on business in Australia. Yes, Ricky is coming home (but he came too late). And her flesh at last had refined to an ethereal delicacy, unrecognisable, and her eyes were flinched shut, and her hand a precious claw in his.

A century earlier, the imperial British had built a narrow-gauge railway into the Himalayan foothills to Simla. Through more than a hundred tunnels and over eight hundred bridges it annually carried the governing elite up from the threatening swelter of Delhi towards the mountains. Steven's parents had travelled with it. In fact, he and Ricky might be settling into the same wooden seats as they had. Just before dawn, the toy-like train started to tug its red and yellow carriages out of the mist and began a five-hour ascent. At first it snaked through tropical vegetation, then levered itself upward in hairpin loops among giant cedars and pines. At noon they saw the horizon break open on a shimmering palisade of snow, and glimpsed the old summer capital spread along precipitous ridges above them.

Steven had no idea what to expect, and they stepped out into nothing recognisable. They searched for a hotel in the centre, and were engulfed by throbbing crowds. Weekend holidaymakers from the plains, Delhi office workers, Sikhs and mountain tribespeople flowed round them in rivers of different dialects and violent colours. People came to Simla now to shop, trek, relax. Jeans and anoraks and bobble hats jostled among turbans and *salwar* trousers; and everyone was taking photographs. No Westerner was in sight. Ricky had brought a map, and tried to trace old landmarks, without success. The world they were seeking had been gone for sixty years. Modern India had overswept it: bright, swarming, newly confident.

Along the main ridge a bronze Mahatma Gandhi walked with his staff and book, his plinth inscribed 'The Father of the Nation'. Vendors of candyfloss and ice cream were milling around him, and children taking pleasure rides on docile horses. Opposite, a statue of Indira Gandhi, the Iron Lady of her day, stood with her back to the steep suburban slopes, and a troop of rhesus monkeys was bustling round her feet.

Slowly Steven and Ricky began to notice round them the buildings that their parents must have known. They stood in a quaint mock-Tudor style that was soon to be despised in their motherland, and survived here in faded anachronism. At one end of the esplanade the neo-Gothic Christ Church was closed, its drainpipes wrapped in barbed wire; at the other, the old town hall had withered to a wraith of glass and rotted timber, the shingles slithering from its dormer windows, and pigeons flying in and out of empty rooms.

That evening, exhausted, they sat on their twin beds as they had as boys, and wondered if they should have come. Ricky had brought with him an old family photo album, and with it a pencil map of Simla's western ridge. Here, in their father's meticulous hand, various government offices were inscribed, and just beneath the grounds of Viceregal Lodge a faded green dot marked where their parents' bungalow had stood. In his youth, Steven had once asked to see this album, and had found himself peering into a time he strained to imagine, until his father had eased the book away again with one of his dismissive quips. But now, while his brother slept, he leafed through its pages with deepening fascination. In its small, faded snapshots, Simla's shopping mall, its churches and its half-timbered offices looked near-deserted: a sepia stage set dotted with stock figures in topis and rickshaws. But there were pictures too of polo matches and viceregal garden parties, of their mother's face shadowed under an enormous Florentine hat, and a military band playing in the background, while his father chatted with colleagues in morning coat and the grey top hat that he'd kept until his death.

In other photographs, closer and more intimate, the couple were sitting on their bungalow's veranda, or in its sunlit rooms. Here was his mother planting a pot of nasturtiums or cradling a Labrador puppy, while his father lounged in a wicker chair reading *Blackwood's Magazine*. They stared unsmiling into the camera. Steven might not have recognised them. His mother's eyes looked blacker and sharper than they were, her hair tightly parted and bunched to either side. Her expression was different from any he remembered; she looked hard, self-protected, even frightened. Yet she'd fallen in love, she said, with the scent of cedars and the Himalayan streams. As he turned the pages, Steven was overcome by the feeling of how deeply his parents were separate from him. They had lived these lives before he was born. His mother had ridden horses at the Annandale race meetings; his father had hunted sambur in the Sivalik Hills. There were blurred snapshots of people dancing. As he looked, his parents became stranger with their time. Inscrutably young, they drifted away from him. He longed to question them: What were you feeling? Were you so different? Yet even in this alienation, he realised that by some trick of time they already seemed to be his parents, and subtly senior. They would for ever be older than him.

In such photographs the servants occupied an opaque hinterland of their own. They wore white jackets and banded turbans, but their dark complexions seemed to retract them into shadow. If they appeared in any photo, they were labelled under generic names – the *khansame*, the *mali*, the *dhobi* – and they walked barefoot. Only the chief bearer laid a guiding hand on the shoulder of a small boy – Ricky – who stood to attention in khaki shorts and a loose, big-collared shirt. And towards the album's end, another child appeared. Steven knew this must be himself. He was lying in the lap of his Indian nurse, his *ayah*, whose bangled arms cradled his head, or he held her hand as an infant schoolboy. Soon both boys wore outsize topis, Ricky already alert and manly, clutching a home-made kite, while Steven's face looked blanched and dreaming. She, his *ayah*, was almost all he could remember of India, and perhaps he had imagined her too. She was a mission-educated Madrasi, his mother had said, and wore a crimson sari. Her face and arms were burnished, dark and oiled, and the corners of her eyes, slanting nearly to her hairline, gave her the gaze of a cat. Of Steven's broken memories barely three survived: a monkey leering from a stone lantern somewhere; the pliant mud from which he'd modelled little animals; and the aroma of this dark woman.

He closed the album and switched off his lamp. Below the hotel window rose the noises and fumes of a late-night bazaar – the smells of woodsmoke and coriander, and the sound of Hindi music. He went out on to the balcony, unwilling to sleep. The hillside below was covered in dimming lights. The familiar excitement of such moments – of unknown lights and sounds – was touched with the melancholy of his parents' absence. One by one the lights went out and the noises dwindled. Then the barking of the pye-dogs started up – a howling that had haunted his mother's nights – and a half-moon was shining over the mountains.

He gazed at this for a long time: the dying lights of the town beneath the illumined Himalayas. Fancifully he wondered if the elation he felt at such sights were not a kind of remembrance. He wondered if the sensations of his Indian infancy, which had followed him through English boarding school in fading images – a leering monkey, a woman's bangled arm – had lingered on in his unconscious, so that his later passion for travel was not a desire to experience novelty at all, but a hunt to recover what he had lost: a pilgrimage whose origins he had forgotten.

Dawn came quickly. The magic of the night bazaar had evaporated. The store shutters were down – it was Sunday – and the pye-dogs lay asleep in the gutters. A cold wind came in from the north. Ricky, who had woken dull-eyed and tetchy, insisted on recalling over breakfast their father's disillusion: how premature the Indianisation of the civil service had been, how interfering the parvenu politicians, how weak-willed the British. Everybody, it seemed, was a fool, even his father. 'He never saw it coming.'

But in the early-morning quiet they could discern at last the insubstantial shape of their parents' world. If you dissolved from your mind the suburbs swarming over the farther slopes – their roofs too brightly red or green – then the cleansed hills would roll untrammelled to the foot of the imperial ridges, and the long, glacial silhouettes of the Himalayas loom closer. From the curve of the old, narrow high street, the lanes dropped precipitously into the valley. The gabled shops that lined it clung to old names and times: Ram and Son 1908; C. Fook Chong & Co, designer of Chinese shoes; Duti Chand Travel Good; est. 1921 . . .

Steven remembered his mother deriding the mall as a centre of gossip and wasted time. She ordered everything through the Army & Navy Stores catalogue, she said, and he was aware of scanning these shops with her indifference. But while he was recreating Simla through her eyes, Ricky was doing so through his father's, and when they found a side door of Christ Church open, they went in to find their father standing in imagination among the bronze memorial plaques to the dead servants of the Raj, lit by Victorian virtues: Prudence, Fortitude, Patience – pallid women in stained glass.

Soon afterwards Steven stumbled on the little Gaiety Theatre, where their mother had acted in one of the amateur plays staged by the British. Its programme was pasted into the album that Ricky had brought along with him – they opened it in the empty auditorium – and there was a picture of their mother in a clinging silk dress, acting in an obscure comedy called *By Candlelight*. Even in a photograph she looked too big for the stage, her gestures and features too stark. A guide told them that nothing since her day had changed: only the crimson decor had been muted to green and gold. Gingerly Steven climbed the stage to the spot where she had stood, and followed her gaze beyond the kerosene footlights to the viceregal box and the banked seats – three hundred and twenty of them. He even thought he felt her stage fright.

It was noon before they reached the old precincts of imperial government. The domestic Tudor architecture had disappeared, and their way was dark with trees. Buildings in heavy stone stood on the slopes above them, half invisible. Ricky walked buoyantly, his spirits recovered, his father's album slung in a hessian bag over one shoulder. But Steven felt a sad frustration. He had thought Simla might bring his parents nearer, that his damaged brain would shape new understanding round them. But instead he sensed them receding into history. Their world was not his, and they were young, far younger than he was now. Ricky, he thought, was more wholesome, more down-to-earth than him. Ricky either cared less or accepted more. 'They were just themselves, Steve,' he said.

They reached the office where their father had worked, but it had become a barracks, inaccessible – the Sikh sentry warned them away. Then came the quaint imperial post office, and at last they were winding up beneath the long, dark-stoned revetment of the drive to Viceregal Lodge, the heart of British power over four hundred million souls. For a long time the place withheld itself, hidden on its tree-thronged hill. Then mown lawns appeared, clipped hedges and English flower beds, and finally the enormous confection of the residence itself. They gazed at it in astonishment. It was at once forbidding and fantastical: a massive architectural hesitation between Tudor palace, giant baronial castle and Mogul pavilion.

They sat on a bench and caught their breath. Here, in an early photograph, their father stood beneath the emblazoned porch, one hand on his hip, posing for an unknown camera. He was barely twenty-five. He must have been on official business, because he was dressed not for an evening reception, but in shorts and knee-length socks. As Steven scrutinised the photograph, he saw to his bemusement a face in which the ingrained sourness of the father he remembered had never been. The mouth that became so tight and cynical was smiling broadly. Under his topi, his expression was cloudless, confident, as if the porch above him were the entrance to the future. In later years, Steven recalled, his father had ridiculed Viceregal Lodge as a mongrel wedding cake, its multi-tiered galleries and mullioned windows, oriels and turrets all blazoned with a heraldry he said he despised.

For a while they walked among the magnolias and irises of the Victorian garden. They heard a peacock cry. Ricky had turned sombre. 'I don't know why Dad stayed so hurt by India,' he said. Steven sensed he was empathising with his father's failure, as if failure were genetic. 'He should have left it behind.'

They walked out of the estate and under the rim of its hill. A tarmac road replaced the track that had once wound beneath their parents' bungalow. Its glade was dense with hemlock and cedar trees. The mangy rhesus monkeys that infested the town had vanished, and a troop of white-maned langurs was plunging through the branches. He and Ricky had little hope of finding even the site of the bungalow. Ricky said he had clear memories of it. Steven had none. There were other houses scattered along the way now: run-down cottages and warehouses, an advocate's office. But the lane was very quiet. Sometimes the langur monkeys leapt with a crash from their treetops on to the corrugated iron roofs, then stillness returned.

They sat for a while on a crumbling wall, in the scent of fallen pine needles, and debated whether to go back. Then suddenly Ricky said: 'There it is!'

They were sitting on its lower terrace, and they saw at once that it was derelict. Above them a thicket of new-grown trees obscured it, and the bank on which it stood was a tangle of grasses. They climbed the fractured steps softly on to the veranda. Ricky recognised the stuccoed pillars, brightly sunlit in the photos, but darkened now by overhanging trees. The veranda paving had splintered into a roughened pool of stones under their feet. Ricky was saying: 'I remember . . . I remember . . .' but his voice was muted, unsure.

They tried the doors, but they were locked. Whoever had last lived here must have left years ago. A web of cracks was spreading over the outer walls, and the frames of steel mosquito netting dangled from the windows. Against one balustrade somebody homeless had laid a few bricks to enclose the cinders of a fire. There were dead leaves, a pair of rotted trainers. But Steven glimpsed the view through trees that his parents would have known: a gleam of mountains where a lammergeier was sailing on the wind. Sometimes, staring about him, he wondered if a few years ago, before his brain surgery, he would have remembered everything. He began to slip in and out of wish-fulfilment. He imagined he recalled his father sipping gin on the terrace, while his mother came and went smiling through the doors.

Ricky had opened their album on a window ledge, and was working out the layout of the rooms. Peering through a window where the shutters had disintegrated, Steven saw only debris and splintered glass. But this, he realised, had been his parents' sitting room, and a single yellowed photograph furnished it again with its cane chairs and chintz curtains and a sofa where his mother was reading. A potted palm stood in the left-hand corner, with a wind-up gramophone beside it. Beneath this snapshot, this now-ruined room, his father had inscribed: 'Our first home'. Steven went on looking through the window, surprised by the prickling behind his eyes. There had been a teak sideboard too, and the skin of a sambur hung on the wall above his mother's head.

She had been happy here. Bored by the round of bridge parties and race meetings, she said, she'd taken up Urdu lessons and had held soirées for Indian wives. She disbelieved the rumoured hatred that was gathering against the British, and years later remembered with nostalgia the fluttering pennants of the Indian cavalry, the day-long picnics in the pine woods, and the sudden starlight of the Indian nights, by which she'd read *Anna Karenina*.

None of this could Steven guess from the faces staring from the album. Only his *ayah* seemed herself, whoever that might have been, her age irrelevant, her upswept eyes fixed on an infant's face. But from an envelope stuck at the album's end, as if in afterthought, there fell out a photo of their mother in the sitting room beside another man. He was delicately handsome, dressed in a knee-length surcoat and carrying a cane: an Indian aristocrat, it seemed, hatless but immaculate, with polished European shoes. He was looking at the camera with anxious, swimming eyes, while she was looking at him, her hand on his arm.

'Let's see.' Ricky was peering over Steven's shoulder. 'That's a strange photo.'

'Her hand . . .'

'An Indian.' Ricky began to smile. 'That was unheard of.'

'I wonder who took the photo.' Steven smiled bleakly, surprised.

'His servant, I suppose.' Ricky suddenly laughed. 'She was never one to play by the rules.'

'You think he was her lover?'

'Simla was notorious for that. Everyone had affairs.'

'I know Father did, but not Mother.'

Then Steven felt a dull sadness, but quite for what, he didn't know. As a boy he had thought his mother beautiful – perhaps every son did – then came to realise her heaviness, her indefinable rawness. Only with old age did some inner frailty paper her skin delicately over her bones, and her gaze was sometimes softened by confusion. He wondered who else had held the hand that reached for his across the hospital bed. Maybe, characteristically, she had thrust the affair behind her; or perhaps, in her silence, cherished it. He wished only that he had known. She seemed farther away now.

'Do you remember him, Ricky?'

'I was only seven!'

Ricky was talking about other things: his first Wolf Cub uniform at the prep school nearby, and how two years earlier he had inveigled himself on to the route of the departing viceroy, Lord Linlithgow, and presented a wobbly salute; and the clouds of butterflies that had once flowed over the school playing fields and into the valleys.

Under the monkey-infested trees they squeezed around a wall to the servants' quarters. A few outhouses were still standing, their tin roofs intact, and a gutted cookhouse. Steven walked beyond them into the remains of the garden, stepping frailly between remembrance and the illusion of it. He stared back at the bungalow's wall, its brick chimneys, the balustrade. Something seemed immanent in them. He found himself treading lightly, as if to make no noise in the present.

Then he remembered the orchard. A kind of sickness overcame him. He was willing his mind too fiercely to enter the past, he knew. But in the undergrowth, the Himalayan apple trees stood gnarled and redolent – they would already have stood tall sixty years ago – and he touched their trunks as though they were familiar. A circle of stone marked where the water butt had stood: a black-painted cylinder that he suddenly recollected, its rim already frayed by rust. No brain surgery had erased it. The stones were rough and damp to his touch. Beyond them he pictured Ricky's young face, saying nothing, and the smell of fallen apples filled his nostrils. Then, in the luxury of willed remembrance, in the orchard's long grass, his *ayah*'s bangled arms were round him, and although he knew that the remembering brain trembles and changes with every recollection, her eyes were shining and his child's lips kissed her, he was sure, and he caressed her dark breast.

*   *   *

Beyond the window the view had dimmed to a flatland of blurred shapes and ashen colours. Wheat and paddy fields left only opaque rectangles in the fog. To the south, the Ganges was invisible. Sometimes a few farmers crossed the mist, or a bullock stood idle in the merging land and sky.

At dusk, Steven dropped into half-sleep in his empty cubicle, inured to the stench of the urinals and to the *chai*-sellers calling along the corridors. On the bare bunk opposite, Ricky had left him a water bottle and some biscuits, and the memory of an awkward farewell. By the time they parted – two elderly Englishmen embracing in the turmoil of Old Delhi station – something of Ricky's old, brusque authority had returned. He might have continued travelling, he said, but India was not his country, he couldn't stand another masala chicken, and there were things he had to do back in England.

To his own surprise, some incommunicable sadness in Steven made him want to return with Ricky, but not yet. He planned to see Varanasi, the great pilgrimage city on the Ganges, and perhaps afterwards to travel south. In parting, Ricky had said: 'Are you still pissed off about forgetting things, Steve? Because your memory's fine. You keep remembering them all: Dad and Mother and all those others . . . maybe too much.'

For eighteen hours the fog blinded the train to snail's pace. It seemed always to be slowing down, but it never stopped. Steven pulled the stained railway sheets and blanket over his head, and lay on his back in jaded insomnia. Belatedly he resented Ricky for the notion that he was slipping back into memory, into the dead. Yet of course there were deaths that continued, deaths that seemed unresolved: Sylvia, the colleague's wife he had loved after his divorce, who had died in a distant hospital; the friend who had hanged himself decades ago; and his mother, yes, who returned to him always, in her unhealed absence, and her new enigma. And then there were those other, lesser deaths – partings and betrayals – that haunted you in the solitude of travel: old friends he had forgotten, women he had failed in love. It was now that the elusiveness of memories most troubled him. He wondered if the intermittent throbbing in his head was self-induced. Sometimes, fantastically, he even imagined there might have been another self, who had known and experienced things more intensely than he, someone of whom he was only a belated refraction.

He fell at last into fitful sleep. The train reached Mughal Serai at four in the morning and he disembarked into a still, clammy cold. The station lights were orange orbs hung up in the fog. An auto-rickshaw found him and carried him through the night, its torn curtains open to the road, towards the Buddhist sanctuaries of Sarnath. For an hour it puttered over the unlit tracks of scattered villages where men crouched over roadside fires, and left him at last in the fog-bound silence of the holy town. He found a Tibetan monastery whose courtyard doors were open, and went in and sat in its concealing mist until dawn. He felt the excitement of his own solitude returning, then rifled through his backpack to find Ricky's biscuits.

Light came imperceptibly, less like dawn than a transparency in the night air. One by one the monks and pilgrims emerged to twirl the prayer wheels round the temple court, murmuring their mantras, and the throb of drums and chanting filled the temple. He sat there for a long time, feeling a subdued elation, listening to the incomprehensible prayers, until an old guest master arrived and assigned him a cell in the cloisters.

In the streets outside, Steven ignored the stalls of gilded souvenirs and the touts for fake antiques, and went into a park where the fog gentled the remains of a monastery city founded more than two millennia ago. Here the Buddha had preached his first sermon, surrounded by early disciples and some attentive deer. A few monks were circling the only memorial stupa to survive – a towering cylinder of stone-faced brick – and pilgrims were lighting candles wherever they believed the Buddha had preached. Around them a vast complex of monasteries and temples, fallen into ruin a thousand years ago, spread its brick foundations into the mist: grass-fringed cells, terraces, avenues, and the empty circles of once-stupendous shrines.

Living monasteries – Japanese, Thai, Chinese, Burmese – filled the town outside. His own Tibetan sanctuary was quietly venerated. In its temple, beyond the low seats and banked altar, the gilded torso of an enormous Buddha loomed, his head invisible in the shrine's tower, while his golden hands descended to inscribe the gesture of his enlightenment, received in the park where Steven had just walked. The walls were covered with rank on rank of frescoed Buddhas, tiny and identical, like echoes of the prayers and mantras chanted here, in the peace of repetition.

His cell was furnished with an iron bed and a defunct fan. Two nights he woke to the low, pulsing prayer in the temple, like a beehive stirring, and in the morning found the monks eating at their makeshift canteen, or walking along the cold cloisters in their magenta robes and woollen hats. Several spoke English, and talked to him in soft, surprised voices. Few of them had ever known their Tibetan homeland. Born in exile, they had found a homeland in their faith. What was Tibet in their minds? he wondered. Was it a lost paradise, or the despoiled country of the Chinese? An old monk, burning with some inner merriment, said that Tibet was present here in India, in the lineage of its teachers. Here was the true country.

To Steven the monks seemed mysteriously cheerful. He found himself asking them naive questions. Talking about karma and *samsara*, they answered him gently, so that he warmed especially to the old man, and to a frail-looking acolyte. The younger fell silent in the presence of the older, so Steven tried to encounter them separately; yet often they echoed one another, as if from the same insight or authority, speaking of the human being always as an entity that ceases and is constantly reborn. Norbu, the old man, described the journeying soul as a wayfarer who takes up his abode each night, then sleeps and forgets, and rises each morning to a new birth. Tenzin, the acolyte, likened such rebirths to a planted tulip that flowers again each year after sleeping in the earth.

Yet no soul existed. There was no lasting human essence, they said. Only the journey itself, the karma of cause and effect. While Norbu boomed his truths in grinning serenity, Tenzin sensed some distress in Steven. His thin fingers twisted at his prayer beads as he spoke, as if they might sweeten his answers, and his eyes flickered. 'Things are different with us' – he assumed Steven a Christian. 'We don't believe in the existence of God. There is no Creator. There are gods who are aids to understanding, but they die. They are illusions.'

Steven was silent, then asked: 'If there is no God, what survives death?' He could hear the breathiness in his own question, as if Tenzin – whose speech was so exact, so certain, yet nervous – might have secret knowledge.

'Something inherited,' the monk answered. 'Something waiting to be perfected.' His hands unfurled from his chest. 'But the previous life cannot be found again.'

'It has no memory . . .'

'If it has memory, it does not know it. Sometimes a person is reminded after many years, maybe prompted by chance. There are stories . . .'

Steven detected a searching for his consolation in the monk's eyes. Yes, there were stories of people remembering their previous lives, but strange stories, unsure. In the end, nobody could find again the loved dead. They were changed, they did not even know themselves. Tenzin said: 'They have already gone. They'll never come again.'

'No.' But Steven could see his tension reflected in Tenzin's face. His gaze dropped from the monk's into silence. 'There's too much past.' He heard the voice of his colleague's wife, Sylvia, who had died in love with him; he still touched his mother's hand; and the hanged and innocent head went on turning in his memory.

The old monk Norbu, seated in a cell almost as bare as Steven's, cheerfully told Steven he did not exist. In fact neither of them existed. Nor did Tenzin. The world began to thin and vanish with the illumination that led at last to nirvana. It was the self that created its surroundings. And these were illusions. And the self too was an illusion: the greatest of all. It was meditation – Norbu had meditated over fifty years – that brought about this purified vision. Once started on the path of meditation – and he patted Steven's arm in encouragement – you could never return. 'You'd lose too much! Ha, ha! You'd die back into suffering. We say that life is a burning house.'

Steven noticed by Norbu's bed a parchment mandala: the painting of a maze-like palace, at whose centre sat a Buddha. This wasn't magic, Norbu laughed, and no, it was not a maze either. It was an aid to meditation, in which you focused on the sacred figure at its heart. This was an act of great discipline and stillness, in which the independent self slowly evaporated, and united at last with the Buddha.

Steven remembered from his teaching days, as from another life, some recent experiments on the brain, proving that prolonged focus on an object, through a complex imbalance of neural flow, produced the sensation of the self and its object merging. For a moment he wanted to tell the old man this, to temper his certainty. But of course the experiment proved nothing. Only that the brain was either the receiver or the creator of divinity. Rapture or grief – or maybe God – were waiting in the mind's dark, to be ignited by the martyr's shrine at Meshed perhaps, or by the confessions of a postulant in the candlelight: either self-induced or divinely precipitated, no one could know.

Steven tried to imagine travelling down this path of meditation, deep into its certainty, its neural transformation, while the old man beamed at him. He might journey on, of course, until return became impossible: until doubt vanished together with the sharpness of grief, and the dead were released into their reincarnations.

In the monk's faith, he realised, only good and evil importantly survived, continuing in a chain of karma that was beyond self, and moving to the salvation of all sentient things.

'When people dream' – it was Tenzin speaking, with his odd, tremulous certainty – 'they imagine that all sorts of desires and terrors are real. But then they wake up. The "I" is like that too. It is dreaming illusion.'

Steven could not recall ever hearing Norbu or Tenzin speak in the first person. Perhaps they instinctively recoiled from it. 'I' was not an intrinsic entity for them. It was only a series of transitory responses, which in memory constructed a recipient for themselves and called it 'I'. 'I' was the story the perceptions told themselves. As in recent theories of the brain, the coherent self disappeared.

Yet he muttered almost inaudibly: 'But somebody wakes up from the dream. There is somebody dreaming.'

'There is nobody dreaming,' Tenzin said.

After a while, a kind of weary impatience grew in Steven. He was starting to equate doubt with liberation, and he wanted to leave. But there was a fragility in his head, he knew. Something had been taken away. It would never return, whatever concentration he exerted. Perhaps it was for this that he determined to insist on 'I', his own singularity. I am walking along this street, he told himself, after he left the monastery. I am looking for a bus. In an hour's time I think I will be in Varanasi. These are my legs, my arms. I . . .

*   *   *

The streets grow dense with pilgrims and traders, all muffled against the fog, long before they reach the Ganges.
Rickshaws and motor scooters thrust and weave between
them. The noise is tremendous. The people have grown
dark and small since Simla, pilgrims from country towns
and villages, led by their *panda*s, their foreheads bright
with *tilak*s. They barely look at me. From time to time a
wooden bier is rushed through the streets. The shrouded
corpse lies rigid, its garlanded head poking out from gold
and crimson sheets, and a handful of mourners follow
chanting *Rama nama satya hai!* Sometimes they look joy-
ous. *God's name is truth!* The air above is jungled with
advertisements and electric cables. Garbage is everywhere,
open sewers and pavement fires. Dogs sleep in the warm
ash, and white cows graze.

I go down alleys to the river. Four, five storeys high,
their walls barely let in light. They are rotted plaster: a
labyrinth overhung by decayed balconies and shutters.
The way is constricted by stone steps and ledges, where
people sleep. The doors give on to darkness. And the
gods' sanctuaries are everywhere: in alcoves and subterranean
chambers, where the stone phallus of Shiva, lord of destruction and change, is wreathed with marigolds and shiny from
anointing. The whole of Varanasi is his. Mystically balanced
on his trident, the city escapes the Hindu cycles of cosmic
time. It is indestructible. Those who die and are cremated
here will instantly enter *moksha*, the Hindu nirvana. So the
place is crowded with the sick and the old, waiting. I am
walking into the heart of an ancient understanding. Seen
with clear eyes, people say, the city is beautiful. The fero-
cious neglect – the drifting rubbish, the open sewers, the

chronic poverty – is the thin cloak of its sanctity. Yama, the lord of death, is forbidden to enter. Only I do not see this. My vision is unpurified. I am just a tourist, and the beggars throng round me, shaking their empty bowls.

I find a hotel near the Ganges. It is dusk now. The river flows oily grey beyond my window. A run-down restaurant serves the masala chicken that Ricky hated – nothing here costs more than a few pence – and I wash this down with Kingfisher beer, and go early to bed. After last night's monastic cell my room looks cavernous; its warm shower brings on a nostalgia for comfort. I sleep fitfully and wake in the night to hear chanting and bells, then fall asleep again. You may take a boat at dawn along the holy Ganges, the hotelier said, while the pilgrims come down to bathe. So I go out into the cold before sunrise, and the boatmen crowd around me calling, 'Uncle! Boat, Uncle!', until I select an old oarsman – he is shivering under a tattered pullover – and we push out on to the river.

The night becomes white around us. Our oars creak forward into a vaporous wall of sky and water. Then the city starts to materialise: an auburn silhouette in the greyness, where a few lights shine. For four miles along the river enormous terraces of steps flow down beneath ancient-looking temples and palaces. The sun rises and hangs like a white coin in the emptiness, void of any circumambient light. And already the people are descending. Men strip to their loincloths and walk waist-deep into the flood. They splash its sanctity over their bodies, their faces. Some submerge themselves wholesale. A holiday joyousness is in the air. Women bathe laughing in their saris. Stout Brahmin torsos, dangling their ceremonial cord, mingle with the spindly, the aged. They make isolated tableaux as we pass. A young man, deep in the cold current, stands raptly facing the east, his palms joined in prayer. An old woman, frail and shaking, is gentled into the water by her daughters, perhaps for the last time.

My boatman rests on his oars. 'You make offer to Mother Ganges?' He sells me a garland to float on the river. 'You want buy silks?'

No silks, no. The polluted current squelches against our prow. The river's edges are seamed deep in refuse. Effluent from factories upriver – chemical plants, tanneries, slaughterhouses – joins the sewage and litter and fragments of cremated bodies, to float past us in a slow, toxic holiness. The palaces and temples that tower over the steps, rising from blank walls into skyline galleries and turrets, look gutted and derelict, their windows unlit. Their walls are broken by faded advertisements for hostels and restaurants, by painted gods, by notices for 'Yogic Voice Consciousness', the Elvis Guest House, and a helpline for abandoned children.

As the day wears on, groups of pilgrims float on to the river in big, slow motorboats. Their engines barely sound under the temples. Far out in the calm, where the eastern shore of the Ganges is a treeless wilderness, they drift suspended in the fog, and women float tiny cups of candle flame on to the water. Along the more popular ghats, priests are settled under saffron umbrellas, and sadhu holy men, smeared with ash or sandalwood, sit before homemade shrines to Shiva and gaze motionless at the river.

I gaze back at them, and wonder what they are seeing. I feel an old urge to capture this whole spectacle on camera, and cross the steps all afternoon in a watery sunlight. Along the quietest stretches, boys are playing cricket with sticks and tennis balls, or flying kites which twitch high in an air that looks unearthly still. Other terraces are gaudy with pink towers and clustered parasols, like some sacred funfair, while downriver shine the everlasting fires of the cremation grounds. Everything seems to arrange itself for the camera in a shock of colour or vivid composition. A temple tilts into the sludge in sheaves of sculpted stone. Flocks of mynah birds shower from a palace roof. A young woman, slim and poor, collects the Ganges water into a little phial and cradles it at her breast. And all along the terraces a telephoto lens can foreshorten the crowds into a brilliant multitude, and angle along the river's edge to capture a collage of glistening, hirsute bodies.

But at dusk, in an alley's shelter, I run these photos back through my viewfinder, and wonder. Some essence has eluded me. It is as if everything visible in this strange city were unimportant, its meaning accessible only to the privacy of belief, even the belief that the sewer of the Ganges is pure. I have merely coerced these scenes to clichés of form and light, and hoped that they would speak.

'You want hashish, Uncle?'

I've heard this all through Africa and Asia. I used to smoke it. Now I see a small brown cake in the man's hand. I buy it, I suppose, because hashish is sacred to Shiva, and

I have a leftover desire to experience things in their place. Munched in the deserted lane, it tastes more bitter than it should.

In the labyrinth of alleys, temples and shrines multiply behind dilapidated walls and doors. Under an unlit gateway somebody sells me a garland for the god, offers a bowl of water to wash my hands, and dabs my forehead with a *tilak*. I shed my shoes into his care. The entrance is hung with notices in Hindi, which I can't read. I find myself in a warren of passages flanked by iron-barred chapels, and the marble paving is ice-cold under my feet. Worshippers are lighting candles on the steps before the gods while a woman whispers the divine names. But the gods sit indecipherable in the dark of their cages. Some are violently painted, others daubed vermilion, still others – these the least worshipped – seem withdrawn into their naked stone. Often I can make out no more than a disembodied headdress or the slope of a jewelled hand. Others are so draped in garlands that only their eyes gleam in the smothered face. The elephant-headed Ganesh squats in a cave of flames; the monkey god Hanuman is a blob of clay, pricked with black pupils.

To a learned elite, these deities do not exist. As with the Buddhist monks, the world and even divinity are illusion. I walk their aisles in bewilderment. No god is himself alone. Each one, in a teeming pantheon, is an aspect or a spouse or the divine antithesis of another. I cannot keep track of them. An old, tingling euphoria is starting up inside my head. Vishnu, the preserver, is the benign manifestation of Shiva the destroyer, who himself creates even as he ravages. They are each, in a sense, one another. Shiva's consort is the gentle Parvati, who may revert at any moment to her alter ego Kali, the bloodstained goddess of dissolution.

The shrines follow one another in zones of flickering light. I go from fire to fire. There is a juddering behind my eyes. Everything is alternately close and far away. I hear laughter and chanting. I wonder if I am really allowed here, in this private netherworld of gods. If the statue's eyes are present, I've read, the god is alive. The eyes, like an icon's, emit light from another realm. My feet drift soundless over the marble. I have a sensation of floating. I realise this is only the effect of hash – I've known it before – but there are doors and passageways here that might lead to near-infinity. I imagine unlocking private chambers where curtained walls part to reveal something else, and something beyond that. When I gaze into the shrines, my hands on the cage bars look far away. The gods loom in and out of focus. They are all one, of course, or nothing. But their stares criss-cross the dark. And they are all accompanied by their mounts, their incarnate energies, which lie at their feet: Shiva rides a bull, Parvati a lion, Ganesh travels by mouse, Vishnu by eagle. I go silently on my own feet, which I cannot feel. But my head throbs.

Behind a bank of candle flame, the light wavers over the god's carved face. The worshippers are all smiling. The god is lapped in the fire of their devotion. He is a masked bull, I think, the bull of Shiva. Perhaps my memory is returning. His horns curl high over his head in the firelight. As if drugged on incense and candle smoke, I reach up to remove the mask, and my fingers meet solid stone. My hand looks like somebody else's. Perhaps, like the gods, I am many others, or have no profound being. I cannot hear myself pray. I've forgotten how. I am only the recipient of sensations. There is no reason, particularly, that I should exist, except in my own imagination. I have never existed before, and never will again. But the smoke smarts in my eyes.

Now the worshippers are clustered before an inner sanctuary. A white-robed priest, concealed behind lattice doors, is bathing and anointing its deity for our sight. The pilgrims form a corridor before it, women on one side, men on the other, and I wait in the smell of incense and stale flowers. Then the gates burst open with a deafening clamour of gongs and drums. The priest is tracing circles of fire before the image, to the sound of a piercing bell. I crane forward. Down the tunnel of worshippers, bathed in brilliant light, dances Kali the goddess of destruction. She is black-skinned and white-fanged, brandishing a severed head and a bowl of blood. Her jewellery is human skulls. Her eyes swerve up like scimitars in her head, sloping back almost to her tiara. They are obscenely beautiful. I gaze back at her, into dereliction. Half obliterated behind her, in concentric silhouette, is her other self, Parvati, a face of formulaic sweetness. The worshippers are bowing before Kali. One of them falls forward, striking his forehead. My nostrils fill with incense and rotting marigolds. I take out my camera to capture her. Her painted eyes glare back into the viewfinder.

Then a man slaps my hand, shaking his head, and I close the lens. She is, after all, holy. In some guises, in a feat of creative change, she devours time itself, then sinks back triumphantly into her abyss. To photograph is to diminish her. A rankling guilt follows me out of the temple and into the cold night.

At first I did not want to go. But a Swedish couple from the hotel said they were going that morning, and for a long time we walk along the ghats together, conspicuously foreign, so that the boatmen and beggars and the vendors of flowers and candles for Mother Ganges swarm around us. Somebody seizes my hand to claim it for Ayurvedic massage; somebody else clamours to cut my dishevelled hair. Close to the cremation grounds on Manikarnika ghat, the offers and threats intensify: invitations to cremation viewing platforms, demands that we pay for bundles of firewood or feed the hospices of people who are waiting to die.

Beyond a palisade of logs and kindling, twenty or thirty feet high, an arena of scaffolding, temple spires and dingy houses is fogged in smoke and lit by an aureole of fire. We peer down, with other tourists, from a temple balcony. The Swedish woman says she is going to be sick. On their different terraces, the various castes are going up in flames. Just beneath us, six or seven pyres are lined up like dormitory beds. The corpses are carried in from the streets, blanketed in crimson and gold, and sometimes heralded by a din of drums. A few male relations follow – women are forbidden – and carry the bier down to dip its feet in the Ganges. Then the funerary sheets are stripped away and the body – bandaged stiff and white – is laid on its allotted pyre, where a caste once called untouchable heaps on whatever logs the family has paid for.

I stare down, numb at first. Most bodies take three hours to burn. The eldest son, his head shaved, circles the corpse anticlockwise and lights it from another pyre – the fire on this site must never die. Then he throws on sandalwood, and the flames start. The man joins his relatives where they sit to watch on the slopes of firewood. I cannot tell how much they grieve. Sorrow is unseemly here. It will offend the dead. Some of the mourners are chatting together. One is reading a newspaper. A few old men are staring in silence. A whole wooden hillside of men, it seems, is waiting: and beyond them on the river there are barges sunk to their gunwales, carrying more stacks of logs which are chucked up to the riverbank, and yet more are piled on the balconies of the disused temples round about.

Beneath us the white-bound heads and feet protrude from their pyres, facing the Ganges. When the fires are slow, the attendants stoke the flames with long branches. In time the shroud is burnt away and in the furnace the body breaks up. Goats and starved dogs scavenge at its foot. If the corpse does not disintegrate fast enough, the attendants beat it with sticks and lever it deeper into the flames. Closest to me, the head has become a charred ball. I watch in frozen fixation. Then the skull cracks like a pistol shot, and a blackened mass spills out into the flames: shards of bone, flesh, memory.

My knuckles are white on the balustrade in front. I do not think of my mother or of Sylvia or of anyone at all. I only repeat inside my head: What is being consumed is not a person. It is just a recipient of sensation, a transitory consciousness. If I mourn, I am mourning the illusion of a self. That is all. The brain is seventy-five per cent water. It can desiccate to a walnut. The Hindu world dies and is reborn in conflagration, and the human being is its microcosm, a fragment of the undying cycle. My throat has turned tight and dry. The individual is nothing. Someone kept Einstein's brain in two mayonnaise jars for twenty years. All that is lost is her hand's touch, the timbre of her voice.

The Swedish woman has forgotten to be sick. As she turns to leave, she asks: 'Are you feeling all right?'

I answer surprised: 'Yes. Why?'

'You are weeping.'

I put a hand to my eyes. 'I didn't know.'

On the nearest pyre, the fire has died. When the fire is dead, water is poured on to the embers, and the ashes find their way into the Ganges. Fragments may survive, of course – the boatmen call them 'floating souls' – but they are left to go to the sea.

If you watch from the hotel windows at dawn, and the fog is not too thick, the pale line of the river's eastern shore appears. It looks no more than a bar of sand suspended there, and by the time I go down to the waterside it has disappeared.

It is to this shore, in the generous diversity of Hindu belief, that the soul crosses on a twelve-day journey to join its ancestors. A boatman, on the other hand, offers to take me there in ten minutes, but volunteers that there is no point. 'Nothing to see there, Uncle. Instead I take you burning ghat. Twenty rupees.'

'Let's go, all the same.'

We push out into the fog. Within minutes Varanasi has blurred to a land as insubstantial as the farther shore, a few lights shining in its vapour. A kite, flown from somewhere invisible, hovers out of the mist above us, then vanishes. Our oars dip into a grey calm. Swallows flitter over its surface. Near the farther bank an abandoned boat shrills with a colony of mynah birds. There is nothing here but sand and etiolated scrub, with the faded start of trees on the eastern horizon. Don't get out, the boatman says. There are bad people beyond the trees. I ask: 'What kind?' But he does not know.

I walk here lightly. The sand is soft as dust underfoot. The boatman repeats that this is a landing stage for souls on their way to reincarnation. But the shore is hemmed in flotsam: sodden garments, withered flowers. A dead dog. Garish funerary sheets, apparently imperishable, glint in the shallows. There are things I do not want to examine. Then an aqueous sun comes out and solidifies the shore we left behind. And it is time to go back.

* * *

Next day he turned south and took a series of buses towards Rourkela. The roads were marked only thinly on his map, and the towns far apart. He was never sure where he would spend the night. It was a mild land at first, edged by low hills under a rainless sky. Plates of rock heaved up from its plains like the backs of tortoises sleeping under the earth, and farming villages were scattered along the paddy fields. Random sights brought a strange comfort out of the blue. They seemed to replace the memories he feared his mind had lost: a view of stone temples on forest hills, a chain of rainbowed waterfalls dropping from a plateau. And the people, slender with poverty, who shared his relay of buses, were sometimes beautiful.

After three days he disembarked and began to walk. His way threaded between rocks and whitened trees. He saw almost nobody. Dried-up irrigation channels latticed empty fields, then faded into scrub and yellow grass. He filled Ricky's water bottle from a trickle of sunken streams, and fed on curried vegetables which he had wrapped in chapattis several days before. Now he was no longer anticipating anything. There was nothing he knew ahead. He spread his sleeping bag under the stars, warm in the early night, and woke at dawn shivering with cold. His body felt hard, but his mind had emptied. In the rusted mirror of a village shop he saw a face shriven to its bones, its eyes fever-bright. He had been walking only five days, and still moved easily over the cracked tarmac. His pack felt light as a shell on his back. He was afraid to stop. Yet he walked sometimes with a feeling of delicacy, separate from his body, as if his gaze was turning back inside his head, and an emptiness ached there. He was afraid of a brain haemorrhage. In the end, he no longer knew where he was. The village names had never reached his map. He did not understand anyone he tried to speak with. Once he spread out the map among farmers, and they ran their calloused fingers over the foreign script of its towns and exclaimed among themselves, and could tell him nothing. He was not sure they could read.

Little by little, he filled with foreboding. Not because of the land and its inhabitants, who seemed only rough and poor, but from his own compulsion to continue, perhaps for ever, through this wilderness of boulders and skeletal trees, towards a horizon that had misted away. To the land's inhabitants he must come from another caste or province. He walked across their gaze and then beyond. And his sense was growing that his surroundings were thinning, reduced at last to the strip of fractured road ahead, while inside his skull this frailty trembled. He felt his head might burst if he laid it too abruptly on the rocky soil at night – he folded his trousers for its pillow – or could implode even with his laboured eating, or with the cold grate of his toothbrush, or with any remembering at all.

One morning a figure came gradually into sight. It was barely darker than the pink soil around it – it might have materialised from the earth – and was sometimes lost among the stunted trees that overlapped the road. It must have been the faint shimmer from the rocks that gave Steven the illusion that the shape was his own reflection approaching him. Neither of them made a sound. After a while he saw by the man's saffron robes that he was a *sanyassin*, a travelling holy man, his trident sloped over his shoulder like a fishing rod. Even as they neared one another, they went on walking. Steven saw now that the man was old, his face daubed white with the ashen bars of Shiva, and that his big, soft eyes were staring straight in front, transfixed by something far away. He passed without a glance.

The *sanyassin*, he knew, would walk for ever. The skyline would recede before him until he stepped from his path to die. Steven gazed after the dwindling figure, and heard the faint slapping of his sandals on the earth, where he left no trace. He watched until the man had gone from sight. After a long time a lorry appeared, and Steven thrust out his arm. His mind remained numb and empty. But he paid the bemused driver a few rupees, and after two days he was entering the turmoil of Calcutta's suburbs, and conceiving his return home.

Months later, in England, an obscure rankling never quite died – as if there had, after all, been a destination that had eluded him.

Only minutes after he had stripped his walls of their traveller's mementoes – the house was burning under him, his brain reeling – he had forgotten that he'd dropped even his Persian vases and Nepalese Buddha into the flower beds below. Choking, he could not raise himself from the sofa. He imagined smoke pouring into the absence where his memory should be. He was staring at bare walls. There was no evidence of his journeys. No evidence, in his suffocating mind, of himself, who might only be sights and sensations, and the horizon he had not yet reached.

Landlord

In the cold starlight, at the predicted hour, the Quadrantid meteors erupt in the northern sky and stream to earth. Their flow, in astronomic terms, is young and narrow, and their fall is clustered densely within a few hours. The darkness seems to be weeping stars. They give the illusion of fanning out from the constellation Boötes – on charts they resemble the explosion of a firework rocket – but they may scatter half the sky. Sometimes a meteor may split in two; others shoot out like celestial tadpoles, with big, flaring heads and tapering tails. In the silence they seem to move with arcane purpose, but in reality, of course, they are only cosmic waste – the detritus of a passing comet – rushing to their last combustion in the dense atmosphere.

A sharp wind rises, and combs the sea into foam. The rooftop observatory only thinly shelters him. He listens to the waves' rise and fall. In the past, during the Quadrantids' height, he trained his camera on a long exposure and recorded the peak-time meteors: their magnitude, colour, length of path. He loved their variety: the blurred teardrops that flashed near the horizon, and the swift, needle-like trajectory of others. But tonight he falls into the kind of dreamy scrutiny he indulged in when young. If he ignores his telescope – even his binoculars – and gazes with the naked eye, the hemisphere of the sky, on a clear night like this, is newly moving. Its dimensions mean little to him. The supercluster of galaxies to which he and all known life belong measures four million light years across. But even this number is small in cosmic space, and there his mind gives up, to concentrate on more perceptible phenomena. The computer erected on the telescope mount can lock within seconds on his chosen stars, like a register of favourite telephone numbers, and he still watches with boyish awe the delicate beauty of them. Their changeless-seeming presence is strangely optimistic (yet he knows they too are dying). There is a double cluster in Perseus that hangs overhead in a jewelled mass, so many that the sky pales and softens round them. And beside the tail of the Great Bear he locates the binary of Alcor and Mizar. One burns golden, the other piercing blue. Some obscure gravitational pull unites them, so that every half-million years or so – a blink in galactic time – they complete the orbit around one another.

Sometimes, as tonight, the sky fills him with an old notion that there is something to be understood there, something undetectable. The restless constellations remind him of his schoolboy days, when solid-seeming bodies were revealed under the microscope to be a universe of moving particles. But he imagines this celestial secret, if there is one, to lie not in the galaxies themselves but in the invisible chasms of black holes which – if the science is right – may outnumber the stars. The unpredictability of this – the flouting of once-accepted science – he finds oddly comforting. Things are not as they seem. Black holes, ingesting all known phenomena, bend space and light rays until previous laws and time itself break down. It may even be that deep within such an abyss, a wormhole leads to an inverse immensity where matter is not sucked in but recreated, and time reverses, and memory returns.

In the radiant of the Quadrantids, the darkness where the star T Boötis once appeared has obsessed him for years. But now the cold, and the stench of smoke from somewhere, and a lapse in the meteor shower, combine to compel him downstairs again. He links his telescope for the last time on the site of the vanished star. He has a sudden feeling that this time, astonishingly, it will appear to him. Then he puts his eye to the freezing ocular, and sees only the dark.

Downstairs, the acrid smell that he had imagined emanating from his old cine projector has fused with a faintest haze of smoke. He peers into the kitchen, but it occupies the innermost recess of his flat, where the smell fades. Casually he switches on the projector to test it, and there arrives on its screen a vista of pinkish African earth, a herd of startled antelope and misted hills. He used to read the labels on his stacked cine films with gratified wonder: Iran, Tanzania, Dar es Salaam, Jerusalem, the Amazon and Ganges deltas. But nothing is stranger to him, as he starts to watch at random – his nostrils inured to the smoke – than his own uninhabited face. After forty, fifty years, it has grown blank with youth: a frightening stranger. Why does he smile that way, as if he's keeping secrets? And those around him, those he must have smiled at – the actress who felt already old, the black woman who stares unsmiling back, knowing what will happen – are the victims of his emptiness.

He tries another reel, and a dazzling light fills the room, where three young men are climbing a headland. Their leader marches ahead, his flaxen-haired disciple following, and their steps appear buoyant in the clear air. Shocking how young they look, how bright with belief. And here is Julian in front of a chapel fresco, marvelling at its absence of an individual viewpoint: the world in the gaze of God.

There are cinematic scenes of the Dorset coast, and a theatre somewhere, and of empty rooms strewn with rubble, the distant cry of a peacock. Then a woman walks in an overgrown orchard. His mother is awkward and big-boned, a feisty housewife with a smile that wrenches his heart. She opens her mouth to speak.

Then the projector blacks out. Irritably he thinks: who will ever repair such an antique? He flicks a light switch and the electricity has gone. In the dark, the stench and smoke feel more intense. He finds a flashlight and opens the door on to the sitting room. The air hangs blue in the torch beam.

Then a cold panic starts in him. The exit from the flat lies beyond a fire door. The fire escape drops from the passage beyond that. When he unlocks the door, it blows open in his face on to an asphyxiating blindness. He stands paralysed, unbreathing. Smoke belches over him into the room. Beyond the door it is suffused by a dull crimson light, and through it, before his eyes smart shut again, he makes out the railings above the stairwell where the crimson deepens and flickers. Muffled far below, there are dull detonations and the crash of exploding glass, and beneath it all a low, breathy roaring. He stands for a second longer, disbelieving. Faintly, almost imperceptibly, he feels the whole building tremble. The fire door that has held back this inferno has become a panel of blistered paint and leaking sealants. He slams it shut with his foot.

The sounds and the light dim. He starts to breathe again, and wipes his streaming eyes. Then, touched by a sad, unexpected calm, he enters the bedroom. His torch beam finds her asleep under the duvet. He sees the rise and fall of her breathing. The smoke hangs only thinly. He thinks: this is how her suffering will end. He lies down behind her, his arms around her shoulders. He doesn't know whether this is for her comfort or for his. Under his hands he feels the heaving of the too-wide barrel of her chest, inflicted by its years-long struggle for breath.

She stirs awake now, mumbles: 'What's that smell?'

He says: 'It's burning. The house is burning.'

She says: 'Oh. Some fuckwit must have left a fire on,' then turns over and goes back to sleep.

He finds by her bedside the bottle of sleeping pills that she takes against night panics. It is almost full. He gets up and pours a glass of water, then tumbles twenty pills into it, and presses it to her lips. She mumbles, 'What's this?' but she has lapsed into confusion, and obediently swallows them. He crams the rest into his own mouth. She says: 'Where are we going, then?' and falls asleep again.

His lips touch the hand curled against her neck. He whispers in his head: Yes, think of it like a journey. Imagine a journey.

There is silence and stillness. On either side glide scarps and domes of ice whose contours, in this elemental light, look as intentional as sculpture. The ship floats on a glacial calm. The air is frozen cold. It is a universe of gleaming immobility, its colours pared to dazzling white and the intermittent black of mountain walls. Sometimes thin floes scatter the sea like icing sugar. Everything inessential – movement, sound, humans – has been shorn away.

It was a fantasy from the start, of course: the idea that this crystalline air might cure her. There is no cure for emphysema. But for years she had wanted to see the mountains of Antarctica, and now she stands for hours at the ship's prow, clutching the cold rails, and watches the towering procession of ice forms in the white silence, and seems at peace. The other passengers avoid them. They have seen her with her concentrator pack, exhausted by climbing the stairs on to deck, inserting the oxygen cannulae into her nostrils; and they assume her need for privacy, or are tacitly repelled by her oddness, as if she might mar their holiday. She laughs at her quarantine. She is happier alone, she says, with him. Although she cannot disembark with the others to photograph seals on the pack ice, she follows through binoculars the colonies of penguins where they waddle along some snow-suffocated massif, and can gaze for hours at the passing icebergs, their blue gleam under the water.

It was this vivid quality of attention that had first arrested him years ago, when neither of them was quite young. He had met her three times before he kissed her startled lips. Later, to his infatuated gaze, her slanted eyes and cheekbones gave her the look of a beautiful gazelle, and her quickened intelligence and mood swings could dilate the same eyes into confusing orbs of alarm or sadness.

He noticed her frailty first on their cliffside walks. She would stop, perplexed, to stare at the view, as if it were this that had taken her breath away. Later, angry, she fought the disease with too-violent exercise, and daily hours of yoga. Often she couldn't rest for coughing, but would sleep exhausted during the day; and all the time – despite hospital intubation to relieve her lungs – her breathing grew shallower, faster, until even when at rest she was wheezing through pursed lips. At length the vibrant precision of her speech faltered, so that her sentences would sometimes die into confusion, she too tired to finish them.

On board ship, for a full week, she sleeps deeply. There are no panic attacks. In the half-dark of the Antarctic summer they often go on deck alone. They watch the ship's prow parting a white flotsam that closes in after them as if they have never been there. They do not know if this is the detritus of a whole ice world melting round them: if they are leaving behind a ruined planet.

Then one night she wakes afraid and is coughing up green sputum. At the ship's prow next morning he hears her banging her fists on the iron parapet, furious, cursing, so that people edge away. This swearing, he knows, is a violent assertion of herself still breathing. Even close friends could often seem strangers to her, because they were on one side of death, she almost on the other. Even he was alien to her sometimes. He would see it in her eyes, as if he had withdrawn to a great distance, and there was mist between them, something that made him not quite there, and she would speak in angry bursts. Because he was going to live on. And sometimes, in retaliation, he would consciously withdraw from her, tell himself that she was beyond loving, to quench the dread of his bereavement.

But these separations would barely last a day. He would only have to catch a helpless semiquaver in her cough, or glimpse the pulse awakened in her neck, to feel a racking sorrow. He wondered if his love for her was too much powered now by compassion, which might demean her: she who had once dispelled his solitude, and redeemed in him a past too full (as he conceived it) of his own betrayals. He had even loved her ageing – eleven years his junior, she was far behind in this – and liked to caress the new lines that crinkled her eyes, and forbade her to dye her hair. He was surprised by himself. Before her disease, he had thought she would always seem young to him. Now he saw her physical beauty transform – her chest and neck thickened, her face gaunt with sleeplessness – and even her radiant mind dimming. Soon, he thought, she might become pure memory, his own, and he did not know what he would be loving.

This, of course, is their last journey. He finds her on the deck at midnight, a night still bleached by refracted sunlight. She says: 'You know it's not working.'

Yes, I know, I know. We always knew. He holds her against him. Her hands touch his back. He thinks: this is my loved one, this is until the end. The Antarctic skies are different from any he has known. Beyond the Southern Cross, even in this half-light, you stare up into the Milky Way as through a great funnel, littered with stars.

The smoke reaches them as he holds her. For a while he imagines he might fall unconscious, still beside her, while the sleeping pills take effect. Now he is unsure if she is breathing. She feels very calm. She does not move as the smoke condenses round them. But his panic returns and he clambers shaking from the bed. He has an idea that he will find an open window, clear sky. A stench of carbonised wood and smelting iron fills his study. His torchlight wavers over everything he ought to save, hoarded from seventy years: letters from friends in schools, seminaries, hospitals, tiers of catalogued photographs, inflammable cine films, astronomy records, neurotic writings on girlfriends, his mother, sister, brother, Africa, Asia, Antarctica. He remembers that items stored in a fridge may survive fire, and scrabbles among snapshots and forgotten correspondence, and empties out a box of old gifts. There is a quaint souvenir of India, bought by Dick; a Greek icon of the Virgin of Tenderness from long ago (but worthless); a Toledo paper knife. He lights on a crystal ball from his schooldays, in which a tiny wizard waves his wand, with snowflakes falling; and finds a photograph of Samantha, still handsome in her last year, its back inscribed with Leonardo's fable of the butterfly and the flame ('I thought I would find happiness in you, and instead I have found death').

He is on the floor, not knowing how he fell. His lungs are rasping. He wants to vomit, his legs gone. A burning void is opening in his chest. For a full minute he tries to get back to the bedroom, but cannot move. But the pain is leaving him now, flowing away. It drains into hallucination. He thinks in a half-trance: My lungs have stopped, my brain is alone. He is swimming away from his body. He knows the brain, of course, how it forgets, and how it can remember without love, if the operation takes you deep into the limbic system. But he has lost his body now, his mind floating. She stares up at him from the hospital trolley. 'Remember.'

The brain may live for minutes after the heart and lungs have stopped. Emotions detach themselves from their causes, and flow free. He feels he dreams what he has forgotten, or what never happened. Maybe he lives the memories of others. Their essence has escaped him, eluded the camera. She wears a salmon-coloured dress, and her hair is twined in gardenias: a house agent for cottages they might have lived in. But he buried her trust under his concrete floor. And he loved her most on stage. She is a perfect Edwardian lady in her cream lace gown. There are others too, their eyes averted, looking in and out of coastal paths and sitting rooms. And then she, shining black in her crimson dress. She gazes back at him like stone. There is nothing you can do for me now. He reaches out to touch her, to kiss her should she allow it, as if to remove a mask and uncover a face.

Crystal-clear this morning, the Antarctic light. On the ship's railings their hands rest side by side. And gently her little finger hooks around his. The hand is as he remembers it, the tendons spread like harp strings. And she whispers, 'Thank you.' It arises from her stillness, almost like breathing.

It is dark now. He begins to part the chapel curtains. There is a dead butterfly on the altar, still glistening. Passages lead off beyond, to other curtains, other rooms. He is nothing now, or somebody dreaming, dreaming of the dark one whose breast in ecstasy he held in the firelit orchard. The house is shaking round him, and its rooms are empty except for his dreams. As the synapses of the brain close down, its memories hang isolated, waiting for their own dissolution. There is no one to awaken them. They constitute a person who has disappeared. He might be sinking into the black throat of a wormhole. Perhaps a light bursts beyond, like the flaming of a once-invisible star. Or it flows over him in a river of fire, until the brain – ninety billion neurons of it – spills out as it might into the Ganges, to reach the ocean at last and disintegrate under the gleam of unfamiliar stars.

ACKNOWLEDGEMENTS

I owe special thanks to William Gray, Professor of Functional Neurosurgery at Cardiff University School of Medicine, for critical information and insight, and for granting me access to brain surgery. Likewise to Andrew McEvoy, consultant neurosurgeon at the National Hospital for Neurology and Neurosurgery in London.

I am much indebted to my sensitive editor Penny Hoare.

penguin.co.uk/vintage